# WORLD OF
# ONE

## Also By Charles Templeton

*The Cat Who Thought She Was a Dog* (1988)
*The Queen's Secret* (1986)
*An Anecdotal Memoir* (1983)
*The Third Temptation* (1980)
*Act of God* (1977)
*The Kidnapping of the President* (1975)
*

*Jesus: His Life* (1973)
*Evangelism For Tomorrow* (1957)
*Life Looks Up* (1955)

# WORLD OF ONE

A NOVEL BY

## CHARLES TEMPLETON

Doubleday Canada Limited, Toronto

Design: David Wyman

---

**Canadian Cataloguing in Publication Data**

Templeton, Charles, 1915–
  World of one

ISBN 0-385-25158-0

I. Title.

PS8589.E46W67 1988      C813'.54      C88-094118-9
PR9199.3.T42W67 1988

---

Published in Canada by

Doubleday Canada Limited
105 Bond Street
Toronto, Ontario
M5B 1Y3

Printed and bound in Canada

For Anna . . . who rescued the perishing.

If God did not exist,
it would be necessary to invent him.


François Marie Arouet (Voltaire)

# PART ONE

# ONE

I first saw Oscar Gladden in the early spring of 1995 in the Manhattan Federal Courthouse on Foley Square. I was one of perhaps three dozen spectators shoehorned into the public benches in Courtroom 318 on the opening day of his trial. He entered from a door to the right of the judge's bench—to my astonishment a spectacularly obese man—and strode with an unexpectedly nimble grace toward the defense table. Bandbox-fresh, a tiny, perfect, red rosebud on the lapel of his exquisitely tailored black silk suit, and flanked by a phalanx of the most expensive legal counsel in the city, he looked, I thought, the embodiment of money and power.

He did *not* look like the spiritual leader of a globe-girdling television ministry, the founder and head of a church whose followers numbered in the millions and whose reach extended to virtually every civilized country in the world.

Exactly one month later I was again in Courtroom 318, having waited in the corridor in a jostling line for the better part of an hour. When the doors were opened, I was borne on a tide of moiling, sweaty spectators to find myself wedged, elbows pinioned, between a modish woman reporter from ABC News and one of that breed of odd hangers-on you see at celebrated or gamey trials, a woman known to us in the newspaper business as Dandruff Annie. Annie is a fixture at such trials, dressed regardless of the season in layers of ill-fitting sweaters and ankle-high work boots. Redolent of garlic and cloying baby-powder, she sits silent and expressionless, clutching a crumpled paper sack containing her lunch. Annie's presence in a courtroom is a guarantee that the trial in progress was the best show in town.

Room 318, spacious and high-ceilinged, is one of the larger rooms in the federal courthouse. Its lower walls are faced with gray and black marble, its upper reaches boast bleached oak columns and ornamented niches. Six large mullioned windows admit the sunlight, which, on this radiant May morning, was casting dazzling diagonal patterns on the marble walls of the inner courtyard. Unlike the grubby precincts so often the law's venue, Room 318 is a pleasant place. Beyond that, it is functional, communicating the majesty of the law and the solemnity of the judicial process, an ambience radically at odds with the electric expectancy and magpie chatter of the onlookers in the courtroom this morning, when the Reverend Doctor G. Oscar Gladden was scheduled to be released from custody.

By normal expectations, a trial such as his should have been a prolonged yawn — "Anti-trust, dry as dust," as the saying goes. Instead, it had become a *cause célèbre*, reported in excessive (and often mischievous) detail in the world press and on radio and television. For weeks, New Yorkers had gossiped about little else, following the detailed revelations of Oscar Gladden's lavish lifestyle and his complex financial and entrepreneurial affairs with the avidity normally reserved for political and show-business scandals or for the internecine squabbles of the *Yankees*.

From the opening day of the trial, when it had taken cordons of police to control the noisy, sign-pumping devotees and the merely curious, Oscar Gladden had been the center of attention. The paradox of the famous but reclusive preacher who was seldom seen in public but whose face was familiar to millions on television drew hundreds to the square. When he entered the courtroom, conversations subsided to silence and the entrance of Judge Hugo Wheeler was an anticlimax. Most defendants are servile and obsequious; Oscar Gladden was arrogant and imperious. He didn't trouble to hide his scorn for the prosecutor—whom he cowed in the first few minutes of his direct examination—and he clashed almost daily with the judge —on a half-dozen occasions avoiding only by a hair being cited for contempt.

It became evident early on that the prosecution had not adequately prepared its case. As his counsel shot holes in the various allegations against him, Gladden thumped a massive fist on the great oak table at which he sat or leaned back in his protesting chair, chortling audibly, only to apologize with thespian humility when reprimanded by the bench.

By the second week it was obvious that the prosecutor would not be able to make the charges stick. (They had to do with the tax-exempt status of an astonishing variety of enterprises owned by or allegedly related to the Worldwide Church of One. The jury betrayed its sympathy for the defendant with slight noddings, unconcealed smiles and an occasional guffaw. Judge Wheeler's patience, never celebrated—he was quipped about in the corridors as Job's alter ego—soon degenerated to testiness. It became evident that while there was undoubtedly an element of "creative bookkeeping" and possibly some conspiracy involved, it was equally evident that when flames threatened to break out they would be doused by the tactics and the rhetorical brilliance of Gladden's chief counsel. His summation was worthy of a Broadway stage. The jury was out just three hours, and that long only because of the number of charges.

When finally the foreman had rendered the verdict and the judge had grudgingly dismissed him, Oscar Gladden stood.

"Your Honor."

Judge Wheeler, who had risen to leave, paused, peering over the top of his granny glasses.

"What is it, Mr. Gladden? What is it now?"

"Your Honor," Gladden said, his round, pink face shining, his dark, obsidian eyes burning, "if I am not incorrect, it is customary to give the accused, if he has been found guilty, the opportunity to say a final word. Having been found not guilty, I would like the same privilege."

Judge Wheeler placed his hands on the bench. I noted that they were trembling and that his gaunt face had gone parchment pale.

"Mr. Gladden," he said in a constrained voice, "you have been fully heard. The charges against you and the corporations you head—"

"Allegedly head," Gladden interjected.

3

"—have been declared not-proven. You are dismissed, and that is the end of it. Good morning." He turned to leave.

"Your Honor."

Judge Wheeler whipped about, his robe flaring like a matador's cape. "Mr. Gladden, that will be all! You have tried the patience of this court long enough. I have heard all I want to from you. There will be no statement. Is that understood?"

"Sir," Gladden said, "I came into your court falsely accused." His words were clipped, his tone crisp. "It has cost me four weeks and large sums of money to rebut the charges falsely and maliciously laid against me. I have been tried here and, vindictively, in the press. The jury has found me innocent—"

"Not guilty," Wheeler corrected.

"Innocent." Gladden emphasized each syllable. "Where there is no guilt there can only be innocence. I have earned the right to make a statement. Justice demands that it be made."

Gladden's chief counsel was tugging on his sleeve, whispering. The spectators who had begun to leave froze in their places. The jurors watched, transfixed. Judge Wheeler remained for a moment, his knuckles resting on the bench, his brows drawn down, his mouth working as though on a chance morsel of food. Then he sat down again in his great chair.

"Mr. Gladden," he said, a slight tremor in his voice, "do I have your attention?"

"You do, sir."

"Then hear me carefully. This court has been patient with you. Lenient. In the face of your arrogance and obvious disdain, this court, though sorely provoked, has refrained from disciplining you. But there are limits, and those limits have been reached. You will not be permitted to turn these precincts into a forum. That will be all. *All*, Mr. Gladden!"

He picked up the gavel and brought it down. The sound rang out like a gunshot.

The two men faced each other in taut silence, like gunmen at high-noon in a dusty western street, I thought. I could hear the wheeze of Gladden's breathing and felt a momentary concern for Judge Wheeler's heart, his face had gone so ashen. After a moment, Gladden leaned forward.

4

"Sir," he said, "I challenge your right to refuse me."

Judge Wheeler banged the gavel again. The handle broke and the head skittered along the bench and fell to the floor.

"Oscar Gladden," he said, his voice rising, "I find you in contempt and sentence you to one day in jail. Bailiff, take the prisoner in charge."


During the course of the trial, my interest in Oscar Gladden had become more than professional, as I shall explain shortly. The man intrigued me. When I returned to the newsroom each afternoon to write my story, I talked about little else to the reporters who would gather around. "He's the genuine article," I told them, "a true individualist, a bona-fide misanthrope. Lives on this enormous estate out on Long Island and travels in two identical stretch-limousines. The second one's a fully equipped ambulance driven by a disbarred M.D. He's a diabetic and, I'm told, a hypochondriac. Physically, the guy is absolutely gross, but he moves like a Nijinsky. I don't know who his tailor is, but he should be given the Needle and Thread Award. Doesn't give a damn for anyone—*anyone!*—nor does he try to hide it. The president once invited him to the White House and he didn't even bother to respond to the invitation. The guy is something else! He's the leader of a world religion and he doesn't believe in God. . . ."

Now, in the company of Dandruff Annie and a jam-packed crowd of working newsmen and gawkers, I awaited the dénouement. The television networks had played the story to the hilt, and the newspapers had been filled with it. I found myself taut with expectancy.

A door opened and Oscar Gladden entered the court. He looked as though he had just come from a restful sleep. Somehow, the rosebud had been replaced and the now familiar tight smile was in place. There was no indication that, having been processed by Central Booking the night before, he had been handcuffed and strung on a running-chain with a dozen or so pimps, petty thieves and drug-pushers and shipped in a police-van to a nearby precinct, to spend the night on a narrow pallet in a bleak cell. It occurred to me that, being a diabetic, he might have been given special treatment, and I made a note to check it out.

All rose, and Judge Wheeler swept in from his chambers. The contrast was remarkable: Wheeler's face was pallid and drawn, dark shadows encircled his eyes and, when he directed himself to Gladden, who now stood before him, his voice betrayed fatigue.

"Well now, Mr. Gladden," he began, feigning ebullience. "How are we this morning? I trust you've managed to calm down and that you are prepared to act like a gentleman."

Gladden made no response. I could see his head come up and knew he was looking full into Wheeler's face. Wheeler dropped his eyes to his notes and delivered himself of a clichéd lecture about the courts being fundamental to justice and the American way of life. All it lacked was a fife and drum accompaniment.

"There are times," he pontificated, "when the system fails, when the apparatus of justice falters." I glanced at Roger Zachs, an old acquaintance who had headed the prosecution team. Color was flooding into his neck and ears. "At such times it is important to rebuke those who think they can, with impunity and through the employment of skilled counsel, subvert justice and scorn the system. Such must endure the rebuke of the courts."

He looked up at Gladden, anticipating a response. None came.

"Good," he said. "We understand each other. There being no further business before it, this court stands adjourned."

No cameras or recorders are permitted in the courthouse, and most newsworthy defendants flee the media by leaving the courtroom through the jurors' door and the building by any of a dozen exits. Gladden chose not to do this, but turned and bulled through the crowd, heading for the corridor, taking not the slightest notice of the reporters' questions, clamorous in the air.

On the sidewalk outside the courthouse, at the foot of the broad stairs, a straggle of reporters was idling. The television cameramen had rested their mini-cams and backpacks on the sidewalk. The still-photographers were wandering aimlessly about, necklaces of cameras and lens-cases dangling. They were stolid, patient men, accustomed to prolonged stakeouts, and in the warm early-spring sun they were a nondescript, sweaty lot.

Now, the reporters preceding Gladden burst from the main doors. There was a throaty roar from the crowd massed beyond the street, and the newsmen were galvanized into frantic activity. In a scramble resembling a football scrum, they swarmed at the bottom of the stairs. Mini-cams were hoisted and backpacks slung. Photographers whipped off lens-caps. Soundmen extended their microphones. The scene grew chaotic as the print reporters began jostling for position.

Gladden had been handed an opera cape by an aide as he left the courtroom. He paused now on the top step.

"Gentlemen," he said, caustic good humor in his voice, "take your time. Take your time."

At the rear of the crowd, as befits a mere newspaperman, I studied Gladden's face. His porcine proportions camouflaged by the cape—as they are in all his public appearances—he was an extraordinarily handsome man. I noted that, despite the smile, there was no laughter in the eyes and that the massive jaw was thrust forward. The thought surfaced: I wouldn't want Oscar Gladden as an enemy.

He appeared to be enjoying the moment. From time to time he commented, "Now, now, don't shove. The man from CBS is right, you newspaper drudges are in the way. This is the electronic age; there is no god but television, and the anchorman is his prophet."

As the chaos eased he murmured, almost to himself, "What a pack of carrion-eaters!"

The questions began.

"Hey, Gladden, how was it in the drunk-tank?"

"Are you gonna appeal?"

Gladden took a crisp linen handkerchief from a pocket and dabbed at the perspiration beading on his face.

"There will be no questions," he said. "I have a statement to make." A silence settled. The sound of traffic in Foley Square crept in. "I have something to say to all of you. Especially"— and there was acid in his tone—"to you *gentlemen* of the press." He paused, looked directly at the cameras, composed a beatific smile and held up a middle finger. There was a gasp from the onlookers. "Oh, sorry about that," he said, feigning a confusion belied by his smile and raising instead his index finger. Then, after a perfectly timed rhetorical pause, he cried out in a ringing voice, "When all is said and done, only one thing matters: *One!* One God . . . One world . . . Oneness . . . That is all there is."

He gave an airy wave of his hand to the crowd across the street—eliciting a thunderous roar—and went off in that astonishingly nimble way of his to the first of the two black stretch-limousines idling at the curb. As he passed, his eyes caught mine and he gave the slightest jerk of his head.

I stuffed my copy paper in a pocket and followed.

# TWO

As you will have concluded, I am a newspaperman. If you read the New York *Register* you will have seen my byline, Anthony Carpenter, on any number of stories. I could present myself as a foreign correspondent or a political analyst, for I have been both, but I am essentially a reporter. In a time of electronic journalism, when anchormen and "television personalities" call themselves reporters, I take some small pride in being a graduate of a system that requires that you serve an apprenticeship in journalism's joe-jobs before you think of yourself as a newspaperman.

My beat at the time of Oscar Gladden's trial was the courts, which may to some sound glamorous. It is, in fact, more often than not as stultifying as doing the egg-count at a chicken hatchery. I got into the newspaper business on my twentieth birthday, knowing that it was no bower of roses but prepared, even eager, to start at the bottom. The bottom on a newspaper can be pretty menial work, but it seemed to me then—as it does now—infinitely preferable to writing advertising copy, which is what my father was pressing me to do, he being employed at that dissembler's art.

But you should know something about me beyond what I do for a living. First, the biographical data. Age: thirty-two. Born: Presbyterian Hospital, New York City. Weight at birth: ten pounds one and a half ounces. Mother, who tends to blame her numerous "women's problems" on my undue size at birth, likes to recount the event, invariably concluding with the words:

9

"He looked just like that heavyweight boxer. . . ." She will then ritually knit her brow and turn to Father, who will supply, "Tony Tubbs." "Yes, that's the one," she will say. "Tony Tubbs."

I was a passable scholar in grade school where most of what you learn is by rote. But in my early years in high school I was a dud. My consuming interest was sports. Football attracted me most, in part because football drew the largest crowds of students—more specifically, girl students. To that point I hadn't been what is sometimes called "successful" with girls—that damned baby-fat no doubt.

But with the onset of puberty that changed. Seeing me today you would never suspect that at one time my friends called me Lard-ass. I stand an even six feet, bear a distinct resemblance to my father and have, I'm told, picked up many of his mannerisms. Not that I sought to, mind you, for I am not crazy about my father and can't remember ever having been. It's not a matter of active dislike; it is simply that he and I have never been close. I think he was disappointed in me, particularly in my appearance as a child. Father is something of a perfectionist, and I was not, apparently, the son he had visualized.

Father is a good-looking man: one of the "black Irish," tall and fairskinned but dark of eye and dark of hair. However, for all his attractiveness, he was never a womanizer, being absolutely devoted to my mother. I account for this in part by the fact that she is the only person he entirely approves of. He has certainly been a model husband: a good provider, considerate and affectionate. With Mother, that is. Not, as I have said, with me.

Father is a misanthrope. He writes advertising copy, apparently with considerable skill, for he is well paid. But he dislikes the people he works for and scorns the people his copy inveigles into buying things. He takes delight in, as he puts it, "coming up with a great selling-line," especially when it is for a useless product, chortling at the picture of "those silly sheep being fleeced."

I was an only child and a lonely child, and as a consequence turned to books: everything on my parents' shelves and anything else within reach. Nor was it bad fare. Father was a member of the Book of the Month Club, and because he more often than not neglected to notify the club that he didn't want the current selection, we had a large, if largely unread, library.

It occurs to me that I have said little about my mother. She was, I suppose, a good mother. She dressed me well and saw to it that I was clean and shorn. She was an excellent cook and took pains to ensure that our cupboards were stocked with those treats I fancied. I can't remember ever returning from school to an empty house. But she found it difficult to express affection. I lacked nothing as a child except enfolding arms. Father's way of commending me was to give me a pat on the top of the head. Once, when I won a prize for an essay I had written, he congratulated me by shaking my hand. That there was affection between my parents I have no doubt; there was daily evidence of it, although little that was overt.

All of which may explain why I married the first girl I fell in love with. Maggie. Attractive, aware, extroverted, irresponsible Maggie. I was twenty, nearly broke, and had just joined the *Register* when I met her. She was a clerk in the Doubleday bookstore on Fifth Avenue. I used to buy books there as an excuse to talk to her, and when that became too expensive I became a browser.

I was interested in books but I was more interested in Maggie. And after our first date—during which I discovered that sex was more than a furtive, short-lived, almost frantic activity—I was out of my mind about her. Maggie was a virtuoso lover and quickly taught me to be more than merely responsive. Her one drawback, as I discovered after we were married, was that she wasn't prepared to husband her talent. Let me amend that: it wasn't that Maggie was promiscuous; it was simply that her skills in bed were such that from time to time she enjoyed giving a demonstration.

I chanced to enter the newspaper business at a time when it was undergoing fundamental changes. Not many years earlier, nearly everyone read newspapers. There was no television, few newsmagazines, radio hadn't yet discovered the revenue potential of news and movie theaters presented only brief snippets of major events. Newspapers had a near monopoly on comprehensive coverage.

But as the world became a neighborhood and the news more complex, the number and variety of news media proliferated and the competition intensified. These were bad times for newspapers, and their numbers shrank dramatically. The reason was simple: advertising dollars went where the bodies were, and a majority of the bodies were slumped, bleary-eyed, in front of television sets. To survive, many a beleaguered publisher began offering his declining readership a daily diet of sex, scandal, opinions and sport, plus a large helping of violence and the appetizer of a big-buck lottery.

The once proud *Register*, I regret to say, had come to this pass. For this and other reasons, I was vulnerable when I followed Oscar Gladden to his car. As I sank into the down-filled cushions in the back seat of the limousine and it moved away from the curb, I said to myself, How sweet it is! Aloud, I asked, "Where are we going?"

"To my place," he replied.

I didn't even ask why. My senses were marveling at the surroundings. We were encapsulated in opulence. The seats, walls and ceiling were covered with royal blue velvet. Knobs, switches and door handles gleamed with gold plate. Quadraphonic sound enwrapped us. On the far side of the compartment was a console of burled walnut encompassing a television screen, a mini-refrigerator, a cellular telephone and a swing-out wet bar. Seen through the tinted glass, other cars seemed rattletrap, and the sweaty, toiling pedestrians appeared grubbier than usual. It would be easy in such surroundings, I thought, to believe yourself superior.

Gladden, grunting with the effort of leaning forward, was in the act of pouring a drink. Lagavulin Scotch, I noticed—what else? Without troubling to ask if I wanted it, he handed me a brimming glass and sank back in the seat to take a great swallow from his own. The car, its motion reminiscent of a yacht's, nosed onto Franklin D. Roosevelt Drive and picked up speed.

"I should check in with the paper," I said, making conversation.

"Use the phone."

"To file a story on your" — I grinned — "your press conference."

"And what would you write?"

"Probably something like: 'The Reverend Doctor G. Oscar Gladden, founder and head guru of the Worldwide Church of One, apparently none the worse for a night in the slammer, emerged from Judge Hugo Wheeler's court this morning to make a formal statement. In paraphrase: he gave the waiting journalists and the absent Judge Hugo J. Wheeler the finger— quickly amended, it should be said, to point to heaven.' "

His chuckling sent seismic shudders through the cushions. "However," I added, when his quaking had subsided, "I don't have to file a story. I was there only as back-up man today."

"Yes," he said. "I heard there was some unhappiness about our little transaction."

"Our little transaction" had been an act of temporary idiocy on my part. I was having serious money problems, all of which had come to a festering head during the second week of Gladden's trial. They had begun when Maggie, my estranged wife, the separation agreement in her hands and a thirst for my blood in her throat, had cleaned out our joint savings account and, on a Saturday morning when I was upstate fishing, had sent a moving van around to our apartment. I returned late Sunday to find that Maggie had picked the place clean, leaving only my clothes, the overstuffed chair with the loose spring in the cushion, the swayback bed in the spare bedroom, the black-and-white television set, my typewriter, an assortment of mismatched china and a herniated wicker hamper overflowing with dirty laundry, mine.

Maggie, as I subsequently learned, had moved to California in the company of a born-again Hyundai salesman whom she had met when he was in town for a Moral Majority convention. I had reciprocated by withholding the alimony payments due her and was consequently under the constraint of a court order to play catch-up. As the process-server put the paper in my hand, I had muttered darkly, "Till death do us part," and he had responded with doleful agreement: "I know what you mean, buddy. Do I *ever!*"

The following morning there came a registered letter from the Internal Revenue Service. An anonymous computer had disagreed with the arithmetic in my most recent return, had calculated that I owed the government the sum of $6,362.01 (note the one cent!) and had typed out a "remit immediately" form, including a list of the penalties to which I would be subject in the event of delay. Attached to the notice was a business card conveying the further glad tidings that I had been selected for an audit and that District Agent R. Larson—his name penned in a crabbed, hieroglyphic hand—would be in touch.

There was also the matter of my car: a much beloved 1959 MGA-1600, a thing of soul-nourishing beauty for all its years and hard times. It was at that moment sitting mantled in dust in a garage on East 29th Street with a piston rod through its crankcase; the rectifying of which, I had been informed by a greasy oaf in coveralls stiff enough to stand by themselves, would require "at least three thou" for an engine rebuild.

All this plus notification of an overdraft at the bank had led me to an appalling lapse in judgment. During a recess in the Gladden trial, when we were all in the corridor killing time and sipping a bilge vended as coffee, I had drawn Gladden aside and, as much in jest as with serious intent, had offered to sell to him for $500 a copy of his standing-obit then resting with others in the *Register*'s morgue. Gladden had looked at me, his dark eyes appraising, and said, "You've got a deal." Unfortunately, word of the "deal" got back to Ed Replogle, my managing editor, and I was summoned to his sanctum to answer for my momentary insanity. My defense—offered with no conviction—was that, inasmuch as Gladden would never otherwise get to read it and was prepared to pay $500 to know what we would say about him when he was dead, what the hell difference did it make?

Gladden now said, "I'm told your editor was not amused."

"The paper's going to hell anyway," I said, sipping my scotch. "Lost a million last quarter and the scuttlebutt is that it's on the block. Hey!" I said suddenly. "There's a good investment for Oscar Gladden Inc. You're a publisher among other things. Buy the *Register*."

He was silent a moment. "If I did, it would be to kill it. Think of the forests that would be saved."

He held his glass aloft, rotating it. "I, Mr. Carpenter, am not an admirer of the news media. Agreed, they perform a neces-

14

sary function—without them we'd know little of what goes on in the world—but they're vastly overrated. Much of what they report is neither trustworthy nor important and most of their editorial comment reflects their biases. Some, like your *Register*, don't even try to report hard news—it's more like back-fence tattle.'' He brought the glass to his lips and drew an ice cube into his mouth, crunching it in powerful jaws. ''History has been defined as the record of the past written with a bias; modern journalism is the record of the present, trivialized and distorted.''

I bridled. ''And journalists are part of a grand conspiracy to distort.''

''Of course not,'' Gladden said easily. ''All journalists are individualists; you'd never get them together long enough to conspire on anything—other than a scheme to increase their income,'' he added. ''There's no grand plot. It's simply mediocrity exacerbated by the pressures of deadlines.''

''You don't like the press,'' I said drily.

''With just cause. But we'll get to that another time.'' He drained his glass and placed it on the bar. ''How would you like a job?''

I blinked at the sudden change of direction. ''I have a job.''

''I mean, working for me.''

''Doing what?''

''Public relations, official biographer—call it what you wish.''

''Whatever I called it, what would the job be?''

''You haven't said whether you're interested.''

''I come pretty expensive,'' I said, fencing, not really interested but curious.

''The *Register* pays you fifty-two thousand a year,'' he said. ''I know a plumber who does better than that.''

''Who—G. Gordon Liddy?'' I was nettled that he had pried into my personal affairs.

''Look, Carpenter,'' he said, an edge of impatience entering his voice, ''you're broke. The *Register* has six months at best before it follows the *Herald Trib* and the *Mirror* into extinction. You've been a journalist most of your life and what has it got you? Break the mold.''

I reined in an impulse to tell him to shove it and to drop me off where I could get a cab. His arrogance, which from a distance had been engaging, was irritating up close. But I was intrigued enough to say instead, ''Why would you want to hire me? I've never done public relations.''

''Because I like your work and I like your style. The article you wrote before the trial was fairly accurate—''

''How faint can praise be?''

He smiled. ''And I like the thinking behind your offer to sell me my obituary.''

I was thinking of Maggie and her court order, of Mr. Larson sharpening his pencils, of my overdraft, of the Hellbox, a hangout for newspapermen where my tab was well past the limit, and of poor old Smedley, abandoned and forlorn, waiting to have his piston extracted.

''I could be interested,'' I said, deciding to play his game. ''Make me an offer I can't refuse.''

He hooked his thumbs in his vest pockets and pursed his lips, looking every pound the caricaturist's capitalist. ''Okay. For starters, twice your salary at the *Register*.''

''Who do I have to kill?''

''In addition, there would be an annual bonus. But it and your salary would be conditional.''

''Ah, the worm in Eden's apple.''

''I don't think the conditions are unreasonable,'' he said equably. ''If I'm going to make you privy to my business affairs and to aspects of my private life I will want some assurance that somewhere down the road you won't use the information to my detriment. There's a lot of that done these days.''

''Agreed.''

''To ensure that loyalty, I'm prepared to deposit in a numbered Swiss bank account, now and on January first of each year, the sum of fifty thousand dollars. At the end of a dozen years, the interest compounding, there will be approximately one million dollars in your account. By the time you're fifty you will be able to draw a hundred thousand a year for the rest of your life.'' He let it sink in. ''Interested?''

''Is a drunk interested in a distillery?'' I said, trying to keep it light but aware of a quivering of excitement.

''There is one further proviso. . . .''

16

*Now* comes the worm, I thought.

"If at any time you betray any of the information you acquire through our association, the entire deal is forfeit. You see, Mr. Carpenter, I am a very private man."

"I'm still puzzled," I said. "Why me? For those bucks you could get Norman Mailer."

"The biography is a small part of the job. You won't be asked to get my name in the paper but to keep it out. More important than that, I need an experienced professional journalist—someone who knows how the media work."

I was tempted to say an immediate yes but restrained myself. The job would mean an end to my money problems. I would no longer have to worry about whether I could land on my feet if the *Register* went belly-up. And from the sound of it, I would have more freedom, more time to myself; perhaps enough time to concentrate on the novel I'd been working on off and on for the past two years.

"Well?" Gladden asked.

My mind was racing. For all that I was intrigued, what would I be getting into? I knew only a little about Gladden and not much more about the religion he advocated. But what the hell —he wasn't asking me to convert, merely to work for him. And any religious organization with ten million adherents couldn't be all bad.

"You want a guarantee of my loyalty," I found myself saying. "What guarantee do I have that six months down the road you won't renege on the deal?"

He reached into his jacket, took out an envelope and handed it to me. In it was a check for $124,000. "As I said: double your present salary. In advance."

"It's postdated two weeks."

"Of course," Gladden said with a smile. "We'll both want a few days to see if we like each other."

I passed the check back to him, relieved to see that my hand wasn't trembling. "Offer it to me when it comes due," I said, cursing that something in me that resists being beholden. "When do I learn exactly what my duties might be?"

"After lunch," he said, putting the check back in his pocket. "In the meantime," he said, picking up the intercom microphone, "I think I'll slip into the ICU car and have Doc check me out. Last night was just a bit rough."

I watched him as he made his way on the shoulder of the road to the other limousine, thoughts ricocheting in my head. There was an electric exultancy in the realization that in his pocket there was a check with my name on it for more than $124,000 and in the promise of my being a millionaire before I was forty. But there was also an odd, irrational foreboding, a distant voice crying, "Take care."

I watched as a towering black man in chauffeur's livery leaped from the limousine and opened the passenger door. Just before Gladden got in, he paused, turned to look at me and held aloft a forefinger. He smiled broadly and his lips formed the word, "One!" I began to smile in response and then realized that he couldn't see me through the tinted glass of the window.

"The son of a bitch," I thought. He *knew* I'd be watching.

# THREE

O scar Gladden, my research had informed me, was born on the ragged edge of the Parkdale section of Toronto, a sedate, heavily treed suburb to the west of the city, comfortable on the shores of Lake Ontario. Parkdale was originally an enclave built by middle-class businessmen and industrialists, conveniently just beyond the sprawling factories clotted about the Canadian Pacific Railway tracks. Many of the homes were large and Victorian and ugly, designed to accommodate the big families in vogue in the latter half of the nineteenth century. As the city prospered and grew and as many of the great houses degenerated to multitenant dwellings, the early residents moved on to the farther suburbs, surrendering the neighborhood to immigrants, monthly renters and to a gradual deterioration.

As a child, Gladden lived at the grubby north end of Dufferin Street between King and Queen, across the street from an abandoned railway station. His father was an illiterate Italian stonemason, his mother worked as a seamstress in a sweatshop in the Spadina Avenue garment district. He had only one sibling, a younger sister, Marguerita, and was a forlorn, lonely child. Both parents worked twelve-hour days and after the evening meal were too busy or too spent to attend to a boy's emotional needs. Oscar reacted by becoming solitary and withdrawn and by acquiring a prodigious appetite. On his thirteenth birthday he weighed 180 pounds.

But he was a clever student and read omnivorously, shunning all extracurricular activity. In his first year at Parkdale Collegiate, he was taunted about his obesity and bullied, especially by one classmate. In the public library he read a half dozen books on the martial arts, then one day set upon his tormenter, chopping, gouging and kneeing him with vicious savagery. He heard no further jibes from his peers.

Then came the night that fashioned the remainder of his life.

In his late teens, sullen and fearing rejection, Oscar Gladden began to keep to himself and to avoid unnecessary contact with his classmates. One summer night, wandering the north Parkdale area, he passed the dark brick edifice of the First Church of the Galilean. Faint sounds of buoyant, rhythmic singing were borne to him on the quiet night air. He peered in the open door. Three or four dozen young people were seated on rows of chairs in the church basement clapping their hands and singing:

> *I'm so glad that Jesus took me in,*
> *Jesus took me in. Jesus took me in.*
> *I'm so glad that Jesus took me in . . .*
> *Glory to his name.*

He had been there perhaps five minutes when he was startled by a hand laid gently on his shoulder. He whirled about, defensive. It was a girl of about seventeen, long brown hair coiled softly on her shoulders. She was smiling, and the open, unfeigned friendliness of the smile made her somewhat plain face attractive.

"Hello," she said. "I'm Diane Palmer. Won't you come in?" She held out a hand. He wiped his palm on a trouser leg and took it, releasing it quickly.

Late that night, lying abed, infused with an unfamiliar sense of warmth, he reviewed the events of the evening: the rhythmic, zestful songs—in which finally, tentatively, he joined—the earnest testimonies about the presence of God in their lives by some of the young people and the unguarded cordiality with which the other young people welcomed him as Diane introduced him around. Now, in bed, the tears came hot to his eyes. And having begun to weep, he was unable to stop until he was spent and fell asleep.

Oscar Gladden began to spend most of his free evenings at the church. Within weeks, accompanied by a small band of young people, he was preaching on street corners and, not long afterward, to groups in other Galilean churches. When he was nineteen, having completed the requisite "course of study"— the reading of a dozen or so books on the Bible and a history of the Galilean church—and having submitted to an oral examination by a group of local preachers, he was ordained a licensed evangelist. As one of them said after the laying on of hands: "You'll do fine, son. What you lack in lightnin' you sure do make up for in thunder."

Oscar's energy was prodigious. Every minute not spent in school or in church activities was devoted to making money. He worked at everything from a *Globe and Mail* paper route to shoveling snow from sidewalks to buying, repairing and selling used bicycles to his fellow students. At one point, a thousand dollars in the bank, he approached his father and asked him to co-sign a loan. He wanted, he explained, to buy the semidetached house next door and convert it into bachelor apartments. His father discussed it with his cousin, a second-generation immigrant and a man of influence in Toronto's large Italian community, and he guaranteed the note. Oscar divided the house into six tiny apartments—the kitchens being little more than a sink and a hotplate —and rented them to immigrant families fresh from Europe and the Pacific rim. Operating with borrowed money and pyramiding the profits, he was worth half a million dollars by his twentieth birthday. On that birthday, having quietly liquidated all his assets, and not troubling to pack his clothes or say good-bye to his parents, he took the train to Rochester, New York, where he had been invited by the local Church of the Galilean to conduct a revival meeting. He took with him only his Schofield Bible and a red reflector from a bicycle, an object that had sat for years on the dresser in his bedroom.


In Oscar Gladden's private limousine, crossed legs outstretched before me, a superb drink in my glass, the car making its hushed and buoyant way along the Cross Island Parkway, I contemplated the future.

In one of my stories about the trial, I had described Oscar Gladden as "the first of the new breed of television evangelists," and he was surely that. Until the 1990s, religious television had been the preserve of the fundamentalist and charismatic preachers. But in the late 1980s the sex scandals, the naked avarice and the sleazy excesses of many had caused a significant waning of their audiences. Gladden was among the first to note this decline, and in it he recognized an opportunity.

He had observed that, for all their successes, the television evangelists had limited their outreach. They confined themselves to the medium's peripheral times and had been content to preach to the converted. And he had noted also that their principal supporters, the faithful who dropped their offerings into the televangelists' bottomless begging-bowls, were predominantly middle-aged women.

Oscar Gladden — himself an itinerant preacher but little known at the time—fashioned a new evangelism, presenting a faith with a wider credibility and a broader appeal. He realized that the complexities of modern life had produced a widespread malaise of spirit and that millions of people, even those outside the churches, needed to believe in something larger than themselves. He set out to meet that need.

He put forward what he termed a ''twentieth-century faith: a religion for modern man in today's language.'' He organized the commonly accepted North American shibboleths about God, family, success and happiness into a plausible system of thought and called it Oneness.

His Religion for Today theme was an immediate success. Within a few years he had become the preeminent television evangelist in North America and his Worldwide Church of One claimed ten million adherents. Much of that success stemmed from the fact that Oscar Gladden knew intuitively how to work effectively within the confines of the television screen. A strikingly handsome man, he heightened the impact of his appearance through special lighting. And he deliberately created a mystery about his person—living reclusively, never going about in public.

There had been allegations at the trial that some of Gladden's business ventures skated on the thin ice of legality, but none of the charges had been substantiated. None of this gave me pause; it was inevitable that such a man would draw criticism. He was an unorthodox and enormously successful television preacher; he was wealthy; he was reclusive; he was arrogant. He wouldn't join the club and he refused to play by others' rules. He was hated by two or three labor unions that had tried vainly to break his ranks and he had publicly ticked-off many important people.

Senator Johnny Gallagher, a prominent Roman Catholic layman and the Liberal-Democrat, had alleged anti-trust violations, and the manipulation of tax-exempt benefits and had propagated any number of unconfirmed rumors. But I knew the Senator, and he was hardly an objective critic; if it served his ambition he was not above a McCarthy-style scattering of unsubstantiated charges.

But beyond the mystery and the misanthropy, what sort of man was this whose offer of a job was so tempting me, even before I quite knew what the job involved? He had already caused me to have ambivalent thoughts about myself. I was, on one hand, flattered that a person of international notoriety was prepared to offer me a position of trust and a lot of money but, on the other, troubled by how easily my head had been turned by the prospect of the money. With only a few minutes' consideration, I was contemplating turning my back on more than a dozen years as a journalist to do what sounded very much like public relations. And for, of all unlikely businesses, a religious organization. I remembered the outpourings of derision at the Hellbox when it was learned that Robin Drake, an old drinking companion and a senior reporter at the *Post*, had gone to work for one of the giant public relations agencies. Sellout, was the general judgment. But if I were to join Gladden, wherein would I be different?

And how could I rationalize the admiration I was feeling for the car in which I was riding? I, Tony Carpenter, car-buff? How often, snug in the right-hand driver's seat of my beloved Smedley, had I scorned Detroit's chromed and ungainly behemoths. Incredible that I could be so easily seduced.

Money corrupts; big money corrupts immediately.


We left North Hempstead Turnpike and headed north. Hegeman's Lane, Chicken Valley Road, Piping Rock Road, Pink

Woods Lane—the names as picturesque as the virgin woodlands through which we were passing. I recognized the area: we were in Matinecock, not far from Oyster Bay. It was lush, verdant country, money country. The road — crowded in upon by an astonishing variety of trees and shrubs—meandered in gentle curves among low hills and the occasional rock outcrop. There were few signs of habitation, only infrequent unmarked drive-ways leading off into the unspoiled woods and granting only momentary glimpses of the great houses secluded there.

On Duck Rock Road the car slowed. We pulled onto the shoulder and stopped. Through the rear window I saw Oscar Gladden leave the limousine behind. The driver had the door open for him and the car dipped as he got in.

"You get the dollar-ninety-eight tour," he said. "The property starts here."

We drove alongside a mortarless stone wall surmounted with barbed wire, turned at a massive ornamental-iron gate, and stopped at the bottom of a red brick road that ran straight as an arrow between rows of poplars to the house. On either side, tailored lawns draped the rolling contours of the land. Flower-beds foamed with rainbow colors. Shrubbery clustered in clots of variegated green. Giant trees reared to cast their shade. The grass! I marveled—it was like broadloom. I'd want to take off my shoes to walk on it.

Within the gates there was a stone gate-house. A barrier was raised and we passed through. I caught a glimpse of three men in uniform, each wearing a gun. One was a dwarf with a sin-gularly ugly face. He lifted a stubby arm in a crisp salute.

"Knee-Hi," Gladden said. "He runs the security system."

The house lay ahead, an appropriate jewel for the setting. Soaring Doric columns. Barn-red brick with white shutters and trim. Flower boxes overflowing on each sill. A front entrance beyond a wide ballustraded porch. Ten-foot-high double-hung doors with heavy brass knobs and decorative hinges. Brass car-riage-lamps on fluted columns. An elaborately carved pediment drew it all together.

"Be it ever so humble," I said, and saw the slightest smile curl the corner of Gladden's lips.

But nothing of the exterior prepared me for the interior of

the house. The front door opened on a high-ceilinged entry hall with an aquarium that ran wall-to-wall and floor-to-ceiling. In its crystalline water swam a variety of fish. Like a boy before the window of a toy store, I put my hands on the warm glass.

"My god!" I said. "Those are barracuda. And that! That's a lemon shark. And those smaller ones—piranha." As I watched, a conger eel slid its serpent's head from a crevice in the coral at the bottom of the tank and then withdrew it. "They're all predators," I said, staring into the unblinking eye of the shark as it slid effortlessly past. "Who feeds them? Or do they feed on each other?"

"Knee-Hi," Gladden said, not trying to mask his pleasure at my reaction. "You must watch some time. It's quite a show."

I turned away. "Some conversation-piece when friends drop by."

"I have no friends who drop by."

"No friends?"

"Only people who work for me. I keep the fish to impress on them that there's enough for everyone if no one gets greedy."

We went into a room off the entrance hall. The walls were covered with trophies and with photographs of Oscar Gladden skeet-shooting and, in his earlier years, as a sumo-wrestler. Mounted in glass cases were perhaps two dozen shotguns, some of them antique, with elaborately chased shell chambers and intricately carved stocks.

"My one avocation," Gladden said.

On the near wall there was a bank of television monitors and a control panel worthy of a metropolitan broadcasting station. Gladden flipped some switches and I saw on the screens various areas of the estate, along with the halls and principal rooms of the house.

"There's a matching set of monitors in the gate-house," he said. "The only parts of the house not covered by the cameras are my bedroom and office, my daughter Josephine's living quarters and the studio where she paints."

We went on, to a living room with great redwood beams; to a dining room, airy and dancing with light, the sunlight pouring in to shatter on a massive crystal chandelier suspended over a banquet-size table; to a study walled with books, the furniture dressed in suede.

We took an elevator to the second floor, passed a conservatory and two offices and came finally to Oscar Gladden's bedroom. I thought I had become inured to the spectacular but in the doorway I gasped. At the center of a circular room an enormous round bed sat on a dais, its four posts spiraling nearly to the ceiling. The bedspread was black satin with a clot of scarlet cushions at the head. The entire room was mirrored: walls, ceiling and floor. At the far end there was a Roman bath with a descent of marble stairs. On the ceiling above the bed were television and movie screens. Gladden touched a button and music enveloped us.

"It's a goddamn sex arena!" I blurted, and Oscar Gladden laughed, loving it. Above the music there came the sound of a soft chiming.

"Lunch," said Oscar Gladden, and led the way.

Spun-glass draperies had been drawn to filter the sun, and the chandelier had been lit. A thousand facets reflected the light onto the linen and silver. There were fresh flowers and bowls heaped with fruit. Happily, for it was barely noon, there was only soup and a salad and crepes. But such a soup! Senegalese, I was told: cold and curried and creamy, with tiny morsels of white chicken flesh at the bottom of the bowl; icy lettuce with chunks of avocado; segments of tangerine and bits of macadamia nuts; crepes folded about a combination of lobster, shrimps and scallops in a cream sauce that hinted of tarragon and Tabasco. And a chill white burgundy. I glanced at the label and saw that it was a Moillard Meursault.

Gladden met one of my expectations: he was a true trencherman, gourmandising the oversize portions heaped on his plate. Having introduced me to his daughter when she came late to the table—"Jo, this is Tony Carpenter. He's a reporter, so have a care"—he gave over to eating and said hardly a word through the meal.

Josephine Gladden was tall and dark and so beautiful that my teeth ached. Her black, shining hair, drawn back softly into a chignon, provided a simple frame for the perfect oval of her face. She had her father's red lips and even white teeth and his pink, clear skin. On her it was breathtaking. Her most extraordinary feature was her eyes; the irises were a startling emerald. She was wearing a black camisole top that bared her pale arms and shoulders, and slim black trousers that emphasized her ballerina's legs. I thought, in short, that I had never seen anyone so beautiful.

I am not normally gauche with women; with Jo Gladden I was a fumble-fingered oaf. I who live by words could find none of the right ones, and so I stumbled and stammered and seemed, I'm sure, a dolt. I spilled my wine and dropped a fork to the floor and on the whole gave an excellent imitation of a pubescent youth on his first heavy date. Fortunately, my gaucheries seemed to pass unnoticed, and she chatted on amiably. By the end of the meal I had returned almost to normal, and when Gladden said, "Josephine, my dear, you might take our guest up to your studio and show him your work," I rose happily to follow her.

Jo Gladden's studio was reached by a spiral staircase that rose from the second-floor hallway. On the way up the stairs, the undulation of her hips at my eye-level so enchanted me I had to concentrate to keep my mind on what she was saying: that her father was her patron and had greatly encouraged her but that he had never been to her studio. The incongruity of Oscar Gladden negotiating the narrow winding staircase didn't seem to have occurred to her.

The studio matched the house for drama. The ceiling was constructed entirely of glass, shaded in part by semi-opaque panels so motorized that they could be travelled to cover as much or as little of the expanse as was desired. Stacked against the walls were three or four dozen canvases. On an easel was a work in progress. It depicted a stylized man of heroic proportions against a forest wasteland of uprooted trees and brackish water. The treatment was bold, and the colors were vivid and seemed to be derivative of American Indian painting. I walked about, pausing before some of the canvases. Even to my untrained eye it was clear that Jo Gladden was no amateur dauber.

She broke what had become an extended silence. "I'm getting ready for a one-man show."

"Where?"

"The Oneida Gallery. On East 57th."

"Yes, I know the owner, Bernie Leventhal." I turned to her. "I don't want to pretend to expertise, but this is very good stuff."

Her eyes shone. "It's my first show. No one but Bernie has seen it." She smiled. "And now you, of course."

"Anything I can do to help publicize it?" I asked. "I could say a word at the *Register.*"

"Oh, you mustn't do that," she said, suddenly intense. "I don't want special treatment. I want to make it, if I do make it, on my own."

We were at ease with each other now, my initial awkwardness having passed. We talked for perhaps half an hour about many things, during which a uniformed maid climbed the stairs with jasmine tea and petits fours. I found myself talking about my two years in London and my frequent trips to Paris. We found to our delight that we shared a number of enthusiasms for the City of Light, including one for Chez Julie, a tiny restaurant near La Place des Vosges.

"Your father," she said, moving the conversation forward. "Is he a journalist? A writer?"

"You could say that."

"I don't understand."

"He writes advertising copy." I grinned and made a sweeping gesture as though delineating a billboard. "*DESTINY!—the pantyhose that shapes your end!*" She smiled. "He had another immortal line, for somebody's kitty-litter: *Don't let your guests know you run a cathouse.*"

She was looking at me from the corner of her eye. "You're having fun with me."

"No, no—that's how he makes his living. There are worse ways, I suppose."

"And your mother?"

"Alive and well and, like my father, old-country Irish. Her family name is Zefferelli. Don't ask me where that comes from; maybe one of those itinerant Italian troubadors who wandered about Ireland a few generations back. It might account for my loving opera but being tone-deaf."

"And you—were you born in Ireland?"

"You could say that. Coogan's Bluff."

"Coogan's Bluff's in Brooklyn."

"When my grandparents moved there it was Ireland."

"And where do you live now?"

"Peter Cooper Village. On the 23rd Street side. Lovely view of the sewage in the East River."

"And you're thinking about coming to work for my father?"

I nodded slightly. "Thinking about it."

She was nibbling on one of the petits fours. "How much do you know about my father?"

"That he's an extraordinary man and . . . ." I cast about for something to add. "Mostly what everybody does: that he's a new breed of television evangelist. Not much more than that, I'm afraid."

"And what would you do for him?"

"He described it as public relations."

The slightest frown had drawn her brows together. "I suppose you know he's not an easy man to work for."

"There'd be nothing new in that," I said, keeping it light. "You should meet my managing editor. Ebenezer Scrooge apprenticed under him."

She was looking at the painting on the easel, or beyond it, I couldn't be sure. Her gaze seemed far off, as did her voice when she spoke. "I may have to go to work for him myself."

"And stop painting?" I said.

She gave her head a quick shake, almost as though freeing her hair. She lifted the teapot to pour me a second cup. Doing so, she glanced at her watch.

"Oh, my," she said, suddenly businesslike. "I'm afraid it's time to deliver you to Father."

She took me instead to a small office and introduced me to Bartholemew: "He's a love."

Bartholemew was Oscar Gladden's more or less male secretary and, as I would learn, his good right arm. He fulfilled his duties with unremitting efficiency and a smile that looked pasted on. *Teeth!* I entered his office once when he was involved in firing one of the day-maids, and even then he looked like someone doing a Jimmy Carter impression. He couldn't have weighed more than 140 pounds but was at least six feet tall. My irreverent imagination pictured him and Gladden side by side —the perfect "10."

He greeted me coyly and offered the bundle of dry bones that was his hand.

"Welcome," he said. "Mr. Gladden's ready for you. Perhaps afterwards I can show you your office."

"I haven't taken the job yet," I said.

Bartholemew flushed. "Oh dear. My error," he said and led me to Oscar Gladden's office.

Gladden rose from behind his circular desk and took me to a pair of low, overstuffed leather chairs set in a corner formed by intersecting bookcases. He indicated a pewter coffee pot and some two-fisted mugs on the coffee table, filled one and sat. There was a great whoosh of air from the cushions. Not troubling to wait until I had filled my cup, he took a long swallow from his own.

"Now, to begin," he said, "let's find out what, if anything, you know about me. First, about my work."

The man certainly isn't given to indirection, I thought. Which was fine with me; I'm usually pretty straightforward.

"Your daughter just asked me that question," I said. "The answer is very little. Most of what I do know I learned covering the trial, plus some digging in the files. You're president and founder of the Worldwide Church of One. You do six television shows a week. I gather from the testimony given over the past four weeks that the church owns a cable network and buys time around the world. There's a broadcast center in Queens, another in L.A. There's a hundred-acre—what shall I call it?—amusement park in San Bernardino. There's a publishing house, a chain of—I have no idea how many—fitness centers and meditation temples, all of them outgrowths of the television show. Plus, as best I can judge, a dozen or so other projects."

I paused. He gave a series of quick, slight nods, as though to say, Get on with it, I'll let you know when you have it wrong.

"I wasn't able to dig out much about you personally—which is, I gather, the way you want it. I do know that you were born in Canada and came here in your late teens, that you suffer from diabetes, that you have excellent taste in scotch and daughters and that your reclusivity makes Greta Garbo look like a glad-hander."

I was beginning to feel intimidated and was compensating with flippancy. There was about Oscar Gladden—despite the overwhelming cordiality he could turn on at will—a hard, inner preoccupation that created the impression you were wasting his time. Fine, I don't need to be loved by the people I work for, but I am quickly made irascible by anyone who treats me as his inferior. With such, I can become uncharacteristically edgy. I decided to establish from the beginning an eye-level relationship.

"Now," I said, "what do you know about me?"

He shot me a quick, appraising glance. "Mr. Carpenter, I don't hire someone I haven't checked out." His voice was wintry. He smiled, and it was like the arrival of a chinook. "The only negative factor is that you're a journalist."

"Nobody's perfect," I quipped.

"Which," he said, "brings me to the reason for our discussion. You know my feelings about the news media?"

"Doesn't everyone?"

"I put it to you: you covered the trial. Set aside for a moment your predisposition to defend your profession—if that's what it is—and tell me if the impression of Oscar Gladden conveyed by the press fairly represented the facts as they came out in testimony."

"I don't think you can lump all—"

He brushed past the defense I was about to offer. "The reports were inaccurate and biased, the editorial comments were prejudiced and the ridicule by the cartoonists was—there's only one word for it—criminal."

I had been about to point out that he had made himself a target. His arrogance, his unconcealed disdain for the court and for the news media had raised hackles and created enemies, especially among those reporters he had skewered during the recesses. And there was the tempting target of his person: the spectacular obesity, the brusque manner, the eccentricity, the twin stretch-limousines purring each afternoon at the curb. Not that any of these could be offered as justification for the lack of objectivity in the coverage. The cartoonists had, it was true, been savage, portraying him as the ultimate capitalist: greedy, rapacious, porcine and, invariably, wearing a halo formed of dollar signs.

"No argument," I said. "You didn't get a fair shake. But then you're not your average country vicar."

That amused him for some reason. "There *were* exceptions," he conceded.

"Mr. Gladden," I said, "I don't think you brought me here to do a number on the sins of the press. I was hoping that you would spell out exactly what it is you want me to do. I don't think you're about to pay me the kind of money we talked about merely to write your biog."

"You're right," he said. The tip of his tongue darted out, moistened his lips and disappeared. "You and I are going to work on a special project. We're going to teach the news media a lesson long overdue. That they are *not* a law unto themselves. That they may *not* intrude in people's lives indifferent to the consequences. And that they may *not* appoint themselves judge and jury and sit in judgment over their peers."

I was about to say, You're comparing apples and oranges; don't put us all in one basket, but I saw that he was in no mood for lightness. I said instead, not argumentively, "They've been doing it a long time." Old loyalties made me amend that to, "The yellow press, that is."

"It's time it stopped," he snapped.

He riffled through some papers on the coffee table, apparently seeking a particular note. His tiny pink tongue flicked in and out. "Beyond that," he said, "the two of us are going to do something about the demagoguery of Johnny Gallagher."

Johnny Gallagher, as I have mentioned, was the Liberal-Democrat senator from New York who was seeking to be returned in the upcoming off-year congressional election. Gallagher was a high-powered orator with a talent for vivid verbal images, a man who knew how to ring the changes on an issue. But grabby issues had been hard to come by, and when a friend in the Justice department tipped him off that an investigation was about to be made by the Internal Revenue Service into Oscar Gladden's business empire, he had seized it as a hungry dog a bone. Gallagher's constituents were mostly blue-collar voters and the conservative right, and Gladden was the perfect foil. In his speeches Gallagher had been thundering: "This blatant atheist and the tax-exempt empire he rules over must be opposed by every God-fearing American."

Gladden had found the sheet of paper he'd been looking for. "We'll get to Gallagher later. Right now, let me tell you what your first project will be." He began to read. "Your job will be to find a man, a prototypically ordinary American, someone whose IQ is average and whose talents and achievements are zilch. A complete nonentity. A guy who hasn't won so much as a bowling prize—"

"A Mr. Nobody," I supplied.

"Exactly! Then, having found our Mr. Nobody, we turn him into a national celebrity overnight."

I shook my head, puzzled. "I don't follow. Leaving aside for the moment the problems involved in making this no-talent nonentity a celebrity, what's the point?"

Gladden leaned forward, his dark eyes glinting. "The point is this: in so doing, we will have exposed the news media for what it is. We will have demonstrated that they are committed to sensationalism. That they are ready to report anything—legitimate news or not, fraudulent or not—if it will pander to the idiots who read their papers or watch their programs; that they will manipulate any nonevent and mount any hobby-horse if it will sell papers or improve ratings." He leaned back in his protesting chair. "We'll exploit the exploiters of others and show them for what they are."

Perspiration was beading on his brow and he was breathing heavily. He took a cigar from a tooled-leather humidor, went through the cigar-smoker's ritual and vented a rolling cloud of smoke toward the ceiling.

I shook my head dubiously. "I don't know. I doubt that you could make it fly. The media aren't nearly as bad as you paint them." But, despite my immediate reaction, I was intrigued. Andy Warhol had said that the day was coming when everyone would be famous for fifteen minutes; we could validate his prediction. I smiled inwardly as the possibilities began to present themselves. It could be quite a caper. I could even use the project to settle a few scores. A chuckle escaped me. Gladden grinned, and as I began to laugh, he laughed with me.

"Here," he said, "have a cigar."

I took it and lit up. Yes, damn it, the possibilities were intriguing. The job could be fun. I would take it. But before I accepted, I would use the two-week let's-see-if-we-like-each-other period to learn what I could about Oscar Gladden.


The limousine halted short of the gate-house. There appeared to be a problem with the hinged barrier; two of the guards were working on the mechanism. Knee-Hi stood in the roadway, bowed legs spread, a square palm held up to stop the driver of my car. He was a grotesquely ugly man. The oversize head was surmounted by a bulbous brow. The eyes were deep-set and glinted like brown beads from beneath fierce, arched eyebrows. His cheeks were nubbly with acne and there was a straggle of steel-wool beard at the tip of the protruding jaw. His eyes were in shadow, and he appeared to be glaring at me with undisguised hostility, an impression that I quickly realized might not be accurate—he was in the direct sunlight. He saw me looking at him and smiled, baring rows of tiny, seed-pearl teeth. I felt a crawling on my skin.

One of the guards approached the limousine. I lowered the window.

"Hullo, Mr. C.," he said with a self-conscious grin. "Remember me?"

I snapped my fingers in recognition. "Gus Longo! Seventeenth Precinct. How are you?"

He seemed unduly pleased at being remembered, but it had been no great feat of recall. When I was new to the police beat he had given me a number of leads and the tipoff that had enabled me to break the IRT insurance-murders story. It had won me a bonus and an award and had raised my stock at the *Register*. In appreciation, I had pulled some strings in the mayor's office and had managed to get him transferred to the Special Squad, an elite group of policemen attached to the Manhattan district attorney's office. It was years since I had last seen him. In the meantime I'd heard scuttlebutt that he'd been busted for taking kickbacks from a member of the Bonanno family.

He shuffled his feet. "You prob'ly heard I quit the force." The expression in his eyes told me he was wondering whether I knew he'd been busted. "Mr. G. was nice enough to take me on. Bein' a cop's a mug's game," he added.

I decided to do a little fishing. "How do you like it here? What are your duties?"

He was offhand. "Fine. I like it fine. I'm one of the guards — " He grinned and looked down at his uniform. "I guess you can see that. There's six of us. I double as a driver when they need me." He gave a what-the-hell kind of laugh. "The money's good an'. . . ." He put a hand to the small of his back, feigned a grimace and looked at his feet. "An' no more poundin' a beat."

"Six guards! What is this? Fort Knox?"

"Not only that, there's live TV cameras on the grounds." He seemed impressed by it. "An' pit bulls."

"But why?"

He shrugged, not avoiding my question but cutting off the discussion. "Don' ask me. Mr. G. wants it that way, an' he's the boss."

The gate levered to vertical, and Knee-Hi signaled my driver forward. Gus leaned a forearm on the window opening, put his head partly within the car and dropped his voice to a whisper.

"Mr. C.," he said, "jus' between you 'n' me, okay? If you're thinkin' of goin' to work for Mr. G., don't. That's all I'm sayin'. Just don't."

The driver was revving the engine. Gus stepped back, and as the car pulled away he gave me a half smile and a salute.

# FOUR

I don't suppose it is necessary to tell you about Oscar Gladden on television. Is there anyone in the civilized world who hasn't watched him at least once? I had seen him mostly only in glimpses while channel-hopping of a Sunday morning, but I knew that if I was going to work for him I owed it to myself to learn precisely what he stood for and something of what he preached. So at the earliest opportunity I tuned in.

Almost despite myself I was impressed. It was one hell of a good show. The presentation itself was dramatic. There was no set. The show opened—after some intricate computer graphics —with the word *One* superimposed on a map of the world, and there, suddenly, without introduction, was Oscar Gladden in close-up. He wore a black suit and was positioned against a jet-black background. Because of the lighting, the outline of his body disappeared and there was no evidence of his obesity. Nor did his face betray it; the staging and the makeup gave him the appearance of a man of normal proportions. Apart from his face, the only color on the screen was the brilliant red of his tie and the matching daub of scarlet that was the rose on his lapel.

Let it not be denied: Oscar Gladden on television was an extraordinarily handsome man. And when he came to the heart of his brief message and the camera moved in for a close-up (and by close-up I mean from just above the eyebrows to just below the lower lip), the show approached high drama.

"Happiness," he was saying. "You want to find happiness. Everyone does. But happiness isn't something you find; it's something you create. You are born with two things: existence and opportunity, and these are the raw materials out of which you can make a worthwhile life. You don't *find* happiness, just as you don't *find* steel—you refine it from the rough ore. The artist doesn't *find* a beautiful statue; he sculpts it from the shapeless marble. The musician doesn't *find* great melody; he composes it out of the eight-note scale. You see, there is a principle at the heart of life: life is not what you find, it's what you *create!* You get a mind; you can use it or let it stagnate. You get 365 days in the year; you can waste them or use them. You get two people living together in marriage; you can turn it into a beautiful relationship or you can make it a hell on earth." The voice fell to a whisper. "You don't find happiness—*you create it!"*

The eyes were mesmerizing. He appeared only twice on the program, at the beginning and in the final five minutes, but his presence gave the show validity. For all that, most of the impact derived from his words: they were precisely articulated, credible and spoken with a quiet, controlled authority, and despite my skepticism I found myself caught up in what he was saying.

I'm aware that I sound like a convert. I am anything but. As you will learn, I came to know the real Oscar Gladden, and he was utterly unlike the spellbinder on the screen who entranced tens of millions of people in 145 countries around the world. But on television, he was—and there is only one word for it—hypnotic.

I checked in at the paper, prepared to explain where I'd been but no more than that. Gillian, Ed Replogle's secretary, saw me and beckoned. Gillian was not an especially beautiful girl but she carried herself with the grace of a dancer. When she walked her special walk through the newsroom all work stopped. I had dated her a time or two but it had led to complications. Replogle, typically, had stuck his nose in and laid on me a few unsubtle hints about "not dipping your pen in the company ink." I looked at Gillian and thought how beautiful Jo was.

"Mr. Replogle's been looking for you," she said.

"Yes?"

"He heard you went off with Mr. Gladden in his car and

told me to track you down. He thought maybe you could set it up to get some shots of Gladden's estate. I tried to call you there but it's an unlisted number.''

''Pictures? Not a chance.''

''Anyway, he wants to see you. He's in a meeting with the publisher and they're going right through lunch. He said two-thirty.''

I told her I was off to do research on Oscar Gladden, a fact, and dropped in at the Hellbox. As I'd hoped, Dunc Robertson was there. He saw me come in and banged on the bar with an open hand.

''Hold it! Hold it! Here's Tony. He can fill us in.'' He was waving an arm. ''Tony, c'm'ere. What the hell were you doing riding round with Oscar Gladden? You haven't got religion?— God forbid.''

I told the story—altering it, of course, making a big deal out of it, milking it for laughs—and had them in the aisles. I noticed that Dunc was working on a gin and tonic, and as soon as I could catch Kono's eye, I pointed at Dunc's glass, held up two fingers and drew Dunc over to my table.

Dunc Robertson is my closest friend in the news business. We met when we were both juniors on the *Herald-Trib*, back when there *was* a *Herald-Trib*. He's older than I, and tougher minded. If I have a mentor, it's Dunc. I've had few secrets from him—whether related to the state of my finances or the state of my marriage—and was therefore ill-at-ease in the knowledge that I was considering joining Oscar Gladden, a move that Dunc would surely disapprove.

Dunc now worked as a general reporter for the *Wall Street Journal*. He is a balding, cadaverous man of forty with outsize hands and feet who shambles rather than walks. And he conceals a knife-edge mind behind an offhand manner. Dunc and I were founding members of the Hellbox, not one of the city's five-star restaurants but for some reason—mostly its proximity to the *Register* and the *Daily News*—an informal meeting place for a number of us ink-stained wretches.

As we sat down, I said, ''Tell me what you know about Oscar Gladden.''

He looked at me with arched brows. "What do I know? *You're* the redeemed sinner at this table."

Kono arrived with the drinks and put the chit before me. I took out a pencil to initial it.

"Sorry, Mist' Tony," Kono said, smiling his permanent smile. "Cash-money. Mr. Ann-berg say."

I glared, but Kono merely rolled his eyes upward in a gesture of capitulation to the inevitable. I dug out a rumpled bill and flung it on the table. "Tell Mr. Annenberg I was planning to bring Frank Sinatra and Elizabeth Taylor in here tomorrow for photo-sessions, but now to hell with it!" As Kono reached into a pocket for change, I gave a dismissive wave. Too late I noticed that I'd thrown down a ten-dollar bill.

Dunc was already working on his drink. "What do I know about Oscar Gladden?" he said contemplatively into his glass. "Not much, except that he's rich as Croesus and secretive as a double-agent. I looked him up the other day in *Standard and Poor's*. Not much there. Nor is there much about — what's it called?—the Worldwide Church of One." He sighed resignedly, taking a swallow of his drink. "The doctrine of the separation of church and state in this country exists to make it legal for some TV church to separate you from your estate.

"There *is* a company, Gladden Inc., listed," he continued. "It's owned by Oscar Gladden and a half-dozen directors, none of whose names appear, so far as I can learn, on anybody else's board. Dummies, probably. It would appear that he has things so set up that, legally, he's once-removed from the management of all the ventures he's connected with but in such a way that the whole ball of wax is, in fact, a one-man show."

"That came out at the trial," I said, adding, "as you know."

"And of course there's nothing wrong with it," Dunc continued. "It's done all the time. Part of the problem in getting a handle on Gladden Inc. is that it's a religious organization and doesn't have to account to anyone but the taxman, and then only if he has cause to inquire. Gladden's auditors are a one-ledger outfit, Peale and Bjornstadt. Gladden's their principal client—probably their only client. And that's about it. Except, of course, that the Worldwide Church of One is a megabuck operation." He took a long pull at his drink and said almost in passing, "There is talk that he's about to lose his tax-exempt status."

"And?"

"So I asked around. Nothing concrete. The talk was started by the people's friend, Johnny Gallagher. It gets credence because Gladden's such a reclusive SOB and so irksomely rich. I'm told his estate's like an armed camp. Did you get a look?"

I avoided enlarging on what I'd said earlier by making a small production out of fishing a lime seed from my drink. Dunc glanced at me. "Why are you asking? Were you thinking of buying some shares?"

I smiled ruefully. "At the moment I couldn't afford a share of common in a lemonade stand."

"In which case," Dunc said, "I'll stand you."

He drained his glass, put two fingers to his mouth and shrilled a whistle that rattled the glasses back of the bar.


It became a long day. I never did get back to the paper. I took a run over to Queens to check out the OneWorld headquarters and was surprised by its size and complexity. It covered four city blocks and included a twenty-story administration building, a taping and editing facility that rivaled the great networks' and, of course, the broadcast center, an octagonal theater with seating for perhaps seven hundred people. The sound-stage was as spacious as Radio City Music Hall's.

In a nearby Burger King I fell into conversation with two men wearing OneWorld symbols on their coveralls. The older was a lighting man and the other some kind of technician. Apart from some *de rigueur* griping about management, they both liked the company and were Gladden fans. I don't know what I'd expected to find.

I spent what was left of the afternoon doing research, and ended up at the Hellbox again, where there were a half dozen slips telling me that Ed Replogle was trying to reach me, and where I spent the evening — until I don't remember what hour—defending my backgammon championship.

# FIVE

Renata was tapping lightly on my bedroom door. "*Senor, telephono.*"

Renata is my cleaning lady. She's Puerto Rican, was inherited from the previous tenant and is the only reason why my apartment has not been declared a disaster area. Each Saturday she restores order to the clutter of pans and dishes in the sink, the profusion of towels draped on anything handy in the bathroom and the melange of books, newspapers, manuscript pages and empty coffee mugs in the living room — not to mention laundering my socks and shorts and tangled bedsheets.

Renata is confirmed in the conviction that I am incapable of looking after myself (true), that I am lonely (essentially true), that I should be married (utterly untrue) and that any woman would be lucky to have me (would that that were true). She believes in the Puerto Rican version of the cliché about the way to a man's heart, and when I sleep late she prepares enormous field-worker's breakfasts for me—I who prefer grapefruit juice and black coffee. On this morning, as I headed for the telephone, I saw one end of the table laid and caught the scent of eggs and bacon from the kitchen.

It was Jo Gladden. She had been in Toronto visiting her aunt and I had left a message asking her to call on her return.

"We're going to the Museum of Modern Art," she said. "Wasn't that the plan?"

"Yes," I said and glanced at my bare wrist. "What time is it?"

"Ten-fifteen, slugabed," she said lightly. "I was thinking that perhaps we might have an early lunch and then go on to the museum. I'm right across the street, visiting a friend at the Veteran's hospital. I could pick you up in an hour, say."

"Will you hold a second?" I said and covered the telephone with a hand. "Renata."

"*Si, senor?*"

"How much longer . . . *Usted trabajo?*"

"*Senor?*"

"How long you . . . *usted vamos? Finito?*"

She beamed. "*Yo comprendo.*" Enunciating exaggeratedly — always the teacher—she said, "*Dos horas. Uno, dos.* Two how-err. Hokay?"

"Hokay," I said. Judging by the scents wafting from the kitchen, she had well started on making breakfast and would not, I knew, be easily dissuaded.

"Jo," I said, "I'm not nearly ready." I didn't want to get into a prolonged explanation about Renata's breakfasts so I simply said, "Why don't we meet at the museum?"

"You have company," she said. There was the slightest fall-off in the vitality of her voice.

"No, no, no," I said. "Just my cleaning lady." I would need time to shower and shave and, after Renata's breakfast, time to work up an appetite. But more important, I suddenly envisioned the elegance of Jo Gladden in my barren quarters and flinched. "Noon at the museum, right? We can have coffee and a snack there."

"Fine," she said cheerily. "See you there."

At the groaning board my kitchen table had been transformed into, I tucked into breakfast. After a while Renata said, "*Senor.*"

"Yes, Renata."

"*La senorita,* she say err name ees Gladden, righ'?"

"Right."

"Ho Gladden, righ'?"

"Jo Gladden, right."

"*Su padre*—err father—ees not Hos-carr Gladden? On the TV? No?"

"*Si.*"

She put a hand to her mouth. *"Madre de Dios! Hos-carr Gladden!"*

I was intrigued. "You're a fan of his? An *aficionado?"*

*"Si!* Yes. I am—'ow you said eet?—a fan. *Si."* Her eyes were wide and shining. I was thinking, Who can measure the reach of television! My cleaning lady is a disciple of Oscar Gladden, the janitor in my building is a devotee of William F. Buckley (the building could burn down unnoticed when "Firing Line" is on), and I have a friend at Columbia, a teacher with a Ph.D. in Romance literature and a string of earned degrees as long as a kite's tail, who never misses "Dallas."

From that point on, breakfast was served against an excited babble of pidgin. If Renata had been devoted to me before, my knowing Oscar Gladden had now elevated me into an object of veneration.


Foot-weary after an hour or so of wandering through the French Impressionist galleries, Jo and I were seated on an upholstered bench in the Monet Room looking down on the courtyard below.

The courtyard at the Museum of Modern Art is sequestered at the bottom of a well formed by the surrounding mid-Manhattan highrises. It is a soul-restoring place, a sylvan retreat at the heart of the frenetic bustle and uproar of the city. Shrubbery, a small grove of Lombardy poplars and a scattering of ironwood and sycamore trees soften the rectilinear area and cast their shifting shadows on the ivy ground-cover. A European weeping birch trails its foliage on the mottled Vermont-marble paving and into the reflecting pool where galaxies of pennies glitter and tiny fountains spout their silver showers. To one side, Rodin's *Balzac* rears imperiously, as though offended at the sight of Picasso's rude caricature of a *She Goat* at his feet. Men and women, mostly young and mostly in pairs, wander about or slump untidily on a variety of chairs.

Neither Jo nor I had said anything for some time. I was suddenly taken by an acute awareness of the woman beside me and turned to her, gazing openly at her for a moment. She seemed not to notice; her eyes were still on the courtyard and her thoughts seemed far away. I got the impression that her spirit was heavy.

"What does a place like this do to you?" I asked.

She drew a deep breath, expelling it before replying. "I don't know whether I can describe it," she said. "The pictures . . . the sense of the artists' presence . . . I can feel my spirit expanding until, well, there are times when it's almost unbearable." Her eyes went to one of the Monet panels and she smiled ruefully. "I come here for inspiration, and then I want to go home and burn everything I've done."

"How long have you been studying?" I asked.

"As long as I can remember. But seriously only since my late teens. I've been in Europe most of the last half-dozen years. In Lausanne, mostly. And then in Paris, as I told you, at L'ecole des Beaux Arts. I've been home only Christmases and on vacations. And even during some of those I was off junketing around the world."

"Then you haven't seen much of your father."

"Father believes that the world is the best university and a travel-guide is the best reading."

"But now you've graduated."

"Not quite. I think of my show as my graduation." She smiled ruefully again. "I have nightmares. Nobody comes. Nobody buys a picture. The critics hate my work."

"I'll give you odds against that."

There was a brief flare of excitement that quickly burned out. "You're being kind."

"I'll still give you odds."

She drew a deep breath and expelled it almost in a gust. "Sorry to be so uptight about it but it's all I've lived for for the past three years. The show, I mean." She glanced at me and then away and laughed a small, apologetic laugh. "I must seem like a spoiled brat. I've never lacked for anything. Anything." She was silent, reflecting. "I suppose I've got the most generous father in the world." There was an odd lack of emotion in her voice. "I worry about him," she added.

"Why?"

"His diabetes. He won't do what he's told." She frowned and looked down into the courtyard again.

"Has your father always been so . . . reclusive?" I'd almost said antisocial.

She nodded, and suddenly her eyes flashed. "Do you wonder—the way he's been treated? In the newspapers? And by the politicians?"

I took advantage of her concentration to study her face. Her skin was flushed with indignation and her eyes were flashing. "You *are* your father's daughter," I said and then amended it. "In appearance, at least. Your mother—do you take after her as well?"

"She died when I was in my teens."

"Sorry."

"No, no, that's all right. Yes, I *am* like her; certainly more than I'm like Father." She was silent for a moment, her head down, her lips pursed in thought. "It wasn't a very good marriage." She looked up at me. "Are you married?"

The sudden interposition of Maggie jolted me. "No," I said. "At least, not any more. Sentence reprieved, you might say. I presume you're not?"

"Oh my goodness, no. I'm not sure I believe in it."

"Somebody disappointed you."

"No, nothing like that. It's marriage itself: the institution. I love the part about the vows, the church filled with flowers, your family and your friends all gathered—I guess everybody does—but I think it's reckless to promise to love, honor and cherish for the rest of your life. How do you know what you'll be like twenty or thirty years from now? Or what the other person will be like? We change. I'd be willing to bet that most couples wouldn't give each other a second look if they met as strangers after twenty years."

"But isn't that the point? After twenty years you're not strangers."

She looked at me, her eyes questioning. "You surprise me. When I asked were you married, you said no, reprieved. And now you're defending marriage."

"I suppose I am," I said, realizing that we had ventured into serious territory but not wanting to draw back.

"Any children?"

"There was no point in compounding the mistake."

"And yet you believe in marriage."

"I've seen my parents' marriage. So, despite *my* scar tissue . . . ."

She frowned. "And I've seen my parents' marriage. . . ."

A silence fell between us. I wasn't quite sure how to react, so I said nothing.

After a moment she raised her head and the frown was gone. "It's none of my business but have you made up your mind about coming to work for my father?"

Her directness momentarily startled me. "I'm not sure," I said. "I'm not sure I'm the right man for the job."

"I don't know what the job encompasses," she said, "but why wouldn't you be right for it?"

I grinned. "Well, your father's a famous religious leader, and I've never been celebrated for my piety."

"You're not an atheist?"

"No," I said. "I certainly am not an atheist."

It may be appropriate to interject here a word about my attitude to religion. I belong to no church; I'm attached to no religious group; I follow no teaching or discipline. If I were required to identify myself with a category, I would have to choose agnostic. I tend to be distrustful of both the zealot and the atheist. For all their antithetical conclusions, they are kin. I find myself wanting to say to the atheist: How can you be so damn sure there is no God?—have you examined all the evidence? Have you unlocked all the mysteries? I want to say to religious zealots: And how can *you* be unequivocal about the nature of the universe? Can the mystery of existence be reduced to dogma? Can the Almighty be captured in a book?

I'd pondered the question of belief in God throughout my youth and early manhood and had finally concluded that there are only two possible answers: faith and agnosticism. I had settled on agnosticism as the only response that I—I being who I am—could make. Some of my friends have chided me about this, insisting that I haven't tried faith. And they're right; I haven't. But it hasn't been by choice. I simply cannot have faith in someone or something that my mind can't posit, and I can't —for all my willing it—envision a God of love in a world whose existence is based on killing. Look about you: the world is so ordered that it is necessary to take life to sustain life. All living creatures are prey or are preyed upon. Animals eat other animals. Big fish eat little fish, and so on down the line to where microscopic creatures consume other microscopic creatures. It's a hierarchy of devouring. We humans, for instance, kill and eat virtually anything we can metabolize. There is no option; the rule is kill and eat, or die. Enough to say that I find it impossible to believe that the immeasurable suffering intrinsic to life could be the reflection of a God one describes as Father. I, certainly, wouldn't treat my children so.

All of which, of course, had made me curious about Oscar Gladden. He certainly didn't fit the traditional preconception of a religious leader. He was, in outlook and lifestyle, the polar opposite of your typical everyday religious. He was arrogant, egotistical, vindictive, gluttonous and touched with megalomania. (My god!—looking now at the way I have characterized him, how did I stay with him as long as I did?)

But I was not about to say any of this to Jo. I didn't want to risk anything that might alienate us.

But her question was hanging. Was I going to take the job her father had offered me? I evaded it by saying, "You mentioned the possibility that *you* might be going to work for your father. Were you serious?"

She didn't answer right away but began to brush at a bit of lint on her skirt. "I'm not quite sure why I'm telling you this," she said slowly. "I guess it's because in a sense we're in the same boat. The reason it's so important for my show to go well is because, if it doesn't, Father wants me to come on his program as a sort of hostess. You know, introducing the show and tying it together. As you probably know, there's something of a tradition in television evangelism of the evangelist's wife or son or daughter appearing with him. I gather the idea is to add— what? — verification, I suppose. You know: 'Look, here are members of my family; the people who know me best. *They* believe in me, so can you.' That kind of thing." She tossed her head in that quick way she had. "I *do* know why I'm telling you this—because time is running out and I'm scared to death."

"I don't quite understand," I said. "You're not a child. You can do as you please."

"No," she said flatly, "we made a deal. Father's kept his part of the bargain and I'll have to keep mine. I was bound and determined that I would paint. Father was dead against it; he wanted me on the show. Talk about fireworks! We sometimes went days without speaking. Finally, he said, 'Okay. Five years. Study wherever you like. Hire the best teachers in the world. I'll build you a studio and pay all the bills. Whatever is needed. And if at the end of those five years, people who know about art, genuine critics, say you're good, okay. But if they don't, you put it behind you and join me.' Well, I took the deal. I shouldn't have but I did."

After a moment I said, "I see now why your show is so important to you."

She gave me a small smile and glanced at her watch. "Oops!" she said and returned her notebook to her bag, preparing to leave. I rose with her and we made our way down the broad stairway to the street level. Outside, one of the Gladden limousines was parked at the curb. The liveried black man I had seen on the drive from Manhattan was standing at the door.

And then she was gone. I stood looking after the limousine until it was lost in the traffic, acutely aware that I was, in the timeworn phrase, falling in love.

# SIX

I am a reporter and thus innately curious. My interest tends to be in the men and women who make the news rather than in the news itself. And I'm a gambler and, as any gambler, prepared to go with the odds. As a consequence I had virtually decided to join Oscar Gladden, even though I was aware that it could be a mistake and that the entire venture could blow up in my face.

Beyond that, I was ready to leave the *Register*. I was at a standstill there. There comes a point in your work for any newspaper where it becomes a matter of move ahead or move on. Either that or settle for being one of the minions who get shifted about like pawns until they are put out to pasture.

Much of my problem was Ed Replogle. He was a difficult bastard, even for a managing editor, and we had clashed from day one. He had been particularly unhappy with me since I had talked him into assigning me to the Albany bureau and had then, after little more than a year, requested Washington. Instead, he pulled me back to New York to sub for Hal McBain, who wrote a general column and had an erratic ticker. When Hal opted for open-heart surgery, I wrote the column for three months and bust my ass to make it work. On McBain's return, I went to Replogle and asked straight-out for a column of my own. He looked at me with those gray, lizard eyes of his, said, "Today, everybody wants to be a star," and assigned me to the Gladden trial. As far as I was concerned, this was full-circle. I'd been a senior reporter for years, covering some of the bigger stories and writing features, had even spent two years with our London bureau, and I felt I was due something better than a return to the courts, even though the Gladden circus *was* a major story. I felt also that I rated a raise.

I said all this in a note to Replogle, and when, on the morning after my museum date with Jo, Gillian handed me an envelope, I opened it with hope. It consisted of a terse three sentences: ticking me off for an insignificant error in a piece I'd done the previous day, stating that management had imposed a moratorium on pay-raises, and ordering me to get my ass over to Johnny Gallagher's campaign headquarters and file a story on a break-in there.


Gallagher's campaign headquarters, on the near East Side, occupied space formerly leased by the Oriental Novelties Co., the ghost of whose tenancy was still visible on the windows despite attempts to scrape it off. Dominant on those windows and on the walls within were enormous blown-up photographs of the candidate, his graying hair carefully tousled, the porcelain caps on his teeth gleaming in a smile absent from his eyes. A good-looking man, Johnny Gallagher: fifty-eight years old and at fighting weight as the result of rigorous daily workouts. An engaging Irish charmer, Johnny Gallagher was most at home on a public platform where his histrionic gifts and anecdotal style could combine to sway even the steely undecided. He was equally effective with individuals. Almost indecently gregarious, he could work a crowd as well as anyone I've seen. He flattered women shamelessly, called total strangers ''Friend,'' clapped workmen on the back with macho ebullience and shook hands at a pace of twenty a minute; managing to leave the impression with each individual that he'd been singled out. And he was a power in Washington, a close personal friend of the president's, a mover and a shaker. Even more prestigious, he was Chairman of the Senate Finance Committee.

He had won the nomination for a third term after an unexpected in-party fight that had ended with ugly recriminations. Gallagher hadn't let that trouble him until a private poll showed him trailing his Republican opponent badly. Needing an issue, he had sought it in Oscar Gladden, railing against his "covert atheism" and the tax-exempt status of his television empire. Then, suddenly, he found another: a break-in at his campaign headquarters.

I was late for the press conference and arrived as the other reporters were leaving. Gallagher saw me at the door and came toward me, affability incarnate.

"I was wondering where the *Register*'s man was," he said, the handshake firm, the brogue orotund, the smile one thousand candlepower.

"You look happy as a pig in shit," I said.

"Happy?"

"It makes a hell of a headline."

"I'm outraged," Gallagher said, turning off the smile and looking suitably indignant. "It's Watergate over again. It's Republican dirty tricks. It's—"

"What did they take?" I asked, pulling a wad of copy-paper from the pocket of my jacket.

"Nothing of value. Not the TV set, not the Xerox, none of the word-processors. Records—they took records. My personal records: my desk-calendar, my correspondence, my files. No vandalism; nothing smashed but the locks on the filing-cabinets in my office. Mark my words: this was no simple break-and-enter."

"Are you saying flat out it was the Republicans? Can I print that?"

Gallagher's trumpeting fell off a few decibels. "I'm not making any charges at this point but figure it out for yourself. Outside of politics Johnny Gallagher doesn't have an enemy in the world, and the Republicans are running scared. Who else would be interested in my files?"

In my business you develop a feeling about a story, and the more I sniffed out this one the less I agreed with Gallagher's conclusions. I knew the Republican candidate, Andy Norlander, and went around to see him. He's a lanky, lugubrious man with a thatch of blond hair like wheat stubble atop his angular head. Looks like a rube but has a brain of Swedish steel. Having none of the graces or artifices, it's something of a small miracle that he has made it in politics. I think of him as the demonstration of Lincoln's aphorism: "You can not fool all the people all of the time." I found him at his headquarters beating on a typewriter.

"Of course it wasn't us," he said. "We certainly wouldn't be dumb enough to repeat Watergate, which was *not* one of the notably successful gambits in political history. Believe me, I'd like nothing better than to nail Gallagher to the wall, but I'm not a gutter-fighter and I'm not a fool."

"Nixon didn't know about Watergate at the beginning. Maybe it was one of your people; somebody with more zeal than brains."

"Let's find out," Norlander said. He turned in his chair and bawled, "Abe!"

A dumpy little man with a gleaming bald head and with the top button of his fly undone to accommodate a belly like a medicine-ball waddled over. He was chewing a cigar that hadn't been lit, removing it between sentences to spit damp specks of tobacco from the tip of his tongue.

"What the hell would we do with Gallagher's papers if we did have 'em?" he asked, looping a brown fleck onto his shirt front. "Gallagher isn't a crook. Stupid, yes, but not venal."

"Some of your people, maybe?"

He shook his head slowly. "Look, I been in politics thirty years; only the dummies play it dirty. Throw mud, you get it on yourself." He sent a shred of tobacco onto Norlander's desk.

"That's everybody's disclaimer. But the mud gets thrown."

"Not on my behalf, damn it!" Norlander said and went back to his typewriter.

I believed him and played the story that way. The other papers led with Gallagher's "Watergate" charges and dumped on the Republicans. I thought they were wrong. Replogle thought they were right and tore a strip off me.


Back in my apartment in a foul mood, I turned on the television. Up came a commercial for the *Register*'s "Jackpot Lotto." I changed channels and there was Oscar Gladden. I reached out

52

to turn off the set but instead sat down to watch him. He had a small telescope in his hands.

"People keep saying: 'Prove there is a God.' I can't, of course. You can no more prove God than you can prove beauty. I may argue that a certain painting or piece of music is beautiful, but if it doesn't seem so to you, no argument will convince you.

"Beauty is known by *experience*. So is the fact of God.

"People keep saying: 'Define God.' I can't. You can no more define God than you can catch a fragrant spring breeze in a paper bag. Catch the breeze and what do you have when you open the bag? A fragrant spring breeze? No, a bagful of stale air.

"Catch God in a definition and what do you have? God? No, you have a collection of words, words invented by men to describe their common experiences.

"'Aha!' you say. 'That proves my point; the whole notion is unreal.' But couldn't you be a little mixed up on what reality is? For instance, have you ever seen or heard or touched an idea? Are ideas therefore unreal?

"Hardly. We've all seen what an idea can do when it takes hold of someone. Think of what an idea did in the life of Columbus, the Wright brothers, Edison, Einstein, Karl Marx. . . .

"Are ideas real? The world is shaped by them. The world is threatened by them. Our lives are determined by them.

"What is love, but an emotion, an idea. Has anyone ever seen love. Of course not. But we've seen how it can change those it touches. How it is the basis of our families, our homes, our society.

"You can't *see* love, but do you doubt its existence?

"It's the same with God. Who has ever seen him? No one. But we can see the evidence of his existence. It is in the laws that govern our universe, our world, our lives.

"Leave him out of your life and you're going to miss the entire meaning of existence. Now, wouldn't that be a foolish thing to do?"

Plausible, I thought. Hardly profound, but at least he's not railing against booze and fornication and trying to get me to speak in tongues. And give him credit; he's reasoning with his viewers, not pontificating. There was nothing outrageous or fanatical in the program; even the appeal for funds had been reasonable. I'd had it at the *Register*, there was nothing else on the immediate horizon and the guy on the television screen was prepared to make me a millionaire, so . . . what the hell!

I sat down and wrote my resignation.

# SEVEN

After the *Register*'s newsroom, the office Oscar Gladden had prepared for me was so impressive it was intimidating. It made me feel like a pretender, and it was the better part of a week before I could work with full concentration.

Bartholemew showed me a bedroom down the hall in which I could stay overnight when I worked late. I learned that none of the help lived in but commuted daily from various nearby communities. He made the point with little subtlety that, while the bedroom allocated to me was mine, I should use it only when absolutely necessary.

"Even I," he said primly, "live in the Port."

He led me outside to the gate-house where Knee-Hi introduced me to the guards on duty as each snapped a hokey paramilitary salute: Gus Longo, whom I knew; Rocco Lombardi, who looked like a *Godfather* reject; an emaciated, muddy-skinned man whose name escapes me but who was referred to as the Spick; and the blue-black Bahamian with the incredible name of Sacred Heart Saywell who doubled as driver of Oscar Gladden's limousines. There were four other guards, Knee-Hi informed me, on duty around the clock.

We headed back to the house. Well to the right of the front entrance was an oversize garage door. Bartholemew touched a button and it rolled up, revealing a great bay in which the two limousines were parked side by side. The walls, ceiling and floor were faced with hospital-white tiles, and as we entered our footfalls and voices resonated.

"The far limousine," Bartholemew was saying, "is equipped not only with the most advanced facilities for the treatment of diabetes but is a miniature version of the intensive care unit in a modern hospital. We call it the ICU car. As well, there's a fully equipped lab through this door." He knocked on it and called out, "Doc!"

Through the door came "Doc" Kildare. He was a stooped man of indeterminate age. Loose skin hung on his face in festoons and his eyes were surrounded by discolored pouches. I was reminded of Sag, a basset hound I once owned. I would learn later that Dr. Robinson Kildare had once been a brilliant practitioner, a specialist in internal medicine whose treatment of young women almost invariably included massage of the chest area and occasional explorations of those portions of the body normally the preserve of the gynecologist. After an accumulation of complaints from parents and from the husbands of three repentant young wives, the Buffalo Medical Association had laid charges of unethical conduct and lifted his licence. He drifted into the employ of Oscar Gladden as a chauffeur, and when his background was discovered he was ordered to bring himself abreast of the state of the art in the treatment of diabetes and related illnesses.

Bartholemew introduced us and Doc gave me a cold, limp hand.

"Mr. Carpenter will be working with Mr. Gladden," Bartholemew said. "Mr. G. thought it might be a good idea if you clued him in. I'll leave you two together."

Kildare looked at me dubiously, shrugged, sighed heavily and led me to the ICU car. The interior was surprisingly spacious; even the trunk space was utilized. There was a sturdy examination table and a leather reclining-chair set alongside an impressive bank of machines displaying a variety of dials and a number of plastic tubes. I recognized an ECG unit and a heart-monitor.

Doc pulled down a jump-seat and sat, crossing his skinny legs. I saw that he wasn't wearing socks and that he had cut a hole in the side of one shoe to ease the pressure on a bunion.

"Do you know anything about diabetes?" he asked, addressing the floor.

I shrugged. As do most reporters, I knew a little about a lot of things, but I had learned not to fake it with experts. "Doesn't it have to do with the failure of the pancreas to produce enough insulin?"

"More or less," he said indifferently and then looked at me. "You don't really want a full rundown, do you?"

He should specialize in euthanasia, I thought; he could kill you with dolor. "It was Mr. Gladden's idea, not mine," I said.

"Okay then," Doc said resignedly. "What we're talking about here is a balancing act. My job is to keep the glucose level in his blood in a reasonable relationship to the supply of insulin. Most diabetics can lead fairly normal lives if they're sensible. Mr. G., on the other hand, isn't. He wants to live as he pleases. My job is to keep tabs on his blood sugar and to take whatever steps are necessary."

"That can't be easy. I've watched him eat."

Doc yielded a wan smile. "It's *his* body."

"But even with you, can he go on forever breaking the rules?"

The smile turned bleak. "Mr. G. *makes* the rules. Thanks to his countrymen, Banting and Best, he can get away with it. For a while."


Of the fourteen senior attorneys working out of the Department of Justice (Manhattan) office, Roger Zachs was the one I knew best and liked least. He and I had lived within a block of each other in our youth, had been academic and athletic rivals through P.S. 128 and George Washington High, contesting with each other at every step until Roger went off to Columbia Law School and I entered an extended period of indecision, wavering between taking liberal arts at City College of New York or betting the next four years of my life that I could make it as a novelist. I settled on novelist to discover a year later that I was restive and often delinquent under the self-discipline required. Suffering from feelings of inadequacy I enrolled at City College.

I heard nothing further of Roger until after I joined the *Register,* when I learned that he had been hired by the Justice department. Some three years later I covered an arson case in which he was the prosecutor. We both made much of our similar background over drinks afterward, during which I discovered to my surprise that there was a bristling between us. Neither of us followed up the reunion; consequently I was surprised when Bartholemew told me that I had received a call from Roger Zachs.

"Have a care," he said pointedly as he left my office.

At exactly noon, settling into our seats at Orsini's, I took advantage of the moment when Roger was ordering the wine to study him. He was wearing a dark blue pinstripe suit and a freshly acquired tan, and as he jollied the waiter he seemed confident, even ebullient. He had seemed anything but when I'd last seen him. Roger had been the chief prosecutor in the Gladden trial and had been in trouble from the opening gavel. He had been up against Milton Goodman, probably the highest-priced legal talent in Manhattan and a man who dominated any proceedings. As I mentioned earlier, there had been some indifferent preparation of the government's case, and Roger was caught out a half-dozen times, the chagrin turning his skin the color of clay and affecting even his normally erect carriage. As the trial progressed, his head came down and his style deteriorated. It concluded with Roger Zachs a deeply discomfited man.

Turning his attention from the waiter to me, he was smiling, affable. "Well now," he said, massaging his hands. "That's done. If I may presume to say so, you'll enjoy the *osso bucco*. It's a specialty here."

"What's on your mind, Roger?" I asked.

"Nothing special. I just got to thinking it's been too long. Since we last got together, I mean."

We made man-talk about politics and sport and did a little harking back, but it was all a shade too hearty and forced. It wasn't until I was dipping into the marrow of my veal bone that Roger said, "I hear you've gone to work for Oscar Gladden."

At last. I continued my excavation and without looking up said, "I would have thought you'd be glad to forget Oscar Gladden."

Roger's tan reddened a shade. "Hank Farr told me you'd

quit the *Register.* He wasn't sure what you were doing, so I asked around."

"Very nice of you."

"It's simply that, as an old friend, I'd be sorry if it was true."

I was irked. I wasn't anxious to have the fact that I'd gone to work for Gladden bruited about and had given oblique replies to friends asking what my immediate plans were. To have Roger Zachs prying into my affairs and taking me to lunch to pump me stirred my gorge.

"You know what?" I said. "I'm afraid you're a poor loser."

Roger's tan now looked more like a bad case of sunburn. "I'm sorry," he said, "but Oscar Gladden is a criminal. It will be my pleasure one of these days to put him behind bars."

I said nothing for a moment, concentrating on removing the last morsel of marrow. "I don't know anything about Oscar Gladden's business activities," I said, "other than what I learned in Courtroom 318. And in Courtroom 318, it seemed to me that with all the resources of the Justice department going for you, you didn't lay a glove on him."

"I'll grant you the preparation wasn't as well done as it might have been."

I shrugged. "It's your department. I heard you'd been preparing the case for the better part of a year."

"There was political pressure to come to trial," Roger said, a trifle lamely.

I'd heard that there had been pressure and that much of it had come from Senator Gallagher but didn't mention it. Now it was Roger who was occupied with his food, excising with excessive care the last morsel of meat from the rind. I decided to take the offensive, not simply because my dislike for Roger Zachs was intensifying with each minute but because I owed it to myself to find out whatever he might know about my new boss.

"You say Gladden's a criminal . . . a child-molester, perhaps? A car thief?"

Roger chose his words with a lawyer's precision. "Oscar Gladden is involved—whether actively or passively I haven't yet been able to determine, and to what extent I'm not at the moment ready to specify—in the skimming of tax-exempt contributions to his ministry almost certainly in New York State and, in all probability, worldwide.''

''That sentence, Roger, could win a Pulitzer Prize for equivocation.'' I felt a roiling anger and wondered whether it stemmed from my dislike for the man opposite or from impatience with myself. Had I walked headlong into something I ought to have had sense enough to skirt?

I said, ''What you seem to be saying is that you think it's within the realm of possibility that Gladden might just conceivably be related in some fashion to some unspecified criminal activity but that you haven't got one jot, much less one tittle of hard evidence on which to base your vague suspicions. Is that a fair reading?''

He was looking hard at me. ''You *have* gone to work for him.''

''So you were guessing,'' I said. ''Jeezus, Roger! No wonder you didn't get a conviction.'' I looked about for our waiter. ''I'd like another drink—or am I off the tab?''

Roger signaled and we were silent until my drink had been fetched, Roger using the interval to light his pipe.

''I'll level with you,'' I said, wanting to nail something down but not wanting to say more than was necessary, ''Oscar Gladden has a project he's asked me to handle. And yes, I'm interested. You said earlier you wouldn't like to see me work for him. Why? Put one hard fact on the table.''

He leaned forward. ''Okay. The security set-up at his estate. Why? The *governor* doesn't have that kind of protection.''

''So he's paranoid. That makes him a capo in the Bonanno family?''

''Let's just stay with the Bonanno family a moment. Two of the guards at the Gladden estate used to work for Bonanno. A dwarf by the name of Neil Hisey—''

''Knee-Hi. I've met him.''

''With a record as long as your arm. Rocco Lombardi—same thing.''

''So, if you're hiring guards do you recruit them at the Salvation Army?''

''C'mon, Tony,'' he snapped. ''If you're one of God's shepherds and you have only sheep to protect, you don't hire wolves.''

60

Roger Zachs hadn't made a case but he had left me worried. As I turned in at the gate I nodded at Knee-Hi. The dwarf peered at me from behind his glittering eyes and made no response. I got a mental picture of throats torn out and blood on fleece.

"Come in! Come in! Don't let the girls bother you."

The bedroom was pungent as a bordello. Oscar Gladden was spread-eagled face down on the great circular bed while two women—introduced to me previously as Jerri West and Merilee —massaged him with musk-scented oils. The two, Bartholemew had told me, came at least once a week to provide their ministrations, and afterward went over Gladden's gargantuan body with what appeared to me to be amateurish kneadings and slappings. Merilee was Eurasian and hardly out of her teens. Her smooth, teak-hued skin, shining black hair and narrow eyes testified to a sino-nordic coupling. Jerri West, who was clearly in charge, was a theatrically beautiful woman in her early twenties with a tumbled mane of honey-golden hair and a voluptuous body only barely contained in the diminutive halter and inconsequential shorts she was wearing.

Gladden obviously took pleasure in calling me in for a conference at the conclusion of these sessions—this made evident by the slight, smug smile that seldom left his lips. I felt ill at ease and voyeuristic and signaled it by averting my gaze and by choosing to sit far from the bed and near the bath, to which he would come when he'd had enough of being the sybarite.

Now he descended from the bed and made his way toward me, his massive body pendulous with pads of fat and gleaming with oil. He descended into the bath. Afloat on his back in the water, a bar of soap lodged in the declivity between his breasts, he said, without so much as a glance, "You've been with me three weeks today. Any problems?"

"Some questions. No problems."

"Take them up with Bartholemew."

"More basic questions than that."

"Well, don't worry about them. Time will take care of it."

He put his head back, took a mouthful of water and spurted

it into the air. (Images of whales, porpoises, elephant seals!) "When do I get your report?"

"The end of the week. Friday, for sure."

He moved to the shallow end of the bath, stood, and began to soap himself vigorously, beginning at his head and working down. His eyes were closed against the soap and I watched him, half in fascination, half in disgust. Tremors moved through his flesh, and the festoons of fat hanging from his upper arms and breasts jiggled and bounced.

He let himself fall forward in the water to rinse, and a wave broke on the marble floor at my feet. Puffing and blowing, he surfaced, climbed the stairs, draped a towel about his middle and took another to dry his face and hair. There were small wicker baskets heaped with fruit and Danish pastries. A thermos jug of coffee stood on a table nearby. He poured for both of us, seized a handful of pastries and sat opposite me.

"Well now," he said with sudden energy. "You've had a chance to watch your employer at work, at play and in his bath — something, I daresay, that never happened to you at the *Register*. You must have formed some opinions. What kind of man is he?"

I didn't hesitate, but stayed in the third-person to soften the impact. "He's prodigal with his money, arrogant about his power, blatantly sensual, exceedingly close-mouthed and, so far as I've been able to tell, no haloed saint." I added with a small smile, "But he pays well."

He bellowed in a laughter that spread Danish across the distance between us. "I take that as complimentary," he said. "I've concluded from observing you that you and I are more alike than you imagine."

I flinched at that and noted that Jerri West and Merilee had tidied the bed and were now at the door waving an obsequious good-bye. Gladden paid no attention.

"It would take two of me to be like you," I said lightly. I tilted my head toward the departing women. "In every way."

He seemed suddenly anxious to justify himself. "You say I'm prodigal, arrogant and sensual, but tell me: what's the point of having money if you don't spend it? What's the point of having power if you don't exercise it? And if it comes to that, of sexuality if you don't get your rocks off?''

I gave a shrug and a tilt of my head, being of no mind to debate. "Life's to be lived, not husbanded," he said. "I know men, and so do you, who work their butts off to get rich and then work their butts off to stay rich. Then, one day, their time runs out and they realize they've missed the boat. Right?''

I said nothing. This was a side of Gladden that I hadn't seen. In our previous meetings he had seldom gone beyond the business at hand. Some days, having come directly from a session with Doc, he would be black-browed and testy. But even then his moods were mercurial, and within minutes he might be buoyant and ready with his great bellowing laugh, continuing sometimes until he was winded and weak. But even at such moments he revealed little of himself. Oscar Gladden was, I was learning, an enigma offering few clues.

His mood had shifted to the contemplative. He was looking off, the remainder of a pastry forgotten between his fingers. "As to my being no saint," he said. "My parents used to get rid of me by shipping me off to Sunday school. Most of the kids turned off their brains because it was church. I didn't. I figured that all the loot to build those buildings and put the gold on those altars didn't come from heaven, so I paid attention.

"Later, I walked on the other side of the tracks with the born-againers. And what did I hear? The greatest concoction of infantile nonsense I've ever listened to. A gospel for fools and deadbeats and failures. The rich man can no more get into heaven than a goddamn camel can pass through the eye of a needle— can you imagine? Ah, but the poor! *Blessed* are the poor. Same with the meek; they're going to inherit the earth! Have you ever heard such bullshit? Blessed are the poor? The hell they *are!* They're miserable and live in slums and don't have enough to eat. The only earth the meek inherit is a spadeful in the face when they're six feet under.''

He took a sip of coffee. "The one thing the Bible says that makes sense is that those who have get more." He excavated an ear with a corner of the towel and glared at me. "Well?''

"I didn't think you wanted another opinion.''

"Well, don't you agree?''

"No, I don't."

"You mean you buy that crap about God and Heaven?"

"Not all of it, of course. But whenever I've thought about it —which has only been off and on—it has always seemed to me that the world works only if you give the other guy the breaks you'd like for yourself." I put my hands before me in an attitude of prayer. "Thus endeth the morning lesson."

Gladden had jammed the last chunk of the pastry into his mouth, and his voice was muffled as he spoke. "Have you taken the time to examine what I teach?"

"Truth to tell, not much. I've been too busy researching the Nobody project. I gather that it's based on numbers."

He gave a snort of impatience. "Not on numbers but on the number *one!* The reason most of us don't make sense of life is because we've never given thought to the digit one. And yet there is no arithmetic without it, no algebra, no geometry, no calculus, no physics, no measuring, no mileage, no counting, no stocktaking, no planning, no order and no meaning. They all depend on the digit one. They have no meaning apart from the digit one. One is the basis of everything. Everything in the universe is a multiple of or a fraction of one. One is the unit by which we measure everything else."

"Sorry," I said, "but you lost me there somewhere."

"Well then, listen," he snapped. "There are many facets to our personality but they are all the expression of one individual. We can only realize our true selves when we become integrated —when we are one. And we can only have a better world when each individual in the world becomes one with us."

"Fine," I said. "But if what we're talking about is a religion, where does God come in? And prayer?"

"There is no praying in One," he said with a show of annoyance. "Prayer is a waste of time; there's nobody listening. Ask yourself: what is prayer predicated on? It's based on the belief that God can be wheedled into running the universe according to the wishes of anybody who gets on his knees. Can you imagine the chaos if everybody's prayers were answered? But beyond that, prayer is a form of self-delusion; our *real* prayers are the way we live. The way we live is the evidence of what we really want in life, no matter what we may say."

"Okay. So there's no praying and there's no God—"

"I didn't say there was no God. The fact is, I don't know. And neither does anybody else. But if there is—and there's good reason to believe there may be—the way to find out what he's like is to study life. If you want to know what Michelangelo was like, study the Sistine Chapel. If you want to know what God is like, look around. Whoever he may be and whatever he's like, he created all that is, and it must bear his imprint. So, while there is no praying in One, there is lots of meditation."

I stifled a yawn. "Mmm," I said.

But he wasn't deterred by my faint praise. He was in full flight. "Meditation," he said, "is only a fancy word for thinking. Reflecting. Pondering. Wondering. Cogitating. Ruminating. Contemplating. Considering. Musing. Examining." He paused for breath. "And when you meditate about the world and the universe, what do you learn? The first thing you learn is that there are laws—physical, moral and spiritual laws—and that you break those laws at your peril. The law of gravity, for instance. Walk off the top of a ten-story building and you don't break the law of gravity; you break yourself *on* the law of gravity. You obey the physical laws or you get broken on them."

His voice had dropped now and his eyes had taken on that transcendent look they sometimes get on television. My mind flashed back to the television picture of the handsome, mesmeric evangelist and then superimposed on it the man sitting across from me, pastry crumbs on his chin and chest, his vast nakedness skirted only by a bath towel.

"But there are not only physical laws in the universe," he was saying, "there are moral laws. And spiritual laws. Laws that govern the body, the spirit and the mind. Your mind, for instance: use it or you lose it. That's the law. Your body: exercise it or it atrophies. That's the law. Give love and you get love. Hate and you'll be hated. These laws are built into the universe. Obey them and benefit from them. Break them and you get broken on them."

I was tempted to ask him if he would count it a law that gluttony leads to obesity, but refrained. His face was suffused by a pleased-as-punch smile. "You remember the Beatitudes?"

"Somewhat."

"Let me give you the Beatitudes of One. They are the basis of what I call Faith Without Cant."

"Can't?"

"Not *can't* but *cant* — pious religious babble." He raised a pudgy hand and began to tick off his fingers as he spoke.

"Blessed are the rich for they shall inherit the earth.

"Blessed are those who hunger and thirst for success for they shall achieve it.

"Blessed are those who dream great dreams for they shall realize great things.

"Blessed are the disciplined for they shall reach their goals.

"Blessed are the adaptable for they are teamed with the universe.

"And blessed are you when you are scorned or ridiculed for the sake of One—it only proves that you are on the right track."

He paused and smiled at me—that professional, humorless smile of his—put his hands before him in an attitude of prayer as I had done earlier and said, "Thus, Mr. Carpenter . . . *thus* endeth the morning lesson!"

This seemed to give him some satisfaction. He pushed to his feet and walked off, looking for all the world like the film version of a Roman senator.

At the top of a piece of paper I printed the words, *Mr. Nobody Project,* underlined them and sat staring into space. Ten minutes later, I leaned back in my chair and pitched my pencil across the office.

I had been working at the project daily, having been down any number of blind alleys, having followed a dozen leads. How in the world do you go about finding a specific man whose principal qualification is that he is utterly undistinguished? I had long since quit searching at the public library or in a newspaper morgue—there is no *Who's Who* of the ruck. No organization draws up an annual list of America's Ten Most Unremarkable Men.

By definition, this man is unheralded, unhonored, unsung. His name graces no plaque, flares from no headline, is engraved in no Book of Remembrance. He is unknown except to friends and neighbors and, presumably, hasn't received public attention since his birth-notice was carried in the classifieds. Walk down any street and you may see him, but who among the throng is he? You can't judge by appearances; some of the world's most celebrated are among its most scruffy. Einstein on the streets of Princeton, New Jersey—a wool tuque on his head, rusty platinum hair straggling from beneath it, a rope substituting for a belt and no socks within his unlaced shoes—looked like a denizen of skid-row. Many of today's most eminent turn up on television in oversize sweatshirts and undersize bluejeans.

How then to complete the quest?

I went to the dictionary. "No-bod-y (no'bod-y) n. a person of no importance, esp. socially, authority or position."

I puzzled over the question. What makes for importance? Surely it is a relative thing. The Driver of the Month at the local Yellow Cab company has certainly achieved some measure of importance no matter how trivial it may seem to others. A private secretary is undoubtedly a cut above the girls in the steno-pool. Then there is the matter of celebrity. The man who is now but one of six salespersons at the Home Sweet Home Realty office in Pompano Beach, Florida, might only ten years earlier have been a class president, a valedictorian, the winner of three high school letters. A somebody—at least for a day.

I realized that I was approaching the problem in an unfocused fashion; there is no such thing as average. The term *the average man* is part of the contemporary jaberwocky used by sociologists and advertising people — a category of convenience. A man in Dothan, Alabama, might be an exact statistical match for a man living in Come By Chance, Newfoundland, but antithetical by every other measure.

Perhaps I should begin by preparing a questionnaire and sending it out to the names on one of those leased mailing-lists. Perhaps my subject was to be found among the subscribers to the *Reader's Digest*. But even if I received a sizeable response, wouldn't I have merely the names of thousands of men and women similar in certain ways and then be faced with the necessity of culling from these a more manageable group? But how to reduce their numbers? Through interviews? But who would do the interviews? And could the results be trusted? Most people guard their private lives; would they not react negatively to questions designed to winnow out all but the ordinary?

Assuming that I did discover the ideal candidate, what then? What of the difficulties in convincing this John Doe that he should submit to the machinations necessary to make him famous? "Now, see here, Mr. Doe, we propose to make you a celebrity. You will be the focus of national attention. You will meet the famous and the infamous. You will be interviewed, photographed, lionized. You will be followed by crowds, badgered for your autograph, offered money, propositioned by star-struck groupies. Your name will become a household word. . . . What do you say?"

Would any but the eccentric say yes? Would they not, rather, judge me mad and flee from me as from a confidence-man?

But even with all these obstacles overcome and my Mr. Nobody identified and willing to cooperate, would I not then be faced with the second and more difficult part of my task—of making him a celebrity? How would I fashion from this anonymous lump of American clay someone so extraordinary that he would attract—and not simply for an hour or two—the spotlight of national media attention? How many men and women of exceptional talent and legitimate achievement try daily to attain to no more than a guest-shot on a national talk-show?

It won't be enough to have him bite a dog, or to leap with a hang-glider from the top of the World Trade Center or eat ninety-seven bagels at a sitting or streak the center aisle at St. Patrick's Cathedral during an Easter mass. Such stunts might win you a mention in the *Guiness Book of World Records* or thirty seconds of attention as the offbeat item at the tag-end of somebody's newscast, but that would be it. Up like a rocket, down like a charred stick. What do you do for an encore? There is an enormous difference between a kook and a celebrity. The kooks you have with you always.

There was, of course, a positive side to my problem: the United States is a fertile field for the sprouting of celebrity. Americans are intrigued by the notorious—their own and others'. Let an actor, a writer, an athlete, a musician, a politician, a television or film performer—even a daredevil, if he isn't patently suicidal—rise above his peers and exhibit a charismatic gleam, and Americans, perhaps more than any other people on earth, will idolize him and reward him in the most prodigal ways. They will rejoice in the most insignificant details of his private life. They will buy the products he advocates, knowing full well that he doesn't use them but, for some obscure reason, needing to achieve an identification with him. They will be astonished but not displeased when he is paid outrageous sums for doing no more than playing a child's game well and will place reproductions of his visage on their clothing or on the walls of their homes. They will line up for hours on the off-chance of glimpsing him in person. They will be fascinated by his choice of sexual partners and take vicarious satisfaction from his conquests. And they will excuse his gaffes and gaucheries and forgive even his boorishness. Oddly, Americans tend not to idolize their women celebrities with quite the same fervor— although exceptions are made for women of unusual beauty who are also perceived as being vulnerable: a Jackie Kennedy, a Katharine Hepburn, a Marilyn Monroe. . . .

I was suddenly overcome by the realization that accepting Oscar Gladden's offer might have been a ghastly mistake. He had presumed that, being a journalist, I was the man for the job. But being a journalist does not necessarily provide the insights needed to understand the public's taste. Who knows better than the man who lives with the news how capricious that taste is? Oscar Gladden had accepted the common misconception that the news media can, at will, create celebrities. In fact, the media have been largely ineffectual when they have deliberately set out to win the public to their causes. A media-blitz does not a celebrity make. Neither advertising nor promotion can guarantee a top-grossing motion picture or a best-selling book. The public must, for whatever reasons, take the object to its collective heart. Word-of-mouth, not double-truck advertising, creates the vogue. The news media may assist but they cannot fashion notoriety from the whole cloth.

I scribbled some notes on the paper before me and sat for a moment staring into space. How in god's name could I fashion Oscar Gladden's silk purse from some undiscovered sow's ear out there in the anonymous world of middle-America? It was a mad idea.

After a while I got out of my chair and went down the hall to Bartholemew's office. He was at his desk, bowed over a stack of paper. I tapped lightly on the door. He beckoned me to enter.

"You look bushed," he said. "Join me for a coffee."

There was a pot brewing on the counter beside his desk and he poured for the two of us. As we settled down I asked, "Tell me how you came to work for Mr. Gladden."

He put his feet on his desk and leaned back in his chair. "Mostly through good luck," he said, smiling reflectively. "Mr. G. had just bought this place—believe me, it was an act of faith; he was just getting started—and he invited me to join him. I was working for a public relations firm in Davenport, Iowa, and I'd been chairman of the promotion committee for his campaign there. He must have liked what he saw; he called me on the phone a week later and said he wanted to ask me two questions: was I a born-again Christian and did I know anything about the Bible? When I answered no to both, he said, 'Good. I just wanted to be sure you weren't carrying any fundamentalist baggage. Maybe I can teach you something. Come work for me.' "

"The man's full of surprises," I said. "I was interested to discover that he never attended Bible school or seminary."

Bartholemew smiled. "He has a favorite comment: 'I'm a self-educated man and I can't think of a better teacher.' He likes to say that his first rule is: 'Challenge the rules; they were probably made by incompetents.' "

"I see what looks like a bicycle reflector on his desk. Is it some kind of symbol?"

Bartholemew smiled broadly. "You could call it that. It epitomizes the man. Mr. G. says, 'When everybody else says stop, it probably means the light has just turned green.' " He sipped his coffee. "He's a remarkable man."

"Has he spoken to you about my project?" I asked.

He shook his head. "Not a word. Mr. G. likes to compartmentalize everything. Don't let your left hand know, etcetera. I do know he was all fired up about it. How's it going?"

"Not exactly gangbusters," I said gloomily. "I'm supposed to find a nonentity and make him into an overnight celebrity.

Then when the media has bought him, we pull the plug and there they are with egg on their face.''

Bartholemew made no comment, but there was the suggestion of a frown on his forehead.

''I take it you're underwhelmed,'' I said.

''No, nothing like that. I just wonder at the wisdom of taking on the press. It's a no-win situation; they always have the last word.''

I sighed heavily. ''I'm up to my gills in research but so far nothing concrete. The problem is, there's no such thing as 'the news media.' The parts of it are as diverse as the *Christian Science Monitor* and the *National Enquirer* or CBS News and the news department of your local rock station. When I *do* lock on a target, I'll run it by you if you don't mind.''

Leaving Bartholemew's office, I passed Oscar Gladden on his way to the broadcast studio. The sides of his face were heavily made-up, the tone shading abruptly to dark as it approached his hairline and jaw. The transformation was startling; it was as though the head of a younger, thinner Oscar Gladden had been transplanted onto his gross body. He went by me without a word or a glance.

# EIGHT

It had become my habit when taking a break from my desk to stand by the window looking out. More often than not—to Bartholemew's sometimes fussy displeasure—I would throw up the sash to freshen the recirculated air. From my window I would watch the activities below: the gardeners, the delivery vans from nearby Port Washington and Oyster Bay, the occasional carpenter or plumber or provisioner, the guards at the gate. In the three weeks I had worked for Oscar Gladden I had come to know each of the guards by sight if not all of them by name. It became evident that Diego Madero and Joey Podertz, a dark gorilla of a man, lived in what had been described by Bartholemew as an old coach-house, the gabled roof of which I could see beyond the trees toward the south end of the estate. In the fragrant warmth of the early summer, the men on duty at the gate often stood about in the open, and their laughter and an occasional snatch of their conversation would rise to my window.

Perhaps once a week, at apparently random times, a large tow truck would enter through the main gate and proceed at undiminished speed down the road leading to the coach-house. On still days, or when the wind was from the south, I could hear the dragon's hiss of air-brakes and the rattle of the diesel as it maneuvered. An hour or so later the truck would return, usually pausing at the gate while the driver had a word with whoever was on duty, but sometimes barreling straight through, headed for Duck Pond Road. It was larger than the tow trucks that normally service cars on a highway and carried, I noted, four oversize truck tires.

I'm a reporter; unanswered questions stick like cockleburs to my mind. Why was a heavy tow truck regularly traveling to what I understood to be the end of the property? It couldn't be to provide tire service; no other trucks used the road. The only vehicle to do so was a black Ford Taurus owned by one of the guards and used to ferry Diego and Joey to and from the coach-house.

I had never explored the property, so one bright and bracing day, on a sudden whim, I set out to do so. I headed south past the parking lot, walking briskly.

"Carpenter! . . . Hey, you! . . . Carpenter!"

It was Knee-Hi, his short bowed legs stirring recollections of the Roadrunner in the cartoons. He caught up with me, breathing heavily.

"You can't go down there," he said.

"Why not?" I asked snappishly. I was having trouble sorting out my feelings about the dwarf. I had disliked him on sight, and that aversion had deepened with each contact.

He pulled a soiled handkerchief from a pocket and wiped his bulbous brow. "They's swampland down there."

"I'll keep an eye peeled."

"No," he said flatly, shaking his head slowly, eyes closed. "I can't let you do that."

"For chrissake, Knee-Hi, it's the middle of the day! I'm not a child."

"Orders," he said. "Mr. Gladden's orders. You wanna argue, go argue with him."

Back in the house, I got a surveyor's map of the area from Bartholemew, took it to my office, unrolled it on my desk, weighted it at each corner and studied it. The property was in the shape of an irregular rectangle and, except for the area about the house, lightly wooded. It was bounded on the east and west by other estates, with the nearest house better than a quarter of a mile away. To the south was Touchwood Creek and to the north, Duck Pond Road. The main driveway was entered through a gate in the great stone wall. Just before it reached the gate-house, it branched onto a dirt road leading to a dead-end

73

at the south end of the property. There, an irregular shape was designated "Coach-house." A slightly larger rectangle bore the description "Barn." Nearby, was a small square designated "Kennels." The entire property was bounded by the stone wall. A link-fence separated the landscaped area of the property from the south on a line beginning just beyond the parking lot.

"Can I help?" It was Oscar Gladden in a bathrobe. There was a towel about his neck and, I noted, a dab of shaving cream high on one cheek.

"I've been wondering about the lay of the land," I said, "and trying to get oriented." I put a finger on the larger rectangle at the south end of the estate. "I presume this is where the guards live."

"Some of them," he said, his voice soft. "The others live in the Port."

"Knee-Hi tells me there's swampland down that way. It doesn't show on the map."

"Knee-Hi is sometimes a fool."

I was trying to interpret his mood. He was oddly subdued but tense. The daub of shaving cream suggested that he had been summoned in a hurry.

"I don't understand," I said. "Why would he lie to me?"

"He thinks of the place as his fiefdom. He should have answered your questions."

"The security arrangements here. . . . I've never seen anything so elaborate."

He went to the window and stood with his back to me, looking out. I waited. It was a moment before he spoke. "I have never forgotten what happened to one of the greatest men this nation has produced," he said slowly. "Charles Augustus Lindbergh." His voice was low and without inflection. "He was, as you know, the first man to fly solo across the Atlantic, and from then on he was bedeviled by the press. They hounded him everywhere he went. Trying to find privacy, he moved to the country, outside Hopewell, New Jersey. That isolation made it possible for an ignorant German immigrant, Bruno Hauptman, to kidnap and murder his only child."

He paused, and I heard the sound of the tow truck as it

approached the gate-house. It stopped, and after a moment roared away, shifting through the gears.

In the descending silence, Gladden continued. "When I bought this property, Josephine was still a child. I was reading a book about Lindbergh and it occurred to me that she, too, might become the target for some twisted mentality, so I set up the system we now have." He turned back into the room.

"Then the south end of the property isn't off-limits?"

"Because of the security system you'd be wise not to go wandering off alone. Anything you want to know about, ask Knee-Hi. I've told him to answer your questions."


With a stubby finger the dwarf drew a rectangle in the air. "Stone fence on three sides: here, here and here. Bob-wire and busted glass on top. Eight-foot-high link-fence everywhere else. That gate there." He pointed at the wrought-iron barrier at the entrance from the road. "It's electrified. If the light's blinkin', don't touch it. You'll glow like a Christmas tree. You already seen the television monitors?"

"Yes."

"Then you know the rest. 'Cept for the dogs." He grinned, showing his little teeth in what was intended as a smile. "They's three of 'em — American pit bulls. Rip your nuts off." The thought seemed to please him; the grin widened. "They run free inside the fences every night after ten. Just so's you know."

"Who designed the system?" I asked ingenuously.

"Me," Knee-Hi said expansively, pointing with a stubby forefinger at his chest. "Me an' Mr. G. Right after I come here."

"And when did you come here, Knee-Hi?"

"Five years this October."

Interesting. At that point Jo was studying in Lausanne.


I met Jo for dinner at Les Croissants on Third Avenue. The *maître-d'* seated us in a leafy courtyard, sufficiently removed from the other tables to give us a sense of being alone. The evening was perfect.

Jo and I had had lunch together in Port Washington on two

occasions, and we met with increasing frequency in her studio after working out together in the fitness room in the basement. Lately, she had taken to dropping by my office for the midafternoon coffee-break. We found much to talk about.

Now, at dinner at Les Croissants, we found ourselves looking into each other's eyes and talking with the openness of long acquaintanceship. The low sun filtering through the leaves cast soft, shifting patterns of light on her face and hair. Her eyes, reflecting the foliage around us, seemed an even deeper green than usual.

"You know," she interjected at one point, "we've talked about everything but your new job. How are you liking it? And how are you and Father getting along?"

I didn't want to get into a discussion about Oscar Gladden. I'd been troubled by a vague sense of apprehension from the day I had driven out to the estate to tell him I was ready to sign on. He hadn't so much as said "Welcome aboard" but had simply reached into a drawer in his desk and passed me the check he had offered on our ride together from New York City. "Have a word with Bartholemew," he'd said, returning to the papers before him on the desk. And that had been it. I had turned and left the office, feeling a small flame of annoyance.

I passed off Jo's question about how much I liked the job by saying, "It's a little early to make a judgment. I will say this: it's certainly different from the newsroom at the *Register.*"

"What I'm really getting at," she persisted, "is how are you and Father getting on?"

I kept the tone light. "A few weeks ago you said he wasn't the easiest man in the world to work for. I may nominate that as the understatement of the year."

She threw back her head and laughed. "You'll learn to read his moods," she said.

The waiter arrived with our salads. When he had gone I said, "Question: Are you an Oscar Gladden disciple?"

She was slow to respond. "If you mean do I believe generally in what he teaches, the answer is yes. But not in many of the specifics." She munched on a piece of lettuce before continuing. "If you're asking if I believe in God, the answer, again, is yes. I suppose I always have, although to tell the truth I've never given it much thought. I don't mean that's it's not important to me — it is — it's just that it has never really occurred to me to *dis*believe. God is — how can I say it? — a given.

"I don't belong to any church," she said, and then amended that to say, "except Father's, I suppose. And it's not a church in the usual sense. But when I do go, I'm moved by the whole . . . the whole ethos. In Paris, I used to go to Notre Dame early on Sunday mornings. It seemed to me you could almost *smell* God there."

"Do you pray?"

"Sometimes. Not last thing at night or anything like that, but yes, when I feel the need to. Not so much when I'm having problems as when I'm happy. Truth to tell, most of my praying is by way of thank-you notes. For beauty. For music. For love. For children's faces. For the happiness I see in families sometimes — things like that. Most of all for being able to paint. How could you *not* be grateful that God has given you the ability to capture an idea, a feeling, the sunlight, the line of a body in repose — to catch it and make it permanent?"

She was silent for a moment. Then she let out a short laugh. "Your question reminded me of the story Father tells about the little boy who was asked if he said his prayers every night. He answered, 'No, not every night. 'Cause there's some nights I don't want nothin'.' "

We went on to talk of other things. I found myself fascinated by what she was saying and by the lineaments of her face and the movement of her lips as she spoke and ate. Toward the end of the meal, almost involuntarily, in the middle of a sentence, I rose and leaned across the table. A glass toppled as she rose with me and our lips met in a gentle, almost pristine kiss. A shudder ran from my head to my heels. I sat down heavily in my chair, breathless and suddenly self-conscious. Some of the diners nearby were smiling. One couple mimed applause and lifted their glasses in a mute toast.

Our waiter arrived, smiling, to remove the broken glass and to take advantage of the moment to bring the cappuccino and the bill. When I had paid it, I glanced up. Jo was looking at me in that direct, wide-eyed way of hers and her face was flushed.

"This is probably an absolutely mad thing to say," she said

and then paused. Her eyes lowered. "I think I have fallen in love with you," she said, her voice uncertain, almost a whisper.

I wanted to say, "And I love you," but it didn't come out. Wouldn't. I knew that to fail to declare what I was feeling might let something surpassingly beautiful pass by, perhaps never to be retrieved, but the words caught in my throat. The wounds that love can deal were too fresh, and my spirit quailed at the possibility of another bout with anguish. But something needed to be said and I heard myself saying with a flippancy that appalled me, "Maybe you've been out of circulation too long. . . ."

Her eyes clouded and she looked away quickly. In a moment she found it necessary to take back her hand to sip her coffee and we were suddenly far apart. A touch of that alienation remained even as we stood on the street looking for a taxi.

We had planned to go on to my apartment — "To see," as she had put it earlier, "where the future Dostoevsky works" — but now she was saying, glancing at her watch, that she'd better get on home. I was taut with rage at myself but very much wanted her to come with me, and pressed her until her reluctance was overcome. We took a taxi, finding mindless things to say to fill the awkward silences.

At the apartment I turned the key, saw through a stranger's eyes the drab, makeshift ugliness of the half-furnished rooms, and was immediately depressed. Striving for lightness, I pointed at the overstuffed chair. "Louis the Fourteenth. Louis Bercovitz — a neighbor. Lives on the fourteenth floor. Borrowed." In the bedroom, before the bed, I mumbled, "The four-poster's out being fitted for a new canopy."

We returned to the living room, ill at ease with each other, and stood looking out at the city. The view of midtown Manhattan from the window is always extraordinary, but with the sun an enormous orange ball on the horizon, the skyline in silhouette and the ten-thousand windows on the midtown towers all agleam, it was spectacular.

She turned, put her arms about my neck and her lips on mine, and I was faint with love. When we broke free, breathless, I whispered, "Jo, I love you." She stepped out of her shoes and settled into my embrace and we kissed long and hungrily. Then, in an unspoken consent, we turned and went hand in hand to the bedroom. My fingers touched the zipper on the back of her dress but she dipped away from me, going to the bathroom and closing the door. I undressed and got into bed, folding back the sheets on the other side of the bed.

It seemed a very long time until the bathroom door opened and she reappeared. She had loosened her hair and, in my bathrobe, looked very small, almost girlish. At the bedside she sat with her back to me, switched off the lamp and, in the darkness, folded and put aside the bathrobe. After a long moment she turned and slipped beneath the sheets.

Then her cool body was against mine and her arms closed almost painfully about my neck. Her body was trembling, almost uncontrollably. I drew her close and she breathed into my ear, ''My darling Tony.'' As I raised myself above her, I heard her say, so faintly as to be almost inaudible, ''I love you.''

# NINE

In the few weeks I had been working for Oscar Gladden, Bartholemew and I had become friends. Because our offices adjoined, we saw each other almost every day and had come to take our morning coffee-break and the occasional lunch together. It had become clear that the operation of most of the Gladden enterprise came within his purview and that, so far as I was able to determine, he ran it without major glitches. For all his delicacy of manner he was direct and could be tart-tongued, and I learned early on not to mistake his preciosity and his perpetual smile for a lack of mental sinew.

But Bartholemew puzzled me. He was completely committed to Gladden and worked long days in his service. However early I might arrive at my office he would be in his, and on the three occasions when I returned to the office to labor late, he was still at his desk. In return, he was treated with what I can only describe as a sadistic cruelty. I had been with Gladden when he had summoned Bartholemew to provide some answers or to give him some instruction. There was no evidence of a camaraderie, no sense of two men working together at a great task. Rather, Gladden was brusque, often to the point of rudeness. Or he would suddenly turn snide or sarcastic, or sometimes, without any apparent reason, obscenely abusive.

Bartholemew's reaction to Gladden's tirades was curious. He offered neither excuses nor explanation. Instead, he seemed to put his eyes out of focus and deliberately turn inward, standing there motionless, his face vacant, until the moment passed.

And yet in my conversations with him about Gladden, Bartholemew never expressed a hint of resentment in either his words or his voice.

One morning when I went by his office for coffee, he was at the window watering some African violets.

"Oops!" he said, putting a hand to his chest. "You startled me." He apologized for not having time for coffee. He had business to do at the OneWorld headquarters complex in Queens and suggested instead that I join him.

"The broadcasts," he said, as we drove there in his car, "are only one of Mr. G.'s ministries. The Oneness Clubs are perhaps equal in importance. There are, as of the moment, 875 of them in the United States and Canada alone. They're based on the telecasts, of course, and have one overall purpose: to integrate the body, mind and spirit of the disciples. Neglect the mind and it deteriorates into ignorance. Neglect the body and you become unfit, a haven for various diseases. Neglect the spirit and you devolve toward the animal." He giggled. "Mr. G.'s words, not mine.

"As a consequence," he continued, "Mr. Gladden has given us Fitness Clubs, where disciples can strive toward health; Cerebration Centers, where his wisdom is taught." We paused for a red light. "Incidentally, we offer a fully accredited four-year undergraduate program and have a publishing arm that puts out anywhere from twenty to thirty titles a year. For the evolution of the spirit we have Meditation Temples where one can concentrate on the attainment of one's better self. There's one at Queens. I'll show it to you after I've given you the grand tour."

The grand tour consisted of a walkabout, mostly on the ground floor. The Fitness Club was essentially a modern gymnasium of the kind that has proliferated in recent years: dozens of elaborate state-of-the-art isometric and body-building machines and a central open space where mass calisthenics could be done. The Cerebration Center was a small dark chapel of sorts, the design vaguely derivative of Christian, Buddhist and Masonic temples. We took the elevator to the penthouse, which was entirely glass-enclosed and offered a view on all sides that stretched for miles. Beyond the foyer was a door covered with gilt-encrusted figures and symbols and a small brass plate that read GLADDEN YOUR DAY. Bartholemew put a finger to his lips, pulled the massive door open, and we were within what appeared to be a black marble cube. Spaced around the four walls were perhaps a dozen doors, each with tiny lights above them, some green, others red. Bartholemew took a key from one of a number of black velvet boxes, used it to open one of the doors and gave it to me. As he did, he put his lips to my ear and whispered, "See you in half an hour."

I entered and found myself in a small stainless-steel cubicle. A sign instructed me to undress and to go through another door. With some slight trepidation I did and found myself surrounded by what seemed to be a roseate infinity. The walls, the ceiling and the floor of what I made out to be a small, circular room were entirely covered with mirrors. At the center of the room was an octagonal pillar about seven feet high. It, too, was mirrored. As I moved into the room, looking about, I saw myself repeated in the mirrors literally hundreds of times. But so warm and pervasive was the light that I was reflected only hazily. I began to climb the steps inset on the near side of the mirrored pillar. The instructions in the disrobing room had informed me that at the top of the pillar I would find an octagonal pad with two vertical chrome supports and that I was to stand on it. I did so, and it began to descend, but so slowly that I felt no alarm.

It was a moment before I realized that I was being lowered into a capsule of lukewarm water. It dawned on me that, as I descended, I was slowly losing all body weight, and finally, as the octagonal pad moved away, I found myself suspended, buoyant and warm in the water. There was a brief flash of panic but it as quickly passed. I tasted the water and found it was saline, which explained why I was more buoyant than normal. My head was entirely clear of the surface. After a minute or two I felt totally relaxed, utterly at ease, every part of my body weightless and warm.

My head was below the top of the pillar, and looking out through the one-way reflective glass I realized that, in effect, I had disappeared. Each of the mirrors reflected others. There was nothing to see but a vast, endless infinity. It is impossible to describe the sensation. I seemed to exist weightless in space.

But the space was warm and welcoming and canceled every sensation normally derived from my body. I had disappeared, and now my body was gone. And I was at peace.

A voice spoke—Oscar Gladden's recorded voice. At first it was only a distant whisper, so soft, so soothing that, when it began, I was barely aware of it. It seemed to be originating from within my mind. It was telling me to focus on the nothingness with which I was surrounded, to entrust myself to the moment. My eyes grew heavy and the lids closed. There was again a momentary flash of fear that I might fall asleep and sink beneath the water, but just as quickly I again felt entirely secure, encapsulated in timelessness.

The voice grew louder: ''You are one with the universe. You and the universe are one and the same. You and all that is are part of the creation of God. . . .''

I opened my eyes. Slowly, stars began to appear. Thousands of them, ten thousand of them, myriad stars and galaxies stretching to infinity. The voice was replaced by music, ethereal, echoing, celestial. It also seemed to originate in my brain and to resonate softly in every fiber of my being.

The voice returned. ''You are one with the universe, one with everything in the universe. One with the sky. . . .''

A summer sky surrounded me: great mounds of heaped-up cumulus, an endless vault of vibrant blue.

''One with the birds. . . .''

The air was filled with them, their colors ravishing, their songs melodious.

''One with the fields . . . with the trees, and the flowers, and the streams . . . the mountains and the seas. . . .''

And there was beauty everywhere.

''And you are one with all the people of the world. . . .'' In space, faces appeared. A few at first and then many, multiplying in the mirrors until there were ten thousand. The faces of children, of men and women, of every race and every color.

''As you are,'' the pervasive voice whispered, ''they are. As there is love and goodness within you there is love and goodness within them. As there is courage and aspiration within you, there is courage and aspiration within them. And as there is selfishness and pride and ill-will in you, there is selfishness and pride and ill-will in them. But beyond all that is the fact that you and they are the creations of the same God. You are made in the same image. You are fashioned from the same mold. . . . You are,'' the voice said, falling off to an intense whisper. ''You are *one* with the world.'' There was an extended silence and finally the words, ''Think on this.''

Then the voice was gone and the faces were gone and I was alone again in the universe.

After what seemed like hours, the lights slowly came up in the room, the octagonal pad rose beneath my feet and I left my capsule to return to the disrobing room. In a warm shower, I was suffused with a sense of well-being.

In Bartholemew's car, returning to the Gladden estate, he explained to me that the Meditation Temples, the Cerebration Centers and the Fitness Clubs were sold as franchises and that there were some three thousand of them across the United States and Canada, with others in various parts of the world. As well, there were OneWorld vacation retreats and cruise ships where disciples could take their leisure and divert themselves in luxurious surroundings.

''And you run it all?'' I asked.

''Of course not,'' he said. ''We have staff people around the world. When we need to meet, I set up a closed-circuit satellite hookup and Mr. G. speaks to them.''

''But they're all accountable to you?''

''Well, yes. But to Mr. G. actually.''

''It's none of my business,'' I said, ''but with all you do for him, why do you put up with the way he treats you?''

He was silent for a moment, making his careful way past an enormous transport-trailer truck. ''It's because of who he is.''

''How long have you been with him?''

''It will be eight years next January.'' There was pride in his voice.

Great, fat globules of rain suddenly began to splatter on the windshield and break into hundreds of droplets, distorting the view. Bartholemew switched on the windshield wipers, but as quickly as the rain had come it was gone. We drove in silence for perhaps half a mile. I took it that he didn't want to continue with the subject when he spoke.

"You have to make allowances for Mr. G.," he said. "This is something you have to learn. He's a man called by God. I don't wonder that he's short-tempered at times. I would be too if I carried the burdens he does."

"But—"

Having begun, Bartholemew was not going to be interrupted. "I believe that God called me to help him accomplish the great task he's been given. And if at times it becomes difficult, well. . . ." He looked across at me and smiled. "The greater the task, the greater the reward."

The voice of the convert, I thought. Little wonder the Aimee Semple Macphersons, the Billy Sundays, the Jim Bakkers and the Jimmy Swaggarts of this world have their forever-loyal followers. Regardless, it would seem, of anything.

Back in Bartholemew's office brewing a cup of coffee, I said, "Tell me about Mr. Gladden's beginnings."

He had been busy scanning a sheaf of telephone-message slips and now put them down. "Actually, he started as a fundamentalist evangelist," he said. "Can you imagine it, our Mr. G. pounding the pulpit in tank-towns all across the country? And not all that successfully either. It was a good thing he didn't have to depend on love-offerings; he would have starved." He poured coffee into my cup.

"Incidentally, being a Canadian didn't help. The heart of the gospel circuit is the South. The most successful evangelists, they're nearly all Southern country boys: Billy Graham, Jimmy Swaggart, Oral Roberts, Kenneth Copeland. Mr. G. would go to these tacky little tents and cinder-block churches and preach his heart out, and at the end of the campaign wouldn't make enough to buy a plate of black-eye peas. Worse, some of those piny-woods pastors would skim off part of the love-offering. You've known Mr. G. long enough to know how he'd react to *that!* Which didn't help," he added.

He perched on the edge of his desk, looking at the carpet. "There's one thing about Mr. G. that is for sure: he was present and accounted for the day they passed out brains. He noticed that the evangelists with the biggest crowds were the ones who put on a good show." He affected a Deep Southern accent. "Lots of hand-clappin', foot-stompin' gospel singin' an' some hallelujah shoutin' an' hollering. Amen, brother!" He grinned self-consciously and dropped the dialect. "Mr. G. had noticed also that, by and large, the healing-evangelists got the biggest crowds. And the more miracles they claimed, the bigger the crowds. Didn't matter that nobody was healed."

"But surely the truth catches up with people like that."

"That's just the point, it doesn't. Nobody ever checks. Even more important is what's called, I think, the will to believe. People want a lift, not a let-down. That's how some of today's television evangelists can lie and steal and fornicate and still keep a following. Many people *want* to believe, *need* to believe."

He sat in the chair beside his desk and took a moment to set the creases of his trousers just right. "Mr. G. figured—and I'll admit I'm presuming in this—in for a penny in for a pound, so he got into miracles." He smiled a wry smile. "I saw one of the promotions he ran back then: *The blind see! The deaf hear! The lame walk! Let Oscar Gladden Your Life!*" He shook his head ruefully. "Then one day he decided that he'd had it with the whole scam and he bailed out. Quit cold-turkey. But it was in his blood. More important, God wouldn't *let* him go." He paused, his eyes glistening. "And that was when he had his resurrection experience."

I'd read that Oscar Gladden had died and in three days had been resurrected, but I'd dismissed it as nonsense, as one of the excesses common to the world of television evangelism. But it was evident that Bartholemew took it seriously. I said, "Tell me about Oscar Gladden's resurrection."

Bartholemew was regarding me closely. It was an appraising look but there was a friendliness in it. "I've never told the story," he said, "but I don't suppose there's any harm in it. And Mr. G. tells me your contract forbids you writing about anything you learn while you're working for him. Not that there's all that much wrong," he added quickly.

"It happened in Toronto, ten years ago last April. Mr. G. had kept Toronto as his headquarters and he'd become friendly with his bank manager. He's always had lots of money—I guess you know that he was a millionaire before he was out of his teens." I nodded. "Well, apparently the safety-deposit boxes in the bank weren't large enough for his purposes, so the manager gave him access to one of the strongboxes in the vault. One Friday he was in the vault at closing time, and the clerk, not realizing that he was in there, closed it for the weekend." His voice dropped. "And there he was — in the darkness of the tomb, as he describes it—from Friday till Sunday."

"But hold on," I said. "There are time-locks on bank vaults and they can't be opened before business on Monday. How did he get out on Sunday?"

"His sister and others knew he'd gone to the bank, and it finally dawned on everybody that he'd been locked in the vault. They were afraid he might smother for lack of air, or panic in the darkness, so they brought in torches and cut their way in. It took from Saturday evening until Sunday morning." I must have had a skeptical look on my face, for he added, "It really happened."

"You don't really believe it?" I said.

"Of course I believe it. I've heard Mr. G. tell the story." He was looking at me, his eyes unblinking. "That's where the whole idea of One was born. In the darkness of that weekend, Mr. G. had a vision. By the time he was resurrected Sunday morning the entire body of his teaching had been revealed to him. And now he's on some fifteen hundred stations and is reaching an audience of fifty million people a day in twenty-six countries around the world."

My god, I thought—it all began in a bank vault!

# TEN

Meet Mr. Nobody: Mary Jane Smith. 127 Main Street, Wichita, Kansas."

So began my fifty-three-page photocopied and bound report to Oscar Gladden on the Mr. Nobody project: the end product of six grinding weeks collating printouts from the Bureau of the Census; demographic studies cadged from my father and friends in advertising agencies; a Ph.D. thesis, "Middle America: Homogeneity amid diversity — the myth of typicality" (a lucky find on a tip from a teaching-fellow at Columbia University); sheets of national income analyses — all assembled and codified by the Department of the Treasury; a half-dozen scholarly books, including Bernardt's *Into the Melting-pot* and Howarrth and Tovey's monumental three-volume study, *The Americans: Sources and Patterns,* plus dozens of newspaper and magazine articles. In the course of my research I had journeyed to Washington twice and to Wichita, Kansas, once; plundered the morgues at the New York *Times,* the *Register, Time* magazine and the Congressional Library; consulted *Books in Print* and a dozen or so other publications (all alphabetically listed in an index at the back of the memorandum and in an annotated bibliography running ten pages), ending with a cross categorization which, when fed into a Census department computer (through the kindness of a clerk, shamelessly flattered and doubtless misled), yielded 2488 names — all "average" Americans.

Hopeless!

Despairing, I had taken a map of the United States, ruled diagonal lines from Puget Sound to Miami and from Maine to southern California. Then I bisected the nation north and south and east and west and discovered at the intersection of the four lines, Wichita, Kansas. The master-list gave me nineteen names within Wichita's city limits. I obtained a map from the Wichita Chamber of Commerce (donated to the city by Everett A. Miller Realty), placed my coffee mug on it and traced its circumference with a pen. Within that circle lived four of my culled prospects. I couldn't restrain a smile when I saw that one of them was named Smith.

Off to Wichita to investigate the four subjects and, as I had anticipated, to encounter problems. Abraham Zachary, first on my list, had moved to Yakima, Washington, so that eliminated him. Next: Edwin James Sylvester. He took me to be an Internal Revenue Service investigator and, for all my disclaimers, would not be disabused of the idea. That eliminated him. Next: the Reverend Arnold Shelby Shellbarger, an ordained minister in the Pentecostal Holiness church. He welcomed me to his tiny "study" in an unfinished concrete-block edifice called Bethel Temple and spent most of the hour he had granted me trying to convert me to "a born-again experience of the Lord Jesus Christ." I managed to escape, unbowed.

My last "potential nobody," Mary Jane Smith, was cordial on the telephone, seemed to accept me as what I represented myself to be and agreed to meet me after work for a drink at the Chisholm Trail Bar in the Holiday Inn. We hadn't specified any means of identification and I found myself smiling at every unescorted woman who entered—getting, to my slight chagrin, only one come-on in response.

Mary Jane Smith arrived fifteen minutes late but unselfconscious about it. She proved to be a comely, relaxed woman in her early thirties, with wide-set hazel eyes, a disarming smile and a sense of herself. As we talked, possibilities danced in my head: here was someone I could work with! After a few minutes our initial reserve passed, and a rapport grew that led to a remarkable candor on both sides. I couldn't help but think as I listened to and watched her, that if this was a typical middle-American, the country was in pretty good shape.

BIOGRAPHICAL DATA:

Mary Jane Smith (nee Jenkins), Wichita, Kansas. Age 32. Born Emporia, Kansas, April 24, 1963. One of three children, all living. Fifth generation American of Scottish and English descent. Father a cattle farmer. Great grandfather one of the settlers who served the terminus of the Chisholm Trail and helped found the city in 1868. Mother's maiden name, Magregor: one of fourteen children (thirteen boys), daughter of a brakeman on the Atchison, Topeka and Santa Fe Railroad.

Mary Jane Smith lives in a semidetached, two-bedroom frame house on the corner of Athenian and Caroline streets, overlooking the west side Athletic Park and with a view of the Arkansas River. She is 5'4", weighs 129 pounds, has hazel eyes and medium-brown hair tinted ash-blond. She has an IQ of 106 (national average, 100), has completed three years of high school, works as a sales clerk in the women's and misses' clothing department at Sears Roebuck and Company, moonlights Thursday and Friday evenings as a checkout cashier at Wall's IGA supermarket, and has an annual income of $24,450. She is separated from her husband after eight years of marriage and has two children—a girl seven and a boy six. She goes steady with Reuben H. Munson, a flight-controller at the Wichita Municipal Airport, whom she dates every Saturday night. Once a week, usually on Wednesdays, he comes for dinner. On Saturday mornings he drops by to do "the man's work" about the house and to look after the kids while she goes shopping. Twice a week she takes the children to dinner at Pizza Hut or McDonald's. Every other week she goes to an early movie, usually with a girlfriend, and then goes bowling. She drives a 1992 Chevrolet Impala, is a member of the Book of the Month Club and subscribes to *People* magazine and *TV Guide*. Favorite television show: "Dallas." All-time favorite movie: *Gone With the Wind*. Favorite movie star: Burt Reynolds. Favorite book: "Anything by Sidney Sheldon." Favorite singer: Kenny Rogers. Favorite food: deep-fried butterfly shrimp. Favorite recreations: bowling and tennis.

I delayed telling her the specifics of the Mr. Nobody project as long as possible. When finally I did outline it, I was surprised at the equanimity with which she reacted. After sitting silent for perhaps thirty seconds, she said, "You know, I've always had the feeling that, one day, something wonderful was going to happen to me. Rube, that's my boyfriend, calls me Pollyanna, but I don't care. I've always thought it would be something like maybe I'd win a lottery, or some relative I've never heard of would die and leave me a lot of money—something like that. I don't mean I dreamed I was ever going to be famous and on television, like you say, but that *something* would happen. Something nice. No, I'm not surprised. And I'm game to give it a try.'

I pledged her to secrecy, promised to get back with more details within a week and, filled with an internal excitement, caught a Braniff flight for New York City. Enroute, I toasted my good luck, neglected to eat, and Jo, meeting my flight, found me a little giddy.


ATTENTION: G. Oscar Gladden
FROM: Anthony Carpenter
PROPOSED SCENARIO: Mr. Nobody project. (Phase One)

(NOTE: It should be understood that the following scenario is not presented as a fully developed proposal. It is put forward primarily as subject matter for discussion. The details—admittedly many and complex—will be worked out after the decision has been made to go ahead.)


## THE INCREDIBLE JOURNEY
Mary Jane Smith obtains a pilot's licence (time required: from twelve to fifteen hours). She will then take further instruction to learn the essentials of cross-country navigation. On the anniversary of Charles Lindbergh's first transatlantic solo flight (May 21, 1927), she will take off from Roosevelt Field, Long Island, as Lindbergh did, in a Cessna-182, ostensibly to log cross-country and instrument time. Approximately twenty minutes later she will land at a farmer's field near Patchogue, Long Island. (See notes and map: p.32ff.) There she will be met by a car and driven to John F. Kennedy airport

91

where she will board an Aer Lingus flight to Shannon, Ireland. From Shannon she will be driven to another farmer's field nearby where there will be an exact duplicate of the plane she flew out of Roosevelt. She will take off and fly at an altitude of no more than 100 feet—thus avoiding Irish coastal radar—to the west coast of Ireland and out to sea for approximately fifty miles. She will then make a 180-degree turn, climb to 5000 feet and come in to land at a predetermined location on the Irish coast. She will explain when questioned that she has always wanted to duplicate Lindbergh's historic flight and has just attempted to do so but ran short of fuel. A check will be made at Roosevelt Field where it will be confirmed that a Cessna-182, piloted by Mary Jane Smith of Wichita, Kansas, and bearing the same markings as the plane she had landed in, had taken off some thirty hours earlier and had not returned. It will be learned that search operations have been instituted.

## BACKGROUND

Two used Cessna-182 aircraft will have to be purchased: one in the United States, one in Ireland. The identification numbers on the wings and elsewhere will be duplicated. The plane in Ireland will be fitted with as many auxiliary fuel tanks as can be accommodated but all will be empty save one. Mary Jane Smith (who has excellent hand-eye coordination; bowling average 218-plus) will undoubtedly be able to solo after the usual twelve to fifteen hours of instruction. I have a cousin in Patchogue, a farmer, who is willing to provide for a landing in one of his fields and will maintain security. Some similar arrangement will have to be made in Ireland and compensation paid. After the transatlantic "flight" has attracted the requisite media attention, it will be revealed as a hoax. Subsequently the two aircraft will be sold and most of the outlay recouped.

## PROGNOSIS

Potential for international media attention, excellent — remember the worldwide attention given to the "Wrong-way Corrigan" flight to Ireland, July 17–18, 1938. (Douglas Corrigan took off from New York for a flight to California but landed in Dublin, Ireland, claiming, tongue in cheek, that he had gotten lost.) See attached photocopies of coverage: New York *Times* and *Daily News.*

Estimated cost after resale of aircraft: $27,000. (See budget breakdown, p. 38.)


Late Friday afternoon I took the bound reports and the relevant research materials to Oscar Gladden's office. I will confess to feeling a sense of dread akin to that which I often experienced during my college years on the eve of final examinations. It wasn't that I hadn't done my job; I'd given the assignment my best shot and was confident that the proposal could be brought to fruition. But I was also acutely aware that, at this preliminary stage, it could easily be shot full of holes.

Gladden looked up at me as I stood in the doorway to his office, two bulging briefcases in my hands.

"What the hell is all that?"

"As promised," I said, "the Mr. Nobody report." I crossed the office, put the bound reports on his desk and the briefcases on the floor.

"You expect me to plow through all this?"

"As much or as little as you wish," I said stiffly. "You'll find two reports. One concerning my candidate for Mr. Nobody—a woman, you may be interested to know—"

"A *woman!*"

"—and a second detailing a proposal designed to get media attention. The briefcases contain research data and relevant documentation. Read as much or as little as you please."

Gladden hefted the reports and glanced down at the briefcases. "What are we planning—a space shot?"

I was aggrieved now and didn't trouble to mask it. "Which is exactly what I feel I've been through, goddamnit!"

He returned to his work. "Give all this to Bartholemew and tell him to put it in my bedroom. I'll talk to you Monday."

# ELEVEN

I slept around the clock and awakened only when the telephone roused me.

"Mr. Carpenter, your car is ready whenever you'd like to pick it up."

Sudden elation! I feel juvenile in confessing it, but one of the great pleasures in my life is my car. I draw a satisfaction from it that I don't expect everyone to understand. I'm not what I think of as a real car buff. I don't understand, for instance, the motivation of people who collect antique cars, spend a fortune to make them all spit-and-polish and then park them in a garage ninety percent of the time. I will concede that some of the early cars are—using the term advisedly—works of art and that they may yield aesthetic satisfaction to the beholder, but a car is essentially a means of transportation. If it's beautiful, that's a bonus, but no more than that. If aesthetic satisfaction is what you're after, you might be better advised to buy something you can hang on your living room wall.

I bought Smedley five years ago—third-hand and neglected —when I was on the rise at the *Register* and had just been given a raise. It's a 1959 MGA-1600 roadster, the first of the 1600 line.

The 1959 MGA-1600 roadster is—with the 1957 Aston Martin, the 1970 Ferarri and the 1967 Porsche—the finest touring car ever built. Its lines are sporty and distinctive but not all that extraordinary—the Bugatti, for instance, is more dramatic. The uniqueness of the MGA-1600 rests in the motoring genius built into every part of the machine. Slide into the Connelly-hide contoured-leather seat, put your hands on the natural wood of the steering wheel and pause to look about you. No gimmicky instrumentation on the walnut-veneer dash; instead, perfect utility. Now, start the engine, slip into first gear and move into traffic. Within fifteen seconds you will realize that you are encapsulated in a piece of precision machinery designed to do one thing superlatively well: make moving from one place to another an experience of almost orgasmic pleasure. The car will accelerate like a jet on afterburners, corner like a cat in a corn-field, and do just about anything you ask it to—so long as you don't ask it to do anything you can't handle. A word of caution if you are ever tempted to buy one: be aware that it may impov-erish you at the gas pump, that the 140 mph marker on the speedometer isn't an empty boast, that the engine will demand more attention than an occasional check-up and that you will feel the road in your tail. That understood, you will be intro-duced to the exalted, almost mystical experience of being at one with a superlative piece of machinery.

No small thing.

I called Jo to tell her that I would hear no argument; she was to put aside her work for one day and join me in a picnic in the country. We had both been so busy that we hadn't seen each other except fleetingly in her studio and hadn't made love for a week, except for one salacious verbal coupling late at night on the telephone. She needed no coaxing and insisted on bringing the food.

I picked up the car and with an electric exultancy in my veins headed out of the city. As I reached into a pocket for money to pay the toll on the Queens side of the Midtown Tunnel, I remem-bered with a jolt that, in my excitement, I'd forgotten to bring my wallet. I found enough change to pass through, hung a hard left and headed back to the apartment. In the parking lot, I delayed for a moment before turning off the engine, marveling at its mellow, burbling sound as it resonated beneath the under-belly of FDR Drive.

I was fanning through my keys at the apartment door when I saw the handle turn. I stepped quickly to one side and froze against the wall. The door opened a crack, swung wide and a man stepped through. I threw a shoulder into him and drove him across the hall into the far wall, kicking at a leg, trying to bring him down. He twisted away, swung about, and with the grunt of the karate fighter bludgeoned the edge of a hand against the side of my head. A knee smashed into my solar plexus, doubling me over and dropping me to the floor. Writhing, face down, I saw only his feet as he raced to the stairwell and disappeared.

It was a full minute before I could haul myself erect. I walked, bent over, to the window of the apartment and looked down. There was no one in sight; the intruder either lived in the building or, more likely, had left by the rear basement door. In the bathroom I crouched on the floor by the toilet bowl, retching.

As soon as I was able to, I called Jo and told her that I would be an hour late but said nothing about the intruder. I counted myself lucky not to have been knifed or shot. A break-in or an assault is no longer a notable event in New York City—I think of it as part of the price one pays for the privilege of living in the most vital and, in many ways, the most beautiful city in the world.

I toured the apartment. Nothing seemed to be missing. A drawer ajar in the desk caught my eye. The intruder had been through it and the other drawers, carefully replacing the contents. Now who the hell would be interested in *my* papers? They were mostly receipts, canceled checks, insurance policies, divorce papers and other documents. I thought of Johnny Gallagher's missing papers and of his cries of "Watergate." Was I, for some reason unknown to me, somebody's Daniel Ellsberg? The only impression I retained of the intruder was that he was white, young and had a thin, ragged beard.

And that he was a hell of a lot better in a brawl than I was.


With the brand-new top down and stored on the rear deck, with Jo in the seat beside me, with the sky azure and the sun hot on our shoulders, with the car like a blooded-horse fighting for its head and needing to be restrained, and with the nausea gone, all the world came right. I put out of my mind the intruder in my apartment and the picture of Oscar Gladden riffling through my Mr. Nobody proposal and rejoiced in the moment.

We drove far out on the Island, nosed into an unused country lane and stopped by a natural clearing in a lovely woods. There was the pungent scent of things growing. The field was dazzling in the sunlight, jubilant in its new growth and dusted with daffodils and phlox and narcissus. We wandered on, idly gathering wildflowers, following the course of a crystalline creek, exploring an abandoned logging-road, finally arriving at a glen where we could spread a blanket and lay out the lunch that Jo had brought.

Later we lay silent beside each other, sated with the food and wine and with our loving. After a long while Jo said, so softly that I could barely hear her, "I know it may sound silly but I want you to know that you were the first."

"Yes," I said. "I know that." I added, "Why?"

"Why?"

"I mean, why did you wait?"

It was a moment before she responded. "I really don't know. It wasn't a conscious decision. It just never became a big issue."

"But you, alone, in Paris," I said, "mixing with other students, many of them artists like yourself. Lonely. . . ."

"It wasn't that I didn't think about it. How could you not? She was silent for a moment. "It had something to do, I suppose, with—I don't know—self-respect. Oh, my! Doesn't that sound pompous."

We lay for a while saying nothing. Her hand stroked my chest and I flinched.

"My poor darling," she said and moved to brush her lips lightly against the angry red blotch where I had been kneed. "Who would want to hurt you?"

I shook my head. "I have no idea."

"Whoever he was, he stole nothing?"

"Nothing."

"But he went through your papers?"

"Yes."

"But why?"

"I've been asking myself that. I simply don't know."

There was a tentative quality to her voice when she continued. "It couldn't have been . . . Maggie?"

"I don't think so. She has what she wants."

"Are you sure? Maybe all the anger she's shown you is because she still loves you and knows that something in you, or perhaps in herself, makes it impossible for her to have you. I could understand that."

The idea made no sense to me. "Maggie doesn't love me. Maggie loves Maggie. For ever and ever, Amen."

"Who, then? Who would want to go through your things?"

"It was probably no more than somebody living by today's logic. The world owes me a living. You've got something I want, so I take it. And don't hassle me or I'll bust your head."

"But it couldn't be that; he didn't take anything."

I shook my head. "Darling, I don't understand it. I haven't a clue."

"It worries me," she said. "Whoever he was, he was looking for something, something specific. If he was after money or jewelry, he wouldn't have bothered replacing things in the drawers."

I was silent for a moment, pondering the questions she had raised. *Could* it have been Maggie? With the details of the settlement being feuded over by our lawyers, was it possible that she had sent someone to look for evidence that I hadn't declared all our assets? But surely not; she knew the state of our finances; that was one of the reasons she had left.

But with Jo's questions the world was back, tough and insistent. I saw Oscar Gladden bent over my reports, his brows down, that now familiar look of disapproval on his face. There was a sinking feeling in my stomach and a sudden touch of depression.

A wind had risen. There was the raw smell of rain and we were both suddenly chilled. We gathered our things, packed up and made our way to the car. The skies were black as we approached Oyster Bay.


When I arrived at my office Monday morning, there was a note from Bartholemew: "Mr. Gladden would like to see you as soon as you come in."

He was at his desk, head down, writing. My two reports were on his desk. He capped the pen and put it aside, picked up my two proposals and hurled them across the office. Like game-birds they tumbled, fluttering, to the floor.

"Puerile crap," he snarled.

I looked at him, startled by his violence. His eyes were dark and malevolent. There was a folded copy of the New York *Times* on the desk. He stabbed it with a forefinger. *"There's* your Mr. Nobody."

I reached across and picked up the paper. It was open at an inside page. Gladden had circled a three-inch-deep story under a one-column heading:

### FINES FOR PROTESTERS
### AT NEW BUILDING SITE

Three men were arrested last night after a protest at the site of the new Republic Motors Building on Third Avenue south of 53rd Street. The men, all members of the Amalgamated Iron and Steel Workers of America, were apprehended by police while spray-painting graffiti on the hoarding that encloses the construction area.

Joshua Crown, 33, Luke Starblanket and Rene Desroches, both 30, live on the Caughnawaga Indian Reserve near Montreal, Canada, and work on the building which is nearing completion. They were charged with being drunk and disorderly and released.

I looked up, incredulity in my face. "An Indian? And a *drunk?* You've got to be kidding!"

"He's our man," Gladden said. "Who's more a nobody in our society than an Indian? Find Joshua Crown and bring him here."

# PART TWO

# TWELVE

The green Lincoln Mark-VI bored through the darkness, silver streaks of rain streaming into the headlights. The speedometer hovered at eighty miles an hour. The *whack-whack-whack* of the windshield wipers matched exactly the cadence of Charlie Pride's "Lonesome Blues" on the radio. Luke Starblanket, the man in the passenger seat, stirred. He'd been sleeping for the past half hour, head against the window, snoring past the phlegm in his throat. He used the sleeve of his jacket to wipe a hole in the condensation on the window.

"Where we at?" he asked.

"Coming up on Morrisburg," Joshua Crown said.

He was a big man, entirely at ease. One tanned hand rested on the steering wheel, the other on the console, finger-drumming to the tempo of the music. He took the car through a curve that sent a pair of sunglasses skittering across the instrument panel. Uneasy in the back seat, I held my breath.

"There's going to be a christly row," Luke said. "Maria," he added by way of explanation. "Stupid fart."

I'd met Maria, Luke's wife, at the party. As I'd pieced it together, Luke had refused to take her to the party and she'd hitchhiked the two hundred miles from Caughnawaga to Brooklyn. I saw her now in my mind's eye: all bosom and belly and buttocks, some fantasy sending her toe-stepping on tiny feet about the banquet hall, body undulating within a shapeless flower-print dress. And later — a half-dozen drinks later, just before Luke abandoned her to catch a ride home with Joshua—

she had been slumped at the center of the dance floor, raising her head occasionally to mutter unintelligible curses at some phantasmagoric memory.

"It was a good party," Joshua said.

It *had* been a good party, of its kind: a boisterous, festive time with lots of booze, much rowdy laughter and high animal spirits in the men. It was a farewell bash for one of the members of Local 40 of the International Association of Bridge, Structural and Ornamental Ironworkers, a skinny man with bowed legs and a prematurely wrinkled face known as Meatless. He'd "gone over the side" three months earlier, falling five stories and landing on a pile of sand. The slope had reduced the impact, and he had sustained only a broken collarbone and some damaged vertebrae, plus a patch of pebbled skin on one cheek where the sand had embedded. He'd read the fall as a signal to quit and was going home to Detroit.

I'd spent most of the evening sitting to one side, waiting for a chance to talk to Joshua, drinking what everyone else was: Molson's, a Canadian beer. There had been brain-stunning music by a frenetic purple-haired combo to which no one listened and few danced: mostly, the women danced with each other. The presentation and the two brief speeches that followed were in Mohawk. I was the only one there who wasn't Indian.

"Find Joshua Crown and bring him here" had been the edict. I'd stormed out of Oscar Gladden's office, enraged at the cavalier dismissal of my proposal and sulfurous with resentment. What the hell did Gladden know about the nature of the problem he'd assigned to me? How in God's name was I supposed to metamorphose a graffiti-scrawling Indian into a national celebrity? What did he expect me to do: announce a photo-opportunity for the news media and holler "Geronimo" as Joshua Crown did a half-gainer into a saucer of tea from sixty stories up?

Early the following morning I'd donned an old leather windbreaker, a pair of scruffy cords and a hard hat and, disregarding the stares of half a dozen ironworkers, had squeezed into the elevator cage for the intimidating ascent sixty-four stories up the exterior wall of the Republic Motors building. At the top, the wind was gusting and, in the cool of the morning, raw and penetrating. The view, reaching for forty miles in every direction, dizzied me for a moment. I made my way across a loose plank floor, stepping carefully over hoses and cables, avoiding buckets of bolts, stacked lengths of steel beams and an untidy heap of crates and cartons. Shouting above the cacophony from air-compressors and pneumatic wrenches, I asked two men carrying a plank where I might find Joshua Crown.

"That's him there," one of them said, pointing a filthy gloved hand at a man in a Montreal Canadiens hockey sweater standing on an eight-inch I-beam above my head.

I stopped to watch him. Another I-beam was raised over the side of the building, reeled in on the horizontal crane and, in a single motion, lowered hard by the massive column that formed one corner of the structure. Joshua Crown seized one end of the beam, walked it to the column and, with the help of a mate, bulled it into position. There was a spud-wrench dangling from the leather belt around his waist. He rammed the pointed end of the wrench into a bolt hole and pried the flange in to register with its mate on the column. Bolts were jammed into holes, the pneumatic wrench juddered and screamed and the beam was set. Two other ironworkers were straining to secure the other end. Joshua joined them, moving nimbly along the beam to beat on the steel with a hammer. More bolts in place, the stuttering cry of the wrench, and the job was done, and done with such an economy of effort that it was a thing of beauty.

I cupped my hands to my mouth. "Hey! . . . Joshua!"

He turned slowly and looked down. "That's me."

"Can I talk to you?"

"What do you want?"

"I'm a reporter from the *Register*."

Catcalls from various points on the structure: "C'n I have your autograph, Josh?" "Hey!—you ain't gonna put *his* ugly kisser in the paper?"

A man in a hard hat with a bobbing belly and a grizzled red face was storming toward me, a roll of whiteprints in one hand.

"Who the fuck are you?" he demanded. "An' what the fuck are you doin' up here?" Then, to the men above: "Back to work, you assholes."

I sweet-talked him into letting me hang around until Joshua

took his coffee-break, promising a mention in my story and making a production out of getting the spelling of his name right. Not long afterward, Joshua and I sat on a pile of planking looking out over Manhattan. The wind was from the east and it had whipped away the saffron shawl that so often drapes the city. The air vibrated with clarity, and the distant buildings and miniaturized cars in the streets below were clearly delineated. Off to the left, over JFK, tiny planes circled like sluggish bees over a hive. Out to sea, ships trailed their pale wakes.

I studied Joshua as he poured coffee into the cap of his thermos, trying to visualize him surrounded by reporters or sweating in the lights of a television studio. There were possibilities. He had what is often called a strong face. The jaw was squarish and clean-shaven. The eyes were an extraordinary amber beneath arching black brows. He didn't look "Indian," which didn't surprise me: I'd done a piece on the Caughnawagans and knew that there were few if any pure-bloods remaining. They have intermarried—mostly with French-Canadians—and while many retain the characteristic broad cheekbones and the shrewd sunken eyes of the Indian, others are indistinguishable from white men.

He looked at me, appraisingly. "You're a reporter?"

"With the *Register*," I said.

"And you want to talk to me about the other night?"

"That's the general idea."

"Not now," he said, drinking deeply of the coffee. "Tonight. I'll take you to a party."


The approach to Morrisburg flowed by. The streets of the sleeping town were gray and deserted and glistening in the rain. On the outskirts, Joshua pushed the car up to seventy. I caught a glimpse of a police cruiser, lights out, in the lee of a Dairy Queen.

"Cop," I said.

"No sweat. They don't bother us 'dumb, fuckin' Indians.' "

A careering turn and we were on Highway 25, five miles from the reservation. On the familiar run for home, Joshua's foot went to the floor and the speedometer touched 110. As we reached the first cluster of buildings, he began to bang the horn.

Lights were burning in many of the houses; families were up as always on a Saturday morning to welcome husbands and fathers, away since Monday in Manhattan or Jersey or any of a half-dozen other places where steel was being raised.

We dropped off Luke Starblanket, and now, turning in at his own house, Joshua cut the engine, switched off the headlights and let the car roll silently through the open door of the garage. The house was dark, and he was careful at the door when he led me in. In the kitchen, he went to the refrigerator, peered inside, produced some cheese and raised an eyebrow of enquiry. I shook my head. He folded a piece of white bread about a chunk of cheddar and opened a can of beer. Down a short flight of stairs, in a recreation room, he unfolded a hide-a-bed, tossed a pillow and some blankets onto it, retrieved his snack and said in a whisper, "See you later."


I don't sleep well in unfamiliar surroundings and was up at around ten. There was nobody about so I wandered outside to sense the morning. Joshua's house was a two-story clapboard structure, with gables and a wide covered porch. The grass needed cutting. Some April resolutions about a vegetable garden had obviously been abandoned, and a plot of earth surrounded by twine strung on fragile sticks had been surrendered to the weeds. Uttering soft mews of friendship, a long-hair tabby sauntered toward me, tail borne high. I picked him up and scratched in the appropriate places. Together, we went idly toward the street.

The neighborhood was pleasant—typically Canadian/American bourgeois. Great oaks and maples and an occasional evergreen cast long shadows on the paved streets and indifferently tended lawns. There were the cries of children at play and the sound of a power-mower. Down the street a man worked on the engine of his car, appearing at a distance to be in the process of being swallowed by a gaping alligator. The street didn't look "Indian reservation," I thought, but then neither did the Lincoln we'd arrived in.

As I mentioned, I'd done a feature on the Caughnawaga Indians in a series I'd written for the *Register* about the recent building boom in Manhattan. They are a small band of mixed-blood Mohawks who live on a parcel of land deeded to them by the Canadian government. It lies on the south shore of the St. Lawrence River, west of the city of Montreal and just below the Lachine rapids. They are a nomadic people of fewer than three thousand, restless as gypsies. It is not uncommon for a family to lock their house, pile into a car and go off for months or years, returning as unpredictably as they went. There are offshoot colonies of Caughnawagans in Buffalo and Detroit, the largest being in the North Gowanus area of Brooklyn. There is a saying that "Brooklyn is Caughnawaga's downtown."

In the seventeenth and eighteenth centuries, Caughnawagan males worked as fur-traders or, as soon as they were old enough, manned the great freight-canoes on the river. Some worked at timber-rafting and built a reputation for daring, running those enormous rafts of oak and pine through the Lachine rapids. Others traveled with circuses; they were the first circus Indians. Others settled on the land to farm, or spent their days fashioning snowshoes and moccasins for sale. Some became shiftless and hung about in the slums of Montreal, doing odd jobs or cadging money from passersby toward a bottle of rotgut brandy.

The Canadian Pacific Railway cantilever bridge at Lachine changed all that. It was begun in the spring of 1886, and soon riveting gangs were working a hundred feet above the St. Lawrence. They found themselves bothered by Indians peering over their shoulders or wandering about the structure with the indifference to height of a squirrel in a tree. Their fearlessness prompted the construction superintendent to try some of them out as riveters. More were hired. Their skill and daring became legendary and soon they were traveling the continent from Sault Ste. Marie to San Francisco, and from the Mississippi to the Florida keys—and especially to New York, where they helped raise the city's towers against the sky.

Caughnawagans seem born to their dangerous trade. From childhood they play on the structural supports of the Mercier Bridge as other children play in fields or on the street. In manhood they will walk a slender I-beam hundreds of feet above the ground with nothing on either side to hold. I've watched them bull columns weighing half a ton while fighting a boisterous wind. I've seen them crouch on a beam, one foot behind the other, fit a long-handled wrench on a nut, and then stand to throw their entire weight on the handle. There is no hesitancy, no loss of balance, no looking down. They live with danger and it has become a familiar.

I butted my cigarette, gave the cat a farewell scratch on the rump and went into the house. There were sounds of someone stirring upstairs but nobody in sight. I wandered into the living room. Shaded by the porch, it was dark, furnished with an overstuffed sofa and chairs. There was a large-screen television set and an absence of books.

Stretched on the largest expanse of wall and almost filling it was an American flag, which surprised me; Caughnawagans are more Canadian than American but consider themselves neither. As treaty Indians they have free access to either country. I looked more closely at the flag. It was old and faded and sagged on the finishing-nails that affixed it to the wall. Beside it was a cheaply framed photograph of a dozen men on top of a building, ironworkers, stripped to the waist and filthy from their labors. Bottles of beer were held aloft as in a toast. Behind them, stiff in the wind, stood the flag. In the distance, indistinct in the haze, were the towers of Manhattan.

Joshua came from the kitchen carrying two mugs of coffee. He gave me one and pointed to one of the men in the picture, a sturdy man gone to fat.

"My grandfather," he said. "Three of the other guys are great-uncles. The flag here—it's the one they used for topping-out the George Washington Bridge." He grinned. "Grandpa stuffed it down his pants after everybody went for drinks. With his belly, nobody noticed." He studied the photograph for a moment, and said, "The good days."

"What was so good about them?" I said, and remembered even as I asked the question.

"Because in those days they built everything with steel. Today most of the stuff going up is reinforced concrete. These are bad times. Right now, half the guys in our local can't get work."

"And that was what you were protesting at the Republic Motors building?"

"No," he said simply and left it there. He raised his coffee mug as though in tribute to the men in the picture and turned away. "Let's get some grub."

In the kitchen I met Jeannie Crown. She was on the telephone but quickly hung up and shooed Joshua from the refrigerator when he began poking around in it. We sat on chairs at a formica-topped kitchen table cluttered with magazines, a half carton of cigarets, a small radio and a variety of unlikely objects. "Hello," Jeannie said, but nothing else. She filled two small glasses with a pulpy tomato juice, pushed the magazines aside and plunked the juice down before us. I saw her sniff the eggs as she broke them into a frying pan. Two pieces of white bread, one of them the heel, went into the toaster. She dug two plates from beneath the clutter of pots and dishes in the sink, dried them with a soiled tea towel, slid the greasy mass of eggs on them and put them before us.

"Don't we have any bacon?" Joshua asked. "Potatoes?"

"I can't think of everything," she said.

I watched her pad around the kitchen in her slippers, a cigaret hanging from her lips, talking mostly to herself. Her unbound hair was on her shoulders, and the soiled hem of her flannelette nightgown dragged on the floor as she rambled on in a muttered griping about a neighbor. I had a go at the eggs, but on the previous night's stomach they were beyond me. Joshua was having the same problem. He asked for more coffee and we wolfed down toast and honey while Jeannie put on the kettle and spooned some crystals into freshly washed mugs.

"Let's have our coffee outside," Joshua said.

He led the way to two chairs fashioned from skinned pine under an enormous oak. We settled in the chairs and talked for the better part of an hour. He was a superbly muscled man, his shoulders and upper arms straining the fabric of his T-shirt, the heavy sinews of his thighs evident under tight jeans. His face and forearms were deeply tanned. He looks, I thought, like a western horse-wrangler.

I found myself liking Joshua Crown. There was a directness about him, an openness, a readiness to laugh, a candor that was often startling. He treated me without deference but didn't seek to assert himself. We went for an idle walk to the foot of the street. The Mercier Bridge loomed above us, rusting metal arcing down to rest on great concrete pads overgrown with grass and weeds. Traffic thumped and clattered high above us. There were children playing tag on the structure. Joshua grinned and said, "Me."

Back at the house we sat again beneath the oak, cans of beer in hand.

"You aren't doing an article about that business in New York," he said.

"Why do you say that?"

"Because most of the things you've been asking me about are the things you ask when you want to get to know a guy. You've gone to a lot of trouble to talk to me. Why?"

Stalling, I took a moment to pick some burrs off a pantleg. I was questing in my mind for the best approach to take and decided on candor.

"I am a reporter," I said, "but right now I'm on another job—"

"I wondered why you didn't take notes," he interjected.

"—for a very prominent man," I continued. "We're looking for somebody who'd be willing to cooperate in a project we're interested in. Somebody who'd be willing—I know this is going to sound ridiculous—willing to become a celebrity." The amber eyes with the tiny black pupils were unblinking. "I said it would sound ridiculous," I added awkwardly.

"That part's okay," he said. "I was just wondering why you're doing this. And why would you want to make somebody a celebrity? And how do you do that? I thought celebrities were, well, like movie stars or politicians or ball players. You've got to, you know, *be* somebody."

I grinned. "Not necessarily. Not today."

His eyes were still on mine, unwavering, slightly disconcerting. "Okay, why me?"

I shifted in my chair. "To tell you the truth, I don't know. Oscar Gladden, the man I work for, picked you. I don't know why."

The eyes widened. "Oscar Gladden? The TV preacher?"

111

I nodded.

"He picked *me*? How does he know me?"

"I don't know. But it has something to do with your writing that graffiti on the wall."

A small wariness came into his eyes. "Is he connected with Republic Motors?"

"I don't think so," I said. "No, I'm sure he's not. You can ask him."

His eyes stayed on mine for a moment and then turned away. "Tell me how you're going to make me a celebrity."

I shrugged. "I don't know. I haven't had time to think about it. The question is: are you willing to consider it? The money's good."

He got out of his chair and stretched; the impression was like one of the great cats rising from a nap. "When I was a kid we used to play 'chicken' down at the bridge. The support beams run up at every possible angle, and we would challenge each other to see who could walk, barefoot, hands-free, up the steepest incline and at the greatest height. I won a lot of nickels and dimes."

"I'm not sure I follow you."

His slight smile widened. "There was some tar near the base of one of the columns, and I used to manage to get some of it on the soles of my feet." He chuckled at the memory. "All I'm trying to say is I like a challenge but I look after me."

"You're saying yes?"

"I have no idea what you want me to do, but it sounds interesting. So what the hell."

I spent the day with Joshua. We wandered through the town, looking at what there was to see, which wasn't much. Every house had a television antenna but, there being no mains, the residents were forced to haul their drinking water. There was a church enshrining the bones of Kateri Tekakwitha, a Roman Catholic teenager crazed by her faith to the point where she chained and whipped and starved herself, went barefoot in the Canadian winter and slept in the open in the snow. In the main street, beadwork and "Made in Taiwan" totem poles and other souvenirs were sold, and the elders gathered in the sun or in a

112

general store to discuss the band's business or the prospects for the Montreal Expos. A longhouse sat on the hill next to the graveyard where men wearing velour shirts and quartz watches sat around a fire smoking the sacred tobacco and rueing the loss of the "old way."

# THIRTEEN

In New York City, I had just pulled up a chair to my table at the Hellbox when Dunc Robertson told me that Judge Wheeler had been murdered.

"Last night. At home. Apparently he surprised an intruder, grappled with him and got a bullet in the head for his pains. You look puzzled."

"Not really." A vagrant thought *had* crossed my mind. "They called Wheeler the hanging-judge, as you know. A lot of guys have sworn to get him. But I'd heard his place has more burglar alarms than Tiffany's, as well as the big daddy of all German Shepherds."

"The dog's dead. The vet had to put him down. Broken jaw."

"A broken *jaw*?"

"I talked to the investigating officer. How, I asked—with a kick? No, he said. Whoever the guy was, he skinned over the fence and, the best they can figure it, leaped astride the dog somehow, grabbed his snout and pulled down his jawbone until it snapped."

"Jeezus!"

"Indeed. After which he broke into the house, and when Wheeler confronted him, shot him. Used one of Wheeler's own guns."

"Which suggests it wasn't premeditated."

"How do you figure that?"

"If he'd gone there to kill him, he'd have brought his own gun."

"Maybe he did and then didn't need to use it. The crazy thing is, with a house full of valuables he takes only a portable TV set."

"He'd probably triggered the alarms. He'd know the police were on the way."

"Then why stop for the TV set?"

"So it shouldn't be a total loss. Or maybe it was deliberate, to make it look like a burglary. You say you talked to the investigating officer. No clues?"

Dunc shook his head. "They found a cheap religious medal in the grass back of the house but there was nothing to identify it. There must be twenty thousand of them in Manhattan alone."

"Broke the dog's jaw! Jeez!"

"Probably higher than Everest," Dunc said. "Most of those break-and-enters are. Give 'em the family jewels, I say."

Dunc's whistle for Kono as usual rattled the glasses back of the bar and woke a guy named Joe Potts, a reporter on the *Daily News*. He and his wife had been feuding about his drinking and she'd locked him out. So each night he would appropriate one of the banquettes at the rear of the dining area, have dinner and sit by himself drinking Harvey Wallbangers until he fell asleep. The cleaning women would get him up in time to grab a coffee and a bagel for breakfast at Grand Central and make it to work on time.

It occurs to me that I may be contributing unintentionally to the impression that reporters are drunks. It's a common misconception. If the statistics were available, I'm sure they'd show that newspapermen drink only slightly more than clergymen (less wine, certainly), about as much as lawyers and considerably less than doctors. One of the reasons they drink as much as they do is because they get offered so much free booze—an occupational hazard or a fringe benefit, depending on your point of view. A further reason is that reporters are, for a variety of reasons, subject to frustration. They are, on average, not well paid, but they commonly move among those who are. Most, fiercely proud of their vocation, are acutely aware — more so than their critics—that much of their product is little better than mediocre and that most of it lacks grace—deadlines do not polished prose make. Some newspaper beats are particularly frustrating because the reporters assigned—who know full well that they have no power and little influence—spend much of their working days with men of power and influence who are patently fools. They are on terms of first-name intimacy with such people and are frequently treated as peers and confidants. Most reporters know that this camaraderie is mere sufferance; they sit at the great man's table because they are a convenience, the necessary evil required to transmit his words and deeds to the public. The uncommitted reporter doesn't stay long in the newspaper business; he tends to gravitate to one of the many aspects of public relations.

When Kono had deposited our drinks, I said to Dunc, "I'll tell you someone who won't shed tears over Wheeler getting shot. Oscar Gladden."

"Hey, that's right!" Dunc said. "I'd forgotten for the moment you'd gone to work for him. What do you do? Turn his prayer-wheel?"

I didn't appreciate the crack and wasn't ready to tell him what I'd been up to, so I swung the conversation to the *Register*. I'd heard some scuttlebutt that the Gannett chain was negotiating to buy it. The stock had reacted, gaining five dollars and, after some fluctuation, holding there.

"The law firm of Haversham and Dukestra is fronting for somebody," Dunc said, "but we haven't been able to track down who. It may not be Gannett. I don't want to sour your day, now that you've left, but the word is that whoever it is has plenty of loot and plans to put up a brand new building and convert the *Register* into a morning paper." He had a pull at his drink. "By the way, I suppose you've heard that Replogle was fired? Well, not fired, kicked sideways into the business end. His job's up for grabs." He glanced at me. "And me saying I didn't want to sour your day."

"Newspapers," I said crankily, realizing that it sounded hollow. "Who needs 'em?"


Although we were running fifteen minutes late, I had difficulty getting Joshua past the aquarium. He paused in the entrance hallway and stood motionless except for his eyes.

116

"This is his *hobby?*"

"One of them."

"What else does the reverend do? Raise cobras?"

In his study, Oscar Gladden, all affability, crossed the floor, hand outstretched. Observing them, I thought I had never seen two men so opposite: Gladden, gross corporeality inhabited by a brooding intensity; Joshua Crown, physical grace with a laid-back, apparently ingenuous openness. Joshua was scrutinizing the man before him with evident curiosity and something of the intentness with which he had watched the predators in the tank. He flashed me a look I couldn't decipher.

Gladden turned on his high-voltage cordiality. "Welcome, Mr. Crown," he boomed. "Mr. Carpenter tells me you want to be a celebrity."

There was the hint of a smile on Joshua's lips. "No," he said. "Only that I'm willing to be one."

We moved to Gladden's desk. Gladden pointed Joshua to a chair and I took another. I was interested to note that, rather than seat himself behind the desk, Gladden took the third chair. Now, leaning back, his manner expansive, he put his chubby hands together, the fingertips touching.

"Well now, Mr. Crown," he said. "As I understand it, Mr. Carpenter has begun to fill you in on what we want. But let's begin with you. Why have you come?"

Joshua gave a small shrug. "To tell you the truth, I'm not sure. A little excitement, I guess. And it's a job. There's not much steel going up."

Gladden began to tap his fingertips in sequence. "Have you had any experience with the press?"

"A few times. When there was trouble in the village."

"The reservation," I interjected. "They call it the village."

"What kind of trouble?"

"The police. The Canadian government sticking its nose in."

"And what impression did you get? Of the press, that is?"

"They're like the gulls. When things smell bad they come around to see if there's anything for them. Sorry, Tony," he added, turning to me. I smiled thinly.

"Do you think you'd be able to handle them?"

"If the president can, it can't be all that hard."

Gladden was loving it. His fingertips were tapping at a merry rate. ''You know,'' he said, turning to me, ''I think he could handle it.''

''Just a minute,'' Joshua said. ''Nobody's told me exactly what it is I'm supposed to handle.''

''First,'' Gladden said, ''there are a few questions. Have you spoken to anyone about this?''

''About what?''

''About coming to see me. I presume Mr. Carpenter has told you that I'm not to be connected with this exercise in any way?''

Joshua nodded indifferently.

''And that, when Mr. Carpenter spells out the terms of the project and you accept them, you do so on your own responsibility?''

''I'm a big boy,'' Joshua said easily.

''I have only one more question. I would like you to tell me what you were unwilling to tell Mr. Carpenter: what is your quarrel with Republic Motors?''

''Why do you want to know that? Tony told me you had no connection with Republic.''

''That's correct. I haven't. But the project I have in mind does.''

I raised my eyebrows; he hadn't mentioned it to me. Joshua frowned.

Gladden said, ''It's very simple; you and your friends sprayed the word *Killer* on the hoarding. Why?''

Joshua shrugged. ''It seemed like a good idea at the time.''

''A drunken escapade?''

''Something like that.''

''*Killer* isn't a word pranksters print on walls. Not without a reason.''

''No,'' Joshua said, ''you're right about that.''

He got out of his chair and strode about the room, gnawing at a thumbnail—a habit, I'd noticed, when he was concentrating. Gladden was watching him, his eyes coldly appraising. I had a mental flash of a horse-trader eyeing a yearling.

After a moment Joshua returned to his chair. ''Fair enough,'' he said. ''If we're going to make a commitment to each other, you have a right to know what gives with me.'' It seemed to me that his face was drawn and that some of his vitality had ebbed. When he spoke, his voice was thick. "Republic Motors killed my best friend," he said.

"Tell me about it," Gladden said, and leaned back in his chair.

Joshua told us the story over the next ten minutes. He didn't tell it well and, as I learned later from others, didn't tell it all. But he did spell it out in some detail and with a surprising candor. When I came to know him better I learned that it was typical of him to spill his guts when the mood was on him or when he'd had too much to drink. Rather than present the incomplete account he gave that morning, I will put the entire story before you as he recounted it and as I pieced the details together later.

Every member of the wedding party agreed that the day Tom Deerfoot and Natalie Greenwood were married was perfect. It was a Saturday afternoon in October, crisp and brilliant and tumultuous with color. The vows were spoken in the exquisite Harry Emerson Fosdick Memorial Chapel in the Riverside Church on Morningside Heights in New York City, and as the bride and groom posed in the sunlight on the topmost step, they looked like ornaments on a wedding cake. Afterward, some three dozen relatives and friends attended a wedding supper in the second-floor banquet room of the Huang Lin restaurant on Eighth Avenue. There was a sitdown meal with endless steaming bowls of Chinese-American food, red and white wine, and California champagne for toasts. Joshua Crown, the best man and the groom's lifelong friend, served as toastmaster. The newlyweds slipped away after the reception, going hand in hand down the rear fire escape to the parking lot where their brand-new Republic Motors Lancer, festive with paper flowers, was parked.

Four hours and seventeen minutes later, the car veered suddenly from the Maryland Turnpike and smashed head-on into a concrete abutment. The groom died instantly, his head severed from his body. The bride's back was broken. She would never again move about except in a wheelchair, nor would she be able to control the voiding of either her bowels or her bladder.

Early the following morning, Joshua Crown was in the garage behind his home in Caughnawaga building a bird-feeder. Over the scream of the power-saw he heard his wife's voice, high-pitched and urgent. He put down the saw and went to the door. Jeannie was standing in the dark doorway to the house. Her face was gray, her jaw slack. He ran to her.

"Tom!" she gasped. "Tom! He's dead."

"Dead?"

"There's a police—a policeman on the phone."

He ran into the darkness of the house. The telephone receiver was rotating at the end of its cord.

"Hello," a voice said. "Are you Mr. Joshua Crown?"

"Yes."

The voice was measured, toneless; an official voice. "This is State Highway Patrolman James Whittman. I'm informed that you are a friend of Thomas Christian Deerfoot?"

"Yes?"

"I'm afraid I have some bad news for you—"

"Tom's dead."

"Yes. I'm afraid so. I'm sorry."

"What happened?"

"It was an accident. An automobile accident." The voice began to read from notes. "At 9:52 P.M. last night, Mr. and Mrs. Thomas Christian Deerfoot were proceeding south on the Maryland Turnpike about thirty-five miles north of Washington. Their automobile apparently left the turnpike and crashed into a concrete abutment—"

"Natalie? Is she all right?"

"Natalie. . . . Yes. Excuse me if I make a note; I didn't have the Christian name. . . . Now. Yes, Mrs. Deerfoot is in the Baltimore General Hospital. I can give you the telephone number later, if you like. Among Mr. Deerfoot's effects was a membership card in the International Association of Bridge, Structural and Ornamental Ironworkers, Local 40, Brooklyn, New York, on which your name was written."

Joshua's voice was hoarse and empty, and he had to clear his throat to get the words out. "He was married yesterday afternoon."

120

"Geez! That *is* rough. I'm sorry. Perhaps you could tell me who his next of kin are?"

Tom's next of kin? There were no next of kin. His father had been killed on a chill, windy afternoon five minutes before quitting time when Tom and Joshua were seventeen and only beginning as apprentice ironworkers. Old Tom, as everyone called him, had stumbled and lurched forward when a piece of warped planking twisted beneath his feet. Tom was working six floors below. Old Tom went by close enough to touch, his mouth open, his eyes wide and staring, grabbing at the air and cursing all the way down. It took two men to pry young Tom's hands from the beam to which he had dropped without a sound. Tom's next of kin? His mother had died in the winter of 1976 sitting in a bathtub; she'd reached out to turn on a portable electric heater. When Tom found her, the skin of her body was wrinkled and parchment-white. Tom's next of kin? No brothers. No sisters. An uncle somewhere, traveling with a circus, performing a bored, jigging dance and selling beadwork.

"There being no known next of kin," the policeman was saying, "would you be willing to have the remains—Mr. Deerfoot's body, that is—shipped to you for burial?"

"Yes."

"I'll have the coroner's office in Baltimore get in touch. Thank you for your help. I'm sorry—"

"Wait a minute. Before you go, what happened? I mean, did a tire blow? Did somebody run him off the road? What?"

"No, nothing like that. There was no other vehicle involved. As far as we have been able to determine, the car just went off the road into the abutment. Nobody saw it, far as we know." There was a brief silence on the line. "They, uh, they'd been drinking, you know."

"Of course they'd been drinking, for chrissake! They'd just got married."

"Sorry. I wasn't saying they were drunk."

Joshua was suddenly overtaken by fatigue. It was as though the strength to remain standing was more than he could summon. He missed the cradle as he tried to hang up the receiver, staggered across the room and fell onto the sofa. In the kitchen Jeannie sat on the floor sobbing into a dish towel.

Three months after the accident, Republic Motors announced the recall of twelve thousand cars of the model Tom Deerfoot had been driving, specifying a potentially defective bolt in the steering assembly. Joshua wrote the company a letter on Natalie's behalf, detailing the accident and enclosing the police report. He received a form letter instructing him to take the car to the nearest authorized Republic Motors dealer and informing him that the potentially defective bolt would be replaced at no charge. He wrote an intemperate letter in which he said, "You overlook a slight problem. The entire fucking front end of the car, including your goddamn 'potentially defective bolt,' is in the driver's seat!" There was no reply. After a number of letters and a half-dozen telephone calls, he talked to a lawyer, and together they pressed Local 40 to institute a suit.

The suit was heard in the 14th Apellate court in the Borough of Queens. The judge found the allegation that Republic Motors was responsible for the death of Thomas Deerfoot and for the injuries sustained by his bride "not proven." The judgment stated that the complainant had failed to demonstrate conclusively that a defect in the steering mechanism of the automobile in question had contributed to the accident. It seemed to Joshua that the decision had been influenced greatly by the summation of counsel for the company:

"I would put before you, sir, one final and, it seems to me, material fact. Speaking in all charity and with some reluctance, but compelled by the candor required of me in fulfilling my responsibility to my client, I would impress upon the court the fact that the occupants of the automobile in question had, but four hours before, come from a wedding supper—quite understandably a festive occasion—at which they were the principal celebrants and during which the thirty-five adults present consumed a total of twenty-one 24-ounce bottles of wine as well as six magnums of champagne. It pains me to say this, but I would be remiss in my duty to assist this court in its consideration of all the relevant facts if I did not mention that, of the thirty-five persons present, all but two were native Indians." There were vehement objections, but the point had been made.

The costs assessed against the complainant were $14,000.

They were paid from the treasury of Local 40 on a motion by Joshua Crown.

As he finished the story, Joshua seemed depressed. He returned to his chair and slumped low in it. I, who had been taking notes, stored the copy paper in a pocket. Oscar Gladden, who had moved to his desk, ground out a cigar and asked bluntly, *"Was your friend drunk?"*

Joshua's head came up quickly. "Of course he was drunk. He was an Indian, wasn't he?"

Gladden was rocking slightly in his chair, the lids of his eyes low. "So," he said, "you've discovered that justice in this country is not only blind but stupid, and you would like to strike back at Republic Motors on behalf of your friend. Good. I approve that. What did you have in mind?"

Joshua was slow in answering, but when he did speak his voice was firm. "An appeal."

"And what makes you think you could win an appeal?"

"The judge was biased. He disregarded the fact that the autopsy showed no significant level of alcohol in Tom's blood."

"Nor, from what you told us, did the inquiry demonstrate that there was anything wrong with the steering of the car." Gladden began to tap out rhythms on the desk top with a brass letter-opener. "What will you do with the money if you win the appeal?"

"Give it to Natalie. She has nothing."

"Are the Ironworkers prepared to finance the appeal?"

"No."

"Is your local?"

"No."

"Do you have the money?"

"No."

"Do you have any idea what it will cost you?" Gladden said, pressing. "There'll be a retainer for your lawyer. Subsequent payments. The cost of transcripts. The preparation and the filing of the appeal. Postponements. The case could go on for years."

"I know all that."

"And do you know what you will have accomplished when

you're finished? Nothing. Believe me, nothing. All you'll do is put yourself in debt. There is no way, my boy, that you are going to beat Republic Motors in the courts. It's your David against their Goliath, only you don't have the sling-shot or the five smooth stones. If you think you can win, you're a fool."

Joshua's head was down. He made no response. Gladden was watching him closely. "Did you hear me? Go after them in the courts, Joshua Crown, and you're a damn fool."

Joshua's head came up. For a moment I thought he was going to lunge at Gladden across the desk. Instead, his jaw working, he looked at him for a moment from beneath his brows, rose from the chair and walked to the door.

Gladden's tone was conciliatory. "Come back and sit down. I was testing you."

Joshua's hand was on the knob. Gladden was smiling now. I was surprised at the warmth, the almost overpowering charm that radiated from him.

"Come, come, my boy," he said, his voice honeyed. "I was just checking on your boiling point."

Joshua remained where he was, but some of the anger had receded. "Fuck you, Gladden," he said. "I don't need you."

"Ah, but you do," Gladden said. "You need me to help you get even with Republic. If I were to give you a way, a foolproof way of doing that, would you be interested? Well then, come over here and sit down."

Joshua hesitated for a moment, then made his way back to the chair.

It was soon clear to me that Gladden had no specific plan in mind. He skated around the subject, begged the question and avoided specific answers on the ground that Joshua and I hadn't yet worked out an arrangement. He brought things to a conclusion by turning to me.

"Mr. Carpenter, I want you and Mr. Crown to firm up the details right away. In the meantime, why don't you show our new friend around the place. And take him up to meet Jo." As we left, he called out to me, "See me when you're finished."

Jo looked tired. She had been working almost without a break, sometimes until dawn, preparing for her show. I embraced her, kidded her about her perfume—Eau de Burnt Umber—and introduced her to Joshua.

His gaze had been ranging around the studio. "The symbols," he said, "they're Mohawk. Iroquois." He walked among the canvases, stopping before some to examine them closely. Jo was watching him, her face flushed.

"They're the totem animals among our people," he said. "The turtle, the wolf and the bear."

"Anowara, Ohkwaho and Okwari," Jo said solemnly. She burst into a laugh. "Don't you *dare* answer me in Mohawk; I only know a few words."

Joshua turned back to the paintings. "I love them."

He moved about the room—I was reminded of a cougar sniffing out prey. Jo watched him, intent. She pointed to the model's stand. "Would you mind getting up there for a minute? Just for a minute." When he stepped on the stand, she added, "Take off your shirt, please."

She began to sketch with bold, sure strokes. I watched for a while, marveling at her skill, and then, feeling redundant, went down the stairs to Gladden's office. He was at his desk, working. Without looking up, he gestured me to a chair.

"Where's our noble savage?"

"In Jo's studio being immortalized."

"I think he's our man," Gladden said. "See what kind of scenario you can come up with."

He shoved a sheaf of paper across the desk, and with it a purse-size date book. "See what you make of this."

I flipped through the papers. They were photocopies of pages from a desk calendar. I saw nothing unusual about them. There were names, some with telephone numbers—appointments presumably—airline departure and arrival times, random jottings.

"Is all this supposed to mean something to me?" I asked.

There was a cryptic smile on Gladden's lips. "Look up January 13 and 26 in both of them."

The pages in the desk calendar were clear except for an American Airlines flight number with a departure and arrival time, the words, "Mayflower Hotel" and a telephone number. The corresponding pages in the date-book were headlined, "Washington,'' and listed some names and telephone numbers. At the bottom of the page were ''Mayflower 11:30'' and the printed initials ''JRG.''

''I still don't get it.''

''JRG. John Robert Gallagher. It's his desk calendar.''

''And the date book?''

''Jerri West's.''

''This is a photocopy of Gallagher's desk calendar?'' I asked.

Gladden nodded, smiling as though at some delightful secret.

''Then how do you come to have it? His desk calendar was among the things stolen from his office in that break-in.'' Gladden's grin grew even more Cheshire. ''Where did you get it?''

''A friend. Somebody who knows how Gallagher's been trying to crucify me.'' Indeed, Gallagher had not been dissuaded by Oscar Gladden's acquittal in Judge Wheeler's court. There had been barbed comments in recent speeches about his lifestyle and about the tax-exempt status of the Worldwide Church of One.

''How I got it isn't important,'' Gladden continued. ''What matters is the significance of it. The date book is Jerri's and those are Gallagher's initials. Here.'' He pushed another paper across the desk. ''Check these dates. Every time he goes to Washington he sees her. He's a customer of hers.''

''So?''

''What do you mean, so? The son of a bitch has been married twenty years. He's got nine kids. He's a Catholic, a member of the Knights of the Holy Sepulchre and the Knights of Malta!'' He riffled through the papers he'd given me earlier. ''He's been given an award by the Pope himself. Here.'' He read, struggling with the words: *Pro ecclesia et Pontifice.* He's vice president of the Coalition for Morality on Television, for chrissake!''

''So, he's a hypocrite. What do you want me to do? Organize a public stoning?''

His eyes flashed but he contained himself. ''I want you to leak it to one of your friends in the media. But not here. Let it come out of Washington.''

I put the material back on the desk. ''I don't know anybody on the *National Enquirer,*'' I said huffily.

The tiny pink tongue darted out and in. The voice was low but there was an edge to it. "Mr. Carpenter, you and I have an agreement. A contract. You had two weeks to make up your mind. I made no promises to clear things with you and you made no conditions to that effect. You will please do what I ask."

I felt a dew of perspiration forming on my brow. "It won't work," I said. "Anybody who prints this is going to have the police coming round. Where'd you get it?"

"It came to me in the mail. Anonymous. I get twenty to thirty thousand letters a month."

"What about Jerri West's involvement?"

"Let me worry about that."

I got to my feet. There was a roiling in my belly. Gladden was beginning to be hard to take: his curt dismissal of the preparatory work I'd done on the Mr. Nobody project, his arbitrary selection of Joshua Crown, and now the order to plant this sleazy story.

"I'm not sure I like being involved in this kind of thing," I said.

"I don't pay you to like it," he said, unsmiling. "Just to do it."


Oscar Gladden on television, the eyes dominant, the red lips moving, the even white teeth gleaming. The face: strong, handsome, compelling, a glint of perspiration on the brow. I found myself caught up in what he was saying.

"The difference between OneWorld and other religions is that OneWorld is not a pie-in-the-sky-by-and-by faith but a faith for *today*; OneWorld doesn't speak of a heaven in some distant tomorrow but of the heaven you can make out of life on earth. Here! Now!

"All your life the church has told you that you are a sinner and that, for your sins, you will be punished. Consequently, you are told that you need forgiveness. Then you are told that you can only find that forgiveness in the confessional or at the communion-rail or at the altar. Oscar Gladden is here to tell you

127

that it is all a lie and that this is the way the church controls you.

"It's all so negative. *Religion* is negative. Thou shalt not do this and thou shalt not do that. Well, hear this! No amount of negations will make you good or bring you happiness. All the minuses in the world can never add up to positive living. You can remove from your life ten thousand things and it won't make you good; it will merely make you empty."

The voice lowered, the camera moved in, the tone dropped to a persuasive whisper. "The secret of successful living is to adapt to the laws of life. Success comes from becoming *one* with the world and *one* with yourself and *one* with the people in it.

"So seek to understand the physical, mental and spiritual laws of life. God's laws.

"You know, for instance, that if you break a traffic law by running a red light you may get killed. What kills you? One of God's laws, the law of inertia. Knowing that, your good sense tells you that it is wise to keep God's physical laws.

"But there are other kinds of laws. For instance, the laws of friendship. Break the laws of friendship and you will be friendless. Break the laws of civility and you will get rudeness. Think mean, nasty thoughts and you will develop a mean, nasty face. Be loving and you'll be loved. Hate and you'll be hated.

"Ask yourself: how do you get a baby to smile? You know the answer: by smiling at it. It's a law.

"So, here is what you must do—"

I suddenly smelled something burning. Oh my god, the frozen turkey pie I had put in the oven! I leaped to my feet and as I did the telephone rang.

Jo! It would be Jo. I hadn't talked to her for three days. She'd closeted herself in the studio, hanging on the door the DO NOT DISTURB sign she'd pilfered from the Savoy in London. I had permission to disregard it, but wouldn't. I had telephoned twice but there had been no answer. (Bartholemew told me later that she had been at the gallery hanging her paintings.) And when she had returned my call I had been out and there was only the machine. Her terse, mechanical message (she found it, she said, "impossible to speak civilly to a piece of plastic tape") had only deepened my longing to see her. I snatched up the phone.

128

"Tony? It's Don Brower. Long time, no see."

Don Brower was a new man at the *Register*. He'd previously been with the Buffalo *Evening News* where he'd developed something of a local reputation as a hotshot. He hadn't made much of an impression in the year he'd been with the *Register* except as a world-class brown-noser. Syd Oliver, the city editor, had summed up the consensus opinion: "Replogle eats beans; Brower farts."

"Hello," I said. "What's up?"

"Nothing special. I just got to wondering how you're doing. Settled in anywhere yet?"

Calls himself a newsman, I thought, and after two months he doesn't know I'm working for Gladden. Not that I'd spread the word around.

"Look, Don, you caught me at a bad time."

"I haven't seen you at the Press Club. We were talking about you yesterday. Bernie Newman—you know Bernie?"

"No, I don't know Bernie," I said acidly. "We've only worked together for the past eight years, you twit." I walked the phone to the television set and turned the volume down.

He continued, unfazed. "Well, ol' Bern told me to tell you if I saw you that he's the new backgammon champ. I told him, 'Sure, Bern, but by default.' And he said, 'Look, if you see Carp, tell him, anytime.' "

"Don, I've got a turkey pie burning in the oven. What's on your mind?"

"Oh! Right. Sorry. It's nothing. It's just that there's some talk that you're working for Oscar Gladden, which is the reason for my call."

"So?"

"I thought you'd like to know his son's in jail."

"He doesn't have a son."

"You're sure?"

"Sure."

"Then maybe that explains it. I'm over at the 17th Precinct this morning and the desk sergeant tells me they've got a Victor Gladden in the cage. Drunk and disorderly. I prick up my ears, of course. 'Any relation to Oscar Gladden?' I ask, thinking there might be a story, and he says, 'We're not sure. The guy says he's not but he's carrying a health-insurance card that lists Gladden as next of kin.' The sergeant says the guy sure doesn't look like he could be Gladden's son—his clothes, I mean. And he doesn't have more'n five bucks on him. Anyway, the whole thing gets me to wondering. I try to call Gladden, but his number's unlisted. I'm thinking of taking a run out to his estate on Long Island, and then I think, what the hell—wild goose chase. Give Carp a call.''

''I can save you the trip. He doesn't have a son. Now look, Don, the whole damn kitchen's about to go up in smoke—''

''You're sure there's no son?''

''Check Gladden's biog in *Who's Who*. One child. A daughter.''

''Well, I'm glad I called. Good to talk to you. I'll tell Bernie I passed on his challenge. You better check that turkey pie.''

''Thanks.'' I put down the phone.

Was it possible that the Victor Gladden in the cage *was* Oscar Gladden's son? Couldn't be, or he would have shown up in Gladden's biog in *Who's Who*. But not necessarily. The subject decides what's to be included. But surely Jo would have mentioned a brother. Gladden himself had only a sister, and she hadn't married, so the man in the cage couldn't be a nephew. I was trying to fish the turkey pie out of the oven, holding my breath against the smoke, when the thought occurred to me— an illegitimate son?

It was none of my business, but I'd take a run over to 53rd Street to see what I could find out.


The 17th Precinct Police Station in Manhattan is unpretentious to the point of being inconspicuous. It sits on the north side of East 51st Street between Madison and Lexington, undistinguished except for a small name-plate affixed to the stone facade, its presence marked most obviously by the NYPD patrol cars parked and empty in front of it. It is a building unloved by the architect who designed it, by the city that owns and administers it and by the men who spend their working hours in it. Unloved, it is untended, and the interior is uniform, unrelieved bleakness. The walls are a pallid gray with a watery blue dado and are dirty, cracked or peeling. The floors are covered with a worn brown linoleum. Harsh lighting glares at battered desks and ancient filing cabinets, at walls and bulletin-boards covered with curling "Wanted" posters and other notices. There is no desk, no table, no piece of furniture that is not dilapidated. Some of the furniture sits useless and abandoned, in out-of-the-way corners or in the officers' room. The detention cage is a cube formed of link-fence wire, barren of so much as a chair. The door is warped, and it bulges from the kicks of many boots. Only the five detention cells, each with a toilet and a bunk, are clean and freshly painted. A suspect, hustled in in cuffs from a patrol car, sees no comely justice, blindfolded and holding a balance-scale. He sees macho men in shirtsleeves, working with cheerful camaraderie in a bleak, unseemly rabbit warren.

"Hey! Tony!" the desk officer greeted me. "Long time."

"Not that long. You haven't made lieutenant yet."

"They don't have no calendar long enough for that," he said, his laugh degenerating into a spasm of phlegmy coughing.

"Tuck your lungs back in and tell me about a suspect you've got here. Victor Gladden."

He buried a cigaret in an overflowing metal ashtray and turned a page in the blotter. "Let's see now. Victor Louis Gladden. Age 20. Male Caucasian. No fixed address. Booked 4:35 A.M., June 23. Officers Malachi and Steiner. Drunk and disorderly. Punched the arresting officer. Used abusive language. Confined in the detention cell awaiting transfer to Central Booking." He looked up. "That's it."

"I'm told he's related to Oscar Gladden. You know, the guy who—"

"I know, I know. The suspect says he's not."

"But he's carrying identification that says he is."

"Look, it's outta my hands."

"Is he still in the detention cell? Mind if I have a word with him?"

"He's not there. He's upstairs in the cage. Lieutenant Donnelly's been interrogating him."

"I'll speak to the lieutenant," I said, starting for the stairs.

"Hold it. Hold it. First we check. The lieutenant don't like surprises." He looked around and then bawled, "Schultz!"

An officer, half asleep in a chair tilted against the wall, came to his feet in a scramble and the chair tumbled to the floor. There was laughter and catcalls from his fellows.

"See if the lieutenant's still talkin' to Gladden an' can Tony Carpenter from the *Register* talk to him."

"Gladden . . . Carpenter . . . *Register*," Schultz mumbled as he disappeared up the stairs. He was back within a minute shaking his head. "He don' wanna talk to nobody. Like, nobody!"

The desk officer turned up his hands. "So we tried."

I pulled out my notebook and scribbled my apartment telephone number. "Give him this, will you?" I tore off the page. "Ask him to give me a call."


There is a perverse side to me that required that I establish whether Victor Gladden was, in fact, related to my employer. I was, at the moment, resentful of Oscar Gladden and found some satisfaction in contemplating the possibility that I had stumbled on a dark corner of his life. There was a message from Jo on my answering machine suggesting that we have dinner, and I decided to raise the matter with her when the moment seemed right.

It certainly wasn't propitious when she joined me half an hour late at an out-of-the-way table at Robinson's Parsley, a pleasant place on Second Avenue. She was fatigued, in one of her moments of self-doubt, and wanted to talk about her upcoming show.

"I'd like to run away and hide and never come out," she was saying. "The critics are going to tear me limb from limb. I know it. I'd cancel the whole thing if it wasn't so late. Lonnie was telling me about a one-man show a couple of months back where they didn't sell a single painting."

"You're going to stand them on their pointy heads," I said.

"I doubt it," she replied, woebegone. "Yes, sometimes I look at my work and it's good. It is. Other times — like this afternoon—I could throw it all on a bonfire." She was silent a moment, gazing with unfocused eyes at the menu. There was a suspicion of tears. "It's not just the possibility of failing, of course; it's the knowledge that everything I've been living for for the past five years could be gone."

"But it wouldn't be. You could still—"

"No," she said, her voice steadying. "I've talked to Bartholemew about it; I won't have the time. Father does six shows a week, and what with rehearsals and all the preparation, I'll be too busy."

"But surely your father will let you off the hook if you talk to him. He must know how important—"

She was shaking her head even as I spoke. "No," she said. "He won't. And I wouldn't ask him to. You make a promise; you keep it."

Because I didn't know what to say I said lamely, "Perhaps you'll even find you like it." She made no response, so I added, "You'll be seen by—how many—ten million people a day?" I lightened my tone. "Hey! You'll be a celebrity and won't even talk to plebeians like me."

Her head had come up and the cloudiness was gone from her eyes. "The show is going to be a *success*," she said, as though willing it. After a moment's meditation she smiled wryly at me. "Maybe I'll be dreadful on television." The smile brightened. "Wouldn't that be marvelous?"

I'd ordered wine when we arrived and had made frequent noddings at the waiter so our glasses had been kept filled. We'd pretty well finished a second bottle now and Jo was beginning to laugh at her own gloom.

"Maybe if I'm a failure on television," she said gaily, "I can get a job modeling garter-belts. Or on 42nd Street in one of those live peep-shows." She looked at me archly. "Would you pay a quarter, or however much it is, to look at me?"

"I'd turn the family fortune into change."

She had shaken her moment of funk and now leaned across the table, taking my hand. "Darling, darling Tony. Have you any idea how I've missed you? Not so much when I'm working, but late at night." Her voice lowered. "I lie in bed and think about us and about the things we do and I—I *lust* for you. I'm afraid that's the only word for it." Her fingers had tightened on mine. "I lie there imagining the most beautiful things, the most sensual things. I've become absolutely shameless. I think of what we do and what I want to do to you the next time we're together, things I never dreamed I'd want to do with a man. You've opened up something in me I didn't know was there." She sat back in her chair, grasping the arms. "Is there any good reason why we have to finish this silly meal?"

On the street as I tried to hail a cab, she clutched my arm and rubbed catlike against it. At the apartment, I moved about turning on lamps, and she followed, laughing, turning them off. In the bedroom she affected a stripper's dance, letting her clothes fall to the floor, and then undressed me, teasing, smiling with comic lewdness. In bed, with only the light from the street, she mock-pinioned me, and with exploring fingers and devouring kisses feasted on my body. Finally, hands and lips sated, she moved above and put her lips to my ear, whispering commands and husky obscenities. We thrust at each other, roughly and with abandon, until finally we were borne away in a seizure of sweet, welcomed agony.

We lay side by side for a while in silence, fingers intertwined. I told her about Caughnawaga and Montreal, and about Joshua's fight to help his friend's widow. After a while, she put on one of my shirts and went to reconnoiter the refrigerator.

"Dessert!" she cried when she returned, holding aloft plastic containers of yogurt, the spoons protruding like antennae. We ate in silence, hungrily, and then the moment seemed right.

"Sitting here, naked and feasting," I said, "may it be presumed that I know you well enough to ask a personal question?"

"I love it when you're personal," she responded, leaning over to put a sticky kiss on my cheek.

I weighed the wisdom of breaking our mood but went ahead. "Do you have a brother?"

I saw her mood alter and cursed myself for having put the question so abruptly. She wielded her spoon vigorously inside the empty container and then licked it carefully. "Isn't *that* a question out of the blue?" she said. "Why do you ask?"

I told her about my visit to the station house. "It's something of a small mystery. He has identification that lists your father as next of kin but he denies it. And I gather he's down and out."

"Is he there now?"

"Either there or at Central Booking."

She got out of bed and began to put on her clothes.

"I'm sorry," I said, thinking she was angry. I was angry at myself, too. "Please don't go."

"I'm not cross," she said, pausing to reach for some facial tissue and dab at her eyes. "I've got to go down and pay his bail."

"I'll go with you," I said, beginning to get dressed.

"No, Tony." The tone of her voice made it clear that there would be no point in arguing. She was buttoning her blouse now, lovely in the ambient light of the city. When she spoke her voice was unsure. "What are they doing to him? It must be terrible."

"It isn't all that bad," I said, knowing that it could be a nightmare.

He would have been handcuffed and taken from the cell at the precinct station. A chain would be run through the cuffs, joining him to other prisoners, and together they would be herded into a van and driven downtown to One Police Plaza. At Central Booking he would be released into a large cage with others—drunks, addicts, pimps, street toughs, sexual perverts—waiting to be processed. He'd be taken out and Polaroid photographs would be taken, four of them simultaneously, to be cut up and attached to four different forms, with his basic biographical data listed. From there he would go into a cubicle to undergo a strip-search, including an examination of all his orifices; afterward he'd be walked through the kind of device used at airports to detect any metal in his body. Then he would be taken to a large holding-tank—which, on a busy night, might contain 250 prisoners—to be summoned finally to a small window where he would be interviewed by the arresting officer and fingerprinted. More interviews, this time by civilian personnel, to find out his background and whether, if necessary, he could raise bail. In the meantime his fingerprints and personal data would have been fed into a computer. If the readout was uncomplicated and routine, he would be given a DAT—a Desk Appearance Ticket—the date being determined by the convenience of the arresting officer. If the printout showed that he had a record, or if there were problems with the fingerprints or unanswered questions, he might be kept in custody. In Victor's case, if he came up "double negative"—no address, no employer and no funds—he might be held overnight. Otherwise he would be given the DAT and released on his own recognizance.

"Are you sure I can't go with you?" I asked. "It's a long ride downtown."

She shook her head, obviously not trusting her voice. I walked with her to the corner of 23rd and Second Avenue and waited until we were able to hail a cab.

# FOURTEEN

The Republic Motors Building prepared for its spectacular rise by tunneling down sixty feet into the bedrock of Manhattan Island. It began its ascent during the deep-freeze days of winter when the muck and the tawny pools of runoff were often iced over and the steel columns so cold that a wet hand or glove would stick.

Coming out of the hole, the view was limited to a few dozen feet by the surrounding buildings. But as the structure rose, the vista changed almost daily. Within weeks the ironworkers at the top could look down on everything within a few city blocks, and each additional floor extended the horizon. The men enjoyed raising the first twenty floors; the weather was good and they seemed like heroic actors on a perilous stage, never without an audience. They watched the pedestrians and the traffic on the streets or looked into the windows of neighboring buildings, and added interest to their day with wolf-whistles at the women in nearby offices and with boisterous macho comments on everything they saw.

A few months and they had jumped to the point where individuals on the street were indistinguishable and the taxis and buses were toys. Now they could see the Hudson and East rivers. On cool mornings the Triboro, the Throg's Neck and the Whitestone bridges rested on a surreal ground fog. Within weeks the Atlantic gleamed in the morning sun and Jersey and Queens and Brooklyn sprawled in untidy rectangles beneath them.

But now the joy was gone. In an almost mechanical boredom, the men kept adding steel, the floor they were erecting exactly the same as the dozens of floors below and the others yet to come. They became indifferent to the fact that on clear days the eye could see some eighty miles into the countryside of Connecticut, Massachusetts, Pennsylvania, New Jersey and New York. Some days the clouds slid by almost within reach, and to look up was dizzying and dangerous. On muggy days the clouds atomized and moved down to envelope them, and they would labor in isolation from even their mates below until a halt was called. Most mornings the coastal waters of the Atlantic shone in the sunlight, and sleek ocean liners, bulky tankers, squat barges and skimming pleasure craft could be seen tracing their fleeting wakes on the glistening surface. Looking east, a man could easily believe that the island of Manhattan was itself a great ship cruising between the Hudson and East rivers toward the Atlantic.

Midmorning on the day of the topping-out ceremony, a flat-bed truck arrived at the site carrying just one column. Ordinarily, the heavy beams or columns in a load will number eight or nine, and as many as three may be hoisted at a time to be off-loaded at the plank floor. But on this day a single column arrived on a clean truck driven by a clean driver, this in itself sufficiently unusual to mark the day as special. The shackles were hooked up in the street so that the column could be picked up and set in place by the craneman in a single operation. At a signal, up it came, the great American flag, already attached, flaring tentatively, seemingly anxious to catch the wind. On the roof, the ironworkers bulled the column into the splice plates, bolted it up and stepped aside. Thereupon a straggle of dignitaries and invited guests took turns standing beside it to have their presence recorded for posterity by the photographers.

The topping-out at the Republic Motors Building was not an uneventful ceremony. The weather was foul, the tail of an expiring rainstorm still lashing. The vice president of the United States was on hand, as was the governor of the state and the mayor of the city. There were lesser politicians, a handful of architects and engineers and perhaps a dozen Republic Motors officials and their wives—the women clutching at their skirts with one hand and at their streaming hair with the other. Clotted in a group near the ironworkers was a nondescript band of reporters from the various news media. Prowling about, freezing from time to time to fix the action on film, were a half-dozen photographers.

The chairman of the board, having insisted on removing his hard hat and irritated because the wind was whipping about the sheaf of hair he normally combed from near his left ear to near his right, grasped his fluttering notes and moved to the spot designated by the public relations man. Receiving a cue that all was ready, he made a last attempt to control his errant hair, and in the effort lost his grip on the speech. The pages went romping like leaves in autumn over the side and, caught in a thermal, mounted into the sky.

Smiling grimly, the chairman leaned close to the microphone. ''Mr. Vice President, Governor Wainright, Mayor Weiss, honored guests and ladies and gentlemen. . . .''

Frantic signals: the sound-system wasn't working and the chairman's voice was inaudible. As he waited for the problem to be rectified, a last dash of rain pelted his face. A public relations man scurried with an umbrella, which immediately popped inside-out and was discarded. Now the microphone was working, but it squealed in feedback and rumbled from the wind and had to be turned off.

The chairman began again. His face dripping and purple with anger, he shouted into the wind, ''Mr. Vice President, Governor Wainright, Mayor Weiss, honored guests and ladies and gentlemen. . . .''

Any possibility of his being heard ended when the motor on the horizontal crane above his head began to reel in cable. The public relations man ran into the line of sight of the craneman enclosed in his tiny cab and began frantically to semaphore with his arms. The operator seemed not to see him. The public relations man, near-manic now, ran to the foreman, shouted at him and pulled on his arm. Reluctantly, for he was a portly man, the foreman went to the base of the column on which the boom was mounted and began to climb. Seconds later he thought better of it and came back down. Urged to do something, he took a hammer from the belt of one of the ironworkers and, fighting to restrain a smile, began to beat on the base of the column.

Suddenly, rising from below, dangling from the end of the cable, an automobile came in sight. As the television portapacks turned and the still-cameras flashed, the car reeled up to the boom, stopped and began to twist slowly in the wind. The front end was a compressed mass of twisted and rusting metal. The wheels were splayed and buckled. The engine, driven into the front seat, could be glimpsed beyond the flattened chrome of the bumper and the radiator. The words KILLER CAR! had been spray-painted in red on both doors.

Unnoticed, Joshua Crown stepped from the small knot of ironworkers and moved to the base of the crane. He scaled the X-braces with the ease of a leopard ascending a tree and walked out on the boom. The wind had eased, and he went swiftly until he stood directly above the dangling car. Legs apart, a striking figure against the scudding gray clouds, he raised his arms for silence.

"Hear me!" he shouted, and the crowd below, necks craning, mouths agape, grew silent. He pointed a long, accusing forefinger. "Look at this car!" he shouted. "*Look* at it! Twelve thousand cars exactly like it were recalled by Republic Motors because of a defect in the steering. This one wasn't. Why? *Look at it, I say!*"

Every eye turned to the car. It hung there, stark and ugly as a corpse on a gibbet, swinging gently now like a giant pendulum.

"Why was *this* car not recalled? I'll tell you why—because it was already on the junk-heap. This car, this killer car, murdered a friend of mine and crippled his bride for life. On the very day they were married, at the very moment they were beginning to live! And what was Republic Motors' response to this tragedy, this tragedy of their making? It was: 'To hell with your friend! To hell with his bride!' Well, my response to Republic Motors is: To hell with *you! Justice . . . will . . . be . . . done!*"

Eyes burning, he stood motionless for a moment, delineated against the sky. Then slowly he raised an arm, paused, and brought it down. The craneman touched a lever. A moment's hesitation and the car, released, dropped out of sight and plummeted sixty-four stories to the concrete plaza below. The sound of the distant crash—the more horrific for the delay and the faint finality of the impact—rose to the topmost floor. In the silence, Joshua Crown swung down onto the cable and, with a foot in the skyhook, was lowered swiftly out of sight.

Standing to one side of the reporters, I smiled at the explosion of activity and clamorous shouting. As I turned toward the elevator, the way was jammed with jostling, cursing reporters, fighting to get in.


Oscar Gladden leaned forward in his chair, the remote-control unit of the television set in his hand. Jo sat on the arm of the chair, a hand on his shoulder, her eagerness matching his. Joshua sprawled in another chair, legs stuck out and crossed before him, feigning indifference. I stood behind them, leaning against the wall, observing.

The freshet of commercials mounted to a torrent and the screen went black. "Don't worry," I said. "It's the summer dog-days. They'll play it big."

"Quiet!" Gladden commanded.

Play it big they did. To maintain an impression of responsibility, the larger networks first warmed over a couple of stories from Washington, reported a rumbling from *Pravda* about an impasse at the arms limitation talks and dropped in a filmed snippet on an Israeli foray into Lebanon. Then they devoted anywhere from two (CBS) to two and a half (NBC) to three and a half (ABC) minutes to the protest at the Republic Motors Building, an allocation of time normally reserved for stories like a presidential press conference, a Mount St. Helen's eruption, or a major Caribbean hurricane. The local stations, happily and unabashedly, went to the story off the top. As I'd predicted, the line-up editors had been unable to resist the shots of Joshua on the boom, hands upraised against the racing clouds, and of the pulverized remains of the "killer car" on the concrete plaza below.

Gladden kept flipping from channel to channel with almost manic glee, muttering beneath his breath and chuckling aloud at such phrases as, "One man's sky-high protest" and "Consumer protests reached new heights today." All the networks had discovered that the man on the boom was Joshua Crown, an ironworker, but, apart from Joshua's words, were unable to offer anything other than speculation as to the significance of the so-called killer car. NBC carried an interview with a spokesman for Republic Motors who dismissed the incident as "the actions of just another kook." ABC concluded its coverage by detailing the planning that had permitted Joshua to escape into hiding and included details concerning the careful roping-off of the area into which the car would fall to ensure that no one would be injured. "Whoever Joshua Crown is and whatever his motives," Peter Jennings summarized, "one thing is certain: the man knows how to make a point."

At the end, Gladden clapped his hands and shouted a triumphant "Hah!" He switched off the television set and got to his feet. "They went for it," he gloated, "like a hungry trout for a fly!" He moved across the room in what was almost a jig, crowing in a jubilant voice, "We got the bastards! We *got* 'em!"

"It was wonderful," Jo enthused. "And you were wonderful," she said, turning to Joshua.

I'd been studying him off and on as he watched himself on the screen. He had raised his body slowly until he was sitting bolt upright on the chair. As the coverage had unfolded, the expression on his face shifted from half-frowning to enormously pleased. Now he was elated, his eyes dancing as he sought to contain a grin that would not be denied.

"Mr. Gladden," he said, "I want to thank—"

Gladden didn't hear him. His face and body twitching, his skin brick red, he was looking at me. "We *did* it!" he crowed.

"Mr. Gladden," Joshua persisted, "I'd like you to know that—"

But Oscar Gladden's thoughts were elsewhere. He stood at the center of the room, his eyes slitted, his teeth bared in a smile that was a horrible grimace. "Now," he said, "we manipulate the bastards right out of their shorts!"

It was almost a shout.


The story developed quickly. A police reporter at the *Times* dug out his earlier story on the graffiti on the hoarding. The *Daily News* tracked down the Ironworkers' suit against Republic and printed portions of the testimony. Officials at the International Organization of Ornamental and Structural Ironworkers provided Joshua's address, and early on the Saturday morning the news media descended on Caughnawaga.

They came in cars and vans and gigantic mobile units. The *Post*, off the mark late, flew in a team by helicopter. Television remote-trucks, portable generators and other traffic jammed the street for a block on both sides of Joshua's house. The networks strung their cables across the lawns, trampling the aborted vegetable garden and, having talked their way inside, set up their lights in the living room. When the freelancers plugged in and blew the fuses, they were cursed for not having brought their own generators. Tripods, cables, cameras, strobe batteries, tins of motion-picture film and supplies of video cassettes were heaped on the front porch in an orderly disorder. Cameramen sat in the shade of the porch, their hands in black cloth bags, loading film magazines. Soundmen ran checks on their equipment: "Testing: one, two, three . . . one, two, three." An enterprising coffee-vendor worked his truck through the traffic and parked on the lawn. He was sold out in fifteen minutes.

Within the house, reporters contended with each other, pressing their questions until Jeannie Crown fled weeping to lock herself in the bathroom, to remain there until the last journalist had gone. Photographers shot pictures of the house from every angle. A network man bearing a portapack fell off a picnic table in the back yard, fracturing his left ankle. Reporters interviewed the neighbors, pestered Father André at St. Francis Xavier church, broke into the usual Saturday afternoon discussion on the porch at Dubois General Store and besieged Natalie Deerfoot's parents' home, cajoling and badgering for an interview with the widow. They left only when her father ran them off with a shotgun.

The question was put a hundred times in a hundred ways: "Where is Joshua Crown?" Bribes were offered for information and, as a consequence, guesses were made, ranging from the Wigwam, a bar in Brooklyn frequented by Mohawk ironworkers, to a shack near the Lachine Bridge where Joshua sometimes spent the weekend. No one thought to refer the reporters to Joshua's twin brother Caleb's longhouse community not thirty miles north of New York City.

There was much to do. The task was complicated by the need to keep Oscar Gladden's and my name removed from the story. I hired a public relations firm, Tad Butler and Associates, and committed their man, Obie Berenson, to secrecy. I had Bartholemew open an account at the Chase Manhattan midtown branch, so that monies paid out would not easily be traceable. I made a reservation at the Vanderbilt YMCA in Obie's name, planning to move Joshua in when he returned to the city. It would be an ideal address. It was central, it wasn't expensive and it offered meeting rooms that could be used for interviews. Obie was detailed to work out the mechanics of a press conference at a time best suited to the various media deadlines. "No free bar," I said. "No pretty girls, no bumper-stickers, no press-kits"—none of the gimmicks that signal PR. I also told him to investigate the possibility of holding the press conference in an automobile graveyard.

I'd decided to keep Joshua out of sight until he met the press. Joshua had told me about his brother. He and Caleb were identical twins, virtually indistinguishable in appearance but, unlike many identical twins, utterly different from birth in attitude and personality.

While Joshua, following the pattern of many of his peers, had apprenticed as an ironworker, Caleb had become a member of a group of dissidents known as the Followers of the Old Way. Mostly young men, they had come to distrust white men and their governments. Their estrangement was essentially emotional but many of their grievances were real. They found their rallying point in a man from the eighteenth century with the improbable name of Handsome Lake. He was a Seneca who, after a long illness, had had a vision and had begun to preach a set of new religious beliefs to the Iroquois. His moral teachings had in them echoes of Christianity, but his advocacy that Indians give up their traditional way of life and take to agriculture was divisive. He made enemies among both his tribesmen and the

Christian missionaries, but thousands followed him. Two hundred years after his death, small bands of Indians still utter as their rallying cry, "Remember Handsome Lake!"

Caleb's community had been established some thirty miles north of New York City on land owned by Peter Stonehouse. Stonehouse was a Mohawk whose wife, a white woman, had left him the property, twenty acres of scrubby, uncleared land, on her death. But he had no interest in farming and, after hearing a passionate speech by Caleb on the need to return to the Old Way, had deeded the land to him. Caleb moved onto the land with a dozen families from Caughnawaga and began to settle it. From the beginning, there were defectors—men who found the simple life too dull or too demanding—but there were even more recruits, and the community grew. At the time Joshua Crown went into hiding there, the community numbered sixty-three men, women and children, living at peace with their neighbors and in reasonable concord with each other.

I'd spent a day and a night in the community when I'd gone there with Joshua to check it out as a potential hiding place. It was Joshua's first visit to the settlement, and he was as curious about it as I was. Arriving, I felt that I'd been caught in a time-warp. We turned off the highway, passed through a young deciduous wood and broke upon a clearing that was neither farmland nor forest. It was dotted with blackened stumps and downed trees. The trees had been felled without axes, by girdling the trunks to cut off the sap, by burning them at the base, and finally by chipping away the char until the tree toppled.

Beyond the stumps and fallen timber there was a cornfield with beans and squash planted between the rows and women bent to the task of cultivation. Farther on, there was a stockade some twenty feet high formed from heavy logs set in the ground with the upper tips sharpened. The ends of the stockade overlapped, forming an entrance to the village and serving to keep the winds out. The enclosed space encompassed about five acres. In the center there were two hulking longhouses and various smaller dwellings, not unlike log cabins, ranging on either side of a dog's-leg main street. Prominent at the heart of the village was a thick post from which the bark had been peeled. It was called the War Post, I was informed, and was covered with drawings in vivid colors. A tomahawk, daubed red and decorated with colored feathers and black wampum, was set in the post. In the early days, I was told, the pictures spoke of battles fought and victories won, of men lost and prisoners taken; now they recorded the history of the settlement.

Caleb, we were informed, was in the sweat-house by the river. It turned out to be not a house but a small, dome-shaped hut constructed of saplings drawn together at the top and covered with deerskins. I put my head through the opening. In the near darkness, a naked man, wet with sweat, lay on a mat. At the center of the hut was a small pit in which hot stones had been heaped. Beside them was a severed gourd half filled with water.

"Caleb Crown? I'm Tony Carpenter of New York City. I'm here with your brother, Joshua."

Caleb extended a dripping arm and we shook hands. After a moment he came from the hut and without a glance at Joshua rubbed himself with sand and plunged into the stream. He had long black hair and skin coarsened by the sun, but there could be no doubt that he was Joshua's twin: there were the same amber-colored eyes under black, arched eyebrows and a set to the head, which, while it didn't mirror Joshua's, did evoke it.

Joshua and I spent the afternoon being shown the settlement and hearing from Caleb how he and the others had given up on the white man's world. He told the story without apology and with none of the proselytizing zeal of the convert. It was eerie watching and listening to him; he was Joshua playing dress-up in buckskin, a sedate Joshua, his eyes free of mischief, his manner formal, his mien reserved. As I watched them together it became obvious that there was a tension between the two men.

In the late afternoon, Joshua went off to visit an old friend from Caughnawaga, and Caleb and I went to the bank of the creek to sit beneath an enormous black willow. I told him what I had planned for Joshua and asked if he might hide from the press in the community. When I finished, Caleb made no comment but broke up a dead twig and cast the pieces onto the stream, watching as they were carried away.

"As you know," he said, "we're identical twins. We were born in our parents' bed with only a midwife to help. I was born without a struggle but it was another eight hours before Joshua came. He was born feet first and the umbilical cord was wrapped around his neck. It was some time before he moved or breathed or cried. The old woman said that, like Flint in our story of the creation, he didn't want to be born the usual way and that, like Flint, he killed our mother.''

He tossed another twig onto the water. It lodged in some grasses. He pitched pebbles at it, trying to free it, but wasn't able to. I was seeing in my mind a tiny bedroom lit only by a guttering candle, and a panting woman struggling to give life while losing her own. I saw the bedsheets stained and bloodied and the gaunt old woman fighting to slap and breathe life into the limp, blue body in her hands. And I heard the piercing cry of triumph from the tiny lungs.

Caleb began again. ''As I said, the old woman called him Flint—the left-handed twin in our story of the creation of the world. She said that I was the child of the sun and that I would love the day, and that is true. Joshua, she said, was the child of the moon and would love the night. Which also is true. And she said that, like the twins in the story, he and I would contend with each other all our lives. And we have. In everything.''

After dinner—a tough deer-meat stew and strawberries—I wanted to stretch my legs, and Joshua joined me. We wandered through an evergreen woods overlooking the settlement. The sun seemed reluctant to surrender the day, gilding the mare's tails at the zenith but delaying its departure behind the great banks of slate-colored cumulus on the horizon. Joshua did most of the talking. He seemed almost under a compulsion to reminisce, perhaps out of a need to balance what he presumed I'd heard from Caleb.

From childhood, he said, he'd been uncomfortable as an Indian. He had learned early on that he would be taken for a white man unless he said otherwise. Sometimes, especially with girls, he had hidden his origins; not, he said, because he was ashamed of them but because there exists in the mind of most whites a stereotype Indian: slovenly, slow-witted, lazy and a drunk. He'd taken pains to counter that impression, keeping his person immaculate, going shaven even on weekends. And, although he'd dropped out of school at seventeen to join a construction gang, he'd read widely, taking care to work newly learned words into his vocabulary.

He was impatient with his people. He thought that most of them had settled for a twilight world, neither Indian nor white. "The stupid bastards hanker for the gadget-happy crap of the American dream, nattering all the while about the preservation of a way of life that's as out of date as lacrosse." He laughed. "It's contagious. I've caught myself — especially after a few beers — sounding off about the virtues of the past, only to remember my Mark VII parked outside and the twenty-five inch TV I just bought Jeannie."

We emerged from the woods and paused on the edge of the escarpment that put an arm about and sheltered the settlement. The community lay below us, unreal, like a set from a John Ford western.

"Is Caleb's way better, then?" I asked.

"Better than what?"

"Than what you've been criticizing—the twilight world. At least he has committed himself."

"So did Jim Jones."

"And what are you committed to?"

"I don't know. Nothing, most of the time. Other times, I surprise myself."

We went down the slope. It was dusk in the community, but in the sky a jet reeled out its feathery contrail in the dying sun. Joshua pointed at it.

"Have you ever thought," he said, "that before our time nobody ever saw a cloud like that? Now they're in every sky. What would my forebears have thought if they'd seen them? I'll tell you: they'd have put them in our legends—the Finger of God, writing. Are the legends they've passed down to us any more or less significant?"


Now, three days later, Joshua was on the telephone.

"Where are you calling from?" I asked.

"The phone booth just outside the community. Why?"

"Just that I'm surprised Caleb would permit a telephone— the way he is."

"Even he's not that stubborn. The parents insisted. If one of the kids gets sick in the night. Like that."

"Anyway," I said, "your timing is perfect. You caught me on my way out the door. I'm off to Washington."

"Hey!" he said. "Maybe instead of making me a celebrity you can make me a senator."

"Much better to be a celebrity than to be a senator. Unless you can be both."

"How'm I doing in the papers?"

"You," I said, "are a hit."

"Tell me."

"The front page of all the papers. Even the *Times* carried a page-one picture. Below the fold, of course."

"Save 'em for me."

"Your local is being driven out of its mind but is loving it. I just had a report from Caughnawaga; the community is in shock."

Joshua guffawed.

"There are requests for interviews from *Time, Newsweek,* the *Washington Post, USA Today* and *People* magazine. And that's just for starters. All the networks. The 'Today' show, 'Good Morning, America,' Carson, Donahue. . . . Why am I naming names?"

"As the kids say, 'Floors me!' "

"All we've got to do now is keep it rolling. I've hired a public relations firm, Tad Butler and Associates. A guy by the name of Obie Berenson is driving up to see you this afternoon. He'll announce a press conference for Monday at ten. Don't worry about it; Obie will prepare a statement for you to read and I'll check it out. You'll have to take questions — does that worry you?"

"I suppose so. No, not really."

"Don't fret about it. We'll figure out everything they're liable to ask, and some of the Butler people will do a rehearsal with you Sunday afternoon. I've booked you into the Vanderbilt Y. It's on East 47th near the United Nations, perfect for our purposes. Obie will talk to you about transportation, clothes, things like that. But not to worry."

"You said you were going to Washington. When are you back?"

"Tonight. By the way, how can I reach you?"

"I don't know. Somebody's scribbled over the number on the phone. Send up smoke signals."

"If I did, you wouldn't know how to read them," I said. "Call me here early tomorrow."

# FIFTEEN

I caught the Eastern shuttle and connected with Jim Ingraham at Jingles, a bar in downtown Washington not far from the Capitol. I'd chosen it because it had skylights and you didn't need to light a match to read. Jim was an old friend from the days when he'd worked for the *Register.* He'd quit in a fit of pique and had been taken on as a political columnist by the new *Sun,* an irreverent and sassy tabloid modeled on the New York *Daily News.*

He went through the pages of the desk calendar and the date book without comment while I nursed a Perrier and tried to shake off the sleazy feeling that had dogged me from the moment we were airborne in New York. After a few minutes he looked up.

"So the guy gets a little nookie when he's out of town."

"Oh, come off it, Jim; he's running for reelection to the Senate on a reform platform. He's vice chairman of the Morality in the Media Committee."

"And, like I say, he gets his ashes hauled when he's here on business. That's as common in this burg as pomposity. Without it, the hotel business goes belly-up."

I felt myself beginning to perspire. "You surprise me."

He looked at me, eyebrows raised. "I do? Why?"

"I read the *Sun* from time to time. Equal parts sex, crime, sports and show-biz. Isn't that the formula?"

"Not my column," he said stiffly.

"Granted. You write politics. Well, what is this but politics, with a little sex for spice and a chance to draw a bead on a pious hypocrite? Politics, sex and hypocrisy—isn't *that* a dainty dish to set before your readers? Let's cut the kidding. No one buys the *Sun* expecting Jim Reston.''

''You sure know how to make a fellow feel good,'' he said, shuffling the papers before him. ''Where'd you get this stuff? Aren't these some of the papers stolen in the break-in at Gallagher's headquarters?''

''Gladden got them in the mail. Anonymous.'' I pulled out a handkerchief and took a surreptitious swipe at my brow.

''Why don't you pass it to the *Register?*'' he said. ''God knows they could use a good story.''

''*That* bunch!'' I said, my tone connoting a harbored resentment.

Jim pursed his lips, shaking his head slowly. ''I don't know, Tony. Look, I appreciate you thinking of me and all that, but it's not my cup of tea.''

''Gallagher's coming here next week for a Morality in the Media rally. You're going to write about it. But what are you going to say that isn't straight reportage? Look at the date book. Every time he's in town there's a late-night stand with a high-priced whore. I agree: there's no story if he's just one of the visiting firemen, but he's riding the morality bandwagon with a bunch of repressed book-burners.'' A droplet of perspiration trickled from my scalp onto my brow. I flicked it away with a forefinger. ''Your editor will love you.''

He was scowling at the material. ''Jeezus, Tony!''

''To hell with it,'' I said, reaching for the papers. ''If you don't want the story, you don't want the story.''

''I didn't mean that,'' he said. ''Leave it with me.''


It was late afternoon when I returned to New York. I was in a bad mood, and that humor was darkened by the need to go out to the Gladden estate to pick up some papers before heading home to the apartment. Coming from the supplies room, I passed Oscar Gladden's office. His door was open.

''Join me for a glass of wine,'' he called out.

He was sitting in one of the pair of leather chairs in the far corner of his office, a delicate wineglass in his hand, an elegant panatela freshly lit between his fingers. He was wearing a burgundy velvet smoking-jacket with black satin lapels, and his slippered feet were resting on a footstool. My eyebrows rose: it hadn't entered my mind that Oscar Gladden ever took his leisure.

He gestured, indicating the coffee table on which there was a crystal decanter half full of an amber liquid and, beside it, a silver bucket of crushed ice in which a bottle of Moillard Meursault nested. I poured myself half a glass and sank into the nearby chair.

"How did it go in Washington?" Gladden asked, drawing deeply on the cigar and watching the smoke rise in a vaporous cloud to the ceiling.

"Okay," I said indifferently.

He waited for me to enlarge on my response, but instead I took a deep draught of the wine. It was cool and agreeable in my throat.

"No more than that?" he asked.

I shook my head.

His eyes flicked toward me, and after a brief pause he said, "Bartholemew was telling me he gave you an abbreviated tour of the Queens complex."

"Yes," I said, refraining from saying anything further. Considering it in retrospect, I now realize that I was spoiling for a quarrel. When he didn't press for my reaction, I lifted my glass and said, a note of cynicism in my tone, "One for all. Or is it all for One?"

He smiled a grim smile. "You're a strange fellow, Carpenter. You've joined me but you're not with me. You do what you're asked to do—and I'll grant that you do it adequately—but you remain forever the journalist: the self-appointed critic holding up his cracked mirror to the achievers in society." He drew again on the cigar and, when I said nothing, added, "I've wondered from time to time if the petty malice of newspapermen doesn't spring from the knowledge that today's accomplishment is tomorrow's fish-and-chips wrapper."

I shook my head as if in wonderment. "Mr. Gladden, your contempt for the press begins to sound like an obsession. Is there no charity in the world of One? Are we all worthless scoundrels?''

I was surprised at how hostile I was feeling. It stemmed in large part, of course, from my resentment of the sleazy errand I had just concluded in Washington. But beyond that Oscar Gladden had a way of stimulating my gorge. I had seldom gone from his presence without muttering ''Sonofabitch'' *sotto voce* and wanting to slam a door. It seemed that he was incapable of inconsequential conversation, of the simple passing of pleasantries, that there was in him an almost narcotic need to bait, to kindle confrontation. I had observed it in his dealings with Bartholemew, with Doc, even with Heddy, the maid who brought us our luncheon trays. And, now, with me.

''You ask is there no charity in One,'' he said, his glass held aloft to capture the light. ''If by that you mean do I believe in saying nothing to avoid saying something that someone might find disagreeable, the answer is no.''

''It's the oil that keeps society running smoothly,'' I said, perhaps a trifle stuffily.

''It's hypocrisy,'' he snapped. ''Just as charity is usually an expression of weakness.''

For all the bluntness of his words he appeared to be in a good mood. A smile was playing about his lips and he seemed comfortable with himself and with the moment. I wasn't and said, ''I thought charity was a Christian virtue.''

''Precisely. And that's why I don't believe in it. Any more than I believe that I should love my enemies. Why should I love the man who'd like to do me in? That's as irrational as the admonition to turn the other cheek. Turn the other cheek to a totalitarian and next time he won't smite your cheek, he'll clout you on the side of the head with a gun butt. We were all taught these addle-headed aphorisms in Sunday school and took them to be true, but they're lies. 'A soft answer turneth away wrath'? Nonsense! In the army, a soft answer is called dumb insolence for which they'll stick you in the brig.' If someone steals your coat give him your cloak also'? Practice that kind of charity and you'll be naked in an hour. 'Give to him that asketh thee, and from him that would borrow of thee turn not thou away'? These days, that's a one-way ticket to the poor house.''

154

He took a deep swallow of the wine. When I made no response, I saw him steal a quick glance at me from the corner of his eye. I deliberately extended my silence until he said, "Well?"

"What do you want of me?" I asked. "A debate? I'm not a theologian. I am—if you'll forgive the obscenity—a reporter. I'd much prefer to ask *you* some questions."

"Ask away," he said airily.

My real preference would have been to enter into a relaxed conversation over our wine. That being unlikely, I would use the occasion to see what further insights I could gain about this extraordinary man in whose employ I had cast my lot.

I said, "Let me begin, then, by asking, why do you call yourself an evangelist? You're as far removed from most of the evangelists I've heard as the Bible is from *Hustler* magazine."

"I call myself an evangelist," Gladden said, "because the word means a bearer of the evangel, the good news about God, and that's what I am. Why should I surrender the word to that ragtag bunch of Bible-thumpers?" He turned to me. "Do you know anything about evangelists?"

"Not much," I said. "Mostly what I've seen on television or dug out in my research."

"And what's your opinion of them?"

"I'd be more interested in yours," I said.

"Then I'll tell you who they are," he said, and paused to form his thoughts. "They are the lineal descendants of those itinerant hucksters who used to hawk miraculous nostrums in the town square. They are quacks practicing spiritual medicine without a licence. They are fools, most of them, but shrewd enough to have made of the Bible a paper pope, knowing that, with an infallible book, they can forgo the discipline of thought and offer 'God's Word' as the answer to every problem in life. They are exploiters of the gullible."

He glared at me as though expecting a rebuttal. "No skin off my nose," I said with a shrug. "But isn't what you do very much like what they do?"

His eyes narrowed. He was turning his wineglass, the stem between his fingers and thumb. "I'll overlook the insult," he said slowly, "and put it down to your admitted ignorance." He drained his glass, plunked it down on the table and shifted in his chair to look at me. "Now, let me ask you a question," he said. "How do *you* think of God?"

I blinked at the sudden change of direction. "As I said a minute ago, I'm no theologian."

"I didn't ask for your theological views. I asked you how you think of God? You must have given the question thought. Everyone does."

Of course I had thought about the question. I had wrestled with it many times: in my youth, as does nearly everyone, but especially during my college years. And later during those black periods when life pushes you to the wall and you find yourself asking the question that comes inevitably to everyone's lips— "What's it all about, Alfie?" But I hadn't pondered it for years, and it was with some hesitancy that I began my response.

"In a word," I said, "I don't know."

He gave a snort of impatience.

"Now, hold on a minute," I said quickly. "It's not simply that I *don't* know — I don't believe I *can* know. That's what I mean when I describe myself as an agnostic. I'm not an atheist. I don't say there is no God. That would be as presumptuous as saying flatly that there *is* a God. How the hell do I know? How the hell can *anybody* be certain, living in a universe that is so . . . so enigmatic, so impenetrably mysterious."

I had expected to be interrupted but he had turned away, tilted his head back and closed his eyes. When he said nothing, I ventured further.

"It seems to me that one ought to keep one's mind in a kind of stasis. Taking care not to have an empty mind, you ought to keep an open mind. There's no requirement to come down flatly on one side or the other. And—to respond to what you were saying a minute ago—I think it's a cop-out to say you believe or don't believe just because some preacher or some atheist is pressing you to make up your mind. The man I can most identify with in the New Testament is the guy who said: 'Lord, I believe. Help thou my unbelief.' "

Gladden remained with his head back, his eyes closed, his lips pursed. "Have you taken the time to listen to me on television?"

"Yes," I said. "Of course."

"And how does it strike you?"

"Much of what you say makes sense. There seem to be echoes of Buddhism, hints of Christianity, a little humanism." I glanced at him. "And a lot of Oscar Gladden."

"But you don't buy it?"

"As I said: some of it makes a lot of sense."

"But you're not convinced."

"I'm not convinced or unconvinced. I'm not looking for final answers. I don't trust final answers. Anybody's. After all, what do we know about ourselves or our universe? Nothing compared to what we *don't* know. I think we should live by what we *do* know. People like things all neatly packaged; I guess I have an untidy mind."

Gladden's face had turned a dark red. His brows had drawn down and his lips were compressed. "The journalist as oracle," he snarled. He was about to go on when the telephone jangled. He jammed the receiver to an ear and barked, "Yes." After a moment, without so much as a glance, he gave a peremptory wave of his hand, dismissing me.

As I put down my glass and rose, he cupped a hand over the mouthpiece and said, "I'm beginning to believe I made a mistake in hiring you."

I shrugged. "Sorry about that."

"You may well be," he said darkly.

# SIXTEEN

The press conference was held at the Dented Fender, a graveyard for junked cars on Bruckner Boulevard in the Hunt's Point
section of Brooklyn. It was owned by Billy Nighthawk, a former
ironworker who had gone over the side from the fifteenth floor
of an office building in Jersey City. On the way down, hollering
"Sonofabitch" at full voice, he hit a load of planks in process
of being raised. The impact slowed his fall and diverted him
onto a slag-heap wet with rain, tumbling him like a boneless
doll into a pool of rainwater at the bottom of the hole. The load
began to see-saw, spilling planks and hurling them after Billy
like huge blunt spears. Two impaled themselves on either side
of him in the form of a rough triangle and were referred to in
the retelling of the story as "Billy's teepee." He broke an assortment of bones, including his pelvis, and thenceforth walked
with a rocking gait that was pure syncopation. The accident
finished him as an ironworker, but, addicted to rusting steel,
he went into the used-car business and from that into the own-
ership of the automobile junkyard. "I'm handlin' better cars
now than when I was in the used-car business," he liked to say.
The Dented Fender was busy—as are most graveyards—and, as
most graveyards are, was busiest in bad weather. The lot contained a more or less ordered chaos of heaped-up automobile
carcasses, jagged mountains of mangled metal separated by
narrow canyons in which a traveling crane operated. Along one
side there were raised wooden racks on which fenders, hoods,
side panels, doors and other relatively pristine segments were
displayed, like a presentation of chicken parts at a butcher's.

The Tad Butler people, needing to demonstrate their expertise, had at first rejected my suggestion that the press conference be held at the Dented Fender, decrying it as "too hokey" but mostly unhappy because one of their people hadn't come up with the idea. After some token grumbling they agreed, and thereupon hoked it up. They created a "desk" for Joshua fashioned from an unhinged car door placed on two beat-up fenders. Over his head a crane suspended the rusted remains of the "killer car." I took Joshua for a tour in advance of the press conference, and he said, "Jeezus! Who got the hot dog concession?"

He was surprisingly in possession of himself. I'd expected him to be as apprehensive as a dental patient and had had one of the flacks from Tad Butler pick him up at the Y in order to preclude any stop-off at a bar. I'd taken pains to write an opening statement for him, providing a number of optional comments and asides. When we did the rehearsal, I was elated to find that he was a quick-study and had the routine down cold.

I was a touch worried that we might have delayed too long after breaking the story but needn't have been. News was scarce, and although the news media thought they scented some kind of promotion, the story was sufficiently off-beat to require that it be covered. The television cameramen came early to scout the setting and to shoot establishing-shots, clambering onto the heaps of mutilated auto bodies, vying for vantage points. By ten, everything was in readiness and Monte Hammel of Tad Butler—subbing for Obie Berenson who had tripped over a detached bumper from a 1979 Dodge Omni and gashed his leg — knocked on the door of Billy Nighthawk's shack where Joshua had been waiting. It had been decided over my objections that Joshua should wear jeans and a red tartan shirt open at the neck to reveal a knotted kerchief. Joshua decided himself to wear a blue T-shirt and a pair of faded denim trousers. When Monte put a monogrammed hard hat on him, he punted it over Billy's shack.

Later I recounted to Jo what had happened at the press conference as we sat on a bench behind the gallery where she was preparing her show. She was in a paint-smeared smock, looking slightly disheveled and the more beautiful for it. I had come bearing sandwiches, dills and coffee from a nearby deli.

"Things went wrong from the start," I told her. "Monte Hammel—you haven't met him; he was subbing for Obie—looked like a pigeon at a cockfight: fluttering around, chest puffed, doing his best to look in charge. He tried to make an opening statement but the reporters rolled right over him.

"Hymie Morris of the *Daily News* said, 'Mr. Crown, this whole deal smells like some kind of promotion. Like, for the Ironworkers, maybe? Or somebody's making a movie about high-steelers and you're in it. Right?'

"Hammel looked like a doctor just told him he had herpes. I was standing at the back holding my breath. There was what gets called a pregnant pause. Joshua wasn't fazed a bit. He just grinned that easy grin of his and, cool as an ice bucket, said, 'You guys are always exploiting people; I'm trying to exploit you.'"

"Oh my!" Jo said.

"Oh my, indeed. Hymie—even *he* was a bit off balance—said, 'Then this *is* a promotion. And that business on top of the Republic Motors Building was some kind of PR?'

"I was sweating gumdrops. I could see our whole plan going down the tube. I was wondering what the hell Joshua was up to and whether he'd smuggled a bottle into Billy Nighthawk's shack. He was just sitting there behind that goddamn door they rigged up, smiling like a guy who just heard his mother-in-law had to postpone her visit. Then, sounding not the slightest bit preachy or wounded-seal, he ran through what happened to his friend when he was killed in that accident. Sincere! The guy should be a funeral director. But contained—not smarmy. He used some of the stuff I wrote for him, but believe me, he'd made it his own.

"'If, because of my carelessness,' he said, 'somebody got killed, I'd get charged. Right? And, unless I was some kind of creep, I'd admit my responsibility. But that's not the way it is when a big corporation is careless. Trying to get them to admit they're responsible is like trying to nail jelly to a wall. So, you take them to court. They hire the best lawyers: guys who know every loophole in the law and every delaying tactic in the book. You hire your own lawyer. Fine. But lawyers cost money, which you don't have much of and which the big corporations have in bushel baskets. Then, if and when you finally get them into court, what happens? Your lawyer is out of his depth: he's a mumbler and a note-reader and has dandruff. Their lawyer is a look-alike for Walter Cronkite and plays golf with the judge. Whether you win or lose doesn't matter. If you win, they appeal. If they win, you either quit or you appeal. And if you appeal there are delays and bills every thirty days from your lawyer and transcripts to be paid for and time taken from work and a million other things. And finally you say to hell with it!' ''

"Joshua said all that?"

"Well, I've juiced it a bit, but, yes, all of that. Anyway, he wound up by saying—looking right into the camera as though he were an old pro—'The Constitution talks about liberty and justice for all. Well, it's a lie. Justice isn't for all; it's for the rich and the privileged. Justice stands there with that bandage over her eyes looking like a saint, but she's a whore. She'll go to bed with the guy with the biggest bankroll. She likes guys in pin-stripe suits who drive expensive cars and fly in private jets and sit on each other's boards of directors and know the Riviera better than they know Brooklyn; guys who support the Met but not the Mets and have mayors and senators and congressmen ass-kissing them. Justice is a whore.' ''

"Wow! You've made him sound like a radical."

"Most of that last was his own. But he's no radical; he's just pissed-off over the dead-ends he's run into since he first tried to get a settlement for his friend's widow. He's been brooding about it a long time."

"So what happened?"

"What was strange — and remember, we're talking here about a pretty cynical bunch—was they let him go on. There were a couple of carpers but they shut up after a while. Most of the questions were friendly, and he fielded them without too much trouble. At the end he said, 'Look, can I go off the record for a minute?' You'd have thought he'd been doing this all his life! He said, 'I told you I wanted to exploit you. Well, I do. I want to light a fire under Republic Motors, and you guys have a monopoly on the kindling.' ''

"He said exactly that?"

"I know what you mean. I couldn't believe it either."

"But did he get away with it?"

"We'll know when we see the papers. My guess is, yes. Our Mr. Nobody is nobody's fool. Somebody—a radio guy I didn't recognize—asked him if he was a Communist. Joshua said, 'Not now. Not yesterday. Not tomorrow. Any more dumb questions?' "

Jo put the plastic cups, the paper napkins and the leavings in the paper sack and dropped them in a waste basket. I noticed that her hand was trembling.

"How close are you to ready?" I asked.

"All ready," she said, a little tightly I thought. "How do we look?"

I took a walk about and was impressed.

"Look familiar?" she asked, pointing at a large canvas dominant on a wall. Though the treatment was radical, the subject was obviously Joshua. There was an impression of an explosion moving out from his belly. He was naked to the waist and the bulge of his genitals was evident in his jeans. I felt my own tighten.

"What's it called?"

She smiled. *"Number Twenty-four."*

"I'm glad it's not *Number One.*"

She turned, put an arm around my neck, pulled me down and kissed me. "You are such a silly goose," she said. Her mood suddenly changed and there was a flash of panic in her eyes. "You'll be here tonight?"

"Right after the news."


We wouldn't know how the newspapers had treated the press conference until early morning but it became clear on the evening news that the television people had decided to let him exploit them. It was one hand washing the other: television needs pictures, and the setting at the Dented Fender had proved to be irresistible. The one smart thing Monte Hammel had done during the press conference was to get the crane operator to nudge the boom slightly. It set the suspended wreck to swinging over Joshua's head like a surreal pendulum, and against the background of distorted metal it made for a hell of a shot. Joshua had posed afterward astride a mound of car bodies and had even taken a turn at the controls of the crane. The pictures were simply too good to be rejected. But, more importantly, the coverage treated him seriously. Only WPIX was tongue-in-cheek, and even there Joshua's presence came through the tube. The fact was, as is often the case, he was more impressive on television than in person.

I looked in on Oscar Gladden. He was at his desk.

"Did you catch the coverage of the press conference?"

He nodded, showing neither satisfaction nor interest. A small flame of resentment smoldered. I wasn't looking for praise, but his indifference irritated me.

"Well?" I said.

He looked up. "Well what?"

"Mr. Gladden," I said, "I've been working for weeks to get this crazy Mr. Nobody thing on the rails. Today was crucial."

"Is there something wrong?"

"I'd like some signals, that's all. Are things going the way you want? I'm not sure any longer what our objective is."

It seemed to me that in junking my original proposal and settling on Joshua Crown we had lost sight of what I had understood to be the goal: to make fools of the news media, to demonstrate their irresponsibility, to get them out on a limb and then saw it off. The Joshua Crown story was becoming legitimate, and I couldn't see at the moment how it could be turned around. Joshua had blown the scenario with his candor and his integrity. He'd said right out: you exploit others, I want to exploit you—and they had bought it. Fine, but where did we go from here?

Gladden turned in his chair. "If things weren't satisfactory you'd have heard from me."

I was growing stubborn. "The Mary Jane Smith scam would have left them with egg on their face. I can't help wonder if you and I are not on different wavelengths."

His face was like granite. "We may very well be. In the meantime, I believe you're supposed to be at Josephine's opening."

As I closed the door, his voice followed. "I'll be looking for some action out of Washington soon."

Jo, her face flushed, was at the far end of the principal room at the gallery talking animatedly to a guy with a beard large enough to park a Honda in. The place was comfortably full, almost crowded, with nearly everybody standing about sipping wine or talking. I traced the perimeter and saw that more than half the paintings bore a tiny red seal signifying that they had been sold. Jo saw me and shot an almost imperceptible wink past the beard. A shiver of exultation ran through me and I realized that I'd been more worried about the show than I'd let myself know. I headed for the tiny stand-up bar and got a glass of wine. My god! — Puligny-Montrachet. That'd eat into the profits.

I spotted Gus Longo, Rocco Lombardi and one of the guards whose name I hadn't yet learned. At a gallery opening? But, of course, Gladden would want to ensure that there was a crowd. I looked about, half expecting to see Knee-Hi, and became aware of something odd about the gathering. Only a dozen or so people were looking at the paintings and there wasn't that slightly manic conversation and high-decibel laughter common to such occasions. Many of the men seemed ill at ease and glum of countenance, shifting their weight frequently and quite clearly putting in time. Many were with women to whom they didn't trouble to speak; the women were gussied-up with moussed coiffures, furbelowed dresses and layers of costume jewelry. I recognized only one reporter: a man from the *Times'* culture beat. And, off to one side, Dunc Robertson.

"What the hell are you doing here?" I asked.

"Art has become a commodity," he said airily. "Not quite like sow bellies or rapeseed, but—"

"You speculate in art?" Too late I saw that he was putting me on.

"Puligny Montrachet '83," he said, raising his glass. "Courtesy of Oscar Gladden, I presume. Like the guests," he added.

"Eli Broder's here." (He was the *Times* man.)

"As are assorted nonentities and even some members of the Bonanno family. Art lovers all."

"C'mon, Dunc!"

"Okay, I'm overstating it. But look over there—there in the corner — that lizard-eyed guy with the lacquered hair pasted

164

over his bald spot. None other than the FBI's man of the year, Dino Pasquale. C'mon yourself, does this look to you like the usual gallery crowd?''

"This is a gallery, they're a crowd. What else matters?'' I said defensively.

"I had a few words with Bernie. He's out of his skull. Sold fifteen paintings in the first half hour. They were lining up to give him money. The most expensive stuff, too.''

"She's going to be an important painter.''

"She's going to be rich,'' he said. "But then she is already.'' He turned away. "Come out in the garden for a minute.''

We went by way of the bar, had our glasses filled and carried them to the tiny garden where Jo and I had had lunch earlier.

Dunc took a swallow of his wine, savoring it. "Ambrosia,'' he said, holding his glass up to the light. "At a gallery opening! Tony, this stuff retails at thirty dollars a bottle.'' He took his time with another sip of the wine, swishing it about as though it were a mouthwash, swallowing it lovingly and then inhaling deeply through his mouth.

"You should drink nothing but good wine,'' I said. "You're the only guy I know who gets more than his money's worth.''

"I've been asking around about your Mr. Gladden, as you asked me to do, and—''

"I know—he's in bed with Dino Pasquale.''

"I'm not saying that. By no means am I saying that. But the guy's a paradox. He's a preacher, but loaded. And I mean, loaded.''

"Hardly unique these days,'' I said.

"True, but I've been trying to find out if he gets his loot legitimately.'' He crossed his arms on his chest and raised his eyes to heaven. "Lay not up for yourself treasures on earth.''

"He was a millionaire before he went into the ministry. And his books sell in the millions.''

"Right, but he makes a big thing of the fact that he doesn't take a dime from them.'' He glanced about. "Incidentally, where is he? I was hoping to meet him.''

"He doesn't go about in public.''

"This I know, but *tonight*—his only daughter's opening?'' He sipped his wine. "Which is the case I'm trying to make.

165

Oscar Gladden's daughter has a one-man show. I'm not competent to judge how good she is, but that's not the point. She sells twenty-one paintings in the first hour. It doesn't happen that way, not to an unknown. Not in this town. Bernie let me have a look at the list of big purchasers. There's Ron Benison, the adonis who hosts the body-beautiful segments in Gladden's television shows. There's Lonnie Michaels, the president of CableNet Inc—a front man, as is well known. There's Austin Peale of Peale and Bjornstadt, Gladden's auditors, and Dino Pasquale, a Bonanno family member. And Joey Podertz. Who is Joey Podertz? You should know, Tony—he's one of the guards at Gladden's Fortress Jehovah, or whatever it's called. And Joey buys what? The most expensive painting in the show." He raised his glass. "Not to forget the wine."

"Oh, come off it, Dunc. So Gladden buys a couple of cases of expensive wine for his daughter's show."

"It isn't a matter of a few cases of wine. I've been talking to Roger Zachs. The guy owns three houses — forget houses, estates. Plus an eighteenth-century castle up the Hudson sitting on a fat two hundred acres. There's a beach-front hovel at Malibu — sale price eight million — a penthouse condominium in Trump Tower and that rundown shack where you work. But none of the titles are in his name. They're owned by OneWorld or Gladden Your Day, Inc. or the aforementioned CableNet Inc. The IRS wants to know how come. The FBI wants to know how come."

"Dunc," I said, "I'm no apologist for Oscar Gladden, but what you haven't bothered to mention in your indictment is that Roger Zachs and his cohorts in Justice have bust their collective ass and haven't been able to come up with one piece of substantial evidence. And in the meantime—damn it!—you're spoiling Jo's night."

"So the aphorism about smoke and fire is outdated?" Dunc persisted.

I flared. "A father invites some of his business acquaintances to the most important day of his daughter's life and all you can do is carp."

"Down boy," Dunc said, putting a hand on my shoulder. "Sorry. I had no idea."

"You had no idea about what?" I growled, shaking off his hand.

He made an apologetic shrug. "Sorry. She *is* a lovely lady." He raised his empty glass. "Happy days!"


Afterward, Jo said she was ravenous. "Lunch today was the first thing I've had to eat for two days." We went to Les Deux Homard where she took them literally and ordered—so help me!—two large steamed lobsters. That done, she left the table to call her father. Her straight-up double martini was warmish when she returned. She drank it in a few gulps but hardly ate; she was on such a high that she seemed almost to be levitating in her chair.

"Did you see the man I was talking to when you came in?"

"The guy who looked like an uncovered hassock?"

"He's from a gallery in Paris. *Paris!* Loved my work. Wanted to know did I have an agent. I told him Bernie. Could we have lunch tomorrow? And how long would it take me to put together another show? So pleased that I spoke French; and there I was worrying that it was getting rusty. And, Tony — twenty-one paintings! Bernie had told me not to worry if we sold only three or four, but *twenty-one!*"

You've read the phrase, "eyes dancing with excitement"— hers *were*. I watched her, enchanted by her breathless excitement, her untrammeled, childish delight.

We took a taxi to my apartment. She sat with her head against my shoulder, hugging my arm, wound down now but glowing with a quiet exultancy. She hadn't touched the lobsters (we'd taken them with us in a doggy bag and she'd given them to a two-hundred-pound bag-lady who looked as if she was wearing her husband's long underwear) so I poached two eggs and slid them on toasted English muffin halves. She made even that difficult by kissing the back of my neck and letting her hands quest until I was twisting and evading.

That night I completely lost myself in our loving. It was the first time that had ever happened to me—no thought of what we were doing, no conscious giving or receiving or sharing,

only a sustained glow of total sensation from which I emerged
—I have no idea how much later—to find her asleep.

There was no sleep for me. I reran the gallery with its misfit
crowd, saw again the sallow, acned face of Dino Pasquale with
its dead eyes and lipless, downturned mouth. I reviewed the
conversation with Dunc Robertson. Then I changed reels and
relived Joshua's press conference and the aftermath in Oscar
Gladden's study. I found myself wet with perspiration.

Carefully, I eased away from Jo, who never stirred, and in
the darkness fumbled into my clothes. I took a cab all the way
to Seventh Avenue before I found a hole-in-the-wall that sold
newspapers. Joshua dominated the section page of the *Times*
with pictures and a feature story. The *Daily News* ran a front
page picture under the headline, JOSHUA FIT THE BATTLE! The photographer had taken a low-angle shot of Joshua with his hands
upraised. It looked as if Joshua had lifted the car above his head
and was about to cast it down.

There was a single paragraph on Jo's opening, buried deep
inside the *Times*.

Gallery opening:
STYLE LACKS SUBSTANCE
Josephine Gladden, a native New Yorker who has studied
abroad in France and Italy and is the daughter of televan-
gelist Oscar Gladden, made her debut last night in a one-
man show at the Oneida Gallery on East 57th Street. The
work demonstrates originality and a venturesome courage
and is ambitious in scope. Regrettably, while the concept
of adapting the French *cloisonné* technique to paintings
strongly influenced by American Indian primitivism is com-
mendable—there are interesting similarities—the end result
of Ms. Gladden's labors lies closer to commercial art than
to serious painting.

A large crowd was on hand for the opening and the
wine served was extraordinary. Unfortunately, the lady's
not for praising.

# SEVENTEEN

The television news industry is essentially a business. Its function is not merely to inform the public about events around the world but also to produce revenue. This it accomplishes by gathering an audience so that others may sell various goods and services to it. And television has become big business. CBS television news, as an example, represents the single largest source of revenue the network has: larger than its most popular entertainment programs.

It has not always been so. As recently as the 1950s, people got their news from newspapers and radio. Television news was watched by relatively few and was regarded by the owners of individual stations and by the networks as an obligation that, while it lent prestige, showed as a debit on the budget.

In the beginning, television news was presented in a staid and straightforward manner. The men who presented the news were staff announcers or former radio newsmen and they did little more than read to the camera. The preparation of film excerpts was a slow, laborious process (as a reportorial tool, television has been aptly described as "a one-ton pencil"). Each step in the preparation—shooting, processing and editing—was time-consuming, and the film portions of the "telecasts," as they were then called, were usually a day or more behind the events they depicted.

But as techniques improved, as film-processing speeded up, and as portable videotape cameras appeared and satellites began to transmit pictures worldwide, the popularity of television newscasts increased. Viewers discovered that the television news was an undemanding and entertaining way to keep abreast of what was happening around the world, a world that had become a neighborhood—in Marshall McLuhan's phrase, "a global village." There was an immediacy, an apparent authenticity to television reporting. You could see the event unfold. There was no one between you and the actuality interposing himself and his biases (or so it appeared). You could sit in your living room and be an eyewitness as presidents were inaugurated or politicians made pronouncements or bombs shattered villages or billy-clubs crunched skulls or firefighters poured their torrents into infernos. And your name became legion.

As the number of viewers grew, the charge for addressing them increased. The income from commercials skyrocketed. "The news" no longer showed as a debit on the balance sheet; it became the source of larger and larger revenues.

Inevitably, the quest for the advertisers' dollar led to competition. Each purveyor of the news sought to provide more news, more immediate news, more visually interesting news. The newsreader gave way to the anchorman with his coterie of "correspondents," and the anchorman became as much a media star as the singers and dancers and comedians on the entertainment side of the industry. Indeed, Walter Cronkite, an anchorman, was selected in a national poll as "the most trusted man in America."

The time allocated to news programs increased. The nightly news was expanded to include the-story-behind-the-news. Commentaries, features and "backgrounders" proliferated. Prime-time spinoff programs were created, featuring investigative reporting or in-depth analyses. The three major networks each devoted two hours weekday mornings to (more or less) news shows. CNN, a cable network, offered nothing but the news. Live coverage of momentous events preempted regular programs and drew audiences in the tens of millions. "60 Minutes," a news program, headed the ratings. The news had become the greatest show on earth.

That very bigness produced problems. The "news-slot" is a voracious dragon and must be fed every day. If there isn't enough news to supply the demand it must be manufactured. There is no option; the allocated time must be filled. If there is a shortage of hard news, gussy-up an inconsequential story to increase its interest. Search out the human-interest aspect of a story. Create a "media event"—thus transforming a nonstory into an apparently significant happening. Develop in-depth stories about "problems" in the society. And, primarily, seek news that yields interesting pictures — "talking heads" make for tedium. A line-up editor is likely to allocate more time to a riot than to a Nobel Prize presentation. A protest provides more lively footage than a press conference. Responsible broadcasters will, of course, strive for a balance between "legitimate news" and the peripheral; others will major in ambulance-chasing, fires and police work.

The problem of feeding the dragon intensifies with summer. Legislative assemblies prorogue or venture little. The "news-makers" do as the masses do and flee to cooler climes. Some-times, especially in some parts of the country, it is simply too hot to make news—except as the heat itself becomes newswor-thy. The pace of life slackens. It is, as it is known in the business, "the summer dog-days," and half the world has "gone fishin'."

These were the circumstances that made it possible to trans-form Joshua Crown from an obscure figure into a national celeb-rity. The time was right: it was summer and news was scarce. The scenario was right: he was the Little Man fighting Big Busi-ness. There was an element of human interest: a loyal friend battling to provide a helping hand to the crippled widow of his best friend. And the protagonist was right. Joshua Crown was an American Indian who didn't look like one and who worked at a daredevil trade. He was a colorful figure: handsome in a rugged fashion, articulate but not glib, and, as the saying has it, "he came through the tube." There was an openness, a candor about him that set him apart from the smiling, oleagi-nous palaverers so common on the screen. His was a fresh face among the caviling politicians, the junketing actors and the endless parade of "experts" on every subject.

They put him on the late-night talk-shows, on the daytime variety shows and on the women's shows, and used him as a celebrity guest on the game-shows. Radio, which had abandoned programming with the advent of television and delivered itself to disc jockeys and phone-in hosts, interviewed him for their news-every-hour-on-the-half-hour shows, eliciting his opinions on issues ranging from acid rain to Central American guerrilla forays. Newspapers, suffering the same summer news drought as television, reported on his background, assigned cameramen to follow him through a typical day, interviewed him on his likes and dislikes, did think-pieces on the American Indian and examined the trade of ironworker. The New York *Times* carried a comparative study of industry-recalls in domestic and imported cars. Joshua Crown became, as one columnist put it, newsmaker of the month.

# EIGHTEEN

I have a question for each of you," said Johnny Gallagher. "Is there anyone here at this great demonstration of concern in the nation's capital who is not troubled by what is happening in America today? We have sown the wind of permissiveness. We are reaping the whirlwind of casual sexuality, teenage pregnancy, venereal disease and AIDS. Stop at any newsstand and run your eyes over the collection of pornography; there is no God but the genitalia, and Hugh Heffner is its prophet. Step into a movie theater and all is lust and violence. Browse in a bookstore and there for any eyes, no matter how youthful, is a glorification of the sordid and the bestial that would make Nero blush. Pick up a newspaper and read the skyrocketing statistics on rape and assault, on murder and mugging. Our homes are no longer secure. Our schools are vandalized. And here, here in the capital city of the most powerful nation in the history of the world, we are not free to walk the streets at night."

The audience of some twenty thousand gazed fixedly at the man on the platform. Against a background depicting an enormous open Bible, his shirt-sleeved figure delineated by a bank of spotlights, veins corded on his neck, spittle spraying on his plosives, Johnny Gallagher reiterated the themes that had been sounded and re-sounded by other speakers through the evening. Now he grasped the climax.

"And where can we lay the blame? On the home? Yes. On parents who, asked by their children for the bread of life, have only a stone to give. On our schools? Yes. This nation under

God has banned the name of God and the Word of God and the creative act of God from the classroom. On our churches? Yes. Too many pulpits have substituted for the thunder of the gospel, the tinkling cymbal of humanist rationalism. Yes, the blame rests with our homes and our schools and our churches.

"But it lies elsewhere, too. With the communications media. With television stations, granted a licence by the people but using that privilege as an opportunity to send into our living rooms a floodtide of filth and violence. With radio stations, most of them pulsing with that discordant cacophony called rock, with its roots in drugs and its lyrics lewd and lascivious. With the magazine industry, their product awash with trivia and sensuality. Our newspapers are filled with stories and features that besmirch the paper they're printed on. Once the principal source of the information a nation needs, they are now—many of them—carriers of the moral virus that infects our time."

He went on for half an hour and at the end had them on their feet roaring approval and applauding with hands held high. He was a more gifted orator than the preachers who had preceded him, more effective than the other politicians. There was no cadence to his sentences. He didn't read his speech but extemporized from notes, and he didn't try for easy laughs with threadbare devices or rhetorical tricks. Standing just inside the doors at the rear of the auditorium, I recognized all the skills of the demagogue, but in the hands of a man of great warmth and apparent sincerity.

I'd arrived in Washington late that afternoon, having gone there not only to hear Gallagher but also to get away from New York City. The previous three days had been nightmarish. The reviews had made Jo physically ill. The morning after the show, she had willed herself well enough to go to lunch with the beard from Paris only to find that he was a lecher who made out with women painters through informed talk about art and the Paris salons, name-dropping famous dealers and wealthy clients. She had fled the restaurant and locked herself in her room. I went to her door from time to time, knocking on it to whisper about such things as the Fauves—Matisse, Braque, Rouault and Dufy —the so-called "wild beasts" who had been derided by the critics but who had laid the foundation for much twentieth-century painting.

She emerged the following morning, looking drawn and pale. She was tense when I held her and preoccupied when we talked. She was going to Toronto, she said, to see her aunt Marguerite and would be back the first of the week. There was nothing to do finally but take her to the airport and in a dispiriting moment, to say farewell.

When I hadn't been occupied with Jo, I'd been on the telephone with the Tad Butler people, stage-managing Joshua. Actually, there was little for them to do; all that was needed was to channel the floodtide. Joshua was in the process of being anointed an American media celebrity. He spent most of his days in radio and television studios. I managed to catch him on the fly by telephone, and we arranged to get together on my return. In the meantime, badgered by Oscar Gladden, who was impatient for action, I had gone to Washington to see if I could stir the pot there.

The Morality in the Media rally was to be followed by a press conference. It seemed the better part of wisdom not to be too visible there, so I hailed a taxi and returned to my hotel to watch it on local cable. As I switched on the set, Johnny Gallagher, his tie loosened and his jacket draped over a shoulder, was keeping a group of skeptical reporters at bay.

"Now just hold on a minute," he was saying, smiling but firm. "As usual, you people are totally misreading what's happening here. Morality in the Media isn't a repressive movement. We're not censors. We're not book-burners. We don't want to padlock the theaters and the bars or to dictate what people may or may not do. All we're trying to do is to demonstrate that millions of Americans are opposed to the daily diet of sex, crime and violence fed to our young people by the media. We think that when they—the people who control the media—begin to realize that the majority of Americans don't want what they're purveying, they'll change. We're not vigilantes. We're not cross-burners. We're not going to storm the saloons, hatchets in hand."

Jim Ingraham had a hand raised.

Gallagher smiled at him. "If you'll wait just one minute,"

he said affably, "I'll be right with you. As I was saying, I have no authority to speak for others, but let me make my position crystal clear: the one thing that will turn this great nation around and put America back on the road to greatness is a return to personal and public morality. And we can do it, you and I. One raindrop is nothing, but a monsoon can flood a nation. One snowflake is nothing, but an avalanche can cover a city. None of us can do much alone, but together we can turn our world right side up."

There were ragged cheers from the people standing around the perimeter. Gallagher beamed at Jim Ingraham. "Now, friend, you had a question."

It was evident that Jim was ill at ease. He was a gangling, awkward man with an uncombable thicket of coarse red hair, and he had a tendency to swallow the ends of his sentences, but he's an old pro and I've seen him put questions to men and women from the president down without turning a hair. But now his sentences were punctuated with "uhs" and "ums," and he was reading from a notebook.

"Mr. Gallagher, I wonder if you would be kind enough to test your memory. I want to ask you about a couple of dates—"

"The signing of the Magna Charta, June 15, 1215," Gallagher interjected. "My wife's birthday, May the twenty-first — I wouldn't *dare* tell you the year." There was laughter and applause.

"More modern history than that," Jim said. On the close-up I could see that he was sweating. "Last year, as a matter of fact. Can you recall if you were here in Washington on any of these dates: January 22, March 3, March 31, May 29? And, on those dates, did you stay at the Mayflower Hotel?"

There was a low murmur from the crowd. Gallagher's brows were lowered. "I'm afraid I don't follow—"

Jim continued doggedly. "I know you can't be expected to remember all those dates, but—"

"This sounds to me very much like a do-you-still-beat-your-wife type of question," Gallagher said, smiling, but with an edge to his voice.

But now that Jim had jumped off the pier he wasn't going

to go down without beating the water. "Take May twenty-ninth. Surely you can remember where you were last Memorial Day."

"Of course," Gallagher said. "I was here in Washington to address the American Legion. And now," he added, "may I ask you what that has to do with the price of tea in China?"

The murmuring of the crowd was louder. Another reporter raised a hand to get Gallagher's attention. Jim pressed on. "Excuse me," he said, "I'll just be one more minute. I think if you check, sir, you'll find that you were in the city on all the dates I've mentioned, and that on each occasion you stayed at the Mayflower Hotel."

"Doesn't everybody?" Gallagher quipped.

"And that on each of those occasions you had as a guest in your suite a certain Miss Jerri West."

An immediate uproar. Shouting. Boos and cries of "Shut up!" and "Sit down!" Somebody, presumably the chairman, had his hands upraised and was shouting, "Order, please! Order!" Gallagher was smiling an easy smile. He had his head to one side and appeared unruffled.

"That's all right," he said. "Let the man speak."

The sound fell away to silence. Jim, who clearly had no stomach for the task, said, "You haven't answered my question, Mr. Gallagher."

Gallagher pounced. "Answer my question, the man says. He means, questions. Not one question but three." His left hand was raised, with three fingers lifted, the forefinger of his right hand ticking them off. "Question one: Was I in Washington on certain specified dates? Answer: With the exception of May twenty-ninth, I don't know. No problem. I'll check. Question two: Did I on those dates stay at the Mayflower? Answer: Yes. In Washington, I always stay at the Mayflower. I wasn't aware that that was a reprehensible action. And now, friends, we come to what I presume is supposed to be the blockbuster—question three. Did I, on my visits to Washington, have as a guest in my room a woman by the name of Jerri West?" He paused, and a silence quickly settled. "The answer is simple and unequivocal. Not only was the lady never in my room, but I don't know any such lady, and until this minute have never so much as heard her name!"

177

Cheers. Whistling. Applause. "Nor do I know *your* name, Mr. Reporter, or who you work for. Could it be the *National Enquirer?* But I do know one thing: I know where you got those dates and how you knew I stayed at the Mayflower." He turned to the onlookers. "Some months ago, ladies and gentlemen, there was a break-in at my campaign headquarters in New York City. What was stolen? Nothing of monetary value. Not the television set, not the radio, not even the petty cash. No, just my personal records. Including," he said, his voice rising, "my desk calendar. And now we know *why!* My opponents, who aren't ready to fight me on the issues, want to get down in the gutter. Well, I'm serving notice on them right now: it won't work! No, sir, it won't work!"

Jim tried to speak but was shouted down. I turned off the set, waited an hour and called him at the paper. I expected him to upbraid me but he was in a rage against Gallagher.

"The lying son of a bitch! I checked the Mayflower and I tracked down Jerri West."

"You did?" I swallowed my surprise.

"They know her at the hotel. She's a thousand-a-night call-girl. I figure the routine is this: Gallagher comes into town, he gets in touch with West—either here or in New York; she works both cities—and she goes to his suite at the end of his day. All that moralistic crap! The guy's lying through his teeth."

"But can you prove it? It's her word against his."

"I goddamn well *will* prove it. He's making another speech tomorrow. I'll have Jerri West there."


In New York City there was a note under my apartment door. It was from Victor Gladden, with a telephone number. I dialed the number and he answered right away. His voice was low, guarded.

"You left your telephone number," he said after I identified myself.

"You left yours," I countered.

"What did you want?"

"That was weeks ago."

"Okay. So what did you want then?"

178

I decided to play hard to get. I hadn't made any effort to reach him since that day at the police station. But I did want to talk to him. There was a disturbing mystery to Oscar Gladden, and perhaps knowing something of the rift between him and his son would help me to penetrate it. It was none of my business; I knew that.

"It was nothing special," I said. "Somebody at the paper told me the police were holding you and I thought I'd see if I could help. I work for your father."

There was silence on the line.

"Hello. Are you still there?"

"I'm still here."

I left the silence with him now.

After a moment, he said, "Okay. Here's what you do. Take a cab. Come along 42nd Street to Ninth Avenue. Take a right and circle the block. That way I'll know if you're being followed."

"Why would I be followed?"

"Look, it was you wanted to talk to me. Right?"

"Well, yes."

"Then we do it my way. After you circle the block I'll be standing on the corner. In front of the bank."

En route I began to doubt the wisdom of what I was doing. I was mucking about in family affairs that were none of my business. Since the night Jo had gone off to pay Victor's bail she had volunteered nothing. She would have her reasons, and I wasn't about to ask what they were. I certainly wasn't going to raise the matter with Oscar Gladden.

As Victor got into the taxi I recognized him as the man who had broken into my apartment. Remembering how easily he had handled me, I felt a moment of chagrin; he was smaller than I and slighter of build. He was wearing a coarsely knit crewneck sweater over a faded tartan shirt, with the inevitable jeans. I studied him as he gave directions to the driver. His skin was fair and pale. He had lank black hair, not after the fashion but through neglect. There was a growth of wispy, untrimmed beard on his jaw. The color of his eyes couldn't be seen in the poor light, but they were too tired and too darkly encircled for a boy of twenty. There was something of Jo about him, but nothing that I could discern of his father.

The cab headed south on 12th Avenue, alongside the Henry Hudson Parkway, passing a line of cargo warehouses and berthed ships. The area was ill-lit and forbidding. We stopped by the shadowy bulk of a ship. Victor got out, leaving me to pay the fare, and went toward a gangplank where a man with a black beard and wearing a pea jacket was lounging. I got out of the cab and took my time, looking around. The ship was an old one, as attested to by its lines and its rusting plates. I don't quite know what a tramp-steamer is but this one fit my conception. There were no lights showing aboard except for those mandatory while riding at anchor, plus a string of gerry-rigged bulbs on the deck and over the gangplank. The sailor at the foot of the gangplank didn't so much as glance at me as I went aboard.

The forward cabin was pleasant enough: oxblood leather chairs, dark wood paneling, mirrors and, at the center, a large box of a table for reading charts. The impression was of art deco and the twenties. On a couch along one side there was a bedroll and, on a small table, a milk carton, a couple of McDonald's hamburger containers and a remnant of what looked like an eggroll but was apple pie.

Victor had seated himself and was waiting for me to take the initiative.

"Do you live here?" I asked.

"No."

Looking for information, I crossed the cabin to a chart mounted on a wall. It mapped the waters around the bay of Sardinia. On a corner there was the impress of a stamp: Aegean Shipping.

"Why did you try to see me at the jail?" Victor asked.

"Don't read anything important into it. It was mostly curiosity. Same reason I'm here."

"Who told you I was there?"

"A reporter on the paper. I told you that on the phone."

"How did he know?"

"It's his beat, for god's sake! Look, as I'm sure you know, I work for your father. I get a call that there's a Victor Gladden in the cage denying that he's related to Oscar Gladden but carrying identification that says he is. Add to that the fact that Oscar Gladden says he doesn't have a son and that your sister has never mentioned having a brother, and I'm curious. Simple as that."

He didn't respond, so I let it lie there. I looked about, apparently idly, but seeking something that would cast further light on why Oscar Gladden's son would be sleeping in a bedroll and eating take-out food aboard an old crock of a cargo ship. I was aware he was watching me.

"I can't figure out why a guy like you would work for my father."

"Why not? What kind of guys work for your father?"

"Creeps. Hoods."

"Was the guy who had my job before me a hood?"

It was a stab in the dark. Gladden had said nothing about my being a replacement, and when I'd alluded to it in passing, he'd shaken his head. Yet it was obvious that my office hadn't been created for me; there were signs of a previous occupant.

"Bill Naylor?" he asked. Good! I had his name.

"Was Bill Naylor a hood?"

"I don't know. I never talked to him."

"What happened to him?"

"I don't know. He quit or was fired. I never talked to him. He wasn't the kind of guy you could trust."

"And here you are talking to me. Does that mean you trust me?"

He made a grimace, suggesting that it wasn't the kind of question he wanted to answer, went to the table, picked up the remnant of the apple whatever-it-was and began to eat it.

I reared back and threw my hard one: "Speaking of trust, would you trust a guy who breaks into your apartment and goes through your things?"

It didn't faze him. "I needed to know about you."

"Why?"

"Because you'd gone to work for my father."

"That's no reason. Lots of people work for your father."

"I needed to know, that's all."

"And you won't tell me why?"

He seemed to consider it, but said, "Maybe later."

I decided to lob one in there to see if I could get him to take a cut at it. "What is it between you and your father?"

No response, nothing but more meditative chewing.

"It's obvious that you hate his guts and, so far as I can see, there's no love lost on his side. He doesn't even list you in his biog in *Who's Who.*"

He turned and spoke with an intensity that startled me. "Is that true? Are you telling me the truth?"

"You didn't know?"

He stared out of the window again, his eyes blinking. Twice he cleared his throat as though to speak, but didn't. After a moment, he walked to the cabin door and opened it. His face was tight and there was a gleaming in his eyes. "I've decided that's all I want to say for now."

It took me twenty minutes to find a cab.


The buzzer on my intercom went four or five times, which meant Oscar Gladden was saying, "Get your ass in here, boy!"

He'd been more or less treating me that way lately. Some mornings he was dark-browed and terse, communicating only when it was unavoidable. Other times he was snarly and abusive. Only occasionally was he relaxed, ready with his seismic laughter. He might come from a session with Doc Kildare to rail against the "sons of bitches" — never specifying who — who were out to get him. When this was his mood, I would let the tirades roll, relieved that I wasn't the target and meditating on Adolf Hitler's rages. It was difficult not to surrender to resentment on the unpleasant days.

When I grumbled to Doc Kildare, he offered justification: Gladden had apparently convinced himself that he had pernicious anemia, that something introduced into the drinking water was destroying the red corpuscles in his blood. He'd ordered an elaborate filtering system installed on the water pipes and had had a new well dug. We lived for ten days with the clanging, brain-reeling din of a driller at work.

I asked Doc why he didn't fake an elaborate examination and

prescribe something. He looked at me with a vinegary expression and said, "I did. I told him to have a new well dug and install a filtering system. Worked like a charm."

"Wouldn't it have been simpler to say, 'There's a new wonder drug, just discovered and incredibly effective'? Then give him an impressive-looking placebo and, presto! In the meantime, we wouldn't be driven out of our skulls."

Doc smiled with the tolerance of a father for a retarded child. "The man reads all the medical journals."

"Then if you can't give *him* something, give *me* something," I said.

Gladden was removing a blood pressure cuff from his arm as I entered his office. "I read a transcript of Gallagher's press conference," he said, rolling down his sleeve and replacing the sphygmomanometer in its case. "He pinned your man's ears back. But there's been nothing in the papers."

"It's not the kind of story that gets play in most newspapers," I said equably. "Especially when the evidence is suspect."

"Don't ask me to believe that. In my case the newspapers were judge and jury, without one scintilla of real evidence."

"So we lose round one. Round two is coming up. Jim is going to confront Gallagher with Jerri West at a meeting today."

I'd expected him to be pleased; he wasn't. He hammered the desk with the flat of a hand. "Absolutely not! Call him and tell him that."

"I can't do that. I fed him the story but it's his baby now. He tracked her down on his own and he's not going to dump her at this point. Certainly not after, as you say, Gallagher cleaned his clock."

On the telephone he said, "Bartholemew, get Jerri West on the line."

He put his doughy hands on the desk before him and set his thumbs to revolving. For a millisecond I was tempted to tell him that I'd met his son—if for no other reason than to discomfit him. That simmering irritability I'd been feeling was coming again to a boil. The moment was right to tell him that I was fed up to the teeth with his arrogance, that I wasn't a lackey to be ordered about, and that if we were going to work together it would have to be on a ground of mutual consideration. I drew breath to speak.

"Carpenter," he said, preempting me, "I'm paying you a lot of money. I'm not at all happy with what I'm getting in return."

"*You're* not happy!"

He didn't hear me. He rose, walked quickly to a window and stood with his back to me. "I put two projects on your plate. Neither has been handled well. I'll get to your Mr. Nobody in a minute, but first Gallagher. You put the matter in the hands of an incompetent in Washington. And what does he do? He makes Gallagher look like an abused innocent. The man's a monumental hypocrite, and Ingraham makes him a beleaguered hero. If that weren't enough, you are about to compound the error by playing into his hands. Do you think for one minute that he can't handle Jerri West in a public confrontation? And have you given a moment's thought to what will happen when that pack of journalistic jackals gets its teeth into her?"

"Mr. Gladden," I said tightly, "may I remind you that it was you who gave me the material. I told you I didn't like it, and that it would be a case of a call-girl's word against the word of a man of considerable—"

His voice rode above mine. He had turned from the window. With the light behind him, his body was in shadow and outlined by a dazzling nimbus. Out of the darkness of his face came the words, "Of course I gave you the material, but I expected some ingenuity. I presumed that, being one with that mangy crowd of journalistic curs, you'd understand them and be a jump ahead of them. And I expected you to pass the story to a man with some imagination. But perhaps that was asking too much —to look for imagination in a reporter."

"Mr. Gladden, I've had about—"

He continued to ride over me. "We'll leave that debacle for the moment and move on to Joshua Crown. How long since you've talked to him?"

He'd caught me off balance; I'd been preparing a defense of Jim Ingraham. "Joshua? I—"

"I thought as much. Mr. Carpenter, do you know the newspaper term, 'a breaking story'?"

"Monday. I talked to him Monday."

He was back in his chair, which protested as he leaned back. He put his hands together, the fingertips touching, tapping in sequence. "When you have a breaking story you stay with it. Around the clock if necessary. You do not lollygag in art galleries or take time-wasting trips to see people off at airports or go on expeditions to the shipping docks."

I felt a rush of blood to my head and neck.

"Nor do you go out of town without covering yourself. Am I right in concluding that, as a consequence, you didn't hear your Joshua Crown—"

"*My* Joshua Crown!"

"—on the television last night?" He reached into a drawer and removed a video cassette and a manila folder. "I took the trouble to do your work for you and recorded the program. Bartholemew had the transcript made. Would it be too much to ask you to put aside your own interests for the next half hour and listen to your protégé?" He passed me the material. "Your Mr. Nobody is outgrowing his britches."

"Mr. Gladden—"

The telephone buzzed. "Yes," he snapped. "Put her on."

He put the receiver to his cheek and looked at me pointedly. "Good morning, Mr. Carpenter."


## TRANSCRIPT: THE DAVE MORTON SHOW

ANNOUNCER: Good evening, ladies and gentlemen. It's that time again! Time for . . . Da-ave Morton! And here, live from Studio A in the heart of Manhattan, is your roving reporter, your window on the world, Da-ave . . . Mor-ton! *(Applause.)*

MORTON: Thank you, thank you. Thank you very much. You're too kind. Thank you. Tonight: two stories for you. The story of a woman, a mother of six, who found her sight after being blind for thirty years; and the thrilling story of a man with nerves of steel and the courage of a lion who has dedicated his life to ensuring that his dead friend will not be forgotten. We'll be back with both stories right after these important messages.

*(Commercials. Applause.)*

MORTON: Thank you, thank you very much. Now for our first story. *(Music in background.)* Next time you're in New York lift up your eyes. *(Film footage of tall buildings and of steelworkers on the job.)* You'll see another world, a world of beauty and danger and courage where intrepid men risk their lives erecting the soaring skyscrapers that make midtown Manhattan one of the wonders of the modern world. *(Film ends.)* One of those men— modern knights who joust with death—is our first guest. Will you welcome please a man who lives life on a permanent high —Joshua Crown! *(Applause.)* Well now, Joshua Crown—listen to *that!* They love you.

CROWN: Thank you.

MORTON: You realize, Joshua . . . May I call you Joshua?

CROWN: Sure. Of course.

MORTON: You realize, Joshua Crown, that almost overnight, America has taken you to its heart. *(Applause.)* Wonderful! Wonderful! But now to your story. You were born on the Caughnawaga Indian Reserve near Montreal, Canada, raised among a noble people, learned your dangerous trade as a boy playing on the steel structure of a bridge spanning the mighty St. Lawrence, struggled as a young man to achieve your part of the American dream, finally making it, literally, to the top in your chosen field. Then, suddenly, tragedy! Your best friend is killed on his honeymoon night. Killed when his car plunges from the highway. And his bride of just a few hours is crippled for life. Now, Joshua, share with us your thoughts when the news came.

CROWN: Well, what happened was I got a call from —

MORTON: And after that first shock had subsided, your heart broken, you did as all of us must do: you went on with your life. Then you learned something. You learned that ten thousand cars just like the one your friend was driving —

CROWN: Twelve thousand, actually.

MORTON: Twelve thousand cars like the one your friend was driving had been recalled and —

CROWN: Can we mention the kind of car?

MORTON: I don't think that will be necessary. The case is before the courts and —

CROWN: Actually, Mr. Morton, it's not.

186

MORTON: Yes. . . . Well, at this point, no good purpose is accomplished by naming the car. So, with your friend's bride crippled for life —

CROWN: It was a Republic Motors Lancer.

MORTON: Uh. . . .

CROWN: Sorry. I just thought the people should know the name of —

MORTON: I think I should make it clear that the Dave Morton Show has no wish to take sides in —

CROWN: You see, the point I'm trying to make is . . . . *(Garbled, both talking at once.)*

MORTON: . . . his views are entirely his own and are not necessarily those of the Dave Morton Show or its sponsors or of this television station.

CROWN: The point I'm trying to make—and I'm sorry if I got out of line—is that the great multinational corporations are controlling our lives and that we have to fight back.

MORTON: Yes. Well now, look, Mr. Crown. Hold on a minute. I respect your right to hold the views you do—that's the American way—but there are two sides to —

CROWN: But that's just it: There aren't two sides when you try to fight against money and power. Republic Motors killed my friend, as you say, and yet they refuse to —

MORTON: Just a minute, now. I did *not* say that Republic Motors —

CROWN: You're right. I'm sorry, I said it. And I appreciate the opportunity to be on your program and to have your help in telling the real story. The truth. The people need to be told these things. *(Applause.)*

MORTON: Mr. Joshua, will you just hold on a minute here. The Dave Morton Show is happy to have you tell your story, but I can't allow you to—*(Voices of the studio audience.)* Can we just hold on a minute here, please—*(More interjections.)* Well, I'm *trying* to. I'm *going* to let him speak, but —

CROWN: Thank you, Mr. Morton. You see, it's only on programs like this that the ordinary American can have his say. A big multinational corporation can make unsafe cars or they can pollute the air or dump wastes into our rivers —

MORTON: Mr. Joshua, I'm going to have to insist that —

CROWN: Sure, we can protest. We can picket them. But that's like a flea on a dog —
MORTON: We'll be back after —
CROWN: The only way the average American can —
MORTON:—after these important messages. *(Commercial.)*
*(Mr. Crown absent when show resumes.)*


Three weeks after the protest on top of the Republic Motors building, Joshua's mail was being forwarded to the YMCA in mail sacks. Letters flooded in from every state and from a half-dozen foreign countries. There were letters of praise and blame, love letters, letters from men and women claiming kinship, letters asking financial help or assistance in getting books published or inventions marketed. He was offered the opportunity to buy a fast-food franchise, to purchase real estate, to own one-tenth of a black middleweight boxer with a record of 13-0 and to participate in a thousand dollar per contributor chain-letter. There were offers of marriage or, simply, cohabitation. His autograph was sought on photographs, baseballs, hard hats, T-shirts, a discarded forearm cast, jogging shoes and bikini panties. He received a cake with a skyscraper outlined on it, an enormous red lollipop with his name embossed in white icing sugar, a representation of his face in macrame and a red, white and blue needlepoint of the American flag with the word *Joshua* emblazoned on it. His advice was sought concerning family quarrels, unrequited love affairs, astrological predictions and the stock market. A number of women sent lipstick imprints with a request that he kiss the impression and return it. Some requested a lock of hair, one a snippet of pubic hair. Another wanted his fingernail parings. He received dozens of pictures of women and some of men, a few in various states of undress or in provocative poses.

His room was overwhelmed by mail. There were letters on every flat surface and on the floor. Packages were heaped in a corner, mail sacks were stacked against a wall.

Greeting me at the door, Joshua apologized for not shaking hands; he had a sheaf of letters in his right hand.

"You're not trying to read all these?" I said.

"Some of them," he said. "It's incredible. You should read a few yourself. Some dame sent me a dildo and wanted me to autograph it."

There was a difference in him that I couldn't quite pinpoint: a darkness beneath his eyes, a slight tremulousness in his hands. But the change was not primarily physical; it was mostly in his manner. He seemed taut, preoccupied. An open bottle of scotch and a glass sat on the table by an easy chair.

"You shouldn't be bothered with this stuff," I said, indicating the mail. "I'll have a word with Obie."

"I don't know," he said slowly. "Some of them are personal. I should write them back."

"And where are you going to get the time? I'm told you're going sixteen hours a day now."

"Maybe if they could get me a secretary for a couple of hours each morning."

"I'll see what I can do."

"Give me a minute," he said, moving to the chair, reading as he went. "I'm half through this one. You wouldn't believe it."

I studied him. One of the reasons he seemed changed was his clothes. The jeans were faded but the detailing announced that they were tailor-made. His sport shirt connoted elegance even though it was conservative of pattern and worn with the sleeves rolled to the forearms. And there was a difference in his hair: it had been fashioned with a blow-dryer and sprayed.

He looked up from the letter. "What are you smiling at?"

"You look like an actor on the 'Johnny Carson Show' hyping his latest picture. You're not letting all this get to you?"

He grinned the easy Joshua grin. "Not to worry." He got out of the chair, placed the letters on a pile and took a sip of his drink. "Pour you one?"

I shook my head. "I watched you on the 'Dave Morton Show.'"

"And?"

"I wasn't all that crazy about it."

"That I took over? I had to. He was using me as a dummy, putting words in my mouth." He smiled slyly. "The studio audience loved it."

"A television studio audience will laugh at or applaud anything or anybody, on cue."

The smile broadened. "And they couldn't edit me out; the show was live."

"You learn fast."

"You don't have to be all that bright."

"As a matter of fact," I said, "I enjoyed that part. I've been hoping to see that smarmy bastard get a pie in the face. What bothered me was what you were saying. You were a hell of a long way from your beef with Republic. I got the feeling you were doing a Ralph Nader impression."

"Not really," he said, a trifle self-consciously.

"More important than that, if you start taking over the interviews you'll cut your own throat. The television people talk to the agency people, and they all know everything that's going on in their little world. You play by their rules or you don't make it to the green room."

He nodded, but only cursorily.

I said, "The Lord giveth and the Lord taketh away. Remember that."

Back in my office, I left a call for Jim Ingraham. He got back to me almost immediately.

"Hey! We really cooled out Gallagher," he said, a gloating in his voice. "The paper's been taking all kinds of flack on the story, and I've been tempted to say to hell with it, but that son of a bitch Gallagher made me mad: prating about the immorality of the media, and all the while getting himself royally laid every time he's in town. At his press conference this morning I asked him whether he'd been able to check on the dates I'd specified. He made jokes and put-downs and generally played to the gallery, but I just kept after him. His records had been stolen, he kept saying. Surely I knew that, he said—it had been in all the papers. Har-dee-har! But surely, I said in return, there are other records: plane tickets, phone bills, hotel reservations, and surely he'd been able to check with his office about them. Finally, he admits that, yes, the dates are right, but denies flat-out knowing anybody by the name of Jerri West. So I say: then

190

may I introduce the lady. You see, I'd learned that, above and beyond any liaisons he's had with her, he'd met her at a party at the Mexican embassy — which, of course, I mentioned. He nearly shit his pants. He began a long, involved explanation, but by that time all the reporters were crowded around West. She handled them like an old pro. Would she confirm that the initials in her date book were Gallagher's? Only, she said, if you tell me whose initials are in *your* date book. Did she know Gallagher? I'm a very friendly person, she says, I know lots of people. Cool! They got nothing out of her on Gallagher, but, my god, the innuendos she dropped about some of the heavies here in Washington. After we were finished, the photographers did half an hour of leg-shots with her.'' He sounded smug.

I went to fill in Gladden on my conversations with Ingraham and Joshua, but he was with Doc in the ICU car. I left a note telling him to watch the news and the papers and that I would be out of town for a couple of days. I didn't tell him I was going to Toronto.


In Toronto I stay at the Windsor Arms. It's a fusty but comfortable downtown hotel just off Bloor Street in an area that has become the heart of the city's posh shopping district. I like it because it hasn't changed much in the twenty years I've been visiting the city—nor, for all I know, since it was built in 1928— and because it doesn't try to ingratiate itself by telling me that its toilet seats have been sanitized or harass me with elaborate questionnaires soliciting my candid opinions on the quality of the service. Then, too, it has the Three Small Rooms for dinner and the Courtyard Cafe where I can amuse myself through lunch watching Toronto's upwardly mobile watching each other as well as such show-business celebrities as may be in town.

I hadn't told Jo I was coming but knew she would be staying at her aunt's and telephoned her there. Her voice seemed flat. When we met for dinner she looked wan beneath her makeup, and thinner. Which only emphasized the exquisite planes of her face and the startling green of her eyes. Looking into them from across the table I felt complete again.

With the cold almond cream soup she talked about her show.

"I suppose it's happened to hundreds of artists. You work hard, and you begin to believe your work is good, possibly very good, and that when you show it to the world it will be recognized as such. You hold a concept in your mind, with all its meaning and all its emotional content, and you feel that you've come close to realizing what you were after. Then, when others don't see it—some because they *won't* look and others because they're incapable—you're left feeling somehow betrayed. When you send your work out into the world, it's not, as I've heard said, your child; it's you *yourself*. And when it's rejected or dismissed, it's not your work, it's *you* that's being scorned."

She sipped a spoonful of the soup. "After I read the reviews —such as they were—I said to myself: so what? The critics have almost always been wrong when a new direction has been taken, and they're wrong about me. I consoled myself: to hell with the critics—the *people* loved my work. And then Bernie let slip about father's friends buying the pictures. Father—trying to buy approval for me just as all my life he's bought me everything else."

"Jo, darling, beyond what the critics say, what do *you* think of your work?"

She was silent, her eyes down. "As of the moment, I'm not sure. That's one of the reasons I wanted to get away, so that when I return home I can look at it with fresh eyes, as something apart from me."

"That's important," I said. "If you don't believe you're good, or at least potentially good, then you never will be. I can offer my opinion but it really doesn't matter; I'm not qualified. But what does matter is, are you striving to communicate something? Do you know what it is? And is it worth stating? If you think it is then you must go on. But if you *can* quit, maybe you should. I've long believed that if someone has real talent nothing can stop it from surfacing. If people quit out of self-doubt or lack of encouragement or because of a lack of money, it's probably just as well." After the waiter had cleared the soup dishes, I added, "You'll do what you should. I'm sure of that."

With the arctic char before us, served with a flourish and with more than enough chatter by our waiter, it wasn't easy to get the conversation going again. Jo was away somewhere in her head, and I was fretting about what I'd said, wondering if it hadn't been a mere filling of the air with clichés, a making of plausible noises in order to give her something to cling to.

I heard myself saying, "Darling, marry me."

She was as surprised as I and didn't notice that her fork had dropped to the table. For a moment we looked at each other, and the surge of emotion had us rigid. Her face was flushed, and for the second time since we'd sat down, her eyes were glistening.

"You wouldn't be trying to be nice to a girl who's feeling down, would you?"

"No."

Her voice was small. "And you wouldn't like a chance to reconsider?"

"No. Please marry me."

She put her head back and drew a deep breath. "Oh, Tony, I love you," she said. "Will I marry you? Yes. Yes, yes."

We looked long at each other and after a moment at our food —neither of us quite knowing what to say next—simultaneously smiled.

"Here we go," she said. "Insulting the chef again." She separated a chunk of the flesh of the char and moved it about on the plate. "I'm just not hungry."

"It's becoming a pattern."

"I know."

"Are you up to drinking a toast?"

She shook her hair as though freeing it. "Oh yes!" she said and picked up her wineglass.

I signaled the waiter. "What's the best champagne in your cellar?"

"Roederer's Crystal '79. Is there something wrong with the wine?"

I said, "Would you recommend that we continue with this excellent wine or that we drink champagne? The lady has just agreed to marry me."

"Then the wine is as water," he said gallantly and with a flourish emptied the glasses into the ice-bucket.

As we left the dining room we were laughing giddily and had linked arms the better to maintain a direction. Our waiter, overtipped, was at the door to bid us farewell with a bow worthy of a European courtier. On the street we decided, giggling, that we were hungry and rounded the corner to a place called Bemelman's, which was noisy but served us excellent crêpes. Then, back to the hotel where we shared a shower and, wrapped in great towels, repaired to the living room where there was a cheese tray and some beer, ordered from room service. We put our feet on the coffee table and ate with our fingers. I risked asking her about Victor.

"It's an unhappy story," she said and sighed heavily. "I don't know all the details; I was just a child. Mother and Father weren't hitting it off. He wasn't home much—too busy trying to make it as an evangelist, I suppose. And Mother—trying to, well, to stimulate his interest, I suppose—did a crazy thing. She started seeing a man, a friend of Father's, a Joe Pinocchio. Pinocchio—that was his name." She smiled wanly. "He didn't have a big nose, incidentally. I used to call him Uncle Joey, though he wasn't my uncle. Just a friend. It wasn't anything serious, I'm sure of that. It was, quite simply, loneliness, and a kind of desperation bid to get Father's attention." She nibbled with little mouse bites at a piece of cheese, reflecting for a moment. "It didn't work, of course." She shook her head sadly. "As a matter of fact it was a disaster. Father was furious. He has a formidable temper."

"Yes, I know."

"He threw Uncle Joey out of the house. Bodily—he's terribly strong. Then he threw all Mother's things out of their bedroom and made her sleep in the spare bedroom. He wouldn't speak to her except to give orders or to yell at her. It was a terrible time."

She drew a deep breath and held it. It seemed for a moment that she wouldn't go on. "Mother found that she was pregnant. I'm *sure* it wasn't by Uncle Joey. I know it wasn't. But nothing would convince Father. I don't think he *wanted* to be convinced. From then on, Mother sort of shrank back into herself and began to drink. Victor was born. He was sickly as a baby—it could have been the drinking; I don't know. Father wouldn't even go to the hospital to see him. Not once. When Mother came home, she pretty well just stayed in bed. The drinking got worse. She would just lie there with tears on her face, not even wiping them away. And when you talked to her, she didn't seem to hear you. It came to where she was . . . out of touch—that's the only word for it—most of the time.''

She flicked away some tears with a forefinger. "Sorry," she said with a wan smile. "Cloudy with showers."

I fetched a box of facial tissue from the bathroom and put it beside her but the weeping had passed. When she began again her voice was soft but didn't falter. "One morning, we found her dead. Sleeping pills. Father's sister, my aunt Marguerita, moved in with us. You know, to run the house and look after Victor and me. Father doted on me. Spoiled me silly. And with the self-centeredness of a child, I'm afraid I welcomed it. Aunt Marg favored Victor, and she and Father had some terrible arguments. Finally, he drove her out of the house. Victor ran away. Just disappeared. I was away in Europe and wrapped up in my own life, and I don't suppose he knew how to get in touch." She bit her lip. "He's had a terrible time."

"Is he your father's son?"

"Oh yes," she said quickly. "You'll see that when you meet him."

"I have met him."

"You have?"

I told her about the business of the cab circling the block, of our odd conversation aboard the ship and about Victor's reaction when I told him that he wasn't listed in Gladden's *Who's Who* biography.

"The poor darling!"

"He's very bitter. But it's more than that. He seems to think your father is involved in—I don't know what else to call it—illegal activities."

"I know. I know. It's his way of striking back. He's so hurt by Father's rejection he can't see straight." She paused. "That's just terrible—his not knowing about the *Who's Who*."

"I'm sorry."

"It's not your fault," she said, trying for a substantial smile. The smile settled in and she looked at me directly. "Still want to marry into this crazy family?"

I pulled the tab from one of the beer cans and slipped it onto her finger. She leaned forward to put her arms about me and her lips on mine and her towel fell away. And then mine was gone and we were wrapped in each other in an awkward flurry of loving on the sofa.

# NINETEEN

In New York City I stopped off at Cartier's on the way from LaGuardia, picked out a bracelet of braided gold bands, gasped at the price but paid it, added a note and had it delivered by courier to the Gladden estate; Jo was to take a late afternoon flight home. At my apartment, I learned from the answering machine that Joshua Crown had called a half dozen times. There were calls also from Dunc Robertson and Roger Zachs. I was in a strange mood. The euphoria I had experienced after Jo's promise to marry me had, on the return to New York, fallen under a shadow, the dark shadow of Oscar Gladden, and I was conscious of a presentiment of (stated flatly, the word sounds melodramatic) doom. I decided not to call either Joshua or Roger; whatever it was could wait until morning. I did, however, telephone Dunc and arrange to meet for dinner at the Hellbox. I was delayed and arrived late. In the interval, as became evident, Dunc had been wasting no time.

I had only pulled up my chair when he said, "I have a joke I've been dying to tell you. There was this hypochondriac—"

"Nobody we know, of course."

"Every day he would go to see his doctor, complaining of a new illness. Soon the doctor was fed up and not about to listen to any more complaints. The guy says, 'Really, Doc, I've got this dreadful disease,' and gives the Latin name for it. The doctor says, 'You don't have it.' 'But I do,' the guy insists. Finally, the doctor says, 'Look, if you *did* have it, you wouldn't know; the symptoms of that particular disease are that you feel absolutely normal in every way.' The hypochondriac looks at him and says, 'My symptoms exactly!' ''

"Was that why you called me?" I asked drily.

He gave me a look. Kono arrived with our drinks. "Compriments de Hairbox," he said. "Rong time, no see."

"No thanks, Kono," I said. Surprised, he moved to retrieve the drink. I wrapped my fist about the glass. "No sir. But put it on the tab."

"You're a real barrel of laughs tonight," Dunc said.

"Sorry," I said, taking a long pull at the scotch. "I'm afraid that Oscar Gladden no longer amuses me."

"Ah," he said, lifting his glass grandly and looking at it meditatively, "then perhaps my bad news isn't all that bad."

I was suddenly attentive. "Tell."

"I had a call from Roger Zachs at Justice. He's been trying to reach you."

"Yes, I know."

"He tells me, off the record, that the IRS walked in unannounced yesterday on Peale and Bjornstadt, who, you will remember, are Gladden Inc.'s auditors. Six examiners. At Zachs' instigation, I gather. He wanted me to let you know. Sounded pleased as hell."

"Roger Zachs' mother was a pit bull terrier."

"My, my! Aren't we in a jolly mood." He cocked an eye at me. "Do I read that you're not interested?"

"Sorry. No, I want to hear."

"What I get is that the investigation has nothing to do with taxes. Apparently their books are in apple-pie order. What the IRS is trying to find out — among other things, I presume — is whether your Mr. Gladden has more income than can be accounted for by his various enterprises. They're of the opinion that he has. Not pin-money, mind you, but megabucks. And they'd like to know from where and how come? I got the feeling they're on a fishing expedition, that they don't have a hook to hang a cat on. Zachs wasn't saying, but he left the impression that, whatever the source, they suspect he's stashing it somewhere offshore."

I remembered the time when Bartholemew had shown me around the OneWorld premises in Queens. We'd stopped for five minutes at what he called the money room. Despite having been passed by two armed guards, he had still to insert a card bearing his fingerprint and to speak into an apparatus that read the intonations of his voice. Passing through what was in effect a vault door, we entered a large, low-ceilinged, windowless room bright with light and amurmur with a surf of sound. A portion of the area was divided into perhaps fifty to sixty cubicles, each no more than six feet square and five feet high. Within the cubicles, men and women sat at telephones, talking and making notes on various color-coded cards.

"They're taking prayer requests and credit card pledges," Bartholemew whispered. "We encourage our Program Partners to contribute by credit card. There's none of the delay then of sending and cashing a check."

Along one side of the room was a conveyor belt bearing letters. Feeding the belt was a complex machine that extracted the letters from a great hopper and sped each one through a slicer that made a slit along an edge. Alongside the belt, seated at tables, women extracted the letters, made brief notations on them and placed them in shallow plastic trays. The currency enclosed—mostly ten and twenty dollar bills—was placed in separate trays. Men in coveralls—without pockets, I noted—collected and stacked the trays and took them through a door that opened automatically as they approached it. Through the door were perhaps two dozen men and women seated before computers.

"Every letter is answered," Bartholemew confided, his lips close to my ear. "By name," he added, "and personally signed by Mr. Gladden."

"Personally signed?" I said incredulously.

He led me to a glass-enclosed area in which a group of teleprinters were chattering and pointed to an apparatus where a stylus whipped about with lightning-speed inscribing what appeared to be a handwritten signature on each letter.

My brain was reeling when we left the area. "Internal Revenue should be so efficient," I gasped.

Bartholemew was wearing a pleased-as-punch smile. "We have to be efficient," he said. "We process two to three million dollars a week."

Dunc's voice returned me to the moment. "Permission to speak, sir," he was saying, snapping a hokey salute. (He *was* beginning to feel the booze.)

"Speak your piece, soldier," I said, adopting his idiom but without much humor.

"Tell me it's none of my business," he said, "but how serious are you about Gladden's daughter?"

"I asked her to marry me last night."

He sucked in a breath. After a moment he leaned forward, elbows on the table, turning his glass gently with two hands, making the ice tinkle against the sides. "Tony, old friend," he said, "ever since you went to work for Oscar Gladden, I . . . ." He was making small bobs with his head and had something of a boy's awkwardness. "What I'm trying to say is . . . No, let me put it this way: if the building comes down, everybody inside, *every*body could get buried in the rubble. I mean . . . What I'm trying to say is that with all the smoke there could be one hell of a fire." He broke off. He lowered his eyes and mumbled, "Nothing but the best of intentions."

"You sure don't spare the analogies," I said, putting a hand on his arm so that he could see I wasn't offended. "The trouble is I'm not free to take a walk. I have a contract with Gladden and I have a covenant with his daughter. Incidentally, aren't you going to wish me well?"

Dunc straightened up and let loose his whistle. Kono arrived at a shuffling trot.

"Two of the same, Kono," Dunc said. "Wait a minute," he added as Kono turned to the errand, "better make it a double for my friend."


In the morning, Bartholemew informed me that Oscar Gladden was in Los Angeles. Jo, I was told, hadn't yet returned to New York and he didn't know for sure when she'd be back. I tried Toronto but there was no answer at her aunt's number. Joshua called to say that he was on the way out to see me; he needed to talk to me urgently.

I went to the window and stood overlooking the expanse of lawn fronting the house. The morning was a benison, with the sky an electric blue and the air vibrant with clarity. The oaks, maples and balsam poplars cast massive shadows on the glinting grass, and the beds of flowers seemed prismatic in the sunlight. It was a definition of peace, but I drew no peace from it. My brain was like a bog from too long a stay at the Hellbox and from too much turning in my bed.

On the road beyond the wall I heard the familiar roar of the tow truck and glimpsed it as it passed the gate. The sound of it had been nibbling at the edges of my mind for weeks. I would hear it enter from Duck Pond Road, pass the gate and rumble off to the south end of the property. Later, when I had again settled down to work, it would shatter my concentration as it thundered toward the road and was gone. And I would wonder: what possible reason could there be for an outside tow truck to make regular visits to the coach-house?

This morning I didn't put it out of mind. I went to the trophy room and studied the television monitors, examining the contours of the land and working out the placement of the cameras. Contrary to what Knee-Hi had said, there didn't seem to be any swampland. It was somewhat hilly, lightly wooded country, with an occasional outcrop of rock and with a creek bisecting the area. I returned to my office, locked the door, and on the map of the estate sketched out a route that would permit me to make my way to the south end of the property unobserved by the television cameras. It shouldn't be all that difficult if I kept generally to the center, paused at predetermined points to await the rotation of the cameras and sprinted across the open areas. I decided to try it that evening at seven when the night shift came on and the guards were occupied in the changeover.

I heard a car on the driveway and saw that Joshua had arrived. He was driving a Mercedes 450-SL with the top stowed. I greeted him as he came from the parking lot.

"Where's the Lincoln?"

He grinned self-consciously. "Haven't you heard? There's talk of a gas shortage." The grin widened. "The Mercedes is a rental."

He was wearing a tweed sports jacket with pewter-gray slacks. A silk sports shirt was open at the neck to reveal the puff of a matching ascot. He was waiting for me to comment, so I said nothing. As we made our way toward a bench beneath a nearby tree, I had a sudden sense of *déjà vu* and smiled. He was acutely aware of my reactions and said, "What's the joke?"

"No joke. I was just remembering that day at Caughnawaga: 'Hey, Mister, want to be a celebrity?' "

"Worked out okay," he said.

"You wanted to see me."

He was suddenly serious. "I need to talk to Mr. Gladden."

"What about?"

"I've been calling for a week now but Bartholemew won't put me through and Mr. Gladden doesn't call back."

"What do you want to talk to him about?" I repeated. He didn't answer. Nor did he look at me, but gazed into the distance, squinting against the sun. "Hey Joshua," I said. "It's me. Tony. Remember?"

His fingers were interlaced, and he was bending them back and forth, cracking the knuckles. I noticed that his fingernails were manicured. "You're making it look like I don't trust you," he said. "It's not like that at all. It's just that, if I explain it to you and you explain it to Mr. Gladden, I can see how he would say, 'Tell him, To hell with that!' "

"Whatever you say. But if I ask him to see you and can't tell him what it's about, you've got about as much chance of success as Arafat in a kibbutz."

"Lemme think about it," he said, frowning.

"So what else is happening?"

There had been an approach by Republic Motors. One of their junior vice presidents had invited the secretary of the Amalgamated Ironworkers to lunch and, as they were leaving the company dining room, had said offhandedly that Republic might be prepared to make a contribution of, say, twenty-five thousand dollars to the fund for Tom Deerfoot's widow. There would have to be an understanding, of course, and some papers signed—an indemnification, which Republic would draft.

"Take it," I said. "But not their first offer. You want fifty thou plus your legal costs."

"I don't know. . . ."

"Joshua, don't be crazy. You're never going to beat them in

court. You could come out of a lawsuit up to your nuts in debt. Take it.''

"I would have to sign a paper guaranteeing not to talk about the case. Look, we're hurting them or they would never have made the offer. They want to shut me up. They know I've got a following. You should read the mail.''

I could see that there was no point in pursuing it. "I'll talk to Obie Berenson,'' I promised, and walked Joshua to his car.


Berenson's advice was to take the money and run. "The media people are cooling to Joshua. Quite frankly, we're running out of gas.''

"Joshua says the mail is heavy.''

"Fair. But that's the great unwashed. I mean, fifty to a hundred letters a day doesn't cut enough ice to cool your drink once a story starts to fade. Right now this one needs goosing. Incidentally, you said there was to be a phase two.''

"Right,'' I said vaguely. "I'll get back to you on that.'' (At the moment I'd forgotten what it was.)

"In the meantime,'' Obie said, "is there anything you can do to get our hero off the ecology kick? He's beginning to sound like a hippie reissue and the requests for him are dropping like the Dow Jones.''

A few minutes short of seven, I came down the stairs leading to the entry hall. I'd taken off my jacket and necktie and pulled on a cashmere sweater. I wanted to change to a pair of Adidas but had none at the office. Then I remembered my golf shoes in the trunk of the car. They'd be ideal. I would take with me a nine-iron and a ball, and if any accounting was required I could say something about working on getting my handicap down.

From the parking lot I saw the car arrive with the evening shift. Two guards got out and fell into conversation with the men going off duty. Knee-Hi came from the gate-house and joined them. A burst of laughter carried on the still evening air.

I ducked low and followed the hedge bordering the parking lot. At the bottom of a gentle hill I negotiated the link-fence, skirted a stand of trees and went quickly along a natural pathway through a planting of evergreens. It was necessary at that point to cross an exposed area, so I went at an easy saunter, swinging the golf club idly, clipping the tops off weeds; if I was to be seen, it was important not to look surreptitious.

Now there was little risk. I was out of sight of the gate-house, no one was manning the monitors at the moment and the dogs wouldn't be loosed until ten. Nonetheless, I moved with caution; someone in the house might chance to go into the trophy room and spot me on one of the television monitors. I ducked my head to scuttle beneath some low branches and reviewed the route I had plotted. All was going as planned; I was coming up on the creek. I paused, searching for the camera that I knew was just ahead. Yes, there it was: mounted high on a pole, peering like a cyclops over a grove of young birches. I waited until it had completed its slow arc and begun to turn away, then went barreling down the slope on a dead run and, with a leap, cleared the stream. Doubled over, I scurried on until I was able to duck beneath the leafy canopy of a willow.

I stood for a moment catching my breath. I would need to be more careful now; the men of the evening shift might have gone to the gate-house and could be watching the monitors. Moving cautiously, I bore to the left, following an old split-rail fence, stopping twice to outmaneuver cameras and coming finally to a line of poplars that marked the edge of the woods. Off to the right there was a box-like structure surrounded by a link-fence that I recognized as the kennels. Some thirty yards beyond it were the coach-house and the barn. Warily, grateful that I was downwind from the kennels, I moved in on the windowless side of the coach-house and from there to the barn. It was coming on dusk.

Through a chink in the boards I could see the interior of the barn. A tow truck loomed large at the center of the open space. The driver was standing with a foot on the running-board, a sandwich in one hand, a plastic coffee cup in the other. One of the guards had mounted the bed of the truck and was struggling with the cinch on the heavy chain that secured the four truck wheels. He manhandled one of them, rolling it to the edge. The driver took a great swallow of his coffee, tossed the plastic cup into a refuse barrel, stuffed the last of the sandwich into his mouth and moved to help. Over the edge came the first wheel, to be arrested on the bounce and rolled through a doorway into a shed off to one side. The remaining three wheels followed in swift sequence, and the door was padlocked.

The driver went to a forklift on which four wheels, similar to those just stored, were stacked. He started the engine and ran in close to the tow truck where he and the guard hoisted the wheels, rolled them into position on the truck bed and secured them with the chain.

I was puzzled. Why the exchange of wheels? Neither set looked new. Nor were the tires flat. And why were they stored behind a padlocked door? Beyond that, why bring the wheels of a great trailer-truck to a remote barn on private property? It wasn't to have them repaired or retreaded; there was no equipment in sight with which they could be serviced, nor would it be possible in the shed in which they were stored, which had seemed to be no more than a dozen feet square.

I was suddenly aware of the faint sound of voices raised in anger. They came from my left. Hugging the side of the barn, I worked my way toward the sound. It was almost dark now and twice I stumbled on some debris, freezing until I was sure I hadn't been heard. The voices were clearer now, and one of them was Oscar Gladden's.

I peered through a small mullioned window, heavily begrimed with years of dirt, and saw what seemed to be a rudimentary office. It was starkly illuminated by a single bare light bulb suspended on a cord from the ceiling. The only furniture was an ancient rolltop desk, a ruptured cane chair, a metal storage rack on one wall and a cluttered workbench opposite. Gladden stood, feet apart, at the center of the room. Facing him was a man I'd never seen before. He was perhaps fifty, of medium height and dressed in a dark gray business suit. The only unusual thing about his appearance was the two strands of white hair that angled in a V from his brow to the back of his head. He was backing away from Gladden, whose face was distorted in a grimace made more horrible by the harsh light directly above his head.

The shouting had ended. In the silence I could hear only the sound of Gladden's breathing. Moving with that incongruous grace that belied his size, he closed in on the man facing him.

As the man backed away, he interposed the chair between himself and Gladden. It was brushed aside and sent spinning to crash into the wall. The man retreated, feinting in one direction or another, but each move was cut off. There was a terrifying relentlessness in the way Gladden maneuvered him toward the corner. Once, the man held up a hand and cried out hoarsely, ''For chrissake, Oscar!'' Twice he leaped at his pursuer, striking with his fists. Gladden merely raised his forearms against the blows and bumped the man with his stomach, sending him staggering across the floor. As Gladden followed, his eyes narrowed to slits, his teeth were bared and the breath wheezed from his lungs in great hissing sounds.

He had the man trapped now, in a corner where the workbench blocked escape. The man lunged once more, with the explosive energy of a cornered animal, snarling, hammering with his fists. Gladden absorbed the blows and bumped him cruelly into a corner of the workbench. The man screamed, put a hand to his back and went down. As quickly, he scrambled to his feet, his mouth agape, his face twisted now in pain and panic.

Gladden moved in swiftly, raised an enormous forearm and smashed it down on the side of the man's neck, driving him against the wall. The man spun, stumbled, and fell heavily to the floor where he lay on his back, spread-eagled, arms and legs upraised limply like a whipped dog offering surrender. Then, as I watched frozen with horror, Gladden stepped in close and dropped to his knees on the man's chest.

There was the sound of ribs cracking and of a scream suddenly cut off. And the sight of a body jerking and convulsing as Oscar Gladden, his eyes closed, his face impassive, knelt there almost as though in prayer.


I remained in my office until ten-thirty, shaken, uncertain what to do. So far as I knew I had returned to the house unobserved. In the entrance hallway, forgetting that I was wearing golf shoes, I had slipped on the marble floor and gone down but was uninjured except for a bruised elbow. Not wanting to be seen peering from the window of my lighted office, I went into the darkened bathroom and looked out on the gate-house. There were no signs of activity. A few minutes after my return, I heard the front door close and the sound of the elevator, and knew that Gladden was back. I waited another fifteen minutes and when nothing happened, chose the moment and went swiftly, golf shoes in hand, down the stairs and out of the house to the parking lot. On Hegman's Lane my body was shaking so profoundly that I had to pull Smedley onto the shoulder and sit for a few minutes to compose myself. In stockinged feet, I went to the trunk, retrieved my shoes, put them on and continued the drive to New York City.

The chilling fact was that there was no aftermath. It was as though the horror I'd witnessed had been no more than an episode in a fading nightmare. The following morning, preparing breakfast, I turned on the television set.

"Love. . . ."

The familiar Gladden face. The tranquilizing Gladden voice.

"The love of a mother for her child. The love of a husband for his wife and of a wife for her husband. The love of a patriot for his country. The love of a man for his fellow-man.

"Surely love is the highest of all of the laws of God. And surely we must obey it—as we must obey *all* of God's laws—or perish in a world awash with hate.

"I have been talking to you in these programs about obedience to the laws of life. Today, I want to—"

I ran to turn off the television set and, as I did, saw my hand was trembling.

Everything seemed as usual at the gate. My casual wave was returned as casually. My office was cheery with sunlight. There was a note from Jo to say that she had arrived late the previous night, had tried to reach me and would see me at ten. There was a note from Bartholemew: "Mr. Gladden would like to see you at eleven sharp. Also he asked me to pass on to you his displeasure over the frequent telephone calls from Mr. Joshua Crown. Please see to it that they stop." The maid arrived with my morning coffee, full of gabble about a family of raccoons that was nesting in the library chimney and about the fact that cook had some lovely freshwater salmon for lunch.

I responded shortly, not trusting my voice or my demeanor, still traumatized by the events of the night before. It was not that I was unfamiliar with violence; I'd spent the better part of three years working the police beat and had seen any number of men, women and children bloodied or dead. I'd ridden with the police on their night patrols and had viewed with them the gore and the agony. But such death as I'd seen had been after the fact. I'd never seen a man killed before my eyes, and my mind kept rerunning the images and the sounds.

Oscar Gladden on his knees!

I'd half expected the police to be about, asking questions, poking into corners. But there was no evidence in the parking lot of any visitors. I went down the stairs to the trophy room to study the monitors covering the south end of the property. They looked like still-photographs of a pleasant country setting. I headed for the stairs to return to my office.

"Mr. Carpenter."

It took me a moment to discover the source of the voice. It was Knee-Hi, near the ceiling of the entrance hallway, standing on a ladder back of the aquarium. In his hands was a plastic pail.

"Lookin' for somethin', Mr. Carpenter?" he said, his tiny teeth showing in a facsimile of a smile.

"Nothing," I said offhandedly, restraining myself from inventing an elaborate reason for my visit to the trophy room.

Knee-Hi emptied the pail. A disgusting mix of dead fish and what I took to be animal organs spilled into the water and began to sink slowly. There was a flashing feeding-frenzy. Within a minute the food was gone except for a few tiny morsels twisting in the aqueous space before being snatched up by the smaller fish. A barracuda, nicked in the frenzy, zigzagged erratically, trailing a pale ribbon of pink. The piranha moved like a cloud to engulf him.

Knee-Hi chuckled. "Rough neighborhood."

"Better watch yourself up there," I said.

He laughed. "Me?—I'd just be lunch. But *you*. . . ."

I started up the stairs, the sound of a guttural chuckling at my heels.

"Mr. Carpenter."

"Yes, Knee-Hi."

"Your golf clubs—they're Jack Nicklaus, aren't they?"

My god! The nine-iron. I'd forgotten it in my preoccupation. I hadn't had it when I returned to the house. Had I dropped it perhaps at the barn or on my return through the woods?

"Nicklaus? Yes, they are."

"One of the men found a club this morning. I thought it might be yours."

"Hey, that's great," I said. "Thanks. I lost it a week ago. I'll pick it up at the gate-house on my way out this afternoon." I started up the stairs again.

"Mr. Carpenter."

"Yes?"

"I thought I warned you about the swampland."

"You did, Knee-Hi. You did."

Jo was in my office, sitting in my chair.

"Hullo," she said with a shy, askew smile.

I went to her and she came from behind the desk into my arms. After a moment she drew away.

"Darling, you're trembling." She looked at me, frowning, concerned. "You're pale. Are you all right?"

"I'm fine. Maybe a little hungover."

"I called you last night. Twice. I wanted you to meet my plane if you could. It all worked out; Father fetched me home."

Incredible! Gladden had come from the barn and, as though nothing had happened, had gone to the airport to pick up his daughter. The picture of the spasming body of the man in the barn flashed in my mind.

"Tony, what *is* it?"

"Nothing, nothing."

"You look terrible."

"Sorry," I mumbled, moving away to avoid her eyes, running the tap in the washroom as a diversion. My hand shook as I raised the glass.

She came to me, the shadow of concern on her face. *Oscar Gladden! . . . Josephine Gladden! . . .* Then she was in my arms again and I was saying, "I love you," and she was saying over and over again, "My darling! My darling!"

We stood there, clutching each other, I with a kind of desperation. We kissed and there was the taste of tears. When we loosed the embrace she laughed and held up a hand and there was a beer-can ring on her finger. She bared her wrist and showed me the gold bracelet. Then again we fell into each other's arms.

Suddenly she started. "Oh my! I was just going to stay a minute. I'm meeting Bernie for lunch. He's bringing a John MacNamara—he's with *Harper's*. Or is it *The Atlantic?* I forget. And there's more good news, wonderful news; I had a long talk with Father." She was already at the door. "I'll tell you later. Seven, at your place?" I nodded and she was gone.

I watched from the window as she emerged from the front door and ran to her car. She waved, and I waved in return and watched until she passed the gate and was gone from sight. As I turned back into the office I was suddenly overcome with a profound sadness.

# TWENTY

$A$t exactly eleven o'clock I went down the hall to Oscar Gladden's office, dreading the moment, wondering if I would be able to control my reactions. He was removing folders from a file and placing them in his attaché case. He looked up with a smile as I tapped on the door and entered.

"Come in. Come in," he said, beckoning. His voice was cordial and his manner relaxed. "I'm leaving for Los Angeles within the hour. I'll be gone two or three days." He snapped closed the attaché case and stood behind the desk, resting his hands on it. "Two things: First, I like what I read of the confrontation between Gallagher and West. My only concern is that she's liable to exploit it. I'll have a word with her. In the meantime keep fanning the flames. Have your friend Ingraham check into the transfer of a block of one thousand shares of Bellknap Construction stock to Gallagher last February 27. Bellknap, he'll find, is tendering a bid for the repaving of a section of the thruway between Syracuse and Rochester."

He seemed entirely himself. His skin was pink, his manner was easy and he seemed more relaxed than he had for a week. I looked into his eyes, seeking I know not what. He returned my gaze, unblinking.

"Now," he said, showing a suggestion of displeasure, "to Joshua Crown. Bartholemew tells me he's being beleaguered with telephone calls asking to see me. What's it all about?"

"I have no idea. I've asked him. He insists on speaking to you personally."

211

"The answer is no. Anything he has to say to me he can say to you." He reached into a drawer, removed a flat snakeskin wallet and slipped it into the inside pocket of his jacket. "Your Indian friend is becoming tiresome. Dump him."

"You said earlier—"

"I'm saying now, dump him. The media have bought him, lock, stock and barrel, a dumb fucking Indian whose one achievement in life is that he can stand on an eight-inch steel beam and not fall off. The point has been made. Dump him."

"But wait a minute," I said. "We—"

"Dump him."

With Oscar Gladden out of town and with no tasks of pressing urgency commanding my attention, I decided to make at least a preliminary investigation into the events in the barn the previous night. First, I called the *Register,* asked who their stringer was in the Port Washington area and was given the name Jocelyn Gunn. I called her—to discover that Jocelyn was a man—and identified myself, hoping that he hadn't heard I'd left the paper. He hadn't.

"I wonder if you could look into something for me," I said offhandedly. "I'm working on a story and, in the course of it, heard that there'd been a murder in your neck of the woods last night that might tie in. I don't have any contacts with the police out your way. Could you check it out for me? Off the record."

Jocelyn had a stammer, and to break it used the device of banging a hand on anything within reach. "I'll be gla—*(bang)* happy to," he said. "The only prob—*(bang)* difficulty is that we may find there was more than one. Everybody thinks of the Port as all moneyed people, but we have ev—*(bang)* all kinds. Can you give me anything else?"

"Male. Caucasian. Around fifty, I'd say. Has two strands of white hair—you know, almost as though they were dyed—running from his forehead back. Otherwise hair coloring is brown. Medium height. Weight? I'd say 170 pounds."

"I'll get back to you."

Bartholemew buzzed to tell me that Jim Ingraham had called. I telephoned him immediately, reaching him in his office.

"No problem," he said. "Everything's gung-ho. I just thought you might like an update. The police pulled in Jerri West for questioning but let her go. It was mostly for show; if they booked every expensive whore in Washington, the downtown condominiums would be half empty. She's making the most of it. Called her own press conference. I remember when you had to *be* somebody to do that. Mostly the tabloids and the out-of-town press. Coy as hell about Gallagher but no facts. Gamey stuff about a certain unnamed general who used to meet her in the parking lot at the Pentagon for a quickie. And about somebody in the National Security Council for whom she wore jackboots and did the goose-step up and down his back."

"But no names."

"No names. One of the big skin magazines has offered her a contract, she says. *Penthouse* or *Playboy,* it wasn't clear. That's how we reward women who become celebrities: pay 'em a king's ransom to display their crotch to ten million voyeurs. She really has clammed up on Gallagher, though."

"I'm going in to see him this afternoon. I feel bad about him."

"I don't. Don't get me wrong; I'm no moralizer, you know that. Any one of us here could write a dozen stories about the swordsmen up on the Hill. Who can blame them? They're miles from home. Lonely. Fighting to get a handhold on the political ladder and knowing that while they're somebody back in Austin or Keokuk or Yakima, they're a dime a dozen in this town. I like politicians. What galls me about Gallagher is his goddamn professional piousness. I mean, God and country till it's oozing out of his pores. And on the take. I don't feel sorry for him at all."

As I replaced the telephone in its cradle, it rang.

"Mr. Car—Tony?"

"Yes."

"Jocelyn Gunn. I've talked to both the county and state police and they don't have anything. Nary a homicide. Sorry." He laughed. "I mean, sorry I wasn't able to turn anything up."

"I could be way off base," I said, disappointed.

"There's a poss — *(bang)* the chance that the body hasn't turned up yet. I'll stay on it if you like."

*     *     *     *

The activity at the Gallagher campaign headquarters was almost frenetic. Every desk was occupied by workers busily stuffing envelopes, filling out cards, checking canvasing results against voter lists, pounding typewriters or sorting campaign materials. The walls were covered with hand-lettered charts and polling reports. People were coming and going. Even those on a coffee-break were engaged in earnest conversation.

Mo Norman, Gallagher's campaign manager, saw me heading for the candidate's hole-in-the-wall office and cut me off. "He's on the phone."

"I'll wait," I said.

"You could go gray; he's expecting a call from the national chairman." He looked at me quizzically. "Didn't I hear you quit the *Register?*"

"You heard right," I said. There was a knotted frown at the center of his brow. It was evidence of Gallagher's problems. Campaign managers tend to be mercurial: gregariousness' model when the auguries are good, near-paranoid when they're not. Mo being the barometer, the reading said batten the hatches.

A door opened. Gallagher put his head out and beckoned to Norman. Seeing me, he called out, "Stick around."

I went on a hands-in-pockets tour of the campaign headquarters. Poll-workers have always fascinated me. Some are there, of course, only to catch the crumbs from the great man's table, but many have a dedication akin to a missionary's. They will work sweatshop hours without pay or hope of tangible reward simply to see their candidate win. They are satisfied with a handshake or an arm around the shoulder or an individual word of commendation from the candidate, and for this will do some of the most unrewarding work imaginable: walking sometimes hostile streets, climbing narrow stairs, knocking on every door, soliciting the favor of strangers. They will endure insults, rebuke and massive indifference with few complaints and undiminished vigor. Part of their recompense is, of course, similar to that which comes to the hangers-on around rock stars: an identification with the celebrity, the sense of being part of something important. But political workers are prepared to do more than bask in a reflected spotlight; they are givers as well

214

as takers. Often they are lonely people. Some are social misfits. Many are one-note bores. But the political process wouldn't work without them, and they are as committed as any group I know.

A shy young woman wearing enormous horn-rimmed glasses, an outsize shirt and an overlong skirt came up to me. "I think Mr. Gallagher's waving at you."

In his office, Gallagher shut the door, settled heavily into his chair, leaned back and put his feet on the desk.

"Want a coffee?" His voice was flat with fatigue. He didn't look good. Any politician in midcampaign, the smile turned off, betrays the near-exhaustion that has become his familiar. The eyes are surrounded with gray. The muscles of the face sag. The skin—even beneath the lie of good health told by the sunlamp tan—is the color of dough, and there is a tendency while talking to massage the back of the neck—which was what Gallagher was doing at the moment.

"You look like hell," I said equably.

"You don't look all that sensational yourself," he riposted. "Sorry, did you say yes to the coffee?"

"Only if you're having one."

"I'm working on a system to take it intravenously," he said, reaching for the telephone. "Two coffees, Jenny."

"How does the battle go?" I enquired.

"You *did* quit the paper?"

I nodded.

"Then the answer is, in a word, shitty."

I indicated the outer room with a jerk of my head. "They're busy as mice in a feed store."

"The organization's fine. It's you SOBS in the media. Everybody hears the accusation, nobody gives a damn about the response."

There was a tap at the door, and an attractive woman in her late thirties entered. She put a steaming mug in Gallagher's hand and a plastic cup with a paper of sugar and a capsule of cream on the desk in front of me. Her eyes were on Gallagher and his were on her.

"Thank you, Jenny," he said, his voice soft. "Do you know this guy, Ingraham?" he asked me when the woman had gone.

215

"The sonofabitch is a real dose of the clap. You couldn't talk to him for me?" he added, a gleam coming to his eye and as quickly fading. "No, of course not." His face was bleak. "It's too late anyway."

I emptied the cream into my coffee and looped the capsule into a wastebasket, feeling like shoddy merchandise. The telephone rang. Gallagher said no three times and maybe once, hung up and put his feet on the desk again.

"I could ride out the Jerri West smear if that was all, but the trouble is, that kind of problem stirs up others. It's like getting shit on your shoe; everybody starts looking at you funny. Even your so-called friends." I had a sudden flash of the wounded barracuda in the tank. "Somebody's feeding lies to the papers. The Securities Commission is asking questions; right in the middle of the campaign, wouldn't you know! Routine, they say. Routine, my ass!" He shook his head and looked at me grimly. "Anybody who runs for public office is certifiable." He sat forward in his chair and turned on the old smile. The transformation was astonishing. "What can I do for you?"

"Nothing, really. I've been thinking about you. Just thought I'd look in and see how you're faring."

"I never will understand what possessed you to go to work for that fat hypocrite, Gladden. You really surprised me with that. Don't say I didn't warn you."

"As a matter of fact, Mr. Gallagher, you didn't."

"Well, if I'd thought of it I would have," he said wearily. "If that nogoodnik Zachs had done his homework, we'd have nailed Gladden's fat hide to the wall." He suddenly seemed uninterested. "Ah well. . . ."

The telephone rang. Gallagher picked it up and sighed heavily. "Okay, put him on." He covered the mouthpiece with a hand. "The national chairman. He's got his shorts in a knot."

I left, feeling like Judas the morning after.


Jo arrived at eight laden with groceries. She was effervescent with news: MacNamara loved her work and was going to do an article on her. The *New York* magazine hadn't been able to send a man to the opening but would review the show in the next issue. Two of Bernie's more discriminating customers had bought pictures. There had been an inquiry from the American Indian Museum in Brooklyn plus other encouraging words. She whirled away from me and did a gay, skirt-flaring dance in the center of the living room, ending it breathless and laughing. I struggled to simulate enthusiasm but knew I was failing. There had been an odd delayed reaction from the night before and I'd spent the fifteen minutes before she arrived retching in the bathroom.

Once the fever of her excitement lessened she could see that I wasn't myself. "What *is* the matter, darling?" she asked.

"I really don't know," I said, making with my best hangdog look. "My whole system's out of kilter."

"We'll soon remedy that," she pronounced, holding up a cerise-colored thermal sack with the name Le Grub Shoppe inscribed on it. "First, a little wine for the tummy's sake, then the most glorious *coq au vin* this side of Paris. You just put your feet up while I go off to do my patented reheating miracles in the kitchen."

I suffered the cajoling, withdrawing to the living room and using the time to pull myself together. Bestirred by the drawing of a cork, I made my way to the kitchen, where I accepted a goblet of a glorious burgundy and perched on a stool to watch the preparation of what was clearly to be a feast. There were thick pink slices of smoked salmon sprinkled with capers and green onion and bits of hard-boiled egg; shredded crabmeat nesting in avocado halves; flaky croissants and two sagging wedges of cherry cheesecake. The *coq au vin* was already wafting its aroma from the oven. China clattered, cutlery clanged and condiments were set out.

She looked up, giving me a long lascivious wink. "First, you feed the brute. . . ."

"Gastronomy, not music, is the food of love," I said, getting off the stool. "But I'll go turn on the stereo anyway."

I returned to perch and watch. Her face was flushed, her eyes were shining and she was obviously fighting to restrain a smile. Suddenly she said, "I was going to save it till later but I can't; I am ready to *burst!*" She put her hands on the countertop, leaning forward to look at me. "Darling," she said, "I am off the hook!'' She raised her head and loosed a howl of exultant joy: "Whee!" I looked at her, uncomprehending. "I've been pardoned!" she said. "Reprieved! I don't have to do the television show. Do you hear me? *I do not have to do the television show!*"

"You don't have to do the television show," I echoed dumbly. And then it broke on me: "Of course. Of course! Now that you're being accepted, you can continue to paint."

"And the most wonderful thing about it all is that Father told me I was off the hook when he met me last night at the airport, before I'd even *talked* to Bernie, before he was able to tell me all the wonderful things that were happening. It was right out of the blue! As we drove away from the airport, he told me he'd spent the evening thinking about me, and that he'd decided, above and beyond anything else, he wanted me to be happy. And that he wasn't going to hold me to my promise."

"That's marvelous," I said, striving to feign an enthusiasm to approximate hers.

"Oh, Tony," she said fervently, "it really is. I know how much he wanted me to be on the show—you know, the whole family solidarity thing." She was pulling on oven mitts, winding down now and resuming her preparations for dinner. "It was all the more wonderful because I'd been dreading coming home. I'd made up my mind—even if it meant going back on my word—that I simply *had* to go on with my work. The first reaction to the show—the review in the *Times*—forced me to look hard at myself. I had to ask myself if I had what it takes. You said something in Toronto to the effect that if I *could* quit, maybe I should. The point is I couldn't. And that was, as they say, the bottom line." She opened the oven and took out the *coq au vin*. "I had my courage all screwed up for a fearful row with Father, and he just took the wind out of my sails." She shook her head, smiling. "It's all so wonderful."

We carried the steaming plates into the living room, to the table set before the window overlooking the city.

"By the way," she said, heading back to the kitchen, "I was talking to Joshua. He's agreed to pose for me again." She returned in a minute. "Get 'em while they're hot," she said in a hawker's voice, placing the croissants on the table and folding back the napkin covering them. "Now where was I? . . . Oh yes, Joshua. He's agreed to pose for me again. But there's a condition. I have to get Father to agree to see him. He says he spoke to you about it but that there's a problem?"

"Well, yes. The last thing your father said to me this morning was, 'Dump him.' "

"Well, we'll see what we can do," she said cheerily.

I'd had a talk with myself earlier while sitting alone in the living room and had determined that I would let no discordant note intrude on our evening together. But the events of the night before would not be banished from my mind, and as we concluded the meal—to which I'd done little justice—I couldn't resist one question. I put it with a simulated casualness.

"By the way, Jo, do you know anyone who works for your father who has two white streaks in his hair? You know, the way women sometimes have it done."

"Of course," she said. "Mr. Naylor. Your predecessor."

I felt that I'd been struck a blow on the head.

Jo was looking at me, frightened. "Tony, what is it?" She came to me and took my head in her hands. "You're pale. You *aren't* well."

The evening only just escaped being a disaster. I recovered enough to return to my unconvincing story about being afflicted by a virus. We both drank more wine than we should have, but rather than revive our spirits it depressed them. We each strove to put the best face on things and, finally, partly in hope, I think, went to bed. But the passion I simulated was mocked by my impotence, and there was nothing to be said about that.

I wanted to explain. I knew that she sensed that my story about the virus was an invention, and I could tell she was hurt that I'd left the lie wedged there between us. But what could I tell her? Could I tell her that her father had murdered William Naylor only an hour or two before he'd met her plane? Could I explain my reaction if I said merely that I'd heard that Naylor was dead? Then how did he die? And how did I know? And if I knew he was dead, why was I asking blind questions about the streaks in his hair? No, there was no explaining it.

There also lurked the possibility that she might subsequently ask her father if he'd heard that Naylor was dead, which would lead to questions as to how she knew. "Tony told me," she would reply, and what might that lead to?

She left shortly after ten. We embraced while waiting for the elevator but the fondness was forced and her "Good night, darling" was strained. We went down to the street to get her a taxi; she wouldn't hear of my driving her home. There were frequent silences as we waited a long ten minutes in a fine, misting rain. From within the cab she blew me a kiss from her fingertips.

Back in the apartment I looked up Bernie's telephone number.

"Bernie," I said, after apologizing for calling him at home, "did you by any chance tell Oscar Gladden the good news about the critical reaction to Jo's show?"

There was an extended silence on the line and a note of caution in his voice when he did speak. "I'm afraid I don't quite understand. Was there some reason he shouldn't be told?"

"No, no. Of course not," I said. "He's Jo's father. And he's one of your patrons. It's just that something Jo said made me wonder if she got the good news from you or from her father, and I was curious."

"Oh, is that all. Yes, she got it from me. At lunch today. She was thrilled to death. I've never seen anyone more excited."

"Then you didn't tell Mr. Gladden?"

Again he hesitated. "Well, yes . . . yes, I did. But I don't think I spoiled anything, if that's what you're getting at. It was obvious, when I told her at lunch, that it was news. What actually happened was that I called yesterday evening to give the news to Jo but she hadn't returned from Toronto. Bartholemew asked if there was a message and I told him that I had some good news for Jo about her show. Well, he insisted on passing me on to Mr. Gladden and, of course, I told it to him. I hope I haven't committed a *faux pas* of some kind."

"Of course not." We chatted briefly about the turn in events and I hung up.


In the closet in my office was a stack of telephone books covering Manhattan and the nearby boroughs. The following morning it took me about fifteen minutes to extract all the William Naylors and W. Naylors. There were eighteen in all. An even dozen were quickly eliminated by phone and another was on 119th Street in the heart of Harlem, which made him unlikely. The rest were no-answers or the line was busy.

I informed Bartholemew that I was going into the city. On the parkway I listened to the news on the car radio. No mention of Naylor's death. But then, why would there be? There are an average of sixteen homicides in Manhattan and the boroughs on a given night. More if it's hot and humid.

I struck paydirt at my first stop in Queens. The house was a pleasant but undistinguished brick bungalow on a street shaded with great horse chestnut trees. The lawns of the houses nearby were well tended, and there were elaborate displays of flowers in what was obviously something of a neighborhood rivalry. Number twenty-seven was an exception. The grass was overgrown and weedy, and the hedges were ragged with unchecked growth. There were handbills strewn around the porch, and the windows were dull with the film of pollution.

I knocked on the door, not expecting a response, and there was none. I went next door and was greeted by a woman of about sixty in a faded chenille bathrobe. She had blue-tinted hair and heavy pancake makeup on exceedingly wrinkled skin. Beyond her, down a dark hallway, I could hear the sounds of a childish sibling quarrel above the mechanical natter of a television set. Could she tell me how I could get in touch with Mr. William Naylor?

"Wouldn't have the foggiest," she said. "I'm just the mother-in-law around here." She turned her head and bawled, "Darlene!"

A younger woman came slapping her slippers down the hallway. She had rollers in her hair and was wearing a vivid green halter with red shorts. The upper part of her body was comely, but from the waist down she was enormous, with mounding hips and marbled, cellulite thighs.

"He wants to know how can he get in touch with next door."

She looked at me appraisingly. "There's lots would like to know that."

"I'm sorry to bother you," I said. "There doesn't seem to

be anyone living there. Would you know of a forwarding address? Or would you know of anyone who would?''

She turned her head and howled ''Shaddup!'' at the tumult at the end of the hall. ''Why don't you ask Mrs. Naylor?''

''Hah!'' said the mother-in-law.

''Where could I reach her?''

''She's in there,'' said the mother-in-law, who had taken up a position behind the daughter-in-law, indicating with a crabbed forefinger over her shoulder.

''In there?'' I said, looking at the overgrown lawn and the debris around the door.

''Never comes out. Hasn't for donkey's years.''

''A month or two,'' the mother-in-law interjected.

At the end of the hallway, the skirmish had escalated into open warfare. There were the shrill sounds of anger and of a piece of furniture crashing, and then of crying and simultaneous accusations. The television set roared with laughter. The daughter-in-law turned to the mother-in-law and said with overdone politeness, ''Will you puh-leeze *do* something before they kill each other!''

''They won't listen to *me*. I'm just the mother-in-law around here,'' the woman said, but nonetheless went off.

''She even has the groceries delivered,'' the daughter-in-law said. ''The phone's still working—you can get a busy signal—but she don't answer.''

I decided to try again and went next door. There was no response, not so much as a shadow at the window or a movement of the curtains. I tore a sheet of paper from my notebook, printed my apartment telephone number on it, and added, ''Please call. A friend.'' I folded it and slipped it under the door but left a corner protruding. It was still visible as I looked back from the street.

''Told you,'' the daughter-in-law called out from her porch.

The other W. Naylor in Queens proved to be a sister, Wanda, a twin. She lived in a highrise apartment, one of a cluster overlooking 98th Street and Queens Boulevard. When I buzzed her apartment from the foyer, she demanded my name and address and what my business was and required me to stand facing the doorway so that she could get a good look at me on the closed-

222

circuit television. When finally I was admitted to the building and knocked on her door, she peered at me through the peephole before letting me in but was soon cordial and nonstop garrulous.

"You can't be too careful. Would you believe, we've had three muggings in the complex in the last month. In the last month! Three. It's just terrifying. I mean, it really is."

I commiserated with her and waited out the recital of her complaints about vandals, neighbors, children, the super's wife and the gang of road repairmen who were deliberately interrupting her sleep with their "clanging and banging" beneath her window at all hours. "And me with a heart problem. The heart, you know," she said, touching her chest. "I have to watch myself." I finally brought her to the point: could she put me in touch with her brother?

Much rueful shaking of her head. "You know, it's terrible to say this about your own brother, and him and me twins, but I haven't heard from him for months now. It must be a year. Yes, it'll be a year in September. Not one word. My only living blood-relative; the rest of them dead. All dead. My sister Joanna. My uncle Chet. Aunt Mavis. Her husband . . . . I never *could* remember his—"

"Your brother?" I prompted. "He has a house here in Queens?"

"In Queens? Oh, that. He left that months ago to go to California. California." She lowered her voice. "That wife of his is still there. Still there." She tapped her forehead. "Less said about that. I was telling Mrs. Watson—she lives down the hall—2506."

I broke in to forestall the minutiae. "Do you by any chance have his address in California? A phone number, perhaps?"

"Burbank, I think it is. Yes, Burbank. I'm pretty sure it's Burbank. Or is it Glendale? I have it written down somewheres. Now, let me see." She pulled at the flap of loose skin beneath her jaw, distracted by the need for concentrated thought.

"Do you know who he works for out there?"

"A trucking firm. Yes, a trucking firm. He used to work for that Mr. Gladden—you know, the one on the TV. Calls himself a preacher; doesn't even believe in God. Can you imagine: a preacher and he doesn't believe in God? I heard Jerry Falwell talking about him the other day. He's my favorite, Jerry Falwell. I used to be a fan of Jim and Tammy, but that was a long time—''

''You said you might have his telephone number written down. Or maybe the trucking firm where he works?''

She went to a small desk and rummaged about in a drawer. ''Bill . . . Bill . . . Bill . . . . Let me see, now. I'm sure it's here somewheres.'' She reached for her glasses, suspended on a cord about her neck. ''Here we are. Now, wait a minute here. . . . No, that's not it. Here we have it! Yes. It's where he works. Tri-Nat. Yes, that's it. Tri-Nat Trucking, Burbank, California. I was right—Burbank. I did say Burbank? . . . Bill was tellin' me they ship things to Canada and Mexico; that's where they get the name — Tri-Nat. You know — the United States, Canada and Mexico.''

Back in my apartment, I ignored the flashing light on my answering machine and placed a call to Tri-Nat Trucking in Burbank. ''Mr. William Naylor,'' I said, crisp, businesslike. ''I'm calling from New York.''

''I'll connect you with his secretary.''

A Miss Adamson was sorry, but Mr. Naylor wasn't in; he was in New York. Was there a message?

''Could you tell me where I might reach him? I'm sorry to trouble you, but it's important.''

''Yes. Well, he's staying at the Park Lane. You might try him there.'' She paused, considering. ''If it's really urgent, you might try this number.'' I scribbled it down.

The Park Lane switchboard reported a ''doesn't answer.'' Absently, I dialed the second number. Almost too late I realized that it was the number at the Gladden estate. As Bartholemew's voice answered by repeating the number, I replaced the receiver on its cradle.

I had only just done so when it rang. The voice, a woman's, was so soft I could barely hear it.

''Are you the man who left the note under my door this afternoon?''

''Yes, Mrs. Naylor,'' I said, trying to sound reassuring. ''Yes, I'm the one.''

"May I ask who you are and what you want?"

She certainly didn't sound deranged; her voice was quiet but substantial and her words were clearly articulated.

"I wanted to get in touch with Mr. Naylor," I said. I'd have to be careful not to speak of him in the past tense.

"Why?"

"Mrs. Naylor, would it be possible for me to come and see you?"

"You haven't told me why. Do you know my husband?"

"Well, actually no, but—"

"Then why do you want to get in touch with him?"

There was no avoiding it. "Mrs. Naylor, I work for Oscar Gladden. Mr. Naylor worked—works for him, and I thought that perhaps he could be helpful to me in—"

There was a click and the line went dead.

# TWENTY-ONE

I listened to the message on my machine: Call Victor Gladden. He wanted me to meet him on the ship. I said I didn't think that was a good idea, for reasons I'd explain later, and he proposed the TransLux Theater on 42nd Street just off Times Square.

The TransLux is a porn-house: barren, decrepit, sleazy. As agreed, I sat in the back row on the left aisle and watched the artless, joyless, passionless sexuality on the screen. It could be like this in a sensualist's hell, I thought: colossal rampant penises, great gaping vaginal maws, nonstop copulation — where the need dieth not and the fire is not quenched.

Victor felt his way into a seat beside me. Dressed in a shirt, sweater and jeans he looked less the vagrant. And he'd had a haircut.

"Why are we meeting here?" he asked.

"Because you suggested it, for god's sake."

"I mean, why not at the ship?"

"Because last time your father knew I was there."

He seemed pleased. "Were you followed today?"

"I don't think so."

Victor's attention was on the screen.

"Victor—"

"Just a minute."

The film broke, and after a moment the lights came on. There was whistling and sporadic clapping from the audience of no more than two dozen men.

"Let's get out of this place," I said. "I'll meet you in the departures lounge at the bus terminal."

The bus terminal at the corner of Eighth Avenue and 42nd Street is a squat, utilitarian building. Constructed of brick, it exposes ugly X-braces, possibly in an attempt to communicate permanence. On the mezzanine, a gesture has been made to relieve the barrenness by suspending flags and introducing gold-leaf decoration, but a visitor feels no welcome. The departures lounge on the lower level is a low-ceilinged room enclosed by smoked glass. Travelers sit on banks of seats, as though in a theater, but have only an unornamented wall to entertain them. I found a seat in the back row. Shortly, Victor appeared and came to sit beside me. I turned my back to the room and, without preliminaries, went to the point.

"Last time we talked, you hinted that your father's business was suspect for some reason or other. What I'm asking you now is this: do you have one ounce of concrete evidence?" Before he could reply I added, "Not suspicions, not speculation. Facts."

He looked at me appraisingly, the slightest smile forming. "What's happened, Mr. Carpenter? You were talking different the last time."

I decided to take a chance. "You remember I asked you about the man who had my job before me?"

"Yes."

"Well, he's dead. And his death had something to do with your father's business."

"How do you know that?"

"I know it. Believe me."

"What are you saying? That my father had him killed?"

"Of course not. I merely said he was dead."

"I don't know anything about that. All I'm saying is that my father is a crook."

"And I can introduce you to a Democrat who has proof that Ronald Reagan was a closet Communist." He made no response, so I said, "What makes you think your father is a crook? Facts, remember."

"Okay. So far, mostly suspicions. But where there's smoke

227

there's fire, right? Among other things, why the eight-foot wall and the barbed wire?''

''To protect your sister, maybe.''

''Sure, sure. Against who?'' He lowered his voice although there was no one within earshot. ''I've made friends with one of the guards.'' He was almost whispering, and I had to bend forward to hear him. ''He doesn't know who I am, of course, but from what he says and the hints he drops, there's something very funny going on. There's a barn on the property, he says. And in the barn, plenty of funny business. That's all I've been able to get so far.''

''Victor, look—''

''Whatever it is is connected with the barn. One of these nights I'm going out there and . . . .'' The sentence tailed off.

''Victor,'' I said, ''may I say something to you? Don't. Just plain don't. I don't want to go into it. Take my word. Okay? The place is filled with booby traps. There are dogs. You could get in deep trouble, believe me. Okay?''

He put a hand on my arm. ''I'll have something hard for you in a week to ten days.''

''Don't do anything foolish,'' I said, rising.

On the street I stopped, suddenly impelled to return to the terminal to reinforce the warning I'd given. I began to retrace my steps.

''Give you a lift?''

I turned, startled by the familiar voice. A limousine was easing to the curb, Oscar Gladden's great head at the open window. Rattled, I couldn't come up with a plausible excuse, so I said, ''Thanks. I was just going to hail a cab.''

Sacred Heart Saywell leaped out and opened a door. I got in. The limousine moved into the traffic, heading east on 42nd Street.

''Where can I drop you?'' Gladden asked.

''If it isn't inconvenient, at my apartment. I was just going to pick up my car and go out to the office.''

''Ride along with me. I'll have Say run you back into town when you're ready.''

I said ''Thanks,'' and settled back in the seat.

Gladden had a folded newspaper in his hand. ''Have you

seen this?" It was a paragraph in a political gossip column: "Insiders say that the Democratic National Committee is putting the heat on incumbent John Gallagher to bow out of the senatorial race. Sagging polls and recent allegations about his sleeping habits in Washington are said to be only two of the reasons."

"True?"

"I was talking to him earlier. Yes, he's got problems."

"Good," Gladden grunted. He leaned forward and opened a small refrigerator. "Something to drink?" I shook my head. "Some fruit?"

"Thanks. Just had lunch."

A bunch of grapes dangled from one hand. With the other he was pitching them into his mouth. "Lunch? At 42nd and Eighth Avenue?" He chuckled. "At the bus terminal?"

"The Oyster Bar at Penn Station," I said. "I was just stretching my legs afterward." I was furious at myself for giving an accounting, and more, for doing it lamely.

Pop, pop, pop went the grapes. "You'll have to be more careful where you go walking," he said. "One of the gay boys may take you home." He was still chuckling.

He seemed in a good mood. His tone, despite the jibes, was jovial. The car was silent except for the hollow popping of the grapes and the tiny explosions as those perfect white teeth bit into them.

"Josephine insists on my seeing that damned Indian," he said suddenly. "What's he want?"

"As I told you, I don't know. He won't tell me." To forestall his asking what I'd done about "dumping" Joshua, I pressed on. "Mr. Gladden, I'm at a loss. We seem to have abandoned the objective you specified the day you hired me. Your purpose, as you explained it, was not only to dupe the media but to expose it as exploitive, sensationalist and careless about facts. As I understood it, my job was to perpetrate some sort of hoax, suck the media into reporting it, pull the rug from under them and leave them with egg on their face. The plan I put before you would have done that. Instead, on a whim, based on a nothing story in the *Times*, you ordered me to use Joshua to manipulate the media. And now you want me to dump him."

"The point has been made," he said. "We've turned a cipher into a celebrity and we've manipulated the media in doing it. I know that. You know that. Why the hell should I care if anyone else does?"

I sought to keep the exasperation out of my voice. "But we haven't manipulated the media into doing anything other than covering a good human-interest story." I shrugged. "If it satisfies you to leave it as it is, fine."

"No, it doesn't satisfy me," he snapped. "But post mortems bore the hell out of me, so let's drop it!" He was silent for a moment, wiping his lips with a handkerchief. "Anyway, as I told you, I've got other fish to fry. Much bigger fish." He gave me a quick sideways glance. "Maybe even one for Mr. Tony Carpenter if he keeps his eye on the ball."

The car turned south on Second Avenue and I spent a moment pondering Gladden's words. I was about to ask him what he had in mind when he broke the extended silence.

"I've been meaning to have a word with you for some time," he said, and paused. When he continued, it was as though, uncharacteristically, he was weighing each sentence. "Josephine is, as you know, my only child. She's very important to me; nothing else is so important." He paused again, looking out the window. "Unfortunately, she seems drawn to you. I'd assumed it would be a passing thing." He leaned forward to turn off the radio that had been whispering in the background. "Josephine is not experienced in, shall we say, human relationships, and I would be very upset if she were, in any way, to be made unhappy." He turned to look at me and his voice was flat. "Have I made myself clear?"

I met his gaze and spoke as deliberately as he had. "Mr. Gladden, if Jo is as important to you as you say she is, I hope you'll have the wisdom to stay out of her emotional life. She is as important to me as she is to you, and believe me, I would be very upset if she were made unhappy."

Our eyes locked. I was looking into a crevasse in a glacier and was suddenly chilled. But if we were talking as peers I would seize the opportunity.

"Mr. Gladden, we seem to be speaking our minds. There's something that's been bothering me for some time. Ours is supposed to be a confidential relationship, so I'm curious as to why you have misled me about my predecessor. It was obvious when I settled into my office that someone had occupied it. And recently two or three people have mentioned in passing that a William Naylor preceded me. Now, it makes no difference to me that someone did the job before me, but I'm curious as to why, when I specifically asked you about it, you misled me?''

I was watching for a flickering of his gaze, a wavering, anything that would betray what he was thinking, but he hadn't so much as blinked. If there was any change, it was that the cold intensified. I decided to press on. ''I wonder, too, Mr. Gladden, if you would tell me why you got rid of Naylor?'' Even that didn't faze him. ''I would like to avoid his mistakes,'' I added. It took all my resolve to keep my eyes fixed on his. Say sounded the horn in traffic and with the interruption Gladden turned away.

''There seems to be some confusion in your mind,'' he said, looking out at the passing storefronts, ''about who is the employer here and who is the employee. I don't account to the people who work for me. Bill Naylor has nothing to do with you, and your work has nothing to do with what he was doing. In a word, it's none of your business.'' He paused and then turned to me. ''I *will* add this: you have one trait in common with him—you have a talent for getting out of line.'' He picked up a small microphone built into the armrest. ''Say.''

''Yes, sir,'' came the voice on the intercom.

''Pull over at the next corner. At the pipe shop.''

The car drew to the curb. Gladden reached into his jacket and brought out a wallet. He extracted a $500 bill and handed it to me.

''Do you see that shop there?'' He pointed. ''I'm short of cigars. Pick up a box for me, please. They know my brand.'' His voice was smooth as poured honey. As I got out of the car, he pulled the door closed. ''We'll go on ahead. You can follow on by taxi.''

The limousine pulled away and left me standing on the sidewalk, the money in my hand.

When I arrived at the Gladden estate, Gus Longo was on duty at the gate. He stepped into the road, hand upraised to check

231

the cab. When he saw that I was within, he waved the driver through. I signaled to Gus that I wanted a word with him, and he approached the window.

"Nice to see you, Mr. Carpenter."

"It's good to see you, Gus. You've been away."

He made a small tilt of his head. "Nothin'. Just a little job I do."

"You're away from time to time."

"A few days every so often. A little job for Mr. G. Like a vacation," he added. For some reason this amused him and he smiled. "Right, like a vacation." He stepped back and the cab drove on.

I decided, first, to see if Jo was around. As I climbed the circular stairway to her studio, I heard voices. When my eyes came level with the floor I saw Jo at an easel and, on a riser, Joshua, feet apart, head held back, looking off. He turned his eyes to me and winked.

"Hold it," Jo said, working with bold strokes on the canvas as she fixed the pose. "Hi, darling. Just be one minute."

I stood behind her, watching, filled with admiration for the skill with which she distorted the lines of the body to communicate movement and life and emotion. Joshua made an excellent model. His body was lean and had a fluid grace. As I watched Jo block in the planes of his face and the tilt of his jaw, I found myself wondering: what is his new life doing to this man?

"There!" she exclaimed. "That'll do for now." She gave me a quick embrace and went to wash up. "We're going down to see Father," she announced from the sink. She was in high spirits. Joshua was betraying signs of nervousness.

"I was with him not an hour ago," I said, "and I don't think the time is right. You know he's said no to seeing Joshua, not once but a dozen times."

"So, this time he says yes. Off we go."

We went down the stairs to the entrance hallway. To the left was the door that led to the parking garage. As we approached the car I could hear the humming of the generator. Jo tapped on the window. "Father?" Gladden's voice told her to enter. She signed to Joshua and me to follow.

Oscar Gladden's bulk was splayed on a reclining chair. Plastic tubes led from an arm to a suspended bottle and to the dialysis machine. He pushed himself upright as we entered. As he saw Joshua, his face darkened. Jo, crouched beneath the low roof, kissed him on the cheek.

"We've come to beard the lion," she said with a laugh, and then said to Joshua and me, "Sit down. Sit down." We settled uncomfortably on jump seats. "Father, Joshua has something he wants to discuss with you. He's being secretive about it, but it's very important to him and I promised you'd talk to him."

As Joshua made a tentative clearing of his throat, Gladden said, "Fine, I've been wanting to have a word with him." He took a sip of water from a glass on a table by his side. "Now, my young Indian friend," he said, turning to Joshua, "when you first came to see me, what did you want? You wanted two things: a way to get back at Republic Motors and some money for your dead friend's widow. You now have both of those things. I'm informed that well over a hundred thousand dollars in contributions have already come in and that the total will probably double that. And, I'm told, Republic is offering to settle. My advice to you is take it. Go back to the reserve or to your job and forget the whole thing. You got what you wanted. How many men can say that?"

"I have you to thank for that," Joshua said, his voice hesitant but gaining in assurance as he continued. "And I want you to know I appreciate it. But the whole picture has changed. The issues are much larger. People are looking to me; I can't turn my back on them. There's a big anti-nuclear protest planned and I've promised to . . . ." He'd begun to flounder under Gladden's direct gaze. "But that wasn't what I wanted to talk about. I was hoping that you might consider—"

"Now you listen to me, Mr. Crown," Gladden said forcefully but not unkindly. "Get out while you're ahead. Forget all this protest crap or first thing we know you'll be marching with a bunch of bearded crazies carrying signs saying 'Save the Great Sea Turtle' or 'Ban Hockey Violence' or some other damn fool nonsense. They'll use you like the tobacco shops once used wooden Indians — as a shill." He settled back in his chair. "Those are my final words on the subject."

"But Mr. Gladden, I—"

"Good-bye, Mr. Crown."

"But if you would just—"

"Good-*bye,* Mr. Crown."

As we rose to leave, Gladden said, "Carpenter, stay a moment." When the door had closed on Jo and Joshua, he asked, "Was this your idea?"

"Partly."

"Well, don't pull anything like it again. And do what I told you. Dump the Indian. He's become a nuisance."

I said nothing, but reached into a pocket and brought out the $500 bill he'd given me in the car. To my surprise, he didn't flare in anger. "Were they out of my brand?" he asked, an amused smile on his lips.

"I don't know," I said. "I'm not an errand boy."

He pushed against the arms of the chair, reclined and closed his eyes. "So you're not an errand boy," he said wearily.

Reentering the house, I met Joshua coming down the main staircase. We paused in front of the aquarium.

"What was it you wanted to talk to Mr. Gladden about?" I asked.

"I haven't given up," he said. I was surprised at his buoyancy of spirit. "Jo says she'll have a word with him about it."

"About what?"

"It's a really great idea," he said. "I want him to put me on his daily show. As a regular. He already has people teaching physical fitness and meditation and so on. I could be what you might call the representative of the ordinary guy, the working man; there's millions of us. It would really increase his ratings."

"But what would you talk about?"

"What would I talk about? There's plenty to talk about. And I've had tons of experience in the medium the last few weeks. Right? I could tell them, for instance, how I, a highsteeler, a nobody, took on the big guys and how, by following Gladden's teachings, they can do the same. It would be especially powerful coming from me, an American Indian."

"But I thought you didn't like to be thought of as an Indian?"

"That was before I learned that what really matters today is exposure. These days you can take a hat-check girl or a cab-driver and, with the right kind of promotion and media know-how, sell them to the public. Even make them big stars. It's a matter of merchandising. Indians were the original Americans; they've got plenty to say to today's Americans. Some of our legends are a lot like what Mr. Gladden teaches. . . .'' His zeal began to flag.

"Obie tells me the personal appearances are falling off," I said. "And the mail."

"That's just Obie," he said with a show of impatience. "I mean, it's not his cup of tea. He mostly promotes authors and movie people—you know, out there plugging a book or a film. One-shot stuff." The lemon shark slid by and caught the corner of his eye, distracting him for a moment. "Right now's the bad time of year."

We were interrupted by Bartholemew, standing at the top of the stairs. "Oh, there you are," he said. "There's a long-distance call for you." He raised an eyebrow. "From San Bernardino. Mrs. Carpenter."


Maggie was sweet as honey-pie. "How *are* you. It's been *ages*."

She'd run into a friend from back east at the Farmer's Market who had told her I had joined up with Oscar Gladden, and "Wasn't *that* this week's big surprise!" I was "the last one in the world" she would have thought would be working for Oscar Gladden. She watched him every morning and that was the reason for the call. That, and remembering all the good times we'd had together.

"Remember?" she asked, her voice silken.

I couldn't resist it, "Speaking of good times, what happened to your friend, the Hyundai salesman? He was on a religious kick, as I remember it. Only it was Jerry Falwell, if memory serves."

"Oh, *him!*"

"Him, yes. And you. And most of our furniture. And our savings account at Chase Manhattan."

"That's not *like* you," Maggie said.

"What's not like me?"

"Being bitter. Holding a grudge. It's not *like* you."

"In this case it's like me."

"What you're doing is letting the bad outweigh the good. There's good and bad in *every*one. In every *thing*. Reverend Gladden was talking about that just this morning: letting the *good* outweigh the bad. Knowing you were working for him, I got to thinking: if you're one of his followers, you must believe, like he says, that good things are more *substantial*—more *positively charged* is the way he puts it—and that they *outweigh* the bad. Think of the good things there were between us."

"I seldom listen to Oscar Gladden," I said.

"I don't *believe* you. You're just saying that. How could you be *around* a man like that and not be different?"

"Maggie," I said, "what's the reason for this call? There must be something you want."

"Now that's not nice. No, there's nothing special. It was just that I was watching Reverend Gladden and thinking about you actually working for him and I thought: well, I'll just ring up Tony and say hello."

"Hello, Maggie. And, sorry, good-bye."

"No, no, no. Wait just one minute. Don't hang up. There *is* something else. I just thought you'd like to know that—that Mark's possible."

"Mark's possible? You've lost me."

"Mark—the son you wanted so badly. I just wanted you to know that Mark's *possible*. I was at the gynecologist's here—Dr. Harmony. He's *very* good. Audrey, you've never met her, told me about him, and he says there's no reason why not. The old problem's all cleared up, he says. And listening to Reverend Gladden talking about how the good outweighs the bad and all that, I thought: I'll give Tony a ring and see how he is."

"Maggie—"

"Don't say anything for just a minute. Okay? Let me just speak my piece. Okay? We *all* make mistakes, right? *All* of us. Okay, I've made my share, I'll admit that. But there's never *really* been anyone but you."

"Look, Maggie, I don't want to nit-pick, but there *has* been someone other than me. Your Hyundai salesman most recently —or at least I presume most recently. And Jim Everton in apartment 801, remember? The rep from Simon and Schuster—Bob whatever-his-name-was. Jeezus, Maggie, the suburban editor at the *Register*—''

''They were *nothing* to me.''

''They may have meant nothing to you, but they bloody well meant something to me!''

''All right. But I've *changed*. Reverend Gladden has helped me to see that I've been *negative*-oriented, and that—''

''Maggie.''

''Yes?''

''It's over, Maggie. Over.''

''Well, it may be for you—and I can understand how you feel—but I'm *positive*-oriented these days and I'm coming to New York. As soon as I can wind up a couple of—''

''Maggie. Don't. Life moves on.''

''No. As Reverend Gladden says: you can't erase the past but you *can* begin a new page.''

''But there isn't going to be a new page. At least for us.''

''I don't want to talk about it on the phone. I'll be in touch when I get to New York. In the meantime, Tony, go with God.''

# TWENTY-TWO

I am obese,'' said Oscar Gladden, ''not because of a glandular disorder but because I choose to live life to the fullest.''

He, Jo and I were at dinner. Gladden had eaten an enormous meal and was topping it off with a bowl of cantaloupe and melon balls drenched in port. He had sustained a positively ebullient mood through the past three days: ready with quips, filled with zest, loosing his tumult of laughter at the slightest provocation. After my confrontations with him over the cigars and my relationship with Jo, I'd expected him to be at his arrogant worst, but, as so often happened, I was surprised by his unpredictability.

Now, after a magnificent feast, with the servants gone, with the chandelier dimmed and with the evening light mellowed by candelabra, Gladden smiled affectionately at Jo and waxed expansive. She had provoked his response by chiding him gently about his weight.

He leaned back in his chair, lofted a rolling ball of cigar smoke to the ceiling, and replied, ''I am a hedonist. I take pleasure from life. From food, among other things. Most people go to the table locked in a struggle with themselves. You, Jo, are so afflicted. So is Carpenter, there. You spend much of your life begrudging the singular pleasures of food. That crusty, buttered roll to which you said a reluctant no beckons me to a second. The dessert you nibbled at ravishes my palate. You frowned and turned away when the chocolated cherries were offered, I had three.''

"Yes, I noticed," Jo said with a mother's tone of reprimand.

"And when you do succumb to the temptations of taste, the pleasure is alloyed by the guilt that dogs you afterwards. I say, to hell with calories! *Enjoy!*"

He drew again on the cigar, raised a vaporous ring above his head and jetted a stream of smoke through it. "I see these health faddists—scrawny, wrinkled, humorless, the lot of them; their lives filled with prohibitions, the lot of them—saying no to most of life's pleasures on the premise that by so doing they'll achieve a long life. They're fools; old age isn't something to be coveted. Ask yourself: what is the lot of most old people? Sentiment aside, are they serene, fulfilled, contented, happy? On the contrary: to a majority of the elderly, old age means loneliness, a sequence of assorted aches and pains, the consciousness of their own disintegration and the daily awareness that their lives are guttering out like a spent candle. In the end they become a burden to their families and an expense against their estate. They give their life savings not to their flesh and blood but to doctors and hospitals, and to the ravens who operate nursing homes. In what age group is the suicide rate highest? Among the old. It's an illusion of the young that old age is good. The 'golden years' are mostly dross."

I was about to interject but restrained myself; it was obvious that he hadn't yet fully made his case. He reached into a dish of roasted almonds and tossed a handful into his mouth, crunching them zestfully.

"Oscar Wilde said: 'The only thing I can't resist is temptation.' I approve that. If I'm tempted by food, I eat. If I'm tempted by a woman—" He glanced at Jo. "You will forgive me, my darling—I make love. I do what I enjoy and to hell with guilt. The pungency of a good cigar gives me pleasure, and I don't spoil it by fretting about whether or not it's good for me. And if I'm of a mind to drink good booze to where I'm tipsy, a pox on all those doomsayers with their cautions and frowns and gloom. All hail the appetites! They sustain life and perpetuate life and make life worth living. So *what* if it's not good for me! The only certainty in life is death, and I refuse to negate most of life by trying to postpone its conclusion."

"Yes, Father, but the strain on your heart."

He smiled at her as he might have when she was a child. "I have a question for you. Why do all those fitness addicts jog or play squash or work out? What's their objective? Isn't it to strengthen their various muscles and to drive up their heart rate so that another muscle—for that's what the heart is—is strengthened? Isn't that why they put themselves in the way of jogger's-knee and tennis-elbow, or sacrifice an eye to a squash ball?"

He paused to draw again on his cigar. "You see, most people totally misread someone who is obese and active as I am. Contrary to what you may think, I'm extraordinarily fit. My legs, for instance, are much stronger than the ordinary man's. Much!" He brought his palms down on his massive thighs with a thud that was transferred to the floor and to the soles of my feet. "They *have* to be. Perhaps you'll grasp how powerful they are by imagining what would happen to your legs if, every day, you carried around with you a 150-pound weight. All day! Standing, walking, going up and down stairs — an extra 150 pounds. You couldn't do it, of course. But suppose you built yourself to where you could. Can you imagine the strength you'd have? The same is true of my back, of my arms, of every part of my body. Surely you've noticed that the world-class weightlifters are full-bodied men."

I saw him absorbing Naylor's blows on his forearms and sending him reeling with thrusts of his belly.

"That may be okay for you, Father," Jo broke in, "but what if you were a woman? A woman doesn't dare be overweight."

"Overweight?" he asked. "Who is the arbiter of what is overweight? I'll tell you who — doctors. Doctors, whose dicta about health are repudiated as often as they're confirmed. Doctors and the fashion arbiters, and the entertainment moguls — all of whom have led us to worship slimness and youthfulness. But what we Westerners forget is that their standards obtain only in our civilization. Can you picture a scrawny Buddha? No. There he sits, his powerful legs entwined in the lotus position, his round face serene, the globe of his great belly attesting to the fact that rather than deny life he enjoys it. I ask you, who is the embodiment of happiness, the rectitudinous Jesus or the serene Buddha?"

Jo was shaking her head slowly in a feigned resignation.

When it became clear that she was going to offer nothing more by way of rebuttal, Gladden turned to me. "No comment by the representative of the press?" he said. He was clearly enjoying himself enormously.

"I've been listening," I said noncommitally.

"But disagreeing?"

"By and large."

"With what do you take issue?"

"It's not a matter of taking issue. It's your view. I happen to see things differently."

"You happen to see things differently," he said, an edge entering his voice, a pinkness beginning to suffuse his face. "Perhaps, then, you will enlighten us. How, differently?"

I shrugged. "It's of no importance. It just seems to me that you stack the cards."

"The representative of the press says I stack the cards." There was a touch of asperity in his tone. "Wherein, pray, do I stack the cards?"

The cigar was lodged in a corner of his mouth now and his teeth were clamped on it. One part of my mind was counseling prudence but another was pushing me to challenge this man who had come to control so much of my life. A break with him was coming; I was beginning to recognize its inevitability. I was approaching the point where—no matter what the inducement might be, no matter how stubbornly I normally resist abandoning a project undertaken—I must part company with this arrogant tyrant. Since that night in the barn, I was beginning to see him as an incarnation of evil. Even more important, my association with him was beginning to siphon off my self-respect. Here he was: this proclaimer of a gospel, this monumental hypocrite, as Johnny Gallagher had called him, typically, boasting of fitness and a zest for life and all the while larded with obesity and bedeviled by the demons of hypochondria. Okay, I would challenge him.

"The indulgence of one's appetite for food and drink does indeed yield pleasure," I said, taking care not to sound confrontational. "But it is followed—as you must surely know; I certainly do—by indigestion and flatulence and, if you will forgive me, corpulence." I hesitated, realizing that I was going to have difficulty choosing my words. "We do understand," I said, looking into Gladden's eyes, "that we are having a discussion, that I am speaking generally?"

"Yes, yes. Of course," he said with an impatient flutter of a hand.

"Very well then," I continued. "The fat man's muscles"—I had considered and rejected the term *overweight* — "may be strong but his arteries are caked with plaque. He can't run without gasping. He can't climb stairs without wheezing. He can't tie his shoelaces without grunting. And it has been my observation that satiety—from food or sex or what have you—leads not to an intensification but to a deadening of the senses."

Perspiration was glinting on Gladden's brow. The smile remained fixed in place but it was now more a grimace. An inner voice was whispering, Take care! But I had had enough of the check-rein.

"You stack your cards," I said, "because you pit gluttony against asceticism. You compare excesses, and that isn't the choice. Personally, I choose epicureanism. I want to enjoy life, too, but not to the point that it may kill me. As for old age, I'll take my chances. And if it becomes intolerable—as it may for anyone, fit or not—it isn't all that hard to have done with."

"Well now," said Jo, folding her napkin and putting it on the table, "isn't *that* a happy thought!"

Gladden's smile was still fixed. "Lately, Carpenter," he said, "you and I seem to be at polar opposites more often than not. Wouldn't you agree?"

"Yes, I would," I said equably. "But surely you wouldn't want a sycophant working for you. Or would you?"

The smile erased. The voice was sharp. "Carpenter—"

Jo pushed back her chair and rose suddenly from the table. A crystal goblet toppled and shattered. "What a lovely meal," she said quickly. "And now, Father, I'm afraid we have to leave you. Tony and I have tickets for the theater and if we don't hurry we'll miss the curtain."

I looked at her blankly—tickets for the theater? She went to her father, touched a cheek to his, and off we went. To drive about aimlessly, as it developed, avoiding any reference to the conversation at the table. And thence finally to my apartment where we made somewhat unsatisfactory love.

The story was carried in the New York *Times* on page fourteen under a one-column head. I noticed it at breakfast only when I spilled some tomato juice on the paper.

## PROTEST RAINED OUT
## AT NUCLEAR REACTOR

Middletown, Conn (UPI) A protest by the Association for Radiation Control against the nuclear power station on the outskirts of Middletown was rained out Saturday afternoon when a violent thunderstorm forced the dissenters to disperse. The storm included winds up to 56 mph and pea-size hailstones.

The demonstration was one of a number in recent weeks mounted by citizens' action groups opposed to the nuclear plant which provides electric power to the area.

Leading the protesters was Joshua Crown, a Caughnawaga Indian who came to national attention through his dramatic protest against a major automobile manufacturer. At one point in the protest, Mr. Crown scaled the urn-shaped chimney at the heart of the complex carrying a hand-lettered sign. High winds forced him down.

State police arrested ten of the demonstrators. Charges were laid and they were released.

William Jermyn of Teaneck, New Jersey, president of the Association for Radiation Control, admitted that the size of the turnout was "something of a disappointment," but attributed it to the weather. Police estimated the number at fewer than twenty-five.

I had Obie Berenson drop by the apartment to wind up the services Tad Butler and Associates had been providing. I hadn't disclosed to him that Oscar Gladden was his client, and it seemed never to have occurred to him to question my interest in the protest against Republic Motors.

"I'm sorry you've decided to terminate our association," he said. "I've enjoyed it. Although, quite frankly, it hasn't always been the easiest account to handle. I trust you're happy with what's been done."

"I am. I am. You said yourself we were approaching the end of the road."

"Yes. Right. Quite frankly there are limits to the milk you can get from a given cow."

"You might bring me up to date on where we stand."

He opened an expensive leather folder on his lap. "To be frank with you, we've pretty well slowed to a walk." He looked up. "Would it be useful if I gave you the figures for the past week?" I nodded. "Here we have it, then. Requests for interviews: network television, none. Local television, one. Network radio, two. Newspapers: metropolitan dailies, none. Other dailies, two. Major weeklies, none. Other weeklies, five — I should explain that other weeklies includes small-town papers, that kind of thing. To be frank with you, not very useful." He went back to the folder. "Periodicals—"

"Thank you. That gives me the picture. How's the mail?"

"Off drastically. Mostly personal letters. Solicitations. Crank letters, of course. They, like the poor, are with us always."

"You said something about the account being difficult to handle."

"Oh, please don't misread me," he said quickly. He put his hands, exactly centered, on top of the folder. "To be perfectly frank, it hasn't been easy for Mr. Crown—the media attention, I mean. No reflection, you understand. Some of the biggest names find the pressure, shall we say, a little too much." He gave a small laugh and mimed downing a drink. "We won't mention names, right?"

"Right."

"I should get nursery-pay for the ones I've had to tuck in bed."

"I'm sure."

"Or, to be frank with you, for finding them company, shall we say, to see them through the night." He looked at me with a raised eyebrow, dying to gossip.

"Off the top of your head," I said, "can you tell me how

244

much money has come in? The last report I saw, it was some-where around a hundred thousand.''

"I'm afraid I don't have that figure. Mr. Crown set up a trust. We've been forwarding everything to him." A touch of anxiety entered his voice when he saw my brows draw down. "He gave me to understand that he'd discussed it with you."

"Yes, of course. I just thought you might have the figure." I rose from my chair and extended a hand. "It's been a pleasure."

"Yes. Right. Absolutely. Tell Mr. Crown good-bye from me. And good luck. I'll be frank with you; he may need it."

Taking him to the door, I saw that a note had been pushed beneath it. I opened the door. There was no one in sight in the hallway. Alone, I ripped open the envelope. The message was scrawled in pencil and was signed with the letter V. "Very inter-esting development. Meet me tonite. The bus terminal. 6 P.M. Urgent."

Trying to reach Joshua, I called the Vanderbilt Y. He had checked out three days earlier and had left as a forwarding address Tad Butler and Associates. Obie Berenson's secretary had no idea where he'd moved to but suggested his home in Caughnawaga. A sullen Jeannie Crown told me she hadn't seen him in weeks and didn't care if she never heard from him again. "If you see him, tell him to send me some money. I don't even have enough for cigarets." The secretary at Local 40 had no recent information. The Association for Radiation Control proved to be an answering machine. I was casting about for some other lead when the telephone rang.

It was Berenson with the suggestion that I try the Wigwam in Brooklyn. "It's a hangout for Caughnawagans. The people in the neighborhood call it the Indian Bank—they cash the iron-workers' checks. I know Mr. Crown goes there. To be frank with you, he's been going there quite a lot lately."

I called, and someone I took to be the barman said that he hadn't seen Joshua for a day or two but that I should call back around nine. "Bein' a Friday, there'll be a lot of the men in." I left my telephone number and the message that Joshua should get in touch with me as soon as he came in.

I'd arranged to meet Jo for dinner at the Hellbox at six-thirty and called to push it back to seven o'clock. Feeling like a refugee from a television movie, I took a taxi to Eighth Avenue at 40th and, making sure that no one was following me, walked the two blocks to the bus terminal. The clock in the waiting room read 5:56. Half an hour later, irritated, I took a cab to the Hellbox. When Jo arrived, I had a two-drink jump on her.

"Why," she asked, "is it called the Hellbox?"

"The hellbox was the bin in the composing room of a newspaper into which lead type was thrown after it had been used," I said. My mood caused me to add, sourly, "This one's a depository for the obsolete."

"Oh my!" she said.

"Sorry. It's just that mere anarchy is loosed upon the world. My little world, anyway."

"Oh my!"

"Well it is, damn it! Everything's screwed up. I have it that Joshua's drinking like a parched camel and I haven't been able to track him down. I'm mixed up in an unsavory bit of business in Washington. I'm having trouble with your father — it gets worse rather than better—and I don't know what to do about it. And," I added, "I'm worried about your brother."

She showed immediate concern. "Something's happened to Victor?"

"No, no. Nothing to worry about. It's just that we were supposed to meet at six and he didn't show. The crazy kid fancies himself a private eye. He's been snooping about your father's property, and—"

"Our house? Does Father know?"

"I don't know. I don't think so." I told her about Victor cultivating one of the guards and about the note under the door of my apartment.

As I talked, she grew visibly troubled. "He can be *so* stubborn. You don't think he'd do anything foolish. Perhaps we should check his room."

"I don't know where he lives."

"I do."

She instructed the taxi-driver and he pulled up before what had once been a middle-class tenement but was now a rooming-house. We climbed to the third floor on a narrow, creaking

246

stairway illuminated by a single bare bulb, flinching at the smell and stepping carefully amid the debris. When there was no response to my knocking, Jo suggested calling the police.

"Stop worrying," I said. "There's nothing wrong. He got hung up somewhere and couldn't make it to the bus terminal on time. He has a telephone. We can call him later."

I was uneasy about the neighborhood, so we walked quickly to Eighth Avenue where I hailed a cab. "Forget the Hellbox," I said with a small show of exuberance. "We'll pick up Smedley and have dinner at the Wigwam. It's in Brooklyn and I'm told Joshua hangs out there. Atmosphere! Authenticity!"

"What's it like?"

"I have no idea. I'm told it's the Caughnawagan ironworkers' home away from home."

The Wigwam wasn't far from what I'd imagined: not fancy but clean and informal, with an old-fashioned dark walnut bar and small tables for those interested in dinner. The menu was hand-printed in English and Mohawk, and I noted that they sold Canadian beer. I ordered two Molson's.

Joshua was at the bar surrounded by a group of cronies. Occupied with recounting some incident that required much acting-out and elicited frequent outbursts of boisterous laughter, he didn't see us come in. For want of a better option we ordered cabbage rolls with home-fried potatoes and corn on the cob. We'd just begun to eat when Joshua saw us, let out a whoop and came, mug of beer in hand, to our table.

"White-eye boss-man come to home of Mohawk," he said, intoning the words. "How."

I took the cue: responding in a sepulchral voice and extending an arm, palm forward, "How."

Joshua grinned. "How? Sunny side up, with bacon well-done and a side order of toast. Yuk, yuk, yuk."

Jo was investigating the cabbage roll with a fork. Joshua sat down, going off-balance for a moment as he pulled back the chair. "To what do we owe the honor?" he asked. He looked at Jo. "An' the pleasure?"

Her voice was contained. "It's a simple matter of the mountain and Muhammad."

Joshua threw his head back, draining his glass. It was

whisked away and another put in its place. He swept the head to the floor with a forefinger and half emptied the mug in a single draught. "I was jus' tellin' the guys 'bout your house. That crazy fish-tank! Whoo-ee!"

"When are you going to finish that pose for me?" Jo said.

"Why not?" Joshua said. "Why'n hell not?" He banged the mug on the table and a gout of beer leaped over the rim onto the tablecloth.

Improvising, I said, "Jo and I are thinking about taking a run up to Caleb's village on the weekend. Come with us."

He looked at me, his head bobbing, the amber eyes dulled by the beer. "Caleb's? You'll be bored shitless. 'Scuse my French," he said, turning to Jo. He leaned his elbows on the table, lost in vague thought for a moment. Then he roused himself. "Hey! What're you guys doin' in the wilds of Brooklyn?" He laughed. "Lookin' for another nobody?" He wiped his lips with a forearm and presented his face to me. "Hey, Mister, how 'bout me?"

"I thought you were enjoying it," I said.

"Great on the way up, eh? The fat man pays the shot an' Tony here lights the match. Like a skyrocket. Whoosh!" He flung an arm upward, shouting, "Look out below!" and released the beer mug. It fell to the floor, shattering. A man came from behind the bar with a short-handle broom and dustpan and swept up the shards.

Jo said, "How about the weekend? Want to come with us?"

He brightened. "Why not? Why'n hell not?" He picked up Jo's half-empty bottle of beer and handed it to her. "Drink up. We're off to see the wizard, the won'erful wizard of Oz. Oz— Ozzie Gladden, get it? The won'erful wizard of Oz." He was beating time on the table with the beer bottle.

It was an awkward half hour before we could extricate ourselves, by which time Joshua's head was on his forearms and his forearms were on the table and he was muttering unintelligibly to himself.

The return to Manhattan was a somber one. There had been a sudden, heavy downpour that had as quickly ended. The streets were gleaming and the gutters were rippling with runoff. Shallow pools on the sidewalks replicated the neon storefronts.

Occasional droplets sent fragments of light skittering like water-bugs on their surfaces. Now midtown Manhattan lay ahead. The laundered air was crystal clear and the fairyland of the city's towers glowed golden in the dusk. Flat gray clouds, their under-bellies lit by the effulgence of the city, had lopped off the tops of the taller buildings as cleanly as a scythe might level a field.

"Whenever the city is as beautiful as this," Jo said in a low voice, "I can forgive it all its seaminess and squalor."

It was the first thing said in the ten minutes or so since we'd left the bar. I was depressed and not in the mood for conver-sation. Jo seemed content to sit in silence, looking out of the window at the empty streets. A tow truck went by, lights flash-ing, a shiny Lincoln behind, its nose high, its rear accordion-pleated.

We were on the Brooklyn bridge when Jo said in a small voice, "Could we please go check on Victor?"

Now that it was dark, the street where he lived seemed even more menacing. I left Smedley at the curb, acutely aware that it might be stripped when we returned. In the gloom at the top of the stairs I knocked on the door to Victor's room. A television set blared from within. When there was no response, I tried the handle and the door swung inward.

*Blood!* On the floor, spattered on the walls, on the drawn window shade, on the face of the television set. *Victor!* On the floor in a pool of blood, one leg twisted bonelessly beneath him, the head thrown back, part of his jaw blown away, the face a grotesque mask of gore.

I stepped in front of Jo, seizing her by the upper arms, block-ing the sight of the body on the floor. Her eyes were wide and staring and her mouth was open. She was panting like an animal but with barely audible sounds. I turned her and, although she was unable to move her legs, managed to get her to the top step and sitting on it. She had begun to weep, with hoarse shud-derings, and was clinging to the newel-post. I went into the room, turned off the television set, which was emitting the stock market quotations, pulled the door closed and returned to sit beside her, holding her very tightly, striving to will strength into her. It was five minutes before I felt that I could leave her long enough to run down to the entrance hallway where I'd seen a pay telephone.

The police swarmed around the body like blue-bottle flies. Two uniformed patrolmen were first to arrive. Another came thumping up the stairs and more or less stood guard until a detective in plainclothes climbed wearily to the landing and took charge. I heard him tell one of the patrolmen to call for the crime scene unit and the medical examiner. Soon the hallway and Victor's room were overrun with men taking photographs, making measurements, dusting for fingerprints, inscribing notes. They searched drawers, cupboards, closets and under the bed. Jo had become almost catatonic and had been taken away on a stretcher by gentle burly men in white. They persuaded me that it would be better that I didn't go with them; she would be put under sedation at the hospital and it would be more helpful if I would go with the sergeant to the station.

The Mid-town South Precinct in Manhattan is on 35th Street, east of Eighth Avenue, and is, if anything, grubbier than the 17th; even the identifying sign outside has lost some of its letters. Its officers speak of being in the "garment district" and, paradoxically, are proud that the precinct is, they proclaim, the "busiest in the world." I drove there with a Detective Sergeant Alex Kosiosko, giving him a lift, noticing only later that my hubcaps were gone and that someone had spray-painted the words "Up yours!" on the trunk.

Kosiosko was a Barney Miller look-alike, but leaner and more taciturn. He led me to a tiny, cluttered, second-floor office in which there were two desks, each heaped with papers and untidy file-folders, where we talked for the better part of half an hour, by which time I was growing testy. I could see that he wasn't happy either.

"Okay now," he said, looking up from his notes, "let's just double back. You and Miss Gladden go to Victor Gladden's room—I'm referring to the first time—sometime around seven-fifteen. Miss Gladden is worried about her brother. She's worried, you said, because Victor was supposed to meet you at six o'clock at the bus terminal but didn't show. Why the bus terminal? Was he coming in from somewhere?"

"No."

"Were you?"

"No."

"It seems an odd place to meet. Noisy. Crowded. Why not at your apartment or at his place?"

"I don't know. It was his suggestion. Maybe because it was only a few blocks from his room."

"Then why not in his room?"

"I've told you, I don't know."

"Now, Victor doesn't show. You tell his sister and right away she's worried and the two of you go to his room and he isn't there. Or at least he doesn't answer the door. Now, what was she worried about?"

"I don't know."

"She says she's worried but she doesn't say what she's worried about. I wouldn't think her brother missing an appointment would be enough to worry her. There must have been more to it than that. But, whatever it was, she didn't tell you."

"That's right."

"And you didn't ask?"

"No, I didn't."

"Then again, on your way back from Brooklyn, she's still worried and wants to check things out. And again she doesn't say what's worrying her and you don't ask."

"He's her brother, for chrissake!"

"And you're her fiancé, for chrissake! Don't you *talk?*"

I banged the table with a hand and got out of my chair, shoving it back so vigorously that it fell over. I set it back on its feet and walked the length of the office and back.

Kosiosko said, "Coffee?"

"How much longer are we going to be?"

"Not much. I could use a coffee, so if you'll excuse me."

He got out of his chair and went out. I paced, glad for the respite. I'd always held the conceit that it wouldn't be difficult for an intelligent man to handle a police interrogation. In my novel I had written a scene in which my protagonist—who, it so happened, was a reporter—had easily parried the verbal probings of an eccentric detective. I wasn't finding it that easy. The problem was I didn't want the police to learn about the rift between Gladden and his son. I was concerned also about

251

another potential problem—that they might talk to Jo before I could and find our two accounts at variance.

Kosiosko was back with the coffee. "Yours was cream only, right?"

He seemed in no hurry to resume. He offered me a cigaret and when I shook my head, lit one for himself, put his feet on the desk and seemed to relish the coffee even though it was machine swill in a cardboard cup. I said nothing, waiting him out.

"Mr. Carpenter, I will explain my problem to you. First, this is no run-of-the-mill homicide. Oscar Gladden is an important man and there's going to be one hell of a lot of noise. Now, I'm sure you know that we know you had nothing to do with Victor Gladden's death. That's obvious. What's not so obvious is why you're telling me a hell of a lot less than you know." He raised a hand to forestall my response. "I have two reasons for saying this. First, you're an experienced reporter. A reporter's training is to notice things and to ask questions. You'll forgive me if I say that you seem to have noticed very little and to have displayed almost no curiosity. Second, we are dealing here with what is clearly a deliberate homicide by a professional. There was no forced entry. There was no struggle, no vandalism. The assailant wore a cheap raincoat so he wouldn't get blood on his clothes and then left it behind. The pockets are empty; even the labels have been removed. It's too early to determine the time of death, but I'm reasonably certain it was prior to your first visit to his room. I just talked to the forensic people and that's their preliminary judgment. I'm also pretty sure that the assailant was in the room when you first knocked on the door."

"How do you figure that?"

"I'm assuming that Victor Gladden intended to meet you at the bus terminal as arranged. But he didn't show. Therefore, one of two things: he was already dead or was about to be. It's my view that he was already dead and that the man who killed him was still in the room."

"Because the door was locked."

"Exactly. It was unlocked when you came back later. The assailant stayed in the room for some time after he shot young Gladden. We know that because he went through everything

252

in the room, everything. Being careful not to leave his prints. Victor Gladden was shot by someone who went to his room to kill him. He was shot twice with a gun on which there was a silencer: once in the back of the head — probably the first shot—''

''How do you know that? And how do you know a silencer was used?''

''Because no one in the building heard the shots and because the assailant planned to stay on and do a search. The shot in the back of the head was the first because the other was through the temple. If the shot through the temple had been first, the deceased would probably have seen the gun and there would be some sign of resistance.''

He lowered his feet from the desk and stubbed out his cigaret in a filthy metal ashtray. ''The assailant was either someone known to Victor Gladden or a stranger who didn't arouse his suspicions. Gladden had some information that someone didn't want known. Thus the homicide and thus the search of his room.'' He was looking at me, his face expressionless, his eyes unblinking.

''Do you have any idea who might have done it? Or had it done?''

''No,'' he said, his voice flat. ''Haven't got a clue. I was hoping that you might be able to give me a lead. Perhaps you'll understand now why I've been pressing you about your appointment with him and about the reason for it.''

''He made the appointment. As I told you, he left a note under my door.''

''But why under your door? He'd have to bypass the security system at your apartment building to get to your door. Wouldn't it be simpler merely to phone you?''

''He may have. Perhaps he hadn't been able to reach me.''

''But you said you were home most of the day.''

''I was.''

''And when you aren't there, you have an answering machine. He could have left a message on it, unless, that is, he didn't want to take the chance that someone else might hear the message. There was no message?''

''No, just the note.''

"And you destroyed the note. You're sure of that?"

"Yes, I'm sure of it."

"It wouldn't be in the garbage at your apartment?"

I shook my head. "I flushed it down the toilet."

"You flushed it down the toilet. An unsigned note that merely asks you to meet him at the bus terminal and you flush it down the toilet." He sighed wearily and got to his feet. "Mr. Carpenter."

"Yes?"

"There are a number of things you're keeping from me. I have no idea why. I would strongly suggest that you have some second thoughts on the matter."

I rose and went to the door.

"Tell me one more thing," Kosiosko said. "How come Victor Gladden lives in a pigsty when his old man is who he is and is stinking rich?"

"They had a falling out."

"Oh? What was the reason for the falling out?"

"I'm sure it has no bearing on your investigation. It was a long time ago. A family thing."

I went directly to the hospital. Jo was sedated, and they wouldn't let me see her. I wrote a note, borrowed an envelope from a nurse, sealed it and exacted a promise that she would pass it to Jo the moment she was awake.

*My Dearest:*

*It wasn't possible to see you, but I want you to know that I'm thinking of you and loving you every minute. And missing you terribly. There is nothing that I or anyone else can say that will ease the pain you're feeling, but do believe me, darling, you will somehow survive it, and impossible as it may be to believe it now, the pain, if not the sense of loss, will one day become bearable. I'll be with you the moment they will let me, and am with you in my thoughts every moment until then.*

*The police will want to talk to you. You don't have to see them until you're ready so don't be afraid to insist on that. Two things are important: say nothing about Victor talking to one of your father's guards and say no more about Victor's estrangement from your father other than that it was a family falling-out. This is important. When you have read this note, destroy it.*

*Dearest, dearest Jo, you have my heart and all my love, now and forever.*

It was past eleven but I drove to the Gladden estate. As I came up the stairs, Oscar Gladden was in the hall waiting for me. He walked into his study and I followed.

"The police are on their way here," he said. "A Sergeant Kosiosko. I don't suppose there's any option; I'll have to talk to him. He tells me that you and Jo discovered Victor's body. Bring me up to date."

I looked at him with hostile eyes. He was in a pale-blue silk dressing-gown that accentuated his bulk. His face was pale and there was tension in his voice and manner.

"Don't you want to know how Jo is?"

"I know how Jo is; I talked to the hospital."

"Do you want the details on what happened to Victor?"

"Yes, by god! But not now. What I need from you now is how the police are treating it."

"Mr. Gladden," I said, momentarily seeing the crimson mask that had been Victor's face, "your son has been murdered."

"Do you think I don't know that?"

I put both hands on the desk and leaned toward him, my face close to his. "Jeezus, man! He's your son and he's dead. They blew off half his face!"

For the first time in the months I had known him I saw vulnerability in Oscar Gladden's face. For a fleeting second the facade fell away. The eyes went empty, the mouth fell slack. But as quickly as it had gone his composure reappeared. And hardened into flinty anger. He lowered himself into his chair and directed me into another with an impatient gesture. I remained standing for a moment, breathing hard, sensible of a feeling of unreality. As I sat down, I became aware that my entire body was trembling.

"Now," he said, his voice hard, "you will listen to me. I pay you to stand between me and the public, and at the moment that public includes the police. You will control your hysteria and give me your best judgment. Do you understand?''

I made no response.

''Sergeant Kosiosko says he talked to you. What did he want to know?''

''Among other things,'' I said, my tone laced with bitterness, ''why Oscar Gladden's son was living in a cheap rooming-house. In a pigsty, as he put it.''

''What else?''

''He asked me if I had any idea who might have killed him. Or had him killed; he's certain it was done by a professional.'' I paused, suddenly stunned by the thought that Gladden might have had something to do with it. Hadn't Victor sought out one of the guards? He may have been trying to pump him. And there had been something about the barn and—as Victor's note had stated—some new development in his investigation. Was it possible that Victor had learned about William Naylor's death? Or the reason for the visits by the tow truck and the exchanges of tires?

''Well?'' The voice was imperious, the tone impatient.

''I said I had no idea why he was killed.''

It occurred to me that Kosiosko, in talking to Gladden, would mention my appointment with Victor. I decided that it would be best if I revealed this before Kosiosko did. I said, ''Did you know that Victor had been questioning one of your guards?''

There was not so much as a flicker of an eye. ''Of course I knew.'' His eyes darkened. ''I have also known from day one that Victor has been talking to you, telling you god knows which of his many hallucinations. You know he's been in Bellevue?''

''No, I didn't.''

''Partly paranoia, mostly drugs.'' He fixed me with his eyes. ''I find it curious, Carpenter, that knowing how things are, you talked to him and that you did it in a surreptitious manner. I won't ask you why. That's something for another day. In the meantime, is there anything else I should know before I talk to this man Kosiosko?''

There seemed no point in not telling him everything I knew. ''He believes the killing was done by a professional.''

"You already said that." He glanced at some notes on a pad before him. "Now I would like you to earn your salary. Prepare an obituary for the Toronto and New York papers. . . . Beloved son of Oscar Gladden, etcetera, etcetera—"

"Beloved son!"

"Beloved son of Oscar Gladden." He pushed a pad of paper toward me. "Here, make some notes. Make the arrangements for the funeral, which will be in Toronto. St. Francis of Assisi Church. Father Lombardi. Interment at Mount Hope; there's a family plot there. Spend whatever is called for. And order a wreath for the casket with the word *Dad* on it."

The telephone buzzed. He picked it up and said, "Tell him I'll see him in a moment." He put down the phone. "Jo will be going with me to Toronto. You'll stay here to handle the press. Now go down and bring Sergeant Kosiosko here."

# TWENTY-THREE

The news media lived off the story for the next ten days. It lacked the sex, the naked avarice and the internecine rivalries of the Jimmy Swaggart and the Jim and Tammy Bakker revelations a few years back but it had all the necessary ingredients to produce newspaper headlines, massive television coverage and cover stories in the news magazines. Predominant was the reclusive and intriguing figure of Oscar Gladden, his luxurious fortress estate with its armed guards and barred gates, the twin stretch-limousines in which he traveled, the Worldwide Church of One empire, the daily telecasts with their millions of viewers, the photogenic daughter and, overarching it all, the incongruity of the slaying of his estranged son by a hired killer.

Until they were moved out by the police, news vans, remote-trucks and dozens of reporters and camera crews jammed the lane leading to the gates. Banished to Duck Pond Road, they blocked traffic from each direction until temporary *No Parking Police Order* signs were erected along one side. Daily, helicopters hovered over the estate, cameramen craning recklessly to get pictures, the rotors beating the air until my brain reeled. A stake-out was mounted outside Morningside Heights Hospital to await Jo's release, and there was a manic scene when she dashed from a side door to enter one of the Gladden limousines. A *Daily News* photographer who leaned inside the car for a grab-shot had the door closed on his head by Sacred Heart Saywell and was treated for a deep cut and abrasions in the hospital's out-patient clinic.

In Toronto, Gladden took over the entire twenty-third floor at the Inn on the Park, and he and Jo—with Aunt Marguerita joining them—ate all their meals in. The Toronto *Star* estimated the crowd outside St. Francis of Assisi Church during the funeral at fifteen hundred and noted that there were only seventeen in the sanctuary. On the recommendation of the deputy police chief—who argued that it would be impossible to handle the crowds — the interment of Victor Gladden's remains was postponed.

In New York an indefatigable crew of investigative reporters was ransacking every available fact that had to do with Victor Gladden, digging for anything that might provide ground for speculation or enable them to update the story. Victor's landlord, a Vietnamese who spoke only pidgin-English, was able to contribute little other than the information that Victor had been a tenant for only three months and was delinquent two months in his rent. Sergeant Kosiosko would say little more than that he had assigned three men to the investigation and that when there were further developments he would announce them. Senator John Gallagher summoned reporters to tell them, in a lacklustre performance, that "the tragedy was the natural outgrowth of a religion that mocks the God of the Bible." The testimony in Oscar Gladden's anti-trust court case was reviewed, as was the extent and nature of his sprawling empire.

Holed up at the Gladden mansion, I had had little to do but fend off the press, having decided early on that "No comment" was the wisest course. I had the satisfaction of seeing my prediction fulfilled that if no news was forthcoming the coverage would fall away to nothing within ten days.


It was some time before Jo could trust herself to talk about Victor. At the private memorial service in Port Washington she had been inconsolable—as she was, I was told, during the trip to Toronto for the funeral. But now she was past that and we were having dinner at L'Auberge, and she was able to analyze her emotions with some objectivity.

"I'm sure that part of what I've been feeling is guilt. I suppose that when anytime you lose someone close you think of the things you might have done, of the times you failed to reach out. I should have stayed in closer touch with Victor. There were reasons, of course—I was off at school, I was thousands of miles away, I was immersed in my work—but those are just excuses. I could have kept in closer touch." She was silent for a moment, occupied with restraining her tears and, with a fingertip, pursuing a breadcrumb on the tablecloth.

"You're hardly singular in that," I said.

"I know. But that doesn't make it any less unloving."

I could see that she was doing her *mea culpa* as a penance and so was careful not to diminish it. She finally picked up the breadcrumb and put it in her mouth to nibble on it reflectively. "I could have been a better mediator between Victor and Father, for instance." She looked up at me, her lashes matted with tears, and she was so lovely that I felt again that sense of dissolving within. "I did try," she said. "I did. Although perhaps not hard enough. But they were both so stubborn. I suppose Father's mostly to blame—if there's any point in assessing blame. But you have to bear in mind that his and Mother's was a very old-fashioned marriage — you know, the husband is head of the house and the wife is subservient in all things—and when Father decided he'd been cuckolded he had a blind eye to the facts and a deaf ear to any argument."

A tear overflowed onto her cheek, and she wiped it away with her fingertips. "The first I knew that Victor was in trouble was when I got a telephone call from Aunt Marg three—was it three? no, four years ago, just before Christmas—that Victor was in Bellevue and in a bad way and wanted to see me. I flew back. I'll never forget it. He looked simply dreadful. All shriveled up, somehow, and ten years older than he was." She shuddered at the memory. "The doctor told me the problem was some type of paranoia—I've forgotten exactly what kind—and that it had been exacerbated by drugs. Anyway, he released him and I took him back to Paris with me." She paused, trying to corral her emotions.

"Please don't tell me about it unless you want to. There's no need to explain."

"No, no," she said. "It's better if I talk about it." She drew a deep breath, held it for a long moment and then went on.

"We had a wonderful time together. I introduced him to my friends, showed him the city, took him to all the tourist spots and he was fine. For about a month. And then, suddenly—it was as though he'd stepped off a cliff—he started in on Father. He hated him. *Hated* him. The accusations! Some of the things he would say—not to take sides—were totally unfair. But there was no reasoning with him when he got like that. I think the hardest part for him was having the name Gladden. Not so much when he was in Paris but back home he would meet somebody and they would say, 'You're not Oscar Gladden's son?' and then go on to rave about what a wonderful man Father was. Or there would be an article about Father in the paper or in a magazine, or he'd turn on the television and there he would be.

"I came back to the apartment one day after a class and he was gone. There was a note, a terrible note accusing me of siding with Father and of betraying him and any number of dreadful things." She paused for a moment, obviously reliving the time. "He just disappeared. Not a word about where he was or what he was doing for more than a year. And then the same pattern over again." There was the hint of tears again. "Poor, poor darling."

When it became evident that she didn't intend to go on, I said, "Did Victor ever talk to you about his suspicions about your father, about his being involved in . . . illegal activity?"

"Of course. Dozens of times. I would simply change the subject."

"I mentioned it to him—to your father, that is—the night Victor was killed. He said in effect what you've just said: that that kind of talk wasn't surprising, that Victor had been in Bellevue and that he'd been treated for drug addiction."

She looked up quickly. "I'm surprised he told you that."

"I'm sorry," I said. "Perhaps I shouldn't have mentioned it."

"No, no, that's all right. It's just that I'm surprised he would mention it to you. He's terribly close-mouthed about family matters."

"Jo," I said, testing, "do you think you could talk for just a minute about the people or the person responsible for Victor's death?''

''I'm all right,'' she said. ''Don't worry.''

''It's simply that the police aren't getting anywhere—I had a talk with Kosiosko this morning; he's stymied—and I thought I might ask your father's permission to sniff about. I'm a reporter, remember. And I have all kinds of contacts.''

There was anxiety in her eyes. ''Oh darling, I don't know. Whoever did it is dangerous.''

''I won't do anything foolish. It's simply that I can't stand to see it end in a closed-file at police headquarters.''

I broached it with Oscar Gladden the following morning.

''So,'' he said, ''in his spare time the amateur is going to show up the police. Just like in the movies. The answer is no. Victor went the way he wanted to, and it ended where it did. There was an inevitability to it. What I want you to do instead is what you were hired to do.'' He began to sort through some papers on his desk, searching. ''I'm told that the *Wall Street Journal* is preparing a series of articles on the various businesses owned by OneWorld. A reporter has been nosing around asking questions. . . . Damn it—what did I do with that note?'' He picked up a scrap of paper. ''Dunc Robertson. Do you know a Dunc Robertson?''

''Yes, I do.''

''Well, talk to him. Don't fly any distress signals but find out what he's after. Looks to me like a fishing expedition. Get on it today.''

Dunc met me for lunch at the Hellbox. I told him straight out my reason for wanting to see him. He listened, his expression unchanging, and when I was finished, he gave a short, self-conscious laugh. ''I feel like the guy in the public crapper without a quarter. I mean, there's nothing I can do.''

''What do you mean, nothing you can do?''

''I mean I can't help you. It's a special assignment. There are three of our people working on it: here, in Washington and in L.A. I was out there all last week. You know the drill: it's a breaking story. I can't talk about it.''

"Okay, you can't talk about it."

"I *can* tell you this—off the record?"

"Off the record."

"We haven't been able to nail it down yet, but one of Gladden's senior people has had a run-in with His Reverence or with somebody in the management at OneWorld and has been shipped out to the coast. He talked to one of our staffers out there and that's what sparked the assignment. Believe me, if half of what he says is true, it's a hell of a story." He looked down at the table and made a wry face. "I'll level with you this much. We're treading water at the moment. But the story's there."

I took a shot in the dark. "Your informant's clammed up, right?"

He looked at me, frowning. "Well, yes."

"As a matter of fact, you haven't been able to reach him for weeks, and without him you don't have a story."

"Mmmm."

"And you've tried to track him down, in L.A. and here, here because he used to live in Queens. But he doesn't return your calls and his wife won't talk to you and his sister doesn't know much about him and you figure somebody's put the heat on and he's gone into hiding."

Dunc had been peering at me over the top of his glasses, blinking rapidly, his face growing slack. Now, he restored his composure and said, "We're talking about Harry Golding, right?"

"No," I said, raising my glass and taking a sip of my scotch —a bit pleased with myself, to tell the truth. "Not Harry Golding. William Naylor."

"You son of a bitch!" he said. "Fill me in."

"On what?"

"Where he is, for starters."

"I'll make you a deal. You tell me what you know and I'll bring you up to date on Naylor."

He writhed in his chair. "Jeezus, Tony, you work for Gladden."

"Which is exactly why I need to know."

I understood his problem. He'd sold his managing editor on

putting him in charge of this great exposé, arguing that because he'd covered the trial he was familiar with the Gladden corporate structure and that, even though the source was in Los Angeles, it was essentially a New York story. The M.E. had bought it and had assigned three men to work with him. But now he couldn't print the story for lack of proof. And here I was with what might be the key.

"Look," I said, "I'll make it easy for you. Don't tell me any of the details. Let's say you were ready to file the story. How would the lead go?"

He looked at the tablecloth for a moment and then said, "I've gotta take a leak." He was gone ten minutes.

When he returned, I looked at him and grinned. "I should have asked if you had change for the pay phone."

He put his head down. "Okay, here's the lead: 'The Worldwide Church of One, one of television's largest ministries and the heart of evangelist Oscar Gladden's financial empire, is skimming millions of dollars from the tax-free contributions of its supporters.' "

I felt a momentary dizziness. "You're serious?"

He nodded.

"Do you know how it's done?"

"C'm'on Tony, you said just the lead." He made a gesture of frustration. "Okay, what the hell—without Naylor we don't have a thing anyway. In a word, the skimmed money is used to buy gold in Mexico. It enters the United States in tires, truck tires."

The tow truck! The exchange of tires in the barn! "But wait a minute," I said. "You couldn't possibly store any quantity of gold in a tire; it would throw the wheel out of balance. You'd get vibration."

Dunc put his head down, concentrating. "Now, let's see if I've got this straight. You've seen those big tractor-trailers on the highways? I mean the really big mothers. Didn't you ever notice that when they're not carrying a full load and don't need to distribute the weight, they run with the middle set of wheels raised. It's called a lift-axle. Cuts down the friction on the road, saves fuel and makes it easier to maneuver. According to Naylor, they store the gold bars in those tires."

"Naylor told you this?"

"Not me, but my guy in L.A., Tim Rawlins. But now we don't know where the hell Naylor is. And Rawlins thinks Worldwide has got the wind up and has cut off all shipments. Without Naylor we don't have a thing."

"Naylor's dead," I said.

His face was bleak. "I thought so. How do you know?"

"I'm sorry, Dunc. That I can't tell you."

"Your boss had him killed. *That's* why we haven't been able to find him." He looked at me, concern in his eyes. "Jeezus, Tony, what have you got yourself into? You'd better get clear, boy!"

It was going on midnight when I left the Hellbox. The bulldog edition of the *Post* was on the street and a bundle lay on the sidewalk in my path. The front page headline blared:

GALLAGHER
SUICIDES.

I worked a copy of the paper free of the bundle and read it in the light from a storefront. "A shotgun in his mouth. . . . both barrels. . . . in the garden back of his home. . . . his brains all over the flowers. . . ."

He'd been alone in the house, the day-maid said. Mrs. Gallagher wasn't there. She'd packed her things and moved to her sister's in Manhasset a week earlier. He'd written his resignation from the party, sealed it in an envelope and gone into the garden. . . .

Weak, I leaned against the building. It was a few minutes before I could walk. There was a slackness in the muscles of my legs and my brain was like pudding. Nonetheless, I walked and kept on walking. Hours later I looked up suddenly to discover I was outside Gallagher's campaign headquarters. It was deserted. No lights were burning except for a gooseneck lamp directed at a safe. Before my eyes, posted on the window, was a blown-up photograph of the candidate. He was smiling and his hands were raised in a victory salute. But the eyes were dull, blank. . . . Dead!

"I knew it would bother you," Oscar Gladden said, "so let's take a minute to get things in perspective. Come with me."

I'd been on the phone much of the night. Jim Ingraham was

265

in the midst of filing his column but he took my call. "If you want to know do I feel like a prick, the answer is yes. But not really. There's all kinds of stuff coming out. A delegation from the National Campaign Committee went to see him yesterday to ask him to step aside. The scuttlebutt is that the *Times* was about to break a story about irregularities in the handling of his campaign finances; apparently he had his hand in the till. I was just on the phone with a guy on his election committee and, off the record, he says that Gallagher's been into the sauce, heavy. It was the Jerri West thing that got his wife, but the story is that he had something else going with one of his party workers on the side and that he and his wife were having trouble long before my story broke."

I followed Gladden down the stairs to the entrance hallway. He led me behind the aquarium. Knee-Hi was already there, wearing a rubber apron. Gladden pointed to a treatment tank in which there was a six- or eight-pound grouper. Knee-Hi grasped it by the gills and flopped it, struggling and slippery, onto a table. Holding it firmly, he took a knife and with one deft cut slit its belly. Then, the fish clasped to his chest, he went up the ladder and loosed it into the water.

It swam in spurts, erratically, hanging motionless for a moment, and then, with a manic wriggling, zig-zagging about the tank. The other fish circled, watching, wary. Suddenly, the shark moved in. Jaws gaped. A threshing about and the grouper was in two pieces. The barracuda struck like silver darts, their dog's teeth tearing chunks from the tattered flesh. The water swirled with frantic activity, the more terrible for its absolute silence. The piranha converged and within a minute the grouper was gone. As swiftly as the tumult had begun it ceased, and the inhabitants of the tank resumed their lethargic gliding. The only evidence of the death struggle was a fragment of fin drifting to the bottom of the tank, slipping back and forth like a last leaf in autumn.

Gladden's voice returned me to the moment. "See what I mean? When they scent blood, there's a mindless closing in for the kill. That's the way it is with the news media and with the party; they're the same kind of predator. It was *they* who destroyed Gallagher. All we did was nick him. You feel bad about it and so do I, but he was a weak man. A liar and a hypocrite. It's a law of life: nature culls out the weak.''

At the window in my office, unable to concentrate, I saw a car pull into the parking lot. Jerri West crossed to the front door, a modish tote-bag swinging from a shoulder, tossing her great mane of hair with that shake of her head and small thrust of her chin that was her habit. She tapped on my door and said in the little girl's voice she so often affected, ''May I come in?''

She was a beautiful woman, there was no denying it. In the morning sunlight her skin was flawless. I looked at her as she came across the office, demure as a child in a pink linen suit enhanced only by a single rope of pearls. She had extraordinarily round eyes and they gave her a look of perpetual surprise and vulnerable innocence. The poet lies, I thought: the eye is not the window of the soul.

''Mr. Carpenter?'' She was tentative, unsure of herself. ''Mr. Gallagher, uh, killing himself like that—I feel real sick about it; I really do. I mean, even though I didn't know the guy—''

My voice was sharp. ''What do you *mean* you didn't know the guy?'' I was heavy with guilt and saw no reason why she should escape it.

''It's the truth. I didn't know him. I wouldn't lie about a thing like that. I never met the guy 'cept once at a party.''

''His initials were in your date book.''

She lowered her eyes and the lashes were long against her cheeks. ''They told me to put them there. Like, you know, on certain days.''

''Who told you?''

''I mean, how'm I s'posed to know a little thing like that could hurt somebody?'' She glanced at the door and lowered her voice. ''I mean, JRG could be anybody. I never said it was Mr. Gallagher. As a matter of fact, I said it wasn't, but nobody believed me.''

I rose from the corner of the desk where I'd been sitting and went again to the window. The freshly laundered skies were a pristine blue and the lawns were awash with autumnal leaves. A pair of cardinals flashed past the window to land on a nearby branch. Below me, Gil, the yard-man, was trimming deadwood from a row of shrubbery. The world was innocent and lovely. I became aware that Jerri was talking.

". . . And I've lost a lot of business. You know, all the publicity, 'n' like that. I mean, all the guys, you know, who used to call, aren't anymore. Even Mr. Gladden. That's why I come here this morning. I used to hear from him every week." She was looking at me, smiling sweetly. "Mr. Carpenter? Tony? I was wondering if maybe, you know, you could say a word to Mr. Gladden. . . ."

Later, Jo came by. "Tony, I'm worried about Joshua. I had lunch with him and this new agent he has. You wouldn't believe the man: the very embodiment of the hot-shot entrepreneur. His suit! That horrible brown gabardine that has an iridescent green shine. A chocolate-brown shirt and a white tie, if you can believe it! A blow-dry haircut that looks like a thatched beehive. Tony, he's promising Joshua the world. Says he can sell a book and a movie based on Joshua's life for a million dollars. He's got him dictating into a machine. Darling, you've *got* to talk to him!"

"Jo, I really can't butt in on his life. I don't have that right."

"I tried to talk to him, but he says he's got to look out for himself. He's really hurt that Father dropped him. And, darling, he's drinking too much."

"Jo, he's a big boy."

"Please."

When I called information for Joshua's number the operator replied, "I don't have a Joshua Crown, but I do have a new listing: Joshua Crown Enterprises on East 57th Street."

"That'll be it, goddamn it!" I snapped.

"I'm doing the best I can," she said.

There was a secretary reading a paperback as I entered. She put it down and I gave her my name. She said, "Oh, yes. Mr. Crown talks about you a lot."

He was sitting in his shirtsleeves behind an impressive mahogany desk. The office was spacious, with comfortable chairs and matching tables and original oil paintings of the assembly-line kind on the walls. The top of the desk was clear, the IN and OUT baskets empty. He smiled at me, eager as a salesmanship school graduate. As he leaned across the desk to shake hands there was a faint whiff of scotch and he looked tired around the eyes.

"Very posh," I said. "Where'd you get the furniture?"

He grinned happily. "You rent it. Lease it, I mean."

"You can lease anything these days," I said sourly. "Even a pet dog."

"Hey, Tony!" he said, disregarding my mood. "How do you like the set-up?"

"Looks like a Donald Trump castoff."

He turned to an imaginary onlooker. "Great kidder, Tony." And now back to me, his zestfulness undiminished. "You've got to meet my partner, Buddy Boyes."

"Buddy Boyes! That's his real name?"

"Francis, actually," he said. "He likes Buddy better. It has a friendly ring."

"Joshua," I said, slumping in a chair, "what the hell are you doing? And who's paying for all this?"

He was a little piqued. "It'll come out of the advance we get for the book and the movie."

"I mean, now."

"We've allocated some of the funds that have come in."

"But they're all in trust."

"It's just an advance, for god's sake! It's like investing it; we'll pay one percent over bank interest." His ebullience had subsided. "Well, goddamn it, Tony, I was prepared to cut Mr. Gladden in on it, but he wouldn't listen."

I sighed. "When do I meet your agent?"

"Partner," he said, and brightened. "He's out on the coast. Touching base, he calls it. He's a really terrific guy. Tell you the truth, he reminds me a lot of you."

"Thanks muchly," I said, wincing. "Would you mind telling me what the deal is? Not that it's any of my business."

"No, that's okay. It's pretty straightforward; that's what I like about Buddy. We do a book on my life as a highsteeler and on the whole protest thing. Followed by a movie. Then there's the sale to one of the networks for a mini-series. And the spin-offs: video cassettes, T-shirts, designer hard hats, a toy high-rise erection set for kids. The whole schmeer."

"What's Buddy doing out on the coast?"

269

"Touching base, like I said. Working on seed-money. Lining up a writer for the screenplay. Talking to producers, distributors, that kind of thing." His zestfulness was back. "It's going to be fantastic."

"In the meantime, you're dictating your life story. How's it going?"

Disquiet rose behind his eyes. "I'll tell you the truth, Tony. Not so good. You're a writer; you know how hard it is to get started." He looked at me, the concern deepening. "I start off telling about being born and about my family and so on, but Buddy doesn't want me to be raised in Caughnawaga. People aren't interested in Indians, he says, except in westerns, and westerns are dead. He thinks maybe I should make it that I was born in a circus family—high-wire artists, you know—and that's where I get my fantastic sense of balance. I was telling him about having a cousin in circus work and that's what got him going. But I don't know where to begin." He looked at me from beneath his brows. "You couldn't give me a hand to get started?"

"Joshua, believe me: the only chance you have to make it work is to tell it as it is."

He shook his head, a bemused smile on his lips. "I don't know, Buddy's real strong on the circus angle. That's what'll sell. You know, the big top. Color. Excitement."

"Can I stick my nose in?"

"Of course."

"Your deal with Buddy—what's the split?"

He cheered up. "Fifty-fifty, right down the line."

"The rent for this place, his airfare and expenses out on the coast—fifty-fifty?"

"Absolutely."

"He's paying his own way, then?"

"Well, I've advanced what we need to get going, of course, but we'll deduct his salary and expenses from his half of the book and movie sale. First item of business, Buddy says. Don't worry, he's keeping careful records. Every penny. The point of keeping careful records, Buddy says, is because, when you hit big, the tax boys move in and everything better be strictly kosher."

I despaired. Ol' Buddy had the hook set and was reeling him in. I could hear the echo of his clichés in everything Joshua said.

"Joshua, the sea is full of sharks. Your Buddy Boyes may be perfectly legit, but at least check him out. Ask him for a list of his film credits. Recent credits. Who are his other clients? For chrissake, Joshua, you wouldn't hire that steno out front if she hadn't taken shorthand and typing."

It turned out that she hadn't, but she was an old friend of Buddy's and "had a great telephone voice." At that point I became testy and Joshua resentful, so I got out of there.


I had felt a prickly rage while talking to Joshua. Yes, he was being an idiot, being gulled so easily by a transparently obvious flimflam man, but haven't we all been taken in by smooth talk at some time in our lives? And everyone has the right to play the fool: whether the reason be a woman or a get-rich-quick scam or, as in Joshua's case, the hope of grabbing the brass ring of fame and fortune. The real truth was, I was heavy with guilt. My churlishness in the face of Joshua's blindness sprang not so much from his naiveté as from my sense that I had betrayed him. The guy had been reasonably content with his steelwork- ers' life until I — albeit at Oscar Gladden's request — had dis- rupted it. Being who he was, it would have been impossible for him to have turned down the opportunity we put before him, especially with times being tough in his trade. Nor had I warned him (as though he would have listened) that the underside of celebrity is, as often as not, tarnished and seamy. I had been delegated to find a Mr. Nobody and, having been directed to Joshua, had — it's the only word for it — used him. And then dumped him. Not that I meant him ill; it was simply that he happened to be the solution to a problem I had to solve. I knew within hours of meeting him that he was ideally suited to the role we wanted to cast him in, and with all my energies focused on the task to hand, I hadn't given thought to whether I might be about to alter adversely the direction of his life. Not to offer justification, but I suppose we all play God at times: pressing our advice on someone, making a decision for someone, pushing someone into a new experience. We do it in any of many ways.

But I had done Joshua one of the great disservices of our time: I had recklessly given him an hour of twentieth-century celebrity. If such notoriety comes to you and you haven't got a solid sense of who you are, it can burn out your perspective and leave you with ashes in your mouth, forever looking backward at what once was.

# TWENTY-FOUR

Johnny Gallagher's suicide lay heavily on me. I'd rationalized my involvement in Oscar Gladden's revenge on the grounds that Gladden had indeed been maligned and that Gallagher was a political opportunist and a hypocrite: railing against immorality in the media and within the hour bedding Jerri West. As Gladden had said in his graphic object-lesson at the aquarium, Gallagher *was* a weak man, and certainly, as Jim Ingraham had discovered, he had other failings. But none of that excused my duplicity in feeding Ingraham the faked date book and then stepping into the shadows.

In the bathroom mirror, shaving, my face was repugnant to me. I could no longer permit myself to drift, to allow Gladden's agenda to carry me along. I had to act. I would undertake a concentrated investigation of Oscar Gladden. But first I would begin by letting Mrs. Gallagher know that the stories about her husband's involvement with Jerri West were false.

Johnny Gallagher's funeral was an event. Politics is a close-knit brotherhood, and, at their death, men who have served their party well are remembered, often fulsomely. Ranks close, feuds are forgotten, old enmities become as naught. Virtues absent during the life of the deceased are discovered and hailed; arrogance, pig-headedness and an undue commitment to self-aggrandizement are interred with the casket. The eulogies spoken over the remains of a man prominent not only in politics but in the church and in the nation, as was Johnny Gallagher, reach for new adjectival heights, and such guilt as may be felt by rivals or outright enemies gets ameliorated by the feeling: "Well, we gave the son of a bitch a good sendoff."

Gallagher's was such a funeral. It took place in St. Patrick's Cathedral. The mourners crowded the sanctuary and spilled into the street. The cardinal archbishop of the diocese of New York officiated. The vice president of the United States and the speaker of the Senate were in prominent attendance, as was the governor of New York and the mayor of the city. Various cultural and fraternal groups turned out, many in their official regalia, the most prominent among these being the Irish.

I watched from the back of the sanctuary throughout the mass and stood with the crowd in the street as the casket was borne to the funeral coach. In Smedley I trailed the procession on the long drive to Gate of Heaven Cemetery and hung about on the fringes of the crowd that was gathered at the grave. I was acting irrationally and in a part of my brain I knew it, but I was burdened with a sense of culpability and impelled by a need to speak a word of comfort to the widow. It was imperative that she not live an hour longer with the lie we'd told about her husband.

Kathleen Gallagher was a handsome woman who had once been a great beauty, but in the shelter of a son's umbrella in the drizzle that had continued unremittingly through the morning, her skin was the color of the overcast and her eyes were puffed and red.

I made my way close to the limousine in which she would leave the cemetery. The crowd was dispersing, and she came toward me on the arm of one of her sons. As the funeral director opened the door of the limousine for her, I stepped forward.

"Just one minute, Mrs. Gallagher. . ."

I was on my back on the wet grass. Blackness yielded to jagged flashes and whorls of light. Strong hands had me under the arms, and I was borne along on stumbling feet by rough-handed men. A car, a door, and I was flung onto my hands and knees on the floor of a back seat. The fog behind my eyes began to dissipate and I realized that I was in a police car. My jaw was a locus of searing pain. I moved it tentatively and the agony rocketed to my brain.

There were two men in the front seat, each wearing the

familiar peaked cap of the police. They didn't so much as glance back at me as the car spun its wheels, threw gravel and pulled away. On the boulevard they went to the siren for no evident reason: I was in no condition to give them trouble.

There was little hassle at the precinct station. I had plenty of identification. One of the officers knew me from my days on the *Register,* and when I explained that, as someone who had known Johnny Gallagher for years, I was simply trying to offer condolences to his wife, there were apologies and I was released.

I took a taxi to the graveyard to retrieve my car, wondering whether the vivid blotch on my jaw would turn blue and whether I would ever again be able to eat solid food. Returning to the city, I saw a news vendor hawking papers and spotted on the front page what was unmistakably a photograph of Tony Carpenter, a dopey look on his face, in process of buckling from a right to the jaw thrown by Mrs. Gallagher's son. I winced and headed for the apartment, where I crushed some ice, put it in a plastic sack, applied it to my jaw, turned on the answering machine and went to sit in the living room with my feet high, my spirits low and my jaw athrob.

The *Daily News* called, as did the *Post, Newsday,* the *Associated Press* and UPI, all of them doing follow-ups, each asking me to call back. Jim Ingraham's metallic voice rasped: "Hey! I hear you were in some kind of fracas at Gallagher's funeral. Call me." Jo's voice said: "Darling, I just heard on the radio that you were in a fight or something at Mr. Gallagher's funeral. Are you all right? Call me as soon as you come in." Dunc Robertson said: "Tony, you must—repeat, must—change your mind and tell me everything you know on Naylor. Even-steven. Very important." Jo, sounding not nearly so anxious, said: "Darling, it's me again. You are *such* a goose! I talked to the police and they say you're fine. What you need is for me to kiss it better." Bartholemew's voice, softly unctuous, said: "Tony, Mr. Gladden would like you to be in touch as soon as you can. Cheers." WPIX, WNBC and the Brooklyn *Eagle* left call-backs. Sergeant Kosiosko's voice was terse: "Please ring me after five at the station. I have some information that may interest you."

I went to the kitchen to brew some coffee and to slosh it

around in my mouth, wondering whether I should be using heat or cold to control the swelling. Feed a cold, starve a fever, my mind said irrelevantly. I telephoned Jo to tell her I was fine, that I was negotiating for a title-bout for the cruiserweight championship of the world, that I was in a rush and that I would see her for dinner: "Nothing tougher than an omelet." I popped two more aspirin and sat down again with my feet on the hassock. Time to do some concentrated thinking.

Why had I not investigated the enigma of Oscar Gladden with the imagination and persistence with which I would have pursued an important assignment for the *Register?* With the exceptions of questioning Victor and trying to track down William Naylor, I'd made only occasional attempts to learn the facts. The reason for my procrastination was, in large part, Jo. If my suspicions about her father were confirmed and I was to move publicly against him, it might destroy our relationship. Her loyalty to her father continued to exasperate me, but her unwillingness to criticize his faults was not too difficult to understand; I have known daughters who loved and defended their fathers even when the men were drunken louts who bullied and beat them.

But there was another reason for my failure to act, and it did me little credit. If I were to expose Oscar Gladden I would lose not only my income but my hope of financial independence. With my experience, I could undoubtedly get taken on by one of the newspapers in town, but it might be a considerable comedown. The best I could hope for would be to match my salary at the *Register.* I was making twice that with Oscar Gladden and would, within a dozen years, be a millionaire. It would not be easy to forgo all that. It was obvious now why Gladden's offer had been conditional on my silence concerning anything I might learn about him while in his employ.

But what option did I have? Three men were dead—William Naylor, Victor Gladden and Johnny Gallagher. I knew I had to do something, but what could I do? If I went to the police, what could I prove? I had seen Oscar Gladden murder William Naylor, but where was my proof? It would be my word against his, and he would long since have established a watertight alibi. If I were to swear to what I saw that night in the barn, would there not be a number of others — the men who were in the barn among them—to swear that nothing of the kind had happened? Wouldn't Jo herself have to testify, in truth, that when her father met her at the airport that same night he was in normal spirits?

I could charge that Victor was murdered because he had discovered that his father was engaged in some kind of criminal activity, but who would listen? And what, precisely, was the criminal activity? According to Kosiosko, Victor was killed by a professional. How could I hope to demonstrate that Oscar Gladden had hired him—*hired someone to kill his own son!*—if in fact he had? I hadn't one jot of credible evidence. Victor had suffered from some form of paranoia and had been a drug addict. He had lived in a shadow world—for all I knew in an underworld. Granted, there had been a long-standing rift between him and his father, but what was incriminating about that? What father wouldn't be unhappy with a son gone so wrong?

The third man, Johnny Gallagher—who was responsible for his death? I as much as anyone. I along with Jim Ingraham and those members of the press who had printed the doctored evidence without checking it. I with Jerri West. I with Gallagher's fellow politicians, who had used him when he was riding high and then, when his weaknesses had begun to vitiate his usefulness, dumped him. I could charge that Oscar Gladden had had Gallagher's desk calendar stolen and Gallagher's initials inserted in Jerri West's date book, but I had no proof of it. And even if, as was unlikely, Jerri could be talked into implicating Gladden, how much credibility would she have?

Perhaps I should enlist the aid of the police. I could go to Kosiosko and tell him about the rift between Gladden and his son and about Victor's suspicions. The note pushed under my door the night Victor was killed suggested that Victor had turned up some evidence. Perhaps Kosiosko, with the resources of the police, could learn what it was. But what *had* Victor uncovered? The note referred only to "very interesting developments." To press Kosiosko to act with no more evidence than the note would surely be fruitless. Moreover, he was already aware of it.

Perhaps I should level with Dunc Robertson and enlist his help. He wasn't alone; he had associates in Los Angeles and in

Washington and had the resources of his newspaper behind him. Naylor had told Dunc's man in Los Angeles that Gladden was skimming millions of dollars from contributions to the television programs, using the money to buy gold and smuggling it into the United States. He had even detailed the method used. Surely this, in company with the fact that I had seen Gladden kill Naylor, would galvanize Dunc's interest. But what might that lead to? Dunc would have to share his knowledge with his editors. Did I want that?

Perhaps I should go the Internal Revenue Service. According to Roger Zachs, they were investigating Gladden's financial affairs. The IRS welcomes tips by informers—even anonymous informers—but what hard information did I have? I could tell them about the *Journal*'s investigation in L.A. and they could check with Dunc, but what did Dunc know other than what William Naylor had told his staffer? I knew that Naylor was dead, but even *that* I couldn't prove. Asserting it would be meaningless; the fundamental legal question would remain: where is the *corpus delicti?*

One further thought: the testimony of Dunc's man in L.A. would be useless in a court of law. It was hearsay. He knew only what he'd been told, and what he'd been told might well be a lie, an act of vindictiveness by Naylor after a falling out with his boss.

No, I would have to go it alone. And do so in the realization that any charges I might make against Gladden would be viewed with skepticism, seeing how he was one of the preeminent religious figures in the nation.

The sky beyond the windows was dark. I turned on a light and glanced at my watch; I'd been ruminating for hours. I got out of my chair, stretched and went to switch off the answering machine. As I did so, the telephone rang.

"Mr. Carpenter?" The voice was unfamiliar, a woman's voice with a Puerto Rican or Chicano accent.

"I'm Carpenter."

"You a frien' of Joshua Crown?"

"Yes."

"You please come get heem outta here. Righ'? You come *now?"*

"What is it? What's the matter?"

"Hee's drun'. You come get heem. Okay?"

The address given proved to be a generations-old brownstone tenement that had once boasted a spurious elegance. There were masonry scrolls and furbelows along the roofline, and a redundancy of wrought-iron railings, some of the segments broken, others rusted to gauntness. Apartment 3-B wore a battered greenish door and was reached after a long climb up stairways musty with ancient dust. In response to my knock, a distant voice shouted, *"Uno momento!"*

The girl who opened the door couldn't have been more than seventeen. Her skin was without blemish. Her eyes were dark and luminous, and she wore a coral-colored lipstick of the kind that glistens as though just wetted. Soft black hair lay on her shoulders, and the flimsy bathrobe she was wearing was open enough to reveal the delicate base of her neck and the beginning of the swell of her breasts. My god, I thought, she could be an eastern princess or a Hispanic film star, and here she is in this hutch for humanity's walking wounded.

Her voice dispelled my romanticist's dream. Her upper lip curled in an unpleasant way, revealing rotten teeth. "Ee's in 'ere," she said, opening a door.

Joshua was outstretched on a sagging double bed in a tangle of soiled sheets, naked. His head was twisted sideways in what would have been an uncomfortable position had he been conscious. His right leg hung over the side of the bed, the genitals lolling on his thigh. There was a smell of vomit, and flecks of it were on his cheek and chest. The room looked post-cyclonic. The floor was littered. A table lay on its side, smashed. The drapes, chintzy at best, were torn and sagging. A pulldown windowshade hung by one frayed corner.

The girl had followed me into the room. "I theen 'ees a regular yohn," she explained, "but 'ee's loco. Crazee!" She pointed at the closet door. The paneling was dented and cracked as from the blow of a fist. The bottom had been kicked in.

"Where are his clothes?" I asked. Bending over Joshua to see if he could be roused, I slapped his cheek. For my pains, I took an elbow to the right side of my jaw that caused me to fall forward into incredibly strong arms where I was immediately immobilized. A knee was seeking my groin. My head was next to his and the stink of vomit was strong. I bit his ear, hard.

"Joshua! It's Tony, for chrissake!"

The arms relaxed. I rose from the bed, feeling my jaw. At least I'd have matching bruises.

The girl said, "Din' I tole you? 'Ee's crazee."

Joshua pushed himself into a sitting position, looking down at his legs and the bed as a boxer might on recovering from a knockout. The girl was picking up pieces of clothing and throwing them on the bed. With her help I got Joshua into his clothes and on his feet. I put an arm about his waist, hauled an arm over my shoulder and started toward the door.

"Where's his wallet?" I said.

"How I know where's hees wallet, chrissake?"

"Give me the goddamn wallet!" I shouted. "You can keep the money."

She reached into the pocket of her bathrobe, took out a wallet, opened it and extracted some bills.

"Put it in my pocket," I said.

As we went down the stairs, she shouted after us, "Fuckin' crazee!" From a window she shrilled at us in the street: "*Two fuckin' crazees!*"


The cab-driver helped me get Joshua to the elevator of my apartment building, and I managed alone the rest of the way. Jo was already at the apartment. We got Joshua onto the bed in the spare bedroom, and Jo fetched a washcloth and a basin and cleaned him a bit. He roused and got amorous, but she fended him off, and he was soon snoring.

We sat with a drink in the darkness of the living room and talked. In bed, she touched and kissed my jaw lovingly, speaking soft, caressing words of commiseration. I was suddenly overwhelmed with a blanket of desolation and began first to weep silently and then to be shaken with great, wrenching sobs. Jo held me tightly and afterward kissed my eyelids asleep. I didn't stir until she awakened me with our breakfasts on a tray. When we'd finished, we went to rouse Joshua with much noisy miming of cheery servants arriving and much calling out of "Your breakfast, sir." But he was gone.


I decided finally not to quit Oscar Gladden but to stay on the job, thus hoping to learn more about him. I reported to him the following morning on my meeting with Dunc Robertson—tailoring it to my purposes. His displeasure was evidenced by the redness of his face, by a prolonged pursing of his lips and then by a rapid darting in and out of his pink tongue. Oddly, despite the discoloration on the skin of my jaw, he made no reference to the episode at the cemetery.

"They traced Naylor east," I concluded, "but there the trail ends. Dunc thinks he's in hiding."

Gladden was drumming his fingers on the desktop. "What else did he say?"

"Not much," I said. "It was obvious he wasn't going to tell me everything he knew. As he said, 'After all, you do work for Oscar Gladden.' "

"So?"

"The clear implication was that one of your employees was involved in smuggling contraband across the border and that the tipoff had come from Naylor. I told him the very idea was ridiculous and that his man in L.A. must have gotten it wrong."

"What did he say to that?"

"What could he say?"

"Regardless, what did he say?"

"He didn't say anything. He just looked at me as though he was trying to read something in my face."

Gladden sat pondering, his eyes blinking rapidly. "Sounds to me like more journalistic malice. But it's got to be stopped. Rumors like that could hurt us. There's enough trouble. I want you to get back to your friend. Find out the name of the man Naylor talked to and let me have a full report on him."

I took a deep breath. "Mr. Gladden, wouldn't the best thing be for me to work on finding Bill Naylor? He's the key."

He didn't hesitate. "Bill Naylor," he said, his voice flat, "is trouble. I had problems with him when he was here and was fool enough to give him a job in Los Angeles. I have no idea where you could reach him. I've been told he's taken a job in England.''

As I rose to leave, he said, ''Jo tells me you're going upstate over the weekend.''

''Yes. A change of scenery.''

''Some kind of Indian settlement run by Joshua Crown.''

''By his brother.''

''Damn fool Indian! I understand Crown has got himself a two-bit theatrical agent and that he's trying to peddle his story for a movie. Probably spilled his guts on his association with me. Why else would anyone pay any attention to him?'' As I paused in the doorway he said, ''Remember, I want the name of the man Naylor talked to.''

''I'll get back to you.''


I reached Dunc Robertson at the paper. ''I am now asking you to give me the name of your reporter in Los Angeles to whom Bill Naylor talked, and you are refusing to tell me.''

''I already told you.''

''You are now specifically refusing to tell me.''

''Why am I specifically refusing to tell you?''

''Because we both would like him to live a long and happy life.''

''Yes, we would. Indeed, we very much would.''

''I am now asking you whether your man in L.A. has passed on what Naylor told him to others on the paper? Do I understand you to be telling me that, yes, he told his senior people and he told you and that you told your features editor and so forth?''

''And so forth. Precisely.''

''Safety in numbers. And are you now telling me that your man in L.A., knowing that I work for Oscar Gladden, has flatly refused to talk to me on the telephone and has told you that there isn't a hope in hell of my seeing him if I were to go out there?''

''My words exactly.'' He laughed.

''It's not funny, Dunc.''

''So I gather. When do you fill me in?''

"Soon, I hope."

"Stay out of dark alleys."

I put in a call for Detective Sergeant Kosiosko. He called me back half an hour later.

"I got your message," I said.

"My message?" He sounded tired.

"On my answering machine yesterday. You left word to call you."

"Oh, yes. Hold, please."

It was a long wait. He came back on the line and said, "Sorry, I had to take another call. Now, where were we? Right. Gladden. Gladden, V . . . Gladden, Victor . . . I have the file. Hold just a minute." I could hear him in conversation with someone. Now he was back. "Sorry to keep you waiting. Look, I've just checked the file. There doesn't seem to be anything new on the Victor Gladden homicide. Sorry."

"Your message on my machine?"

"Yes. We had a lead. It didn't check out."

"It didn't check out." I was growing testy. "It's now what —weeks?—and you've come up with nothing."

"Mr. Carpenter, the Victor Gladden homicide was a contract killing."

"You knew that weeks ago."

A weary patience in his voice. "Let me spell it out to you: the chance of apprehending a suspect in a contract killing is about ten thousand to one. The assailant has no motive. He probably doesn't even know the victim. He's from out of town. He flies in, does his job and leaves. He uses a stolen gun and discards it immediately. If we find it, we can't trace it to the suspect because it's registered under another name. Even if, by some unlikely circumstance, we do pick him up, it won't help. He'll have an alibi. Ironclad. Even if he doesn't, it won't lead us to the man who hired him; he may not know who he is. And if he does, he won't squeal, not if he doesn't want to get himself killed. No, he'll take his medicine and, likely as not, be back on the street in three to five years."

"What I hear you saying, Sergeant, is that to all intents and purposes, Victor Gladden's is a dead file."

"We don't have any dead files in homicide."

"For chrissake, Kosiosko, don't play semantic games with me. The fact is—"

"Mr. Carpenter, if any game is being played it's by yourself. You know and I know that you haven't told me half of what you know. You may have good reasons; you're the only judge of that. In the meantime, I've got more pressing business. There were close to two thousand homicides in New York City last year. We've had 114 in this precinct so far this year. We do what we can. Good-bye, Mr. Carpenter. Call me when you have something to tell me."


Gus Longo lived on the near side of LaGuardia Airport, just off Northern Boulevard in Queens in a small simulated-brick cottage, identical in almost every respect to his neighbors'. The street was pleasant in the afternoon sun and noisy with the play of children. I parked Smedley at the curb, immediately attracting some children, and rang the doorbell. The corner of a curtain moved and Gus opened the door.

"Hey, Tony!" He drew me inside, looking past me to the street. "Hey, man. Long time! Come in. Come in."

In the living room, he opened a narrow gap on one side of the drapes and said, frowning, "Your car. . . .I don' know. . . .Wadda ya think?"

"It'll be fine."

"I don' know. The kids. Here, gimme the keys. The guy owns the pizzeria at the corner's a buddy of mine. I'll park 'er in back there." He held out a hand. "I'll feel better," he said.

While he was gone I looked about. The living room was small and gloomy, made more so by heavy velvet drapes and by the brown velour sofa and chairs. On one wall there was a dummy fireplace, a mechanical fire flickering. On the walls hung floridly Catholic pictures in rococo plaster frames. Over the mantelpiece was a mounted tarpon, the lacquered surface beginning to peel. A missing eye had been replaced with a green button, giving the fish a distracted air. There was a scent of oregano. The only

284

sounds in the room were the muffled piping of children's voices from the street and the portentous ticking of a massive grandfather clock in the entrance hall. I saw no evidence of either woman or child.

Gus was back, hearty and effusive.

I said, "Were you really worried about my car? It's a nice neighborhood."

He gave an apologetic shrug. "Kids. I mean, why take chances?"

"You didn't want my car sitting in front of your house."

He looked at me, smiling reproachfully. "Now, wadda ya wanna say that for? C'mon, sit down, sit down. A beer? Wadda ya say, Tony boy?"

He returned with two dewy bottles and passed one to me. "You don' wan' no glass, right? Goes better straight from the bottle." He tilted his head back, looking past the bottle at the street.

"Gus, what's the matter?"

"What's the matter? Somethin's the matter?"

"Are you expecting somebody?"

He shook his head vigorously. "Expectin' somebody? Who'd I be expectin'?" He lifted his bottle, let at least half the contents gurgle into his throat and then wiped his mouth with the back of a hairy forearm. "Hey, Tony! Good to see ya! How goes?"

"It goes," I said, watching him. His legs were crossed and one foot was jigging. "I shouldn't have come."

"Hey, don't say that. Who's more welcome in Gus Longo's house than Mr. Tony? I never forget you." He gave me a friendly but empty smile.

"Gus, the first day I came to the Gladden house you said, 'Don't work for Mr. Gladden.' Why?"

He tilted his head and grimaced. "I said that? You gotta be kiddin'."

"'Don't work for Mr. Gladden.'"

He cast about with his eyes. "Why? Nothin'. I didn' think you'd like it, that's all. You know, Mr. G.'s not an easy man. That's all."

"No, it was more than that."

"Hey, willya cut that out? Anyways, so what? You took the

job. You're doin' okay, right?" Sudden solicitude. "Hey, you ain't touched your beer." He took another pull at his bottle.

"Gus, what happened to Bill Naylor?"

It was like a cloud crossing the sun. "What happened to Bill Naylor? You gotta be kiddin'. How would I know? C'mon Tony, for chrissake! Askin' me what happened to Bill Naylor." He looked at his bottle and did a little pantomime about being surprised that it was empty. "Ready for another?" Seeing that I wasn't, he said, "Be right wit' ya."

I followed him to the kitchen, which was tidy and shining clean and gave an impression of being seldom used. As he dug out a beer and twisted open the top, I leaned against the refrigerator.

"Gus, what happened to Naylor? I've been to his house. He hasn't been there for ages. His wife won't answer the phone or the door. A reporter from the *Wall Street Journal* talked to him in Los Angeles a month or so back. Naylor told him that Oscar Gladden is involved in bringing in gold bars from Mexico. He was supposed to get back to him but didn't. Naylor comes back east but nobody's seen him since. He was staying at the Park Lane but he never checked out. I asked Mr. Gladden where he was. He said he didn't know and didn't want to know but he'd heard he'd gone to England. Gus, I don't like it. Be a buddy and tell me what's up. I've got Naylor's old job and it worries me. I mean, what am I into?"

There was no response other than a small shrug. He pulled a box of Ritz crackers from the cupboard and raised an eyebrow in a question, replacing the box when I shook my head. I waited, letting the question hang. After a moment he took a swig from the bottle and again wiped his lips with the back of a forearm. "Wadda ya want from me, Tony?" he asked. There was a plaintive quality to his voice.

"Help," I said. "I'll tell you the truth, I'm worried. Two men are dead." His head came up. "Victor Gladden and Bill Naylor. They both—"

He had been looking at me from beneath lowered brows. "Who tol' ya Mr. Naylor was dead?"

I caught myself. "What else? Where is he? He's disappeared.

He didn't even check out of his hotel. They're holding his bag. He's not in England. So he's dead."

His face was somber now. He preceded me back to the living room and turned on the radio. "Tony," he said, "do me a big favor. Forget it. Okay? Just forget it."

"Gus, I'm in up to my nuts. I should know what I'm into."

Gus was at the side of the drapes again, peering out into the street. He turned back into the room and, in a reflex action, began to raise the bottle toward his lips. Instead he put it on an end-table. His brow was furrowed and his lips were pursed.

"Tony, that first day—when you come to Mr. Gladden's—I tol' ya not to work for him, right? You didn' listen. Okay, I'm tellin' ya now—*listen.* Forget Bill Naylor. Forget Victor Gladden. Don' go stickin' your nose in. Okay? Believe me, there's no percentage in it." His shrug was a mute plea. "I mean, what more can I say?"

I made a stab in the dark. "Gus, I'm told that when you're off doing those little jobs, as you call them, for Mr. G., you're driving a tractor-trailer and it's to haul gold bars from Mexico. I hope I'm wrong."

He shook his head slowly as if in disbelief and then raised his eyes in an appeal to heaven. Now he came to me, reaching out to clasp my shoulders, squeezing them with strong fingers. "Tony, you're a buddy of mine. I mean, you looked after Gus, so I'm gonna tell ya what happened to Bill Naylor an' maybe you'll be smart an' listen. Victor Gladden I don' know from nothin'. I got some ideas but I don' know an' I ain't about to guess. Okay? Bill Naylor. He stuck his nose in. Just like you're doin'—I'm sorry, Tony, but just like you're doin'. Tony, *listen to me*—this is your buddy talkin'. I could get my ass in a sling. Ya wanna know where Naylor is? I'll tell ya where he is. Jeezus!" he said in an aside, glancing again to heaven. "I must be nuts." He dropped his voice and I had to lean forward to hear him over the sound of the radio. "He's at the bottom of the East River, wit' a truck engine chained to his feet."

# TWENTY-FIVE

The George Washington Bridge spans the Hudson River between upper Manhattan and Fort Lee on the Palisades of New Jersey. From tower to tower, it leaps 3500 feet in a single bound across the Hudson, the center span suspended 600 feet above the water. On a busy day, its two levels and fourteen lanes carry as many as 250,000 cars, buses and trucks. At dawn on the morning of the first Monday in September, the eastbound flow of traffic slowed, backed up and, amid a mounting cacophony of horns, came to a stop.

One hour earlier, Chuck Harder, a sportscaster for WNEW Radio, had been commuting to work across the bridge when he thought he saw movement high on the steel grid of the east tower. The traffic was light, so he eased to the right lane, lowered a window and leaned out to check. It was difficult to see clearly in the predawn darkness, but he had binoculars in the glove compartment and there was sufficient illumination from the lights on the main cables to confirm what he had only vaguely glimpsed: a man was climbing the tower, moving up the exposed X-braces with surprising speed. He was now approaching the top.

Harder took the first exit ramp, curving right onto the access road leading to Riverside Drive, and at the first emergency telephone contacted the bridge to ask whether maintenance staff worked on the towers at night. Told no, he reported what he had seen and, from the first pay telephone he could find, called in the story to the radio station. At first light, WNEW ordered its

288

"Eye In the Sky" traffic helicopter in for a look. The pilot reported seeing a man wearing a tartan shirt, a down vest and jeans standing on top of the east tower. A Michael Jackson recording was cut off in full tumult and the report went to air.

The opposition stations reacted swiftly. WTOP's "Great Gettin' Up Mornin' " show was first with a detailed report: "Little Airborne Annie has been able to confirm that the man on top of the east tower of the George Washington Bridge is not a potential suicide, but none other than that incredible man of steel, Joshua Crown, the man who only weeks ago caught the attention of the nation with a spectacular protest on the top floor of the new Republic Motors Building. And now, here's Annie with an update from the scene."

"Thank you, Barry. At the moment I'm circling the east tower of the bridge and can confirm that Joshua Crown—that's who it is, all right—is standing on the metal platform at the very top. He's holding over his head a hand-lettered sign with the words . . . hold on a second . . . now I've got it. The sign reads: 'Acid rain — the Devil's dew!'. . . That's D-E-W, incidentally. Believe me, it's an incredible sight. He's four hundred feet above the traffic and another six hundred feet above the waters of the Hudson. The wind is whipping his sign and threatening to blow him off his high perch, but he is absolutely fearless. Whoops! . . . Hold everything! . . . The sign is gone—the wind just ripped it out of his hands! I think he's all right. . . . Yes, he's fine. Wow! As a matter of fact, he just waved at me and gave me a big smile. Incredible! The guy is absolutely without fear. This is Little Airborne Annie reporting, live, to WTOP from over the east tower of the George Washington Bridge."

By seven-fifteen traffic was backed up five miles on the New Jersey approaches but had begun to move again. Two dozen policemen were posted between the lanes, shrilling their whistles and waving drivers forward. There was some cursing and horn-blowing as drivers sought advantage in lane changes and one fist fight between two commuters whose bumpers had locked. Two older cars began to steam but were waved on. The problem was exacerbated when a fifty-eight-year-old accountant from Teaneck, New Jersey, suffered a coronary infarction and, despite the attentions of a team of paramedics, expired.

At eight-fifteen, Hyman Weinbarger, manager of the George Washington Bridge, arrived and was joined a few minutes later by Michael R. Bosley, director of Tunnels, Bridges and Terminals for the Port Authority of New York and New Jersey. Reporters swarmed about him as drones about a queen bee. He made an ambiguous statement to the effect that the problem would soon be resolved and, badgered by his questioners, retreated in a sheet-lightning storm of flashbulbs to the administration offices at the base of the tower.

The NYPD Emergency Services Division was already on the scene and, having completed an appraisal of the situation, began to suspend nets around the tower. It is not uncommon for exhibitionists or would-be suicides to climb the various bridges in the New York City area. Nor, in most cases, is it difficult to do. The George Washington Bridge is suspended from four main cables, each approximately five feet in diameter. They rise to the towers in a gentle arc from the center of the bridge, and maintenance men walk them with little difficulty, climbing or descending by holding two small cables rigged to serve both as handrails and as anchors for their safety lines. Most intruders on the structure are soon dizzied by the height and, if they don't fall, are usually immobilized by fear. The ESD squad goes after them—and the occasional daredevil climber— coaxing, cajoling, closing in until they are near enough to seize the intruder, handcuff him and put him in a ''body-tie'' — a complicated series of knotted ropes around the man's neck and chest and thighs that enables the rescuers to lead him safely to the ground.

A half-dozen helicopters now circled the east tower, five from news-gathering agencies and one from the Port Authority. The first of what would be a flotilla of small craft made its way up the river, maintaining positions beneath the bridge or slowly circling the base of the tower. Spectators began to line the brink of the Palisades. On the Manhattan side, a few made their way to the water's edge on the parkland south of the bridge.

I heard the news of Joshua's exploit while in my bathroom shaving and began immediately to switch back and forth on the radio dial. WNYC seemed more on top of the situation than the others, reporting almost simultaneously the birth of a baby in the back seat of a car trapped in the slow-moving bridge traffic and the fact that the ESD squad had decided, over the protests of Mr. Weinbarger, to wait Joshua out. Apparently, a team of four ESD officers had taken the tower elevators to its limit and had then scaled the structure to the top, a flat rectangular area comprising a steel grid covered with riveted steel plates. As they moved in on him, Joshua swung over the side, sliding down the X-braces. As the police followed, he eluded them easily and went swiftly again to the top. This game of aerial hares-and-hounds continued for perhaps twenty minutes, with Joshua easily countering each move to corner him. The ESD squad does not lack courage but neither is it foolhardy and, having tried vainly to talk the quarry into surrendering, completed the rigging of its nets and descended. A member of the squad talked to a WNYC reporter: "Look, the guy's like a monkey on the steel. It would take a dozen men to corner him, and somebody'd get killed. He's not gonna jump. We'll just have to wait him out."

I considered it but decided that there was no point in my going to the bridge; there would be nothing I could do there. I managed to reach one of Weinbarger's assistants in his office at the World Trade Center, introducing myself as a close friend of Joshua's and offering to help in any way I could. He seemed hardly to hear me, nattering on in a distracted manner about the traffic problems Joshua was causing. I called the city desk at the *Register* to see if they had anything I hadn't learned from the radio. Nothing. On impulse, I called the Wigwam and, representing myself as an assistant to Dan Rather, got the home telephone number of the barman. His wife had to rouse him from bed.

"On top of the George Washington! Christ almighty! I knew the crazy bugger had somethin' on his mind." It seemed that Joshua had spent most of the previous evening in the bar. "He was really down, know what I mean? He's usually the life of the party—laughin', kiddin' around—but not last night. The top of the George Washington. Jeezus!"

"Did he say anything about—"

"Hey, wait a minute—I just remembered something. Sorry, I'm still half asleep. He had the kitchen make him up two dozen sandwiches to go an' put 'em in a tote-bag he was carryin'. An' half a dozen Molson's. And he put three or four handfuls of pretzels in his pockets. I figured he was goin' to a party or somewheres. Sonofabitch—on top of the George Washington. He won't be lonely — his grandfather helped build the damn thing.''

There was no point in glooming about the apartment so I drove to the Gladden estate. Bartholemew was atwitter with excitement and asked a sequence of questions. I resisted being drawn into a conversation. A few minutes later there was a summons to Oscar Gladden's office.

''Your boy learns fast.''

''Learns fast?''

''The publicity stunt on the bridge. Whose idea was that? Not yours, I hope.''

The thought rocketed into my mind: Buddy Boyes! PR for Joshua's book! ''I don't think it's a stunt,'' I told Gladden. ''I was just talking to somebody who was with him last night. He was pretty depressed.''

''Well, just stay clear of it.''

''I've already offered to do anything I can. He's got them stymied.''

''Call and tell them the Olympic target-shooting champion's in town. I saw him on the news last night.'' He shook with contained laughter at his wit. For a fleeting second I considered leaping across the desk and throttling him. ''Back to business,'' he said. ''Did you talk to your friend Dunc Robertson?''

I swallowed my anger. ''Wouldn't tell me a thing. Not the name of his man in Los Angeles, not the details of what Naylor told him. I asked if I could get something out of his guy in L.A. if I went out there. Absolutely no dice. He's playing it very close to the vest. I did manage to get out of him that the *Journal* is pushing their investigation from the top down. I got the impression that they've got a line on Naylor's whereabouts.''

''Did he say that?''

''Not in so many words. It was an impression from something he said.''

''And what was that?''

I shook my head. ''I don't remember exactly. Just something in passing.''

Back in my office I asked myself where a Buddy Boyes would stay in Los Angeles if somebody else was paying the tab, and called the Beverly Hills Hotel. It would be just past eight on the coast, but Californians are notoriously early risers and I was able to reach Boyes at breakfast on the patio. As the switchboard operator was ringing his table, I got a mental picture of the little bastard in his iridescent brown suit, seated in the morning sunshine with his juice and croissants and coffee at a strategically chosen spot that would permit him a view of the other tables and of the entrance to the patio.

"Good morning!" The voice had that overdone cheeriness characteristic of evangelical preachers and morning-men on radio. "Buddy Boyes here. How can I be of service to you?"

I gave my name and said, "I presume you know that your client, Joshua Crown, is perched on top of the George Washington Bridge."

"Yes," he said, suddenly solicitous. "I heard about it an hour ago. Anything new?"

"And I presume you know Joshua's a friend of mine?"

"Yes, Tony, I do. I do indeed. He's told me a lot about you. We must get together for lunch when I get back. Perhaps we can do each other some good."

"The reason for my call is to find out whether this bridge thing is a PR stunt of yours?"

"My god, no! I didn't know a thing about it till I called back east this morning. It's not on the news here."

"You didn't put him up to it as a way of promoting the book?"

"Hold a sec, will you?" His voice was suddenly distant on the line. "Hi there, Mr. Spielberg — Buddy Boyes. Fantastic morning. Loved your last picture. Absolutely sensational. I'll be in touch." He was back. "Irv Spielberg," he said by way of explanation. "He's very high on a project of mine."

"Not the Joshua Crown story?"

"No, no, no. As a matter of fact, I told Joshua we were going to have to put his story on the back-burner for a while. He's done nothing, absolutely nothing about getting it on tape, and they're not buying product these days without it's down in black and white. At the very least, a treatment." He paused for what sounded like a sip of juice. "You know, Tony, you just might have come up with a sensational angle. The stunt on the bridge could be just the thing to make the whole project fly." He was suddenly excited. "If we could find a way to get the national media on the story. *People* magazine, maybe *Time*."

"Buddy—"

"Maybe I should hire a writer to work with him—"

"Buddy! Hey, Buddy!"

"Sorry. I get carried away."

"You know what you are, Buddy Boyes?" I said, straining to contain my fury. "You are an elephant's asshole."


It wasn't a productive day. I kept breaking from my work on the half hour to turn on the radio, hoping for news that Joshua was safely down. I wanted to talk to Jo about it but didn't feel I should interrupt her. She'd gone to her studio at nine, and it wasn't unusual for her to have a sandwich and coffee sent in and work through to the dinner hour. Nor was there anything she could do if I did interrupt her. I worked through the afternoon, left a note for her and drove into the city feeling heavy with sadness and close to tears. I considered dropping in at the Hellbox to see if there was any scuttlebutt going, but decided instead to head for the apartment, to monitor the various news programs and get to bed early.

Joshua was everywhere on the tube. Some of the aerial shots were breathtaking: the camera slowly circling the tower, Joshua standing at the focal point, legs apart, both arms raised in a V-for-Victory salute, the wind from the chopper blades fluttering his clothing, the tower and the massive cables receding in perspective beyond him to the moving ribbons of traffic and the tarnished silver of the Hudson River. I dubbed one of the shots onto my VCR and studied the close-ups. He had some sheets of bristol-board pinned beneath a foot, each bearing a crudely lettered message. Bulges in the down vest and the fat form of the tote-bag disclosed that he was conserving his food. He was wearing a hard hat. I noted that the metal plate on which he was standing was not small and square, as had been reported, but rectangular, and had a steel grill at its center. I was relieved to see a safety line snaking from his belt to the metal grillwork. But, my god, to sleep there, with no protection from the wind and with nothing to warm him but what he was wearing.

Two of the television stations had mustered the ingenuity to talk to him: one, by shouting through a bullhorn and picking up his answers—only occasionally intelligible over the beat of the helicopter rotors—on a directional microphone of the type used on the sidelines at football games. WNBC hovered over the tower and lowered a microphone on a weighted cable. Except for the wind-roar, the sound was excellent. Joshua talked non-stop, regurgitating clichés about humanity being buried in its own garbage. He finished with a demand to speak to the mayor of the city, adding that he would stay on the tower until the request was met. I shook my head sadly. Poor Joshua; he didn't know that the mayor had a phobia about flying and wouldn't get in a helicopter if it meant missing the St. Patrick's Day parade. Nor did he realize that he posed no political problem to the mayor. The Port Authority was a bi-state agency, with sole jurisdiction over all bridges, airports, and bus and marine terminals within a twenty-five-mile radius of the Statue of Liberty. The mayor couldn't have cared less about the ultimatum but was more than willing to respond at length to the assembled press, feet planted firmly on the inch-deep broadloom in his office.

There was no lack of officials ready to be interviewed, each thumping his own drum, each protecting his own ass. There were authoritative predictions that Joshua would be down within twenty-four hours because of the chill night forecast by the weather office. And there were various proposals to force him from the tower, none feasible. Two boozy members of the Amalgamated Bridge, Structural Steel and Ornamental Iron-workers, Local 40, lusting for a piece of the attention, volunteered to scale the tower, hog-tie their brother and bring him down. A window-washer employed by the Empire State Building belittled the height of the tower and proposed that he be lowered to the top by helicopter, guaranteeing to talk Joshua into descending. A team of mountaineers, just back from Nepal and an assault on Everest, explained to a newsman why their rescue techniques offered the best possibility for a solution. A wild animal procurer, in town to do business with the Bronx Zoo, suggested that Joshua be shot with a tranquilizer dart and then lowered from the top by a police rescue team.

"Darling, I just heard the news. Why didn't you let me know?"

"I didn't want to interrupt you. And there's nothing you or I can do. He's in no danger. Not Joshua."

"But what's he doing up there?"

"I don't know. He seems himself, more or less. At least he hasn't flipped his wig."

"But we've got to do something. He'll freeze. He's not dressed for it."

"Don't worry. They'll find a way to get him down. The unpardonable sin in our society is to obstruct traffic."

"But we've got to *do* something."

We discussed half a dozen possibilities but ended where we'd begun — frustrated. That sense of helplessness led us to agree to forgo meeting for dinner. Exhausted, I was asleep by nine o'clock and groggy when the alarm went at six-thirty the following morning.

The inbound traffic jam Tuesday morning was not much worse than usual. Port Authority police were stationed every few yards on the bridge and brooked no nonsense. Anyone slowing in hope of catching a glimpse of the man on the tower was waved furiously on. The Civil Aeronautics Association banned flights within a mile of the tower, thus ending the circling by helicopters and small planes and, consequently, the hourly updates. During the night, the wind had carried off Joshua's placards and he was unable to deliver any more messages, even to the telephoto lenses. He scribbled phrases on pages from a pad of paper and released them in the wind. One, recovered by a patron of a Burger King in Hackensack, New Jersey, bore the message: "Remember Three Mile Island!"

Tuesday afternoon, the Port Authority helicopter flew in close, and Tommy Ducharmes, chief of the Caughnawaga reservation, in company with Clint Eastwood and Vanna White, urged Joshua to come down. He gave them a middle-finger salute. The Tuesday evening outbound traffic flowed without major incident. Two members of the Emergency Services squad ascended to the top of the tower and spent the better part of an hour trying to talk Joshua down. Vainly. It began to rain an hour before dusk and a dramatic telephoto picture in the *Register* showed Joshua sitting huddled, arms about his legs, his back to the wind, his hair streaming forward.

By Wednesday, the story had assumed the shape of a great lark. Joshua jokes were to be heard everywhere. Johnny Carson did a takeoff, dressed in Indian garb and seated atop a totem-pole. T-shirts and bumper-stickers bearing the legend "High Steelers Make Better Erections" were hawked by street-vendors. A rock group rushed out a single, "The Joshua Rock":

> Do it in the sky,
> Do it in the air.
> Do it, do it, do it, do it,
> Do it everywhere.
>
> Do it in a low-rise,
> Do it on a tower.
> Do it, do it, do it, do it,
> Do it every hour.

The Pete's Pizza Parlor chain ran a full-page ad in the *Post* under the headline: "When Joshua comes down it'll be for a Pete's Pizza. *You* can beat him to it!" Three teenagers, high on crack, tried to climb the Brooklyn Bridge and had to be rescued by the Emergency Services squad. A graffiti artist emblazoned "Crown Joshua" on the statue at Columbus Square. A few dozen young people gathered on the bank of the river south of the bridge and chanted, "C'mon *down!* Joshua *Crown!*" Another group catcalled, "Jump! Jump!" and finally, "Chick-*en!*"

Thursday noon, I phoned Dunc. "Dunc," I said, "let me off the hook on the gold contraband story. Let me talk to the police about what you told me. I promise to feed you anything I get."

297

"I was just going to call you," he said. His voice seemed uncharacteristically subdued.

"You sound down."

"You could say that."

"You've been fired."

"Nothing that pleasant."

"You don't want to talk about it."

"Not now. Not on the phone."

We met for drinks and talked for ten minutes at my table at the Hellbox before he broached it. He asked in a listless fashion about Joshua, and I told him I knew nothing more than what was in the papers. I explained that I'd decided to stop playing coy with Sergeant Kosiosko and that I was going to tell him everything I knew and try to enlist his aid. And I told Dunc that I would need his cooperation.

"Who, precisely, is Kosiosko?" he asked.

"Sorry. He's a cop in homicide at the Mid-town South Precinct, the guy who's been working on Victor Gladden's death. I'm sure I can trust him. I want to fill him in on exactly what Naylor told your guy Rawlins. It could be that what Naylor told Rawlins would confirm what Victor found out but didn't get to tell me."

He sat staring into the drink he'd hardly sipped. "Tim Rawlins is dead."

A roll of thunder in my brain. "Dead? What happened?"

"An accident. He was driving home late last night—he lives in La Canada, in the hills back of the canyon—and his car went off the road and down a cliff. Burned."

"Dunc, I'm sorry."

"Yeah," he said emptily. "So am I."

"Are they sure it was an accident?"

"That's what they're saying."

"No witnesses?"

He shook his head. "It was around one-thirty in the morning. Unfortunately, Tim had had a few."

I sat silent for a moment, stunned. Was it possible? Was that why Gladden had seemed unconcerned when I told him I hadn't been able to get the name of the man who talked to

298

Naylor? Was that why, as I'd learned later, Saywell had gone with Gladden on the trip to Los Angeles? Impossible!

"Did you tell the police about the assignment Rawlins was working on?"

"Yes."

"What did they say?"

"Not much. Very polite. Said they'd check it out. But there was no evidence of anything other than that he didn't make the turn and went off the road."

"What do you think?"

"How the hell would I know?" he said, flaring. There were tears brimming in his eyes. He brushed at them roughly with the back of a hand and turned away. "Where the hell is that goddamn Kono? This is the lousiest goddamn drink I've ever had. I don't know why the hell I come into this goddamn place."


Kosiosko put down the telephone. "Your man had a 1.02 alcohol level in his blood. Definitely impaired. There was nothing about the skid marks on the road or on the shoulder to indicate anything but that he went into the turn too fast."

"Is it possible he was forced off the road?"

"Of course. But they don't think so." He pulled a notebook within reach. "Tell me more about this William Naylor." He printed the name at the top of the page and underlined it.

I told him everything I knew except the scene in the barn. I knew if I told him that he would go to Gladden with the accusation. Nor did I recount what Gus Longo had told me. I left it that Naylor had simply disappeared.

"That's not a hell of a lot to go on," he said, making further underlinings beneath the name. "I'll put out a missing-persons on Naylor and fill in Los Angeles. Don't expect too much." He began to doodle: arrows, all of them pointing to Naylor's name. "Let's go back to Victor Gladden. You say he was alienated from his father—which isn't hard to understand, having talked to him—the father, that is—and that Victor was convinced that his father was mixed up in some kind of illegal activity. He makes friends with one of the guards at his father's estate and leaves you a note suggesting that his suspicions were justified. Within hours he's murdered.'' He looked up from the paper. ''You realize what you're saying: that Oscar Gladden, the Reverend Oscar Gladden, ordered the execution of his own son?''

''Yes.''

''You don't think the whole thing could have been in the son's imagination and that he was killed because of some other connection, about which we know nothing?''

''But you get the same pattern from Los Angeles. Naylor says Gladden is involved in a rip-off of the contributions to his television church and within days he's killed.''

''You say within days he was killed. You said a moment ago merely that he was missing.''

I blinked. ''It makes sense, that's all. Well, doesn't it?'' I said, turning it back on him.

''Very few things in my world make sense,'' he said, sighing heavily. ''Let's see what we've been able to turn up at Bellevue.'' He punched three digits on the telephone. ''Manny? Alex Kosiosko. Anything on Gladden, Victor?'' He was silent, making notes. ''Thanks.'' He hung up the phone.

''Victor Gladden was hospitalized twice last year. Once, September 7 through 18, for drug overdose and subsequent treatment. And again for two weeks in December for treatment of delusionary paranoia. He's been hospitalized half a dozen times in the past five years. In each case his bill was paid with a check written by G. Oscar Gladden.''

He had put on his glasses to read his notes. Now he took them off, lifted his shoulders and turned his hands outward in a gesture of resignation.


That night at the apartment I ranged the television channels looking for news of Joshua. The only reference was on WPIX, which closed its newscast with the sentence: ''Day Four for Joshua Crown.'' I turned off the set and looked from my window in the direction of the bridge. I couldn't see it, of course; the towers at midtown intervened — one of them the Republic Motors Building. It was coming on dark and the nightly miracle of the city's lights was being performed. Wind buffeted the window and tossed the tresses of the trees below. The weather forecasts had warned of a sharp drop in temperature, of rain showers, and of winds from the northeast, winds that the banks of the Hudson would channel past the bridge.

I put on a pullover and a raincoat, picked up Smedley and drove north on the Henry Hudson Parkway. Just beyond the bridge I swung left and looped onto the southbound way. At an emergency parking area I left a note in the windshield-wiper to the effect that I would be back in five minutes—so hoping to forestall a tow-away—and made my way down the grassy slope to the bank of the river. The wind was rambunctious. It whipped my open raincoat about and, in a gust, whirled it above my head.

In so close, there was little hope of seeing Joshua, although possibly he was that tiny daub of color atop the gray of the tower. But I saw him clearly in my mind. He would be seated, hunched, hugging his knees—as in the picture in the *Register*— his back against the blast, the cold beginning to stiffen his muscles and penetrate his bones. How bitter his thoughts must be! The helicopters had been withdrawn. His cards had blown away. The pad of paper was gone. Surely his food would have run out. Even the idly curious atop the Palisades and on the bank of the river had gone—some of their debris lay at my feet. He could shout, but who would hear? He could listen, but there would be few sounds of life this night, nothing but the howl of the wind in the cables. And beyond his discomfort, there would be no sensation but the vibrations of the traffic below traveling to his bleak platform. The lowering clouds and the gathering night would soon erase the city, and he would be isolated, cut off from all life but his own.

I returned to Smedley to fetch my flashlight and to start the motor so the interior of the car would be warm when I returned. Perhaps I could beam a light to him. Perhaps it would carry to the top of the tower and he might wave his arms in the beam, grateful that someone had remembered him. But when I returned to the river bank, the rain was driving. It stung like ice pellets on my upturned face. I turned on the flashlight, but clouds now obscured the top of the tower and I could project only a vaporous, shifting lance of light. I waited for perhaps half an hour, hoping for a break in the clouds, but none came. After a final try I turned back to the car. Within its warm sanctuary I bent over the wheel, my teeth chattering, and wept.

Joshua! . . .

# TWENTY-SIX

Caleb Crown stirred the fire with a dog's-leg branch of dead beech and the sparks spiraled into the darkness to join the stars. The night was clear but moonless, and in it there was an augury of winter. Far off, a dog barked, testing the night. Caleb was crouched on his haunches before the fire. The flames illuminated the lower planes of his face, giving it a theatrically malevolent look. In the shadows on his face his eyes glittered and his teeth showed unnaturally white.

I pulled the blanket more snugly around Jo's and my shoulders. At her insistence we had driven from the city Friday afternoon and had spent the waning evening wandering pathways on the hills above the settlement. For the past hour we had sat with Caleb, talking about Joshua and our concern for him. He had listened without a question or comment and, when we finished, had remained almost motionless, his eyes closed, thinking. Now he stirred the fire again. It blazed almost immediately, and from my position Caleb himself seemed to be aflame.

"When you were here before," he said, "I told you the story of the left-handed and the right-handed twins. They're part of the Iroquois legend of the creation of the world. You may have found it childish or you may have found wisdom in it; it doesn't matter. I had hoped that knowing the story might help you to understand Joshua."

"It did," I said.

Caleb moved from his haunches to sit cross-legged. He found

his pipe and began to pack it with tobacco. Then he lit the pipe and paused until he had it drawing properly.

"Joshua," he said, "is like most Americans—like most Iroquois—a man of today. Since he was a child he has wanted to live for the day and for tomorrow, and he has been impatient with the past. He has tried to forget who he was. I don't think we can do that. We are what the past has made us and each of us is more like our parents than we believe. I have read what your teachers say: that we are what our fathers and mothers were, and we have no choice in this, but that we are also what we choose to be. And this is true. I look in the mirror and sometimes it is my father who looks back at me. Others see my mother in my hands, in the way I walk and talk.

"And yet we are not our fathers or our mothers. Joshua and I are from the same seed, the same womb, and our flesh is the same, but *we* are not the same. Our father, like his father before him, was a wild man. He liked to drink and he liked to fight. And when he would fight it was as though he cared nothing for his own life or for the life of those he fought. When he would drink there was a madness in him. I am not like that. Joshua is not like that. We have spoken of this and have agreed that we are glad we are not like our father.

"And yet I *am* like my father. My father believed in the old ways. He knew nothing of Handsome Lake, but in many ways it was as though he was his son. And in this way I am truly my father's son. Joshua scorns such ways. He thinks a man is a fool who, if he can buy corn in the store, would trouble to grow it. He cannot understand that for the man who grows the corn, life can have a different meaning. Joshua thinks a man is a fool who, if he could ride in an automobile, would choose to walk. He cannot understand that to walk is to find the time to think. The man who drives sees only the road. The man who walks sees the world about him. He hears the birds and the sounds of the stream. He smells the flowers and the fields. Joshua would say, yes, he sees the birds and the fields and the stream, but the world passes him by and leaves him standing in the dust of the past.

"Do I say that Joshua is wrong in this? No. Who am I to say that he is wrong and that I am right? And who can say what is right? The Iroquois legend of the creation of the world says that in the beginning there was a right-handed twin and a left-handed twin and that from their birth they contended with each other. And they created the world. As every legend concerning the beginning of things must, our legend speaks of good and evil. But with us, good and evil are not opposites. They are the way the world is—and they often complement each other.

"So it has been with Joshua and me. We are brothers but we have contended with each other from the day of our birth. I know that I cannot be as Joshua is. I was born an Iroquois. It is what I am, it is what I am content to be. Joshua, too, was born an Iroquois, but in his heart he has wanted to be a white man. Your Mr. Gladden wanted to make him a famous white man, and you have helped him in this. I have wondered from the day I heard about it whether this could be; whether the white man would let an Iroquois be a famous white man. If you ask me what I think, I think they will not."

The longhouse in which Jo and I were to stay the night bore on its gable end a carving of a bear. We entered through a bark door, hinged at the top, and found ourselves in a vestibule of sorts in which firewood was stacked alongside barrels filled with dried food. The interior of the longhouse smelled of wood-smoke, cooking and people. A central corridor of trampled earth about eight feet wide ran from one end to the other, interrupted only by bowl-shaped hearths dug in the ground where, we were told, the women cooked in winter. On each side of the corridor there were compartments — small wooden platforms raised a foot above the ground and open to the corridor. Each was occupied by a single family and was separated from its neighbors by a storage closet. Possessions were stacked on the shelves. Over-head, seed-corn and dried foods hung from the rafters. On the floor were sleeping-mats of woven corn husks and, to one side, folded blankets of deer- and bearskin.

The night was cold. In the bed, the chamois suppleness of newly tanned deerhide was soft against our nakedness. The darkness was total and filled with night sounds: a minute of murmured soprano-basso conversation in the cubicle next to ours; a baby's vexed crying ending in the soft sibilance of nursing; a virtuoso performance of snoring from the man in the cubicle opposite ("The philharmonic tuning up," Jo whispered); occasional unidentifiable rustlings that Jo was certain were rats—which notion I pooh-poohed but didn't doubt; extraneous sounds from without—the tremulous hooting of an owl, a brief dogfight of terrible intensity.

Jo and I each knew the other's body with something of the tactile sureness of the sightless. When we were together, the renewal of our passion could utterly absorb us, and we would often lose all sense of time and place. As lovers do, we had a need to share and would often talk, even while making love: light chaffing talk, murmured endearments, lascivious whisperings. We marveled at softness, at hardness, at touch and taste and smell. There would be relaxed times of casual fondling, and other times of a fierce, exultant glorying in our flesh. Now, as the need for completion would brook no more postponement, Jo whispered, "Shhh," and covered my mouth with a hand. Even as, when a moment later her time came, I put my lips on hers.

In the darkness we heard footfalls approaching. Perhaps we had been overheard and were about to be rebuked. Caleb's breathy whisper came from just above our heads: "Get dressed and come outside."

We dressed in the darkness, feeling for our clothes, awkward with embarrassment. In the darkness, hand in hand, we walked carefully in the direction Caleb had gone, stumbling once into one of the fire-pits but making it finally to the rectangle of lighter darkness where the bark door was being held open.

"The telephone," Caleb said and, offering no further explanation, set out for the exit from the palisade. I saw a shadowy figure following and concluded that it was the man who had heard the ring of the telephone and awakened Caleb.

"Who could it be at this time of the night?" I whispered and felt the tension in Jo's hand as it tightened on mine. In the darkness of the telephone booth I found the dangling receiver. There was the roaring hum of a bad connection.

"Hello! Hello!"

"Tony?"

"I'm here," I shouted. "Who is it?"

"It's Obie Berenson. I've been trying everywhere to reach you."

The static on the line suddenly intensified. There were whistles and a hissing and random beeps. I could hear Obie's voice as if he were in a distant echo-chamber but could catch only an occasional phrase. Then there was a click, and it was as though he was in the booth with me. " —something wrong with this goddamn connection."

"It's okay now. I hear you perfectly."

"Yes, that's much better."

"Obie, for chrissake, what's up?"

"I'd lost the number there and finally I had to—"

"Never mind that. What's the problem?"

"I thought I should let you know," he said. "Joshua's dead."

That Friday morning the Port Authority helicopter had swung by the east tower to prepare an update for the director and had found Joshua gone. All that remained was an unopened bottle of beer wedged neck-down in the steel grillwork. The harbor police immediately began a search, starting at the base of the tower and working their way downstream. Early Monday morning Joshua's tote-bag was discovered in the midst of a dog's-vomit of flotsam bobbing in the lee of Pier 81, where the *Hudson River Day Line* berthed. Deputy Commissioner Ivan Pilsudski of the harbor police told a reporter for the *Daily News* that, while he would not rule out the possibility that Joshua Crown had jumped to his death, it was probable that, there being no moon, he had fallen while descending the tower during the night.

# PART THREE

# TWENTY-SEVEN

A shaft of dazzling sunlight cast a radiant rectangle on the floor of the studio. Jo stood at its center, bent as though old. Her face seemed bloodless. Her eyelids were swollen and her eyes were without luster.

"There was no need for him to kill himself," she said. The voice was flat, despairing. "We could have saved him. I could have. You could have. We don't know how to love. We don't know how to care." She thrust with a closed fist as though striking at something invisible. "*They* killed him—the newspapers, the radio, the television—making a circus out of his protest. Turning him into a freak." She began to gather her sketches and paintings of Joshua. She took the scalpel she used to sharpen her pencils and slashed one of them. The blade whimpered through the canvas.

"Jo, don't!"

"He's been exploited enough." Her arm rose. I seized her wrist.

Oscar Gladden, who had toiled panting up the narrow staircase, had been watching, saying nothing. As I restrained her, he said, "Let her mourn," and went clanging down the stairs.

Jo sank slowly to her knees, her head down, weeping silently. I put a hand to her head and pressed it against my thigh, holding it there. After a while she gathered herself and said in a controlled voice, "I'm okay. I'd like to be alone for a few minutes, please."

I went down the staircase toward Gladden's office, wondering why I had no tears and remembering that day in Caugh-nawaga when I had first come to know Joshua Crown. He had come through the door of his house into the morning sunlight, walking with the ambling ease of the athlete, two coffee mugs in his hands and a piece of toast between his teeth. I had been predisposed to dislike him (after all my research, to have an *American Indian* foisted on me!) but was drawn to him almost immediately. Joshua, the left-handed twin. How unlike his orthodox brother he had been, and how much more engaging. I tend to like flawed people. I found it easy to understand why, in the Iroquois legend, the grandmother from the Sky World might have favored the boy called Flint.

I paused at the door to Gladden's study, gathering myself, telling myself: No speeches. No heroics. No recrimination. Just say it.

I tapped on the door and entered. The office was empty. Enervated, I went down the hall to the bedroom and knocked.

"Mr. Gladden?"

His voice called out, "Come."

Jerri West, in a wisp of a brassiere, her nipples protruding, a triangle of cleft lace at her crotch, reached for a robe and put it on. Gladden was standing by the great bed removing his shirt. His jacket and tie were on the floor. Busy with the buttons, he didn't look at me.

"You know Jerri," he said, casting the shirt aside, his pale breasts jiggling.

"For chrissake!" I said.

Hands on his belt buckle, he looked at me, sighed wearily as though at a difficult child and nodded at Jerri. "Five min-utes." He sat on the bed, his great Buddha's belly supporting his bosom. "Well," he said brusquely as Jerri left, easing the door closed, "what is it?"

"Mr. Gladden," I said in a voice dead of emotion, "I want out. I've set up two people and they're both dead. Johnny Gallagher and Joshua Crown, dead."

"Don't dramatize it, Carpenter," he said, smoothing the satin sheet with the palm of a hand, watching the ripples run before it. "They killed themselves."

"No, I killed them. We killed them. We manipulated their

312

lives. We played God. We made Joshua a celebrity because it suited our purposes, and we brought down Gallagher because he didn't.''

Gladden rose from the bed, stepped down from the raised platform and went to the bar. He chunked some ice cubes into a glass, poured a scotch and took a long swallow. Then he sat down and said listlessly, ''Come over here.''

As I moved to the other chair, he hoisted one foot across a knee and, grunting, began to untie a shoe. ''Let's stop right now,'' he said, ''and try to get things straight. What did we do for Joshua Crown? We made it possible for him to raise a hundred and thirty thousand dollars for his friend's widow. That's bad? We explained in advance what was wanted. We spelled it out and he went along. When he began to get off on that ecology crap, I warned him—you were there—I said, 'Quit now! Forget it!' He wouldn't listen. He was hooked on the glory. Is that my fault? Your fault?'' He peeled off a sock, tossed it aside and hauled up the other foot. ''Johnny Gallagher? Gallagher was an opportunist, a hypocrite and a thief. It would all have come out sooner or later. Did we put the gun to his head?''

''But you rigged the evidence. Jerri put his initials in her date book even though she didn't know the man.''

''But you forget—she *told* the press she didn't know him. But they preferred to believe the lie. Of course, it made a better story.''

''But his initials. The specific dates.''

He shrugged. ''So we helped things along.'' He rose from the chair and dropped his trousers and shorts. His tiny penis poked like a fledgling from the nest at the juncture of his belly and thighs. He picked up a bathtowel, draped it about his waist and returned to stand in front of me, pink and bulbous, his hairless skin shining with a dew of perspiration.

''The break-in at Gallagher's headquarters,'' I said. ''Your people did it, didn't they? Wasn't that how Jerri knew what dates to put in her book?''

He put his hands on his hips, looming massively above me. ''What the hell *is* this? A grand jury hearing? And who the hell do you think you are? Some half-assed D.A.? Gallagher and that dumb Indian killed themselves because they couldn't hack it when the heat was on. They were grown men. They knew what they were doing." He reached for his drink. "And who the hell are you to question me?" He went toward the bed.

I said again, "I want out."

He spun around, his face and body inflamed. "Where the hell do you think you are," he roared, "back at the *Register?* You don't quit Oscar Gladden. Nobody does."

I took dead aim. "Bill Naylor did."

The shot went home. His color deepened to a mottled red. I saw him deliberately rein in his rage. When he spoke his voice was silken but the more menacing for it. "More and more, you remind me of Bill Naylor. Take my word for it—that's not good."

He was watching my eyes, watching for a flicker that might betray something of my thoughts, wondering surely whether I knew what had happened to Naylor. After a moment he turned away and padded to the door.

"Carpenter," he said, "I offered you a deal. A good deal. You had two weeks to make up your mind and you decided to come in. You're in. So let's cut the cry-baby shit and get on with it." He opened the door and shouted, "Jerri."

I went back to my office and, as I had so often in recent weeks, stood at the window to sort out my thoughts. The atmosphere seemed close and it took an effort to fill my lungs. I threw open the sash. The air, pungent with the scent of fading flowers, rotting leaves and harvested fields, flowed over me. I breathed deeply, filling my lungs and emptying them, trying to vent the miasma that was smothering me.

There would be no more temporizing. Goddamn it, I would nail Oscar Gladden to the wall!


The face on the television set: "How often in life we blame others for our failures. My wife is to blame. My husband. The boss. My parents. The government. . . ." Oscar Gladden's dark eyes peering penetratingly from beneath the perfect crescent brows, the red lips moving: "How easy it is to condemn others, how convenient to shift the responsibility. But who is to blame for that expanding waistline? Someone else? For your failure to get that raise? Someone else? For the lawn overgrown with weeds, for that C-minus in your final exam, for blowing your stack at that guy who cut you off on the freeway?

"Okay, sometimes it *is* somebody else's fault. But as often as not it isn't. It lets us off the hook if we can—as the song says —put the blame on Mame, boy. Put the blame on Mame.

"But what a fatal mistake! Keep blaming others and you'll never change. And that's the end of you, because change is of the essence of life. Let me put it another way. Blame others and you'll never grow, never adapt. Don't adapt and you begin to be history. . . . ''

I pushed the off-button and Oscar Gladden's image collapsed. In the ensuing silence I heard the sound of the tow truck and returned to the window. The truck was paused at the gate, the engine idling. Knee-Hi and Rocco Lombardi were chatting with the driver, whose face I couldn't see. How long had it been since I'd heard the truck on what had been a regular weekly run to the barn and back? Three weeks, a month at least. I examined the truck with particular care. There were the usual tires on the flat-bed section. Had the Mexican contraband junkets been resumed?

I went to the telephone and made an appointment to meet Roger Zachs for lunch.


I told Roger nearly everything: about my conversations with Dunc, about Bill Naylor's charge that Gladden was skimming millions of dollars, about Bill Naylor's disappearance (withholding what I had witnessed in the barn) and about Victor Gladden's murder—about which, of course, he knew most of the details. I'd been hoping that, with the zeal if not the skill he'd demonstrated earlier, this latest news would kindle a fire in his belly. But he had listened without interrupting, nodding but impassive, and all the while scoffing chunks of veal *cordon bleu* and washing them down with frequent swallows of the white house wine.

No comment volunteered, I said, "Well?"

He was wiping the plate with a chunk of bread. "What would you like me to say?"

315

"Jeezus, Rog, last time we talked you were so hot to put the arm on Gladden you nearly pissed your pants."

I had to wait until he'd finished chewing the bread. "Believe me," he said, "nothing would please me more than, as you phrase it, to put the arm on Oscar Gladden. But I've learned not to dive in until I know how deep the water is."

"The fact that Naylor has vanished? Gone? Is probably kaput?"

"We're talking to Scotland Yard about that."

"The reporter Naylor talked to—dead?"

"I'm sorry, Tony, but you're putting two and two together and getting five. He was drunk and drove off a cliff."

"The IRS investigation? The audit at Peale and Bjornstadt?"

He shook his head. "Nothing so far that we can proceed on." He was swabbing the shining plate with another chunk of bread. "I'm sorry, Tony. You haven't given me anything I can make stick. The guy may be a monumental crook, but we rushed to judgment last time and got our ass royally kicked."

"Nothing less than a smoking gun. Is that it?"

He said nothing but withdrew a cigar from a leather pocketpack, did the sniffing, moistening and clipping-the-end routine, reached into a vest pocket for a gold lighter and fired up. His every move said, Tomorrow, the lieutenant governor's mansion.

My tone was snarly. "I get the distinct impression, Roger, that Oscar Gladden is a don't-touch. He could burn down the White House and you wouldn't charge him with playing with matches."

He leaned back in his seat, smiling tightly. "I should walk out and leave you with the check."

My anger ran out with the suddenness of the last grains in an egg-timer. Roger wasn't going to do anything and I could understand why. He'd broken his lance trying to make a case against Gladden in the anti-trust indictment and, so I'd heard, had had his tail kicked by the governor, who wasn't about to alienate Gladden's millions of viewers. The wise general only fights battles he can win.

"Instead," Roger was saying, "I'm going to do you a favor. I'm going to have our people guard you around the clock."

"Don't bother," I said. "I wouldn't want to interfere with their arresting old ladies who don't stoop-and-scoop after their teacup poodles."

"Have a care, Tony," he said, placing his credit card on the check. "Your friend plays for keeps."


Bartholemew on the telephone: "Tony, Mr. G. asked me to call and see if you would be free for an hour around ten-thirty. If so, he'll come by and pick you up. Would that be convenient?"

"Well, yes," I said slowly, wondering what was up. "Of course, if it's important."

I was fighting to bring my concentration into focus. It was Sunday. I had risen early in order to devote the entire morning to my novel, and when the phone rang had been deeply immersed in the world in which my protagonist lived. It had been four days since the showdown with Gladden. I had tried vainly to see him in order to tender my resignation. I had once caught Bartholemew in the hallway but had been able to talk to him only on the fly. He was busy setting up Gladden's annual meeting with his OneWorld franchise holders, and since it involved simultaneous two-way satellite transmissions to a hundred or more cities across North America and around the world, he was near-frantic as he sought to draw together the final details of preparation.

Incidentally, Oscar Gladden's franchise owners were never given the opportunity to meet him personally although he communicated with them regularly through a newsletter and made much of such events as birthdays, sending them an audio cassette inscribed with a personal message and presenting the more successful with a one-ounce wafer of gold engraved with his signature. When circumstances required it, he would meet with the seven members of the board of directors of the Worldwide Church of One. But his was a one-man show and those occurrences were rare. In the months I had been with him, the directors had come to the estate only once. I had studied them from my office window as they arrived. There was nothing about their appearance to distinguish them. They looked like typical businessmen, all in their middle years, conservative in dress

317

and each carrying an attaché case. They arrived in expensive cars, three of them chauffeur driven. Seeing them reminded me of Oscar Gladden's response when I had asked him if he maintained the aquarium to impress friends. "I have no friends," he'd said. "I keep the fish to impress on the people who work for me that there's enough for everyone if nobody gets greedy."

"Since your apartment building is set back from the street," Bartholemew was saying, "may I suggest that Mr. G. pick you up on the southeast corner of First Avenue and 23rd."

"You won't tell me what's up?" I asked, conscious of a small stirring of apprehension.

"I don't really know," he said. "No, that's not quite true. I do, but I'd rather leave it to Mr. G. I will say this: I think you'll find what he has to say very interesting."

Doc at the wheel, we headed north on Third Avenue and turned left at 42nd Street, passing the *Daily News* building.

"Familiar territory?" Gladden asked and I nodded. "Take a right at the next corner," he said into the intercom, "and pull over to the curb."

We were parked across the street from the building that housed the *Register.* Gladden leaned across and pointed at the adjoining property, a nondescript fifteen-story building, distinguished only by its conventionality of design and its decrepitude.

"The T.G. Hamblin building," he said. "We begin to raze it next week. Then, in a year or two, we'll take down the *Register* building. In their place we're going to put up this." He removed a whiteprint from a tubular container and unrolled it. It showed an architect's representation of a towering rectangular building covered entirely with reflective glass and unadorned except at the highest point, where the word *ONE* was superimposed on the face.

I turned to look at him. His eyes were glittering with excitement and his skin was flushed. I expected him to say something and waited for it. When he added nothing, I asked, "Are you trying to tell me that you've bought the *Register?*"

There had been scuttlebutt that the paper was for sale. Dunc had mentioned that he'd heard the Gannett chain was interested.

"We're in the process of dotting the i's and crossing the t's," Gladden said. "I bought the Hamblin building three months ago. We'll be announcing very shortly our takeover of the *Register*. I wanted you to be among the first to know." There was the slightest smile on his lips as he rolled up the whiteprint and continued. "You've been asking why I aborted my plan to strike back at the news media. I can understand your concern; that was what you were hired to do. We had a go with the Mr. Nobody project, but it bombed. After my anger cooled it became obvious to me that I had taken a wrong turn and that any further action along that line would be counter-productive. Nobody wins an argument with the press; they invariably have the last word. I began to see that what I really needed was not vengeance but a voice. I have a voice now, of course, but I'm not fool enough to use my television broadcasts for political ends— Jerry Falwell and Pat Robertson made that mistake a few years back, and I'm not about to repeat it."

He looked out of the window at the *Register* building. "But a newspaper! Now, that's something else! And, down the road, a *chain* of newspapers—newspapers that do what a newspaper should do, namely, cover the news, but that also have an editorial voice that can be brought to bear on politicians and governments and institutions, and," he emphasized, "on the media. This country is going to hell in a handbasket and somebody needs to stand against the people who are taking it there." He placed a hand on my shoulder. "And that's what you and I are going to do. Your job will be to run the news department. I'll handle editorial policy."

I won't attempt to describe the surge of emotion that seemed, quite literally, to explode within me. So many thoughts ricocheted in my mind that my brain dizzied.

Gladden read my reaction, smiled and asked, "Well, what do you say?"

I was aware of the thumping of my heart and of a tremulousness throughout my body. I could not yet believe what I was hearing—Tony Carpenter, editor of the New York *Register*! It was necessary to will myself calm.

"Mr. Gladden," I said, and had to clear my throat before

continuing, "I really don't know how to respond." I raised my shoulders in a gesture of bewilderment. "What can I say?"

"It's quite simple. Say yes."

I had recovered my balance now and my guard was coming up. "I'm at a loss," I said. "You and I haven't been exactly hitting it off. I don't follow."

He paused a moment before replying, looking at me intently, his eyes narrowed to slits. "I'll be frank with you, Carpenter: I'd pretty much given up on you. You're not an easy man to deal with. But, all else aside, I will give you this: you've done your job and done it well. It's become obvious that you have a good mind and know more about the news media than I do. So, when I decided to buy the *Register* and began to think about finding someone to run the news end, you were the first person to come to my mind." He inserted the whiteprint into its tube and tapped it into place with the palm of his hand. It gave off a hollow sound.

"Then, of course, there is the matter of your and Josephine's relationship. From the moment I saw it developing I was dead set against it. I told you that. I told her that. But she has a mind of her own—comes by it honestly—and I've had to accept the fact that, despite my objections, she is going forward with her plans. And there isn't a damn thing I can do about it." The slightest of smiles softened his face. "I have always believed that if you can't lick 'em, join 'em, and I've told Josephine you have my blessing."

I was having some considerable difficulty adjusting to an Oscar Gladden who wasn't caustic and insulting. For a fleeting moment I found myself drawn to him, and then remembered the crushed and quivering body of William Naylor, the mass of gore where Victor Gladden's face had been.

"Thank you," I said evenly. "I'll have to think about it—the job, that is."

"What is there to think about?" he said sharply. "You'll have complete autonomy. The starting salary will be double what I'm paying you now, and our original arrangement about your account in Geneva still stands."

He continued to press me, finally growing testy, even as I insisted on time to think it through. In my confusion, I had him

320

drop me off at the Hellbox, hoping that Dunc would be there so that we could talk, but, it being Sunday morning, the place was closed. I hailed a cab and returned to the apartment, my mind in tumult.

I could scarcely contain my excitement. How many times as a journalist had I said to myself—while grinding my teeth at some aggravation—I, goddamn it, could run this madhouse better than the idiots in charge. And now, here, out of the blue, I was being offered the opportunity to direct a great metropolitan daily, to fashion it as I saw fit, to put in practice ideas that I had nurtured for years. Surely I must be dreaming! No, on the evidence, the proposition was genuine. Oscar Gladden was offering me the opportunity to turn my wildest dream into reality, the opportunity to change the practices that had turned the once prestigious *Register* into a form of entertainment rather than a serious journal. Incredible!

A vagrant, malicious thought intruded: there would be a delicious icing on the cake—the opportunity to see Replogle's face when he heard the news! *Fantastic!*

I couldn't take the job, of course. But the contemplation of it was like the savoring of a great wine, and for a few minutes I held reality at arm's length while I relished it.

No, no matter how much I might want to accept Oscar Gladden's offer, I could not. It had become clear to me over the past few weeks that I had no option but to do everything in my power to bring Gladden down. He was a corrupt and evil man. The news that he was about to buy the *Register* and extend his influence only deepened the conviction that I must expose him. I didn't buy one word of the song and dance he had engaged in as we viewed the site. He hadn't made the offer because I was the ideal man for the job but because it would keep me in his employ and thus within his control. (Not, let it be understood, that I couldn't have hacked it as editor of the *Register*; I'd paid my dues.) But Oscar Gladden realized that I wanted out and that, inevitably, I would go. He knew also that sooner or later I would pose serious problems for him. I had sufficient knowledge of his activities to expose him to the world as the monstrous fraud he was, and he knew that.

God, I thought, smiling grimly, wouldn't I *love* to do an

exposé on the Oscar Gladden I had come to know! I salivated at the thought: The Reverend G. Oscar Glutton: Obscene voluptuary. Vicious murderer. Monumental hypocrite. Liar. Tyrant. Bully. . . . And, with the exposé, a sidebar on his "Fortress Jehovah," as Dunc called it, with its fish-tank full of predators and its collection of hoodlums to guard its gates.

Gladden's concern about such actions as I might take would be heightened by the fact that Jo and I were planning to marry. I represented a potential rift between himself and his daughter; I might very well bring about his estrangement from the one thing he held dear in all the world.

But it was not only his problem, it was mine. If I were to move against Gladden, how would Jo react? Especially now, knowing that her father had forgone his opposition to our marrying, had already given us his blessing and was prepared to bestow on the man she loved an open door to eminence and financial security.

It was a complication I had not foreseen.

# TWENTY-EIGHT

$W$e would go to Jones Beach, Jo and I, to a secluded place I knew; on the Monday morning when, October's time onstage begun, she had focused her beneficence on an Indian Summer day of unalloyed perfection.

There had been a hard rain Sunday night, and the downpour had erased all footprints and left the beach as virgin. The sun was hot on our bodies. The sky was a poster-paint blue, brush-stroked with mare's tails. The ocean was mounding long, lazy combers and the air was pungent with the rank scents of the ebb tide.

I'd spent Sunday afternoon committing to paper all I knew and everything I suspected about Oscar Gladden. Finished, I had sealed it in an envelope, inscribed it with the words, "Not to be opened until after my death," placed it in another envelope and mailed it to Dunc Robertson. As it dropped in the post box I'd suddenly felt like a melodramatic fool and wished I could retrieve it.

I had decided to tell Jo of my attempt to resign from her father's employ, of her father's first reaction and of his subsequent offer. I had decided, too, that I must let her know in some way—as obliquely as possible while still getting it said—of my suspicions about her father and of my plans to track them down. I realized that there was a risk in doing this. I might anger and alienate her. Moreover, she might feel she had to discuss it with her father and this could put me in jeopardy. Regardless, the matter had to be raised.

323

At the moment, she and I were lying on towels on the sand, touching at shoulder and hip and hand. There was no sound other than the muffled explosions of the breakers and the sibilant run up and retreat of the waves on the beach. Perhaps five minutes earlier, she had murmured, "I love you, my darling." I had responded, "And I love you," and we had been content to leave it at that. Now, acutely conscious of the exquisite woman lying so still beside me, I felt a gathering in my groin and rose onto an elbow. She rose with me and put her lips on mine. And so we remained for a moment: sensate, overwhelmingly aware of warmth and softness and of a mounting drumbeat of passion.

We fell back to the blanket, breathless. After a moment I said, "I'm going to cool off," and got to my feet. We walked to the shoreline and stood for a moment ankle-deep in the water. Then, with wild cries, we dashed forward hand in hand and plunged headlong into the curl of a collapsing wave.

The water was chilling but clean, and for a short while we romped like children. Beneath the surface my hands sought her breasts. She said, "Lecher," slipped her shoulder straps and pulled aside her bikini bottom. In the midst of the cold there was a sudden, fiery warmth.

We returned, shivering, to the towels. We talked about many things, including her work. Now that fall was here, she said, she would have to apply herself with unremitting discipline. I told her how my loving her had made me reexamine the relationship between the protagonists in my novel, and she put a hand on mine, squeezing it tightly.

"It's true," I said. "Loving you is the single most important thing in my life. Before I do anything these days, I find myself asking how it might affect us. Right now I'm struggling with a problem, and when I'm trying to decide what to do, which course of action to take, there you are, overarching everything."

"I sound like . . . a responsibility," she said, smiling.

"No, no, I didn't mean that. I meant simply that there is nothing in life as important to me as you are. I see everything in a context of you." I broke off. "I sound like a theological undergraduate struggling with I-Thou."

"Am I permitted to know what the problem is?" she said.

"It relates to my job with your father. And to things I feel responsible for."

"Joshua's death?"

I nodded. "That's part of it."

We were silent for a moment. I was debating whether to press on. She said, "You know, I never *did* understand what you and Father were up to with Joshua."

I was tempted to bypass the implied question, but if I was going to talk to her about my problem with her father, perhaps the Mr. Nobody project was a good beachhead from which to proceed. I told her the story from the beginning. She listened without interruption, making swift sketches on the sand with a forefinger and then erasing them.

At the end she said, "But I don't understand. How could Joshua's story be used to show up the newspapers? It was a wonderful story."

"Exactly. I told your father that. But by that time he'd lost interest in it."

She erased her last drawing with quick little pats that left imprints of her palm on the sand. "Do you blame Father for what happened to Joshua?"

I shook my head. "Not really. It wasn't my idea but I went along with it. Nobody put a gun to my head." I had a second thought and added, "I do think it was wrong to dump him so cavalierly."

"Yes," she said, "Father feels badly about that, too."

"Really?" I said.

"The morning we got the bad news about Joshua and I was feeling so guilty about having failed him, Father did a really extraordinary thing. He took me down to the aquarium and had Knee-Hi make a small cut on the spine of one of the fish and put it in the water. The other fish simply tore it apart." She shuddered. "He did it to demonstrate how predatory journalism is and how what had happened in the tank was very much like what happened to Joshua." She paused for a moment. "There were tears in his eyes as he talked to me about it."

She reflected for a moment. "I really think Victor's death and then Joshua's has affected him deeply. In all my life I'd never seen him cry until the funeral in Toronto. When he took me down to the aquarium, it was obvious what he was doing. He was trying to ease my pain about Joshua's death, yes, but what he was really doing, even though he may not have known it, was trying to convince himself that what had happened wasn't his fault. As I say, he was in tears. And afterwards he went to his bedroom and didn't come out all day.''

I was remembering that day: Jo's grief as she slashed her painting and the vast nakedness of Oscar Gladden bawling at the door of his bedroom for Jerri West. I turned to her and took her hands in mine. ''Jo dearest,'' I said, ''there are some things I must tell you.'' I leaned across and put the lightest of kisses on her lips. ''Please hear me out.''

There was the suggestion of a frown on her brow. ''Sounds ominous.''

I cast about, looking for a place to start. ''I presume your father has talked to you about buying the *Register* and offering me the job as editor?''

''Yes,'' she said, her face brightening. ''I've been waiting for you to mention it. Isn't it exciting?''

I wiped my hands on the towel and passed it to her. ''Yes, it is. But you should know that I'm not going to take the job.''

Her brows drew down. ''I've had the feeling that there was something wrong. Father told me all about it at dinner last night, about his plans to buy the paper and about his conversation with you yesterday. He spoke of the job as . . . a sort of wedding present. But, even as he was telling me, I sensed that something was wrong.'' Her expression was troubled. ''Darling, I don't understand. It seems like such a marvelous opportunity.''

I reached out and took her hand. ''Jo, I'm sorry, but it's no longer possible for me to continue working for your father. It's not simply that—you'll forgive me—that he's impossible to get along with, it's much more than that. I really am sorry to have to say this but—'' I faltered, not quite ready to say it. ''Well, he's not the man you think he is.''

She was polishing her sunglasses and said quietly, ''If that's what you feel, perhaps you should quit.''

''I tried to,'' I said. ''That same day, the day we got the news about Joshua. He said, 'Nobody quits Oscar Gladden.' ''

''Are you sure he put it that way?''

"No. You're right. He didn't. He said, 'Where the hell do you think you are—back on the *Register?* Nobody quits Oscar Gladden. Nobody.' "

"Darling," she said, "let me see if I can help you to understand him a little better. Yes, he can be domineering. Yes, he can be downright rude. Sometimes he puts even *me* in a rage. And, yes, he treated Victor badly. But he wasn't alone in that; we all failed Victor. But you must try not to misjudge Father. He has a side you've never seen. I've already told you how much Joshua's death bothered him."

An unreasonable irritability had begun to gather in me. "Yes," I said, "he was so bothered by it that, within the hour, he had Jerri West in his bed to comfort him. And that performance he put on for you—wounding the fish and putting it in the tank. You may be interested to know that he and Knee-Hi went through that exact same routine with me when Johnny Gallagher died."

She looked at me levelly for a moment and then dropped her gaze. "You really do dislike him."

"It has nothing to do with liking or disliking him, it's simply that—"

"Okay, so you dislike him. And let's say for the moment that you have reason to—knowing Father, I can understand how that could be. But what I don't understand is why you feel the need to turn me against him? You think I don't know him? I know him better than you ever will. As I say, he can be difficult —impossible at times—but he has another side, a side you've never seen. He can also be loving—no, don't shake your head —*loving!* In all my life, for all his faults, he has never once let me down. Not once."

"Loving," I said. "Was he loving to your mother? And to Victor?" I regretted the words the moment they were out. And why, I raged to myself, had we gotten involved in a discussion of Oscar Gladden's relationship to his wife and son?

"Damn it, Tony!" she said. "That's unfair. You didn't know my mother. You don't know what happened back then. You take Victor's side because it lets you get at Father. You haven't the slightest idea of the problems he had with Victor." She broke off, close to tears.

I was about to offer a defense but restrained myself. I'd already pressed close to the limit and didn't dare risk going further. I was taken by a sudden impulse to put my arms about her but for some reason couldn't quite bring myself to do it. She was sitting cross-legged, slumped, her head down, and when she spoke her voice was unsure.

"It's a terrible thing. Here I am: loving two men and torn between them. I haven't said anything about this because I thought it would only make things worse, but just as you've tried to turn me against him, Father has tried to turn me against you. I don't know what to do, I really don't. What do you want me to do? Do you want me to stop loving him? Because if you do, I can't. He *is* my father. And I can't turn love on and off like a spigot. You've told me about your father, and I can understand why you don't have very deep feelings for him—he's been indifferent to you—but my father hasn't. True, he didn't want me to marry you, and I gather he's been pretty unpleasant about it, but isn't he like ten thousand other fathers in that? Maybe that's why he's been so disagreeable with you. But now he's changed. He's come around. And he wants to help us."

"I'm not asking you to stop loving him," I said. "All I'm saying is don't be blind to the kind of man he is."

She was angry now. "Oh, and what kind of man is he? Are you saying he has faults? Is he unique in that?" She lifted her eyes to mine and they were unblinking. "Is any of us perfect?"

I felt somehow betrayed and was aware of a fury rising behind my eyes. "All right," I said. "I'll stop the innuendos. I was hoping to soften the blow that's coming but better you learn the facts from me than from the newspapers. Jo, your father isn't the man you see. He's a calculating criminal. He is responsible for the death of two men. I myself saw him—" The look in her face stopped me. Her eyes were wide and full of pain.

"Tony," she shouted, "stop it! Stop it!" She looked about distractedly. "I can't *believe* what's happening! I can't *believe* it."

"Jo, you've got to listen to me."

"No, I don't. And I won't. I won't hear another word." Her eyes were brimming with tears. "Tony, I love you so much. Why do you want to spoil everything?"

My anger was about to best me when I saw the man. He was about fifty yards away behind a dune staring through binoculars. I might not have noticed him had he not moved. I got up and strode toward him. He was seated on the sand, looking out of place in a jacket and slacks: a lean, almost scrawny man with heavy-rimmed, thick-lensed glasses and a seamy, elongated face. As I approached, he let the binoculars drop around his neck.

I was in a rage. "Who are you and what do you want?"

He looked up at me, frowning. "What do you mean, what do I want?"

"Why are you following us?"

"Following you? What are you talking about?"

"You followed us here and you've been watching us through those binoculars. Who are you?"

I heard Jo behind me. "Tony. . . ."

I was spoiling for trouble. "This son of a bitch has been spying on us. I'd like to—"

The man had risen. He was angry now. "Hey, wait a minute. Who the hell do you think you are? Do you own this beach or something?"

"You were watching us. I saw you."

"Why would I be watching you? Who are you, anyway? I didn't even see you till you come up to me. I come here every day. I watch the shipping on the run up the coast." He pointed off to our left. There was a clear view of the ocean beyond the dunes. A tanker was beating upwind.

Jo had my arm and was drawing me away. "Tony. . . ."

"What do you take me for?" the man said. "A goddamn peeping Tom?"

My rage was swiftly receding. I let Jo prevail and followed her back to our towels. The man was shouting after us.

"It's just that your father has had me followed," I said lamely.

"Had you followed? How do you know?"

"He as much as told me himself. Darling, trust me."

"I do. I do. But what do you mean, he as much as told you?"

"That night, after your opening, when I followed you to Toronto. He knew about it. Did you tell him? I certainly didn't.

And he knew exactly when and where I'd met with Victor. Twice. How did he know? He certainly didn't get it from Victor.''

"Tony,'' she said, taking my hand, "please help me with this, I'm having trouble. There were just the two times, right? Isn't it possible—just to give Father the benefit of the doubt for the moment—isn't it possible that he talked to Aunt Marg and that she mentioned you were in Toronto? Or that somebody saw you at the airport that night and mentioned it to him? I don't remember, but I may have—I talked to him on the telephone once or twice from Toronto. And with Victor: think back now, did Father actually say he knew you'd met with him?''

"He told me I had more important things to do than hang around the shipping docks. What else could that mean?''

"Oh, Tony,'' she said, her voice dispirited.

"Well, what else *could* it mean?''

She sighed heavily and began to shake out and fold her towel. I did the same and we went in silence back to the car. Clouds had heaped up on the horizon and by the time we reached Port Washington the sky was overcast.


In the morning there was a note waiting for me at the office:

*Dearest Tony —*

*I despair for us sometimes, but I will never stop trying. You are life to me—I can't even imagine the possibility of existence without you. And we'll find a way past this little impasse. We will.*

*I had a talk with Father last night while driving him to the airport. Told him everything; even your belief that he is having you followed and your resentment at the way he treats you. And for the first time in my life I told him how I felt about his treatment of Mother and Victor. He didn't grow angry, as I thought he might, nor was he the least bit critical of you. On the contrary, he asked me to tell him everything that was on my mind and yours. I told him how his thoughtlessness, his rudeness and his lack of consideration have infuriated you. He seemed genuinely surprised. And, darling, give him this much credit—he has promised to straighten things out with you as soon as he gets back from Washington. He still wants you to take the job. Please meet him halfway.*

*I won't see you until Wednesday. I'm spending the day in the country with Susie Treadwell. But I just couldn't leave without sending this note to you.*

*I love you forever,*
*Jo*

# TWENTY-NINE

There was no reason why I shouldn't be able to get into and out of the coach-house undetected. I knew the routines. The guards at the gate changed at seven. The lights on the grounds came on at dusk. The dogs were released at ten and penned again at seven in the morning. Dinner was served at eight, but with Gladden and Jo away it would be offered on a tray at seven. I called the kitchen, ordered dinner and notified the cook that I would be going into Port Washington on my lunch hour.

In town I went shopping. I bought a small crowbar, a square yard of opaque window-shade material, a box of push-pins and a flashlight that could be attached to my head with an adjustable band. In a drug store I bought a Minolta flash camera and slipped it into my breast pocket.

Through the day I kept watch on the lane that lead from Duck Pond Road to the coach-house. There was little traffic. A panel truck bearing the legend "Adolph Cream—Provisioner" passed through the gate to the house at 3:43 and departed at 3:51. Fifteen minutes later, the Ford that I associated with Rocco Lombardi came from the coach-house and went toward Duck Pond Road. I knew from previous observation that he would be back in an hour to an hour and a half. He was. At 5:17 he turned in at the gate, spent a minute or two talking to one of the guards and went on to the coach-house.

At seven sharp, Heddy arrived from the kitchen with my meal. I had no stomach for food and toyed with the soup, picked at the roast chicken, left the hard rolls and the peach melba untouched but drank all three cups of the coffee in the china pot. I flushed the leftovers down the toilet, arranged the scraps to give the impression that I'd eaten heartily and called for the tray to be removed. Casual questioning elicited from Heddy that she and the others on the kitchen staff were going in a group to see a new James Bond film in Glen Cove.

At seven-thirty, I telephoned the Golden Dragon restaurant, using the name Neil Hisey, and ordered dinner for four: Korean shrimp, double servings of chicken chow mein, egg rolls, pork fried rice and fortune cookies. I asked that the order be delivered to the gate-house as close as possible to nine o'clock.

At eight forty-five, I put on my Adidas, donned a black pullover sweater, put my car keys in a hip pocket, slipped the crowbar through a belt loop—tugging at it to ensure that it was secure—and shoved the roll of opaque material into the top of my trousers. In the bathroom, I fitted the flashlight to my head, loaded the camera, tested the flash and turned out all the lights. I noticed that my hands were trembling.

At the window, I saw the car leave with the kitchen staff. Their laughter hung on the evening air. At ten past nine, I was taut as a bowstring and had begun to perspire. Cursing softly, I was dialing the number for the Golden Dragon when I saw their station-wagon turn in at the gate. Within the minute I was down the stairs, out the front door and poised behind the shrubbery. Knee-Hi could be heard arguing with the driver of the station-wagon.

Crouched low, I ran to the parking lot, ducked behind the hedge, sprinted along the path, leaped for the top of the link-fence and scrambled over it. I'd reviewed the route through the woods so often that I was able to follow it with sure, silent swiftness. The overhead lights cast dense shadows, making much of the way unfamiliar, but presented no problem. I located the television cameras without difficulty and paused briefly each time, waiting for the arc to swing away. Within minutes I had reached the south end of the property and was standing in the lee of the barn.

A light burning on the coach-house porch illuminated the driveway. There were other lights in what I took to be the entrance hall, the living room and a bedroom on the second floor. I waited in the shadow of the barn, alert for any sign of an alarm within the house or from the kennels. There was no sound but the faint quip-and-laughter sequence of a television situation-comedy. There had been one brief burst of barking from the kennels but it had subsided.

The porch light cast such a wide pool of illumination that I dared not enter the barn through the great double-doors. I crept softly to the window through which I had watched the tires unloaded from the tow truck and worked at it with the crowbar. With gentle leverage it swung open. In a moment I was over the sill and within the barn. I waited until my pupils adjusted to the deeper darkness and made my way on tiptoe toward the room in which I'd seen the truck tires stored. The door was padlocked. Finding the hasp, I inserted the crowbar and began slowly to ease the screws from the wood. It took no more than a minute and made no sound that would carry.

Inside, I switched on the flashlight. It was a small room, unfurnished except for a large mechanism of the kind used to remove tires from rims. At the far end of the room was a massive steel door that extended from wall to wall and almost to the ceiling. My heart was pounding; so this was the vault where the gold was stored. I went to it and, almost reflexively, tugged at the handle. It didn't move. I took a series of photographs and left, closing the door behind me.

Inside the room where I'd seen the death struggle between Oscar Gladden and Bill Naylor, I covered the window with the opaque material, fixing it with the pushpins. Satisfied that no light could leak, I switched on the flashlight.

The room was as I'd remembered it: the rolltop desk, now closed and locked, the padded chair, the cluttered workbench, and a plain chair against a wall. Leaning on another wall were two truck tires and a set of metal shelves on which there was a variety of odds and ends. On the top shelf there were neatly stacked piles of Pliofilm sacks. I slipped one into a pocket and took a photograph of the remainder. On the workbench there was a mechanism plugged into an electric outlet. I examined it. There were no working parts except for an insulated handle. I switched the on button. There was the smell of heat and I realized that it was a device for sealing the Pliofilm. I flashed a picture, moved to the rolltop desk and pried it open.

The sound of a car!

I turned off my flashlight and froze. The sound drew closer and the car turned into the driveway of the coach-house. There was the *beep-beep* of a horn. Oscar Gladden's voice: "Rocco?"

"Hello? Oh, it's you, Mr. Gladden. You're back early."

"I have to pick up something in the office. I thought I'd better let you know I was here."

"Need any help?"

"No, no. I'll be fine."

"Okay then, have a nice evening, sir."

The sound of the engine ceased. There was the slam of a car door, the crunch of footsteps on gravel and the squeal of hinges as the barn door was opened. Shoes scuffed on the concrete floor and the door to the room in which I was hiding swung open. Light flooded in. There, silhouetted in the doorway, was the formidable figure of Oscar Gladden.

"Bartholemew thought I might find you here," he said.

He flipped a switch by the door, and the single, suspended light bulb illuminated the room. He stood for a moment, his eyes taking in the flashlight on my brow, the camera in one hand, the crowbar wedged in the opening to the rolltop desk. He closed the door behind him and, his eyes never leaving mine, rolled one of the truck tires in front of it.

"You never did have the sense to mind your own business," he said. The voice was like a father's finally out of patience with a trying child.

I guarded my voice lest it betray the fear that had congealed in my chest. "What did you expect? I'm a reporter."

"You're a fool."

He came toward me, his arms hanging loosely in front like a sumo wrestler's. I saw Bill Naylor retreating in terror before that same figure, striking out ineffectually; it would be equally hopeless for me. Testing his reflexes, I threw a punch at his head. He took it on a forearm. I kicked out at a shin and felt a jolt of pain in my toes; the Adidas would be of little use.

He came toward me now with a terrible deliberation, slowly, a half smile fixed, his white teeth gleaming. I backed into the truck tire, stumbled and went to one knee. He leaped with a surprising quickness and I had to scramble apelike on all fours to avoid his hands. I looked for something to use as a weapon. I considered pulling down the metal shelving to impede his progress but realized that this would reduce the area in which I could maneuver. I considered a dash for the window; perhaps I could open it and escape. No, he would be upon me before I could mount the sill and I would be on the floor beneath his knees. Perhaps I could haul the workbench to the center of the room and, with it between us, circle opposite him. I seized it and pulled. It was fixed to the wall. I whipped the desk chair toward him, rocketing it on its casters. He raised a foot and sent it careening into a corner. The tire! I edged near to it and sent it rolling toward him. It bounced against a thigh, went wobbling across the floor and flopped, spinning to the floor. And still he came on. I picked up the smaller chair and thrust it at him, as an animal trainer might to keep a lion at bay. One of the legs struck his brow. There was a red gash and then blood ran. He cursed, caught a rung on my next thrust, tore the chair from my hands and flung it aside.

He was winded now and paused, leaning against the door, sucking air. Brushing the back of a hand against his brow, he looked at the blood and then at me.

"You're dead, Carpenter."

"I won't go as quietly as Bill Naylor," I said. "A lot of people will be asking questions."

"An accident," he said, his belly heaving, the words punctuated by his breathing. "You had an accident. You slipped off the tow truck. The wheels crushed your chest. We'll give you a big funeral."

I'd decided that I would have a better chance in the dark and waited for him to catch his breath, planning a feint that would draw him from the door so that I might reach the light switch. Where had I left the crowbar? There it was, protruding from the rolltop desk. But he had been watching my eyes. He went to the desk, seized the crowbar and tore it loose.

He had caught his breath now and came toward me again. I worked him to the right, gathered myself, made a feint and leaped past him to the door. He turned and swung the crowbar, missing and going off balance. My hand went to the switch.

Darkness! Silence! Each of us listening for the other.

I realized that I must move from the door. Knowing I was there, he could simply barge forward, arms extended, the cruel hook of the crowbar extending his reach. I went softly, crouched low, pausing with each step. Something crunched beneath my foot and I heard him coming. I spun away but blundered into his grasp. I found his right wrist and seized it, but I couldn't match his strength and my fingers began to loosen. A thrust with his belly threw me off balance and drove me against the workbench. I renewed my hold on his wrist and with a sudden jerk smashed his knuckles against the bench. The crowbar clanged to the floor.

But I was pinned against the bench, bent backward by the massive bulk thrusting against me. The edge of the bench cut cruelly into my back. My hand touched metal—the heat-sealing mechanism for the Pliofilm sacks. I felt for the handle, found it, brought it to where I knew Gladden's face would be and pressed it, hard. There was a scream, a scent of seared flesh, and he backed away. I went down, whirled about on all fours and found my feet.

He had returned to the door. The light came on, dazzling me. The sight of his face was startling. Rivulets of blood from the gouge on his forehead had traversed one cheek and were dripping from his chin. There was a livid patch on his nose and left cheek where he had been burned. His face was running with sweat. I seized the cord of the heat-sealer, pulled it from the outlet, whirled the mechanism around my head in great circles and let it fly. Gladden raised an arm to ward it off. It scored a red furrow across the back of his hand. As he glanced down at it, I leaped into the air, smashed a fist against the light bulb and we were in darkness again.

In the darkness I crept silently on all fours toward the window. My hand touched metal and closed on the crowbar. I clanged it three times on the concrete floor, as a warrior might smite his shield with his sword.

Now the advantage was mine. I tensed, listening for his breathing. He was still by the door. I pulled the camera from my pocket, directed it toward him, tripped the flash and leaped at the figure momentarily revealed. The claw end of the crowbar thudded into flesh and I heard a grunt. I held the camera at arm's length, flashed the light in a swift sequence and immediately moved aside. I wanted to impair his vision, to fill his pupils with circles of light. More flashes. As in a stroboscopic film, I saw him raise a forearm to shield his eyes.

For a moment, neither of us so much as breathed, each waiting for the other to make the first move. I considered leaping at him, striking with the crowbar at where his head would be, but knew that he would be expecting such a move and that, if I missed, he would seize and overpower me. I heard him moving away from the door and knew by the sound that he had removed his shoes. Was he trying to lure me into a dash for the door, knowing that, while I was struggling to roll aside the tire, he would be on me? Regardless of the risk, I must try it soon; confined by the room, he would surely find me before long.

There was a ripping sound, and the room was suddenly filled with a dim light. Gladden had torn the opaque covering from the window. He cast it aside, picked up the wreckage of the smashed chair and, holding it before him, advanced on me. I swung the crowbar at it, but the blows clanged off the wooden seat. Another swing and the bar slipped from my hand to skitter across the floor and disappear beneath the workbench.

"*Now*, you son of a bitch!" he snarled.

He flung the chair aside and advanced on me, wheezing like a great steam engine. I threw the camera through the window, hoping that the noise of the pane breaking might bring someone —*any* intervention would be preferable to remaining alone with the looming figure now driving me into the corner beyond the workbench, the place where William Naylor had been trapped and where the life had been crushed from him.

I threw myself at him, driving my fists at his face. His massive forearms absorbed the blows. He made no attempt to seize me, but bumped me with his belly and sent me reeling. Twice I tried to go around him. Each time he cut me off. The distance was closing. I swung a fist into his stomach, putting my body behind it. The impact drove a gust of air from his mouth and sprayed my face with spittle, but it was like trying to bring down an elephant with a blow of your fist.

I began to beat against him, blindly, frantically, shouting hoarsely. Twice he bumped me and sent me stumbling. Once I went down but managed to regain my feet. He stood there glowering, knowing now that he had me cornered, savoring the triumph. His hair had fallen forward on his brow. Sweat mingled with blood streamed down his face. His nostrils flared and his mouth was agape as he sucked in great gulps of air. In his eyes there was pure malevolence.

He raised an arm and whipped it down. It clubbed aside my defense and struck the side of my neck, spinning me to one side. I crashed into the wall. Another blow to the side of the head staggered me. I fell to the floor on my back, helpless. He moved in swiftly, looming above me. I saw his knees flex as he began the drop. I rolled away and, as his knees hit the concrete, kicked with every ounce of force I could summon. My foot sank deep into his groin. He screamed and fell back, writhing on the floor.


I fled the barn to shouts from the coach-house and raced through the woods, disregarding the cameras, heading for the parking lot and my car. I heard the tumult behind me as the dogs were loosed and set baying on my trail. Chest afire, my legs grown leaden, I reached the upper link-fence. Twice I failed to scale it, and only managed to haul myself over with the dogs in sight and snarling toward me.

In the parking lot, my hands trembling, I wasted precious seconds trying to insert the key in the ignition. Dark figures were running from the gate-house, flashlight beams probing erratically. On the third try Smedley roared to life. Tires spinning, the rear end fishtailing, the car barreled out of the lot and toward the gate. The guards had their guns out, but if they fired I didn't hear the shots over the roar of the engine and the scream of the tires. The barrier lowered as I bore down on the gate. There was a crash, a sudden cobwebbing of the windshield, and ragged chunks of wood ricocheted to each side. I made a hard right and, within seconds, was on Duck Pond Road and then on Hegman's Lane, lancing through the traffic.

Only then did I realize that I had lost one of my Adidas and had ripped a leg of my trousers almost to the hip. Only then did I realize that I was without my wallet, without identification, without a driver's license. I slowed, but only slightly, peering past the damaged glass of the windshield, watching in the mirrors for the police patrol. I didn't want to be stopped now; there would be too many awkward questions. In the meantime, I had to stay ahead of the pursuit, get to the apartment, get a pair of shoes, a change of clothing and a checkbook.

At Peter Cooper Village, I parked under FDR Drive and ran, off-stride on one stockinged foot, to my apartment building. There would be enough time to change; surely I had outdistanced any pursuer. And it was unlikely that the guards would have sufficient presence of mind to head directly for my apartment.

As I opened the door, the telephone was ringing. Should I answer it? No, it would betray that I was there. In the bedroom I pulled on corduroy trousers and stepped into a pair of loafers. The bell continued to sound, loud and insistent. It might be Jo. It was.

"Darling, you're out of breath. What's the matter?"

"I just got here."

"Oh, Tony, I just had to talk to you. I've been trying for at least an hour."

"Jo—"

"Something's wrong?"

"Jo, I'm sorry, but I've got to go."

"Please, just one minute? Please? It's terribly important. I've been talking to Aunt Marg—"

I broke in. "Hold just a minute." I went to the light switch and turned it off. At the window, I looked down into 23rd Street. A car, running with only its parking lights on, turned the corner from First Avenue, moving slowly on the inner drive. I watched until it drew abreast and parked. No one got out.

"Jo?"

"I'm here."

340

"Now, darling, listen to me carefully. I can't take the time to explain, but I've got to go. I'm sorry."

"Please, Tony!" There was an urgency in her voice. "Just one minute. I promise. After our talk on the beach, I called Aunt Marg. I told her everything—about Father and you, I mean. Everything you said. She's been like a mother to me and—" She broke off, obviously fighting her emotions. I walked the telephone to the end of its cord, to where I could look into the street. The car was still there, its parking lights on. "She was loyal to Father, of course; he's the only member of her family still alive—"

"Jo—"

"I'm hurrying, I'm hurrying. She finally admitted that she worries about him, that—"

"Darling—"

"Quickly, then. It was obvious that she was trying to tell me something but that she didn't want to be disloyal. I told her I wanted the truth, whatever it was. At first, all she would say was that there are a lot of things wrong. Terribly wrong. And then finally she said—" Her voice faltered. "I'm sorry. I can't say it on the phone. It'll have to wait until I see you."

Two men were out of the car and walking quickly toward the apartment. Because of the trees lining the walkway and the semidarkness, I couldn't be sure, but one of them looked like Sacred Heart Saywell.

"Jo," I whispered, my lips brushing the telephone, "your father tried to kill me tonight. And some of his people are after me."

"Tony, no!"

"Believe me, it's true. I'm sorry, but I've got to go. Goodbye."

As I put down the phone I heard her voice, tremulous, frightened: "Run, Tony, *run!*"

My hand was on the doorknob when the telephone rang again. I was about to go on but realized it might be Jo calling back. It could be something important, something she needed to tell me. I ran back and picked up the phone.

"Carpenter?"

"Yes."

There was a click and the dial tone sounded. As I replaced the telephone on its cradle, cursing myself for having answered, I heard the sound of a key being fitted in the lock on the door. I leaped to one side and flattened myself against the wall. The handle turned and the door opened slowly, swinging toward me. Whoever it was had paused on the doorsill. I crouched, gathering myself to hurl my weight against the intruder — if possible, to knock him down and get out of the apartment.

"Hello? Anybody home?"

"Maggie!"

There she stood, pushing the door closed behind her, lowering a suitcase to the floor.

"Tony? You frightened me. I didn't know *what* was going on for a minute. What are you *doing*; hiding in the dark, for goodness sake?" She reached for the light switch. "There, now. That's better."

"Maggie, what in the world are you doing here?"

"Well now, isn't *that* a welcome home," she said lightly. "I've been calling ever since I got into LaGuardia, and no answer. I still have my key, so I thought: what I'll do is just go on and surprise him."

"Maggie, look—" I didn't know what to say. I had to get out of there, but how could I explain to her the urgency of the moment. Nor could I simply go, leaving her in the apartment alone, in jeopardy. An explanation would take too long, and she, a Gladden disciple, would never believe for one moment that his people were after me, bent on killing me.

"I know I should have given you some warning," she was saying, "but, you know how it is. I didn't want to try to explain on the phone what I've been thinking." She had been unbuttoning her jacket and now slipped it off. "So I said to myself: for goodness sake, Maggie, he's your *husband*. Go *talk* to him. You're both adults. Surely between the two of you, you can—"

There was no option. Without a word I picked up her suitcase, opened the door and, seeing no one, put the suitcase out in the hallway.

"Tony! What are you *doing*? For goodness sake, Tony!"

I put my arms about her, pinioning her, picked her up and

plunked her down outside the door; she would be safe in the corridor.

"I'm sorry, Maggie," I said. "I'll explain everything later." I pulled the door closed behind me. "Talk to you later."

At the elevator there was the hum of a car rising from the lobby. I went quickly to the stairwell. Maggie's voice followed me, rising in volume and virulence. "Do you know what you are? You're a real bastard! A dirty, rotten son of. . . ."

The parking lot serving City Park Apartments and the riverfront area lies on the west bank of the East River beneath Franklin D. Roosevelt Drive and runs from 20th to 23rd Street. Even in daylight it is an unprepossessing place, dirty and scattered with debris. At night, ill-lit, the massive concrete pillars rearing to the roadbed above, the rows of diagonally parked cars deserted, it can cause trepidation. An active imagination can readily visualize an assailant crouching in any of dozens of places and contemplate the fact that, in an emergency, any cry for help would be muffled by the roar and clatter of the traffic overhead.

I had the key in the door of the car when I heard Rocco Lombardi's voice.

"Tony." Rocco was coming over to me, emerging from between a row of parked cars nearby. He was perspiring heavily but was all heartiness, a wide smile on his meaty face, his voice echoing from the concrete above. "Hey, Tony. What a break! I been lookin' for a cab for half an hour an'—you know how it is —shit outta luck." He was a lousy actor. "I said to myself, I said: Tony parks roun' here somewheres. Maybe he'll give me a lift." He was standing to the rear of Smedley, blocking my exit. "Just somewheres I can catch a cab is all."

There was no point in refusing; he surely had a gun. I got into the car, leaned across to unlock the far door and started the engine. Rocco came to the open door, tilted the seat forward and said, "I think maybe I'll ride back here. In the jump seat."

As he raised a foot to get in, I jammed the gearshift into reverse, floored the accelerator, and shot the car backward. The open door carried Rocco back and flung him to the concrete. I braked, slammed into gear and, tires smoking, roared off down the access lane, the inertia swinging the door shut. On the ground, Rocco got off a shot. I heard a pop and looked up to see a hole in the fabric of the top. Damn! Only weeks ago it had cost me $450 to replace the old one.

# THIRTY

It was to be a long night followed by a longer day.

I had trouble finding a place to stay; I dared not return to the apartment. I telephoned Dunc, hoping to bed down at his place, but there was no answer after a number of tries. I went by the Hellbox thinking I might see someone from whom I could borrow a hundred dollars. But there was no one there I knew other than to nod to. I considered for a moment spending the night on one of the banquettes at the rear of the dining room, but after a look decided that nature had not fashioned me for so confining a bed. I called the Plaza where I knew the night manager. It was his night off; regardless, there was no room at the inn. I tried a couple of old friends, but there were no answers. I ended up at two in the morning on a narrow, lumpy cot in an airless room next to the elevator shaft at the McConkey Hotel, a seedy dive just off Herald Square, parking Smedley in a littered lot back of the hotel. Even the McConkey gave me a hard time. I had no wallet and thus no credit cards or other identification, so the young hood-in-training who registered me agreed to take my check only if my Piaget wristwatch was left as surety.

By dawn's early light I was up and out, spent the coins in my pocket at a nearby Nedick's for what passed for breakfast and caught the night-man at the nearby car-rental agency asleep in his chair. (I'd decided overnight not to drive Smedley; he was too easily identifiable.) Piqued at having been found napping, the night-man was happy to discover that he could legitimately frustrate me.

345

"Mr. Carpenter," he said, in a tone suggesting that I'd just confessed to child-molesting, "you have no credit cards and no driver's license. It's simply impossible."

"Have you no faith?" I asked, having run out of other pleas.

"Only in God," he said with the fundamentalist's sweet certitude.

I walked the eighteen blocks to my bank and had been shuffling my feet at the entrance for half an hour when, at long last, a clerk came to perform the various unlockings. The manager listened to my improvised story about how I'd lost my wallet, smiling knowingly as he took note of my stubbled jaw and pink-rimmed eyes. Ah, newspapermen—a wild bunch. Regardless, within ten minutes I had a thousand dollars in one of the bank's plastic wallets, which didn't suffice for Hertz or Avis or Budget —I had no driver's license. In a graffiti-inscribed pay phone, the door hanging askew and the coin-return jimmied open, I called the Mid-town South Precinct and asked for Sergeant Kosiosko.

"Mr. Carpenter. Of course I'll see you, but before you come here I should inform you that there's a warrant out for your arrest."

"For *my* arrest?"

"Sworn by Oscar Gladden this morning. Two charges: aggravated assault and break-and-enter. I'm told he displayed some impressive cuts and bruises."

"*He's* charging *me!* That's ridiculous!"

"Nonetheless, the charges have been laid. It was brought to my attention first thing this morning, and although I could get my tail kicked for it, I've put everything on hold. You should know, though, that if you come here I will have no choice but to charge you."

"I can't believe this."

"What I'd like to do, Mr. Carpenter—and this is on the presumption that you're now prepared to cooperate — is to get together with you and Agent Mordecai Green of the FBI. Would you be agreeable to that?"

My mind had been racing as he spoke. They would end up wanting me to lay assault charges, and where would that get me? Gladden would have the burn on his face and the cuts and bruises to buttress his case, not to mention plenty of ready witnesses. There would be a crowbar with my fingerprints on it and the evidence of its use on the window, the office door and the rolltop desk. How would I justify my breaking in, wearing a headband flashlight and carrying material to cover the window? I could tell them about the vault, but securing your valuables is hardly a criminal act. Moreover, the camera, with its evidence, was gone; I had thrown it through the window and couldn't even prove that the vault existed.

On the other hand, it was important not to alienate Kosiosko. With the warrant in hand, he could have me picked up any time he pleased. Despite his obvious displeasure I insisted on a few hours to think it over.

I took a taxi across town to pick up Smedley, planning to park him indoors. As I paid the hotel bill and reclaimed my watch, the desk clerk asked, "Isn't that your sports car out back?"

"I have a sports car out back. Why?"

He gave me a watery smile: "You got a problem."

Outside the McConkey Hotel I could have sat down and cried. Smedley's top was slashed to ribbons. The windshield, the windows and the headlights were smashed as with a hammer. Even the windshield-wipers were bent. Within, the seats were slashed, the glass on the instrument panel was broken.

A policeman was making notes. "This your car?"

I nodded.

He gestured with his notebook. "They threw dirt in your gas tank." I circled Smedley, mourning. The policeman continued to write with a labored hand. "You should've known better'n park a car like that in here," he observed.

"They told me there was a guard dog."

"There was. She's over there," he said, indicating with a nod of his head. "I had to shoot the poor bugger."

The dog, a part-Lab, part-German shepherd, lay on its side against the fence. It had been shot through the ear. There was a lot of blood. The white tongue lolled on the dirt. The lower jaw lay against the neck.

"Its jaw's broken!" I said, and suddenly remembered Judge Wheeler.

"Wouldn't I love to get my hands on the creep what done

that!'' the policeman said. He continued with his pains-
taking notes. ''Any idea who might of done this to your car?''

I shook my head.

He looked at me obliquely. ''Somebody don't like you.'' I
tested a door. It resisted, groaning. ''You won't be able to drive
her. My partner's on the blower callin' for a tow truck. Mean-
while, maybe you could help me make an estimate of the
damage.''


Perhaps I could entreat Gus Longo to go with me to Kosiosko
and tell what he knew. It was a frail hope but worth a try. I was
able to borrow a car from a friend on the *Register* and drove to
Gus's house in Queens only to find that he wasn't home and
that all the drapes were drawn. There was a newspaper on the
front porch. Leaving, I glanced back. Did I imagine a movement
at the window?

In order not to worry Gus, I had parked in back of the pizzeria
on the corner and walked to his house. Now, returning to pick
up the car, my imagination filled the sunlit street with menace.
That man across the way—was there something odd about his
manner? I stopped to untie and tie a shoelace, resting my foot
on a hydrant, glancing back past a shoulder. Was it coincidence
that he too paused at that moment, ostensibly to light a cigaret?
That dark gray Plymouth parked near the corner, the man in it
reading a folded newspaper; did he just happen to turn his head
away as I passed? And why, as I entered the parking lot, did he
start up his engine?

I backed into the street and turned onto Northern Boulevard.
The Plymouth was two cars back. He was still there five minutes
later. I made a left at the next light, deliberately crossing in front
of the oncoming traffic as the yellow went to red, and, having
circled back three blocks, returned to the boulevard. He was
nowhere in sight. I'd lost him—presuming that is, that he'd
been following me.

I checked the rear-view mirror from time to time. Nothing.
As I approached Queens Boulevard and the turn leading to the
Queensboro Bridge I smiled wryly, chiding myself for my
heightened imagination. Suddenly it broke on me that, each

348

time I'd looked for the Plymouth, there had been an Oldsmobile station-wagon two or three cars back. More incipient paranoia? I would find out, damn it!

Coming off the bridge on the Manhattan side, I hung a hard left, turning 180 degrees into 59th Street. In the middle of the block I made a U-turn, and running against the one-way traffic — to the accompaniment of curses and a cacophony of auto horns—returned to Second Avenue and turned south.

I'd lost the station-wagon. There could be little doubt about that as I continued on, checking every few blocks in the rear-view mirror. But, waiting for a light at 39th Street, I saw the Plymouth working its way past a bus half a block behind. My heart began to hammer and there was a metallic taste in my mouth. I'd been heading toward my apartment, planning to park on 20th Street, walk across the complex and approach the building from the rear, but I realized now that that would be a mistake. In the meantime, until I could decide what action to take, I would have to avoid solitary places and stay on heavily traveled streets.

A glance showed that the Olds had fallen in behind the Plymouth. Approaching 34th Street, puzzling as what I might do, I thought of Herald Square: there was no busier part of Manhattan. Macy's, Gimbel's, the McAlpin Hotel, Korvette's . . . safety in numbers. I turned right onto 34th, and while crossing the square, turned on my headlights and made a sharp right onto Broadway, hugging the curb, heading into the oncoming traffic. I would take my chances on a collision. If a policeman stopped me, that would be just fine.

Which is exactly what happened. An officer, posted at the north end of the tiny park, stepped into the street, shrilled his whistle and, hand upraised, walked toward me. An anguish of squealing tires and admonitory horns surrounded me.

"What the hell's the matter with you?" the officer yelled. I smiled vacantly. He thumbed me closer to the curb. I turned off the engine and sat back in the seat, aware that I was shivering and wet with perspiration.

A second policeman materialized and began to divert the oncoming traffic around me. As the first sauntered toward the car with that exaggerated casualness that policemen affect, a

thick-set man in a gray suit intercepted him, produced something from a pocket and began to talk animatedly, pointing at
me. When he went off, the policeman approached.

"All right, you," he said, banging the flat of a hand on the
side panel of the door, "start the car but stay right where you
are." An amused crowd had gathered on the sidewalk, and
there was much craning, peering and wisecracking. The uniformed officer had taken a position to the front of the car, a
proprietory hand on a fender, and seemed to be waiting. The
Plymouth was suddenly in sight and pulled to a stop to the
south of me. Blowing sustained bursts on his whistle, my policeman raised an imperious hand and halted the oncoming traffic.
That accomplished, he began making energetic circling move-
ments with an arm, which I interpreted to be instructions for
me to make a U-turn. With the fear freshly back and banging at
my ribs, I did as instructed. The policeman was suddenly at my
window, pointing to the Plymouth.

"Follow that car," he shouted. He banged a hand on the
roof. "Okay, fella, *move* it!"

I fell in behind the Plymouth. In the mirror I saw the Olds
following, boxing me in. It was a long ride downtown. It was
only as we approached Federal Plaza, turned onto Duane Street
and took a left down a ramp into an underground garage, that
I realized that my escort was the FBI.


As I climbed out of the car, puzzled and angry, two men
approached. One was in his thirties and almost film-star handsome, the other was the man I'd seen at Herald Square. He was
middle-aged, overweight and balding. Such hair as he had was
trimmed short, suggesting a monk's tonsure, but he had the
concave nose and scarred eyebrows of a former fighter. Both
men were dressed in medium gray, the younger man modishly,
the older in rumpled ancients. The older flashed his badge.

"Federal Bureau of Investigation," he said pleasantly.
"Agent Green. This is Agent Zapulski. May I see some identification, please?"

My hand went to a pocket automatically. "Oops, sorry," I
said. "I don't have my wallet." In an inside breast-pocket my

fingers found my press pass, which included a photograph. I passed it to him. He glanced at it and said, amiably, "Your driver's license, please."

I shrugged. "Sorry. I don't have my wallet. What's wrong with the press pass?"

"They're giving them as prizes in Crackerjacks," Zapulski said.

I had often wondered about the location of the FBI offices in Manhattan, never having had cause to go there. They occupy the twenty-fifth to the twenty-eighth floors in the Jacob Javitz building. To reach them you take one of a bank of public elevators. Enroute, with Green and Zapulski flanking me, I recognized a friend from my fitness club who fell into conversation, chiding me for my infrequent attendance.

"How about a game of squash, tomorrow at four?" he asked.

Fancying myself witty, I said, "If I'm free."

The reception foyer on the twenty-fifth floor was empty save for a receptionist behind a desk. Zapulski disappeared. Green led me to a small, brightly lit, windowless room. It was sparely furnished with four chairs and a wooden table on which there were a number of grubby metal ashtrays. The walls were painted an industrial beige. Flecked gray broadloom carpeted the floor. Green pointed to a chair and sat beside the table, pulling out a small notebook. Zapulski entered, took a chair, placed it behind me and sat.

"Well now, Mr. Carpenter," Green said in a cheerful voice, "perhaps there's something you would like to tell me."

I considered acting enraged, demanding explanations or even going on the offensive, peppering them with questions. In the end I merely said, "Would somebody please tell me what the hell is going on here?"

Green looked at me as a teacher might an obtuse student. "Sorry. I presumed Sergeant Kosiosko had made that clear."

"Excuse me, men, if I try to get oriented," I said. "Am I under arrest?"

Green looked at me in an aggrieved manner. "Nothing like that. We're just having a talk."

"Then I'm free to go?" I said, moving as though to rise from the chair.

"Mr. Carpenter," he said quickly, "why don't you bear with us for a few minutes while we try to clear up what is in all probability an unfortunate situation. I read the *Register;* I know who you are. I would much prefer that what is happening wasn't, but. . . ." He rubbed a palm over his bald spot, looked at it and wiped it on a thigh.

"There *is* a warrant for your arrest," Zapulski broke in.

"Yes, there is," I said, swinging around in my chair. "So why haven't you served it?" I turned back to Green. "Look, why did you follow me? I told Sergeant Kosiosko I'd be glad to talk to you. Later," I added, lamely.

Green's eyes were wide with innocence. "Why then, when you noticed we were following you, did you take evasive action?" He shook his head in mild reproof. "Turning into the oncoming traffic."

"What should I have done? I was being tailed by two cars. I didn't know you were the FBI."

Blithely: "Who did you think we *might* be?"

I didn't miss a beat. "I had no idea. But I didn't like it. Not one bit."

"Actually," Green said, "to clear that matter up, we were looking for Mr. Longo when you turned up."

I heard the flipping of the pages of a notebook behind me. Zapulski said in a curt manner, "You work for Oscar Gladden. Is that correct?"

"You know I do, Mr. Zapulski," I said, gazing with exaggerated patience at the ceiling. "And why the hell don't you sit where I can see you?"

"What precisely are your duties?"

"Mostly public relations," I said wearily. "I act as liaison with the news media and the public."

"Would you describe this as complex work? Difficult?"

I swiveled around. "I'm not having very pleasant thoughts about you, Mr. Zapulski," I said testily. "What is this sitting-behind-me technique? Are we rehearsing an episode for 'Today's FBI'?"

He didn't look at me; his eyes were on his notes. "This work you do for Gladden—it *is* very complex?"

"If you mean does it take a graduate degree from MIT? No."

His voice was laden with insinuation. "Then you must provide other services?"

I bridled. "Meaning what?"

"Simply that you are very well paid for whatever it is you do. And you were given a pretty healthy advance when you started. Right?"

I picked up my chair and turned it so that I was facing him. "Mr. Zapulski, there was a time in this country when your bank balance was sacrosanct and your business arrangements were private. Unless you can give me one good reason why you've been nosing about in my private affairs, I am going to raise one hell of a public stink."

He wasn't fazed in the least. "In the course of which, Mr. Carpenter, you would need to explain a salary advance of eighty thousand dollars and a numbered bank account in Switzerland for providing what you concede is something less than a unique service. The public might also want you to answer some questions — as indeed we would — about your employer and about your predecessor, a man with a long criminal record."

"William Naylor?"

"The same. Grand theft, auto, 1978. Two counts of fraud, 1982, another of income tax evasion the following year—"

"Naylor?"

"William Granby Naylor."

Green brought his chair around and joined us. "Look, Mr. Carpenter, we've been interested in your employer for some time, and when a missing-persons bulletin came through listing Naylor as one of his employees, we thought we should have a talk with his successor. Particularly in light of the criminal records of the various people your Mr. Gladden employs." He nodded to Zapulski, who looked at his notebook.

"Augustus Longo, whose home you visited last week and again today: dismissed from the Special Police Force, Manhattan District Attorney's Office, for activities related to trafficking in narcotics. Neil Hisey: assault with a deadly weapon, aggravated assault, statutory rape. Rocco Lombardi: illegal possession of a firearm, armed robbery, half a dozen assault charges. Joey Podertz: living off the avails, Mann Act violations. Sacred Heart

Saywell: assault, illegal possession of a firearm; Bartholemew Marks—''

''Not Bartholemew!''

''Bartholemew Marks: a.k.a. Marcus Barthelmes, Mark Bartlett: fraud, grand theft, buggery. . . . It goes on.''

Green said, ''Then, of course, there's the matter of the recent contract killing of Victor Gladden under circumstances that indicate that it was more than a typical homicide.''

I said nothing. I could think of nothing to say that would begin to explain the circumstances that had brought me to this moment. Green, who had been watching me closely, said, ''Perhaps now you can understand, Mr. Carpenter, why we followed you today and why we wanted to have you in for this little talk.''

I said, ''What do you want from me?''

''Some information.''

''Of what kind?''

''About your employer. For years now there have been a great many questions about his business connections, but no satisfactory answers. He's been investigated by this office, by the Justice department, by the IRS. I'm being candid with you, Mr. Carpenter, simply because at this point I'm bankrupt of other options. I'm of the opinion that you are what you seem to be and I need your help.''

''You want me to be an informer.''

''I'd call it being a responsible citizen.'' He was watching me closely. ''I can understand your reluctance: you are, I gather, emotionally involved with Oscar Gladden's daughter. You're in a difficult position.''

''You've been talking to Alex Kosiosko.''

''Yes. Of course.''

''Then surely he's told you that I don't know anything that could help you.''

''No, he didn't tell me that. He told me that he's pretty sure you're withholding important information. As a matter of fact, so am I.''

I looked at him levelly. ''And if I insist that I'm not?''

He shrugged.

''Give me five minutes,'' I said.

''Certainly,'' Green said, rising. ''Coffee?''

"Thanks. With cream."

Alone, my hand wrapped about a plastic cup, I paced. Six steps and turn. Six steps and turn. Now, I instructed myself, forget everything peripheral—what's the bottom line? In one word, Jo. Despite what her aunt may or may not have told her about Oscar Gladden, he is her father and suspicions won't be enough. Before I implicate him I must have incontrovertible evidence. He's a murderer—my eyes are witness to that—but am I prepared to tell her and the police what I saw through the window of the barn that night? More important: what do I know that I can prove? Together, Kosiosko, Green, the IRS haven't been able to turn up anything damning. Will my testimony alter that? I can pass on my suspicions, but they have plenty of their own. I could add what Gus Longo told me, but if they were to drag the river and not find Naylor's body—an entirely likely circumstance—what then? And certainly Jo would never forgive me if I publicly charged her father with the brutal murder of William Naylor—with even the death of his own son—and my story went unsubstantiated.

There was no option. I would follow my own course and let the police and the FBI follow theirs.

And walk with care.

I had decided that I should get out of New York until I could determine what action to take. I left a message on the answering machine to the effect that I had gone to Los Angeles, giving the telephone number of a friend, a reporter on the *Times*, and briefing him to say that I was staying with him but was not in. I called Jo on her private telephone and left word on the machine that I would telephone the following morning between nine and ten. And not to worry.

Now, some thirty miles north of New York City, I turned off the thruway onto a state highway and after a few miles onto the side road that led to the longhouse community. A child informed me, pointing, that Caleb was in the sweat-house by the river.

I called out, "Hello," and put my head through the opening.

In the near darkness, a naked man lay on a woven mat, gleaming with sweat.

He extended a dripping hand and I shook it. In a moment, he came from the hut and, without a glance, rubbed himself with sand and plunged into the stream. I was surprised to note that he had cut his hair. As he came up from the water he was smiling broadly. Other than the shorter hair there was something odd about his appearance; the skin seemed fresher and less lined by the sun. The smile broadened even further as he wrapped himself in a robe.

"Good to see you, Tony," he said.

The voice. "My god!" I said. *"Joshua!"*

We threw our arms about each other and beat on each other's shoulders, laughing wildly—I almost unbelieving.

"Hiding out again," he said with a grin, adding, "This time from the twentieth century." He punched me lightly on a shoulder. "It's your fault, you know. You made it so I couldn't go into a McDonald's."

Later, supper over, we walked the trail atop the bluff that overlooked the village.

"We were sure you were gone," I said. "Jo will be so excited to hear the news."

We sat on an overhang of rock that jutted out from the summit of the hill, our feet dangling. The sun was about to bed down on a great bank of cumulus and there was that quiet reverence in the woods that so often comes as the day begins to die.

"It never occurred to me at the time that people would think I had fallen or had jumped," Joshua said.

"There was that tote-bag in the river," I said. "And that bottle of beer. I guess anybody who knew you should have known you wouldn't leave a beer behind."

He yielded a small smile and then was silent for a moment. Finally he said, "I was up there four days. The first two days were wild, everybody getting into the act—which was what I wanted when I went up there, I suppose. But the last two days. They were—I don't know—a kind of dying." His voice had fallen and flattened, and as he went on it was in a near monotone. "You wouldn't believe how . . . absolutely god-almighty *alone* you can feel with hundreds of people only a few feet below you and with maybe ten million more within a few miles. I could see them daytimes, of course, but at night—especially the last two nights, when the weather was christly—the only way I knew I wasn't alone in the world was by the vibration from the traffic in the seat of my pants.

"People think I jumped—at least that's what the papers said. And, I'll tell you the truth, I nearly did. On the Thursday night." He shifted position, bringing his knees up to hug them to his chest, much as in the photographs in the newspapers. "I was half frozen. The choppers were gone. The boats. The gawkers. Much of the time I couldn't see the ground. Black thoughts? You better believe it! I mean, I found myself asking: Who am I? Nobody. I got to thinking I was somebody, but I was just a dumb, fucking Indian who stuck bolts in holes, something any knot-head dumb enough to risk his neck on an I-beam could do."

I said nothing, and after a moment he went on. "Anyway, I finally decided, to hell with it all, and got up and went over to the edge and stood there. There was a break in the clouds for a few seconds and I could see the ground. I unhooked my safety line and—you won't believe this—somebody, God knows who, was down there on the bank of the river in the wind and rain with a flashlight. A *flashlight*." His voice thickened and he had to clear his throat before going on. "And he was looking for me."

After a while we got up and went down to the village in silence.

# THIRTY-ONE

Joshua, I'm at a loss. I've been to the police, I've talked to the Justice department and the FBI. I've told them nearly everything and they *know* that at least two men have been murdered. But after all that's happened they still say they don't have enough to go on. It's incredible! I had lunch with a guy from the Justice department last week—he has a personal score to settle with Gladden—but when I finished my story, he said, 'Sorry. No dice.' I can't prove it, but I saw Bill Naylor killed before my eyes. I saw Gladden's son with part of his face blown away. And forget anybody else—Oscar Gladden tried to kill *me!* And *still* I can't get anybody to act.''

I was with Joshua and Caleb in one of the cubicles in the longhouse. Caleb, who had said nothing, now spoke.

''What do you want of us? A place to hide? A place to stay?''

''I don't know. I really don't know.''

''Is it counsel you want?''

''Again, I don't know. I doubt that there's anything anyone can say that I haven't said to myself. I suppose I just needed to talk to somebody.''

''Will you tell it to the elders?'' he asked.

''You'll forgive me, Caleb,'' I said, ''but what would be the point?''

''Who knows? They see through different eyes.''

As much out of a sense of obligation as anything else, I agreed, and that evening told again the convoluted tale—without much zeal, I must say—to a small circle of scruffy-looking

358

men: the elders, as Caleb called them, although some appeared to be approximately my age. We were seated on the ground, ringing a small fire built in a shallow pit—now mostly embers, pale with ash but glowing occasionally in greeting to a vagrant breeze.

After I finished, the silence went unbroken for perhaps fifteen minutes while my back and thighs went from discomfort to agony to numbness. Caleb had warned me not to expect lively discussion. "People wonder why Indians say so little and often sit for long periods without speaking. It's because our way of thinking is different from yours. We believe that silence permits the brain to gather wisdom."

Well enough, except that it did appear that half of the men in the circle were asleep; the others stirred only occasionally, some to shift their positions, some to scratch or belch or to puff on their pipes. Finally, the eldest put aside his pipe and spent some time hawking the phlegm from his throat, spitting satisfactorily into the fire. He was a thin, dark-skinned man whose corrugated face had the appearance of old leather. From the center of his flat face, black, rheumy eyes stared unblinking at the fire.

"When the first white men came to our shores," he began, "they asked only for a place to sit down." (My god! I thought, I'm in for the entire tatty history of Indian–white relations.) "They were a pitiful people, pale and skinny. Our people felt sorry for them. Some of our people thought they had a sickness. Others thought they had come off the surf of the sea, that they had just popped out of the white foam that comes in. So our fathers said, 'You can have as much land to sit on as a deerskin is big.' So the white men took the deerskin and cut it into a strip and made a place many times larger to sit down in. Our fathers said nothing because they had told the white men that they could have a place to sit down on as big as a deerskin. But they remembered it." He took up his pipe, sucked on it vainly for a moment and then continued.

"The friend in our midst has spoken of his dealings with the white man. He has learned, as we have, that the white man does not keep his word and that it is no use to appeal to the keepers of the white man's laws. This is something we know.

They will not believe you, and to speak against wrongs done is of no more use than to rebuke the wind."

He reached toward the fire, picked up a twig only partly consumed, blew on it until it flamed and used it to relight his pipe.

"Our people have always believed that if one of us does wrong—does something that is bad for all the people—it is best if this is established not from the mouths of others but from the mouth of the one who did the wrong. Others may speak of the wrong being done, they may even speak of seeing the wrong done, and they may be believed. Or they may not. But if the man who has done the wrong says out of his own mouth that he is wrong, then all will be in agreement and the matter can be set right. Perhaps our friend should think on ways to get his enemy to establish in his own mouth what he has done."

After a moment, it became evident that he had finished. I looked around the circle, expecting someone else to speak, but no one did. I addressed myself to the old man and found myself speaking in his formal fashion.

"I agree. If the man of whom I speak would confess, it would resolve everything. But there is no chance of that happening. Why would he? What reason would he have for doing so?"

"I do not know your enemy," the old man said. "I cannot tell what he may or may not do. But I do know this: in the days of our fathers, when we were at war with the white man and wished to know what was in his head, we would sometimes take one of the white men prisoner and put him in the charge of the women, to do as they wished. They had ways of learning what the prisoner had in his head."

I'd read of the Iroquois custom in which the warriors delivered their prisoners—white men or Indians—into the hands of the clan mothers, and of the tortures inflicted by the women. Nearby, Kate, the Bear Clan mother, a matriarch of about sixty and built like a silo, was supervising some children in the gathering of firewood. It took little imagination to transport the scene back two hundred years. The night suddenly seemed chill.

"I appreciate your counsel," I said to the old man, "but there are two problems: there is no way I could capture my enemy and, even if I could, no way by which I could force him to confess. And there is something else: in the white man's law, a confession may not be forced from a man.''

''That may be,'' said the old man. ''But think on it.'' He rose stiffly to his feet. ''When there is no way sometimes a way will appear where there was no way.''

The old guy's seen too many late-night westerns, I thought. But I did think on it. Hard.


Standing in the back seat of the rust-pocked 1965 Pontiac Parisienne convertible, I had a clear view of the highway for a mile in both directions. I was able to confirm two black Cadillac limousines approaching. I lowered the binoculars and touched the shoulder of the man at the wheel. ''Here they come. Start up, and flash your lights.''

In the car with me, crouched low, were four youths from Caleb's settlement. Stripped to the waist, feathers dangling from their hair, bodies and faces painted with lurid colors, they were chaffing and whispering in grinning excitement. A hundred yards down the highway, hidden behind the drapery of an enormous weeping willow, a dozen dilapidated cars and pickup trucks started into life. The clatter of their engines carried to me. An ugly smear of oily smoke drifted across the road and disappeared.

The limousines were approaching: swift, silent, imperious. In the binoculars I could see Doc Kildare at the wheel of the lead car; his gaunt face impassive, dark glasses shielding his eyes from the sun. Ensconced in the rear, Oscar Gladden would be reading or asleep, lulled by the pneumatic movement of the limousine. The guard everyone called the Spick was at the wheel of the ICU car.

I had predicated my plan on the knowledge that, unfailingly, on the first Friday of each month, Gladden made the journey to Haarlem House, a great stone castle he owned. Built by the Dutch, it was almost a fortress and sat high above the Hudson River north of the town of Stony Point. Early that morning, Caleb had posted a lookout on the highway south of the longhouse community. At the cutoff leading to the settlement, two men in coveralls and hard hats stood by. Alerted, they had hustled a barricade onto the highway, with a sign reading, DETOUR, and an arrow pointing to the side road. And now the two limousines were bearing down on us.

As the lead limousine rolled by, my driver burst onto the highway, wheels smoking, and with his hand banging on the horn forced his way between the lead and the ICU car. Doc Kildare's jaw went slack as the painted men in the convertible with me leaped to their feet, brandishing rifles and whooping like madmen.

Ahead, at the bottom of the hill, another barricade blocked the road. A man in coveralls was directing the lead limousine onto a trail to the left. Doc braked. We bumped him hard. His inertia and the downhill lie of the road forced him into the turn and he emerged beyond the trees, moving slowly into an open field. The ICU car followed. As it did, an outlandish assortment of beat-up cars and trucks converged from all sides, each over-flowing with painted, half-naked Indians, all beating on the sides of their cars, firing rifles and whooping like wild men.

Doc spun his wheels and took off across the field. The Indians swung alongside, cutting him off, herding him toward the center. I caught a glimpse of Oscar Gladden banging on the glass that separated him from Kildare, shouting. Doc hauled on the steering wheel, trying to circle back to the highway. A dune buggy made a sudden turn and rocketed toward him, head-on. Doc had no option: he stood on the brakes and came to a lurch-ing stop. A cloud of dust overtook the limousine, rolled over it and passed on. The ICU car pulled alongside and stopped.

Now the rattletrap pack of trucks and cars formed a line and, wheels spinning and throwing up dust, the men aboard hooting and screaming, began to circle the beleaguered limousines. Around they went, the air shattered with the roar of engines, the shouts and yelps of manic excitement, the blowing of horns and the rattle of rifle fire. I saw Joshua in one of the cars, unrec-ognizable behind the geometric patterns on his face. He was hysterical with laughter.

# THIRTY-TWO

$H$e looks, I thought, like a gargantuan elephant-seal.

Oscar Gladden was balanced on a three-legged milking stool at the center of the Bear Clan longhouse. I sat opposite him on a packing case. A ragged circle of men, women and children were gathered around the perimeter. Gladden's clothes were rumpled, and his touseled hair fell forward on his face. Perspiration was dripping from his eyebrows and from the tip of his nose, running in rivulets from his cheeks onto his neck; but he seemed in no way intimidated. Indeed, although for the first time in our relationship I was in the dominant position, I was still conscious of his interior authority.

"The games children play," he was saying, his tone derisive. He turned toward me and his voice dropped to a whisper. "You, Carpenter, you're dead. Believe me, you are dead!"

"We'll see," I said, affecting an indifference I didn't feel. I had an odd sense of being an actor feeling his way through the first reading of a bizarre movie scenario. I felt awkward, self-conscious. And when I spoke, my words had a stilted sound in my ears. I half expected a director to call out, "Cut!"

"All right," Gladden said curtly, "let's cut the crap. What the hell's going on here?"

His words eased something of my insecurity. There was a hint of anxiety in his tone, almost imperceptible but there.

"First question," I said. "Where's Gus Longo?"

I could see the mind at work behind the eyes. "He's back at the house."

"He's alive?"

"He's alive." He looked at me from beneath his brows. "I'm saving him. And you."

I nodded to Caleb. He said something in Mohawk. The women moved in, surrounding Gladden. There were curses and a sharp, short struggle. When they moved away, Gladden stood naked, the gross hairless body running with sweat. A whisper went sibilantly among the watchers. A child giggled and put a hand to her mouth. Gladden, a black rage in his black eyes, sat down again on the stool. The only sound in the long-house was the wheeze of his breathing.

"Doc Kildare," I said.

The Clan Mother moved on piano legs to the door and called out in her man's voice. Two women came from the out-of-doors holding by the arms a pale and unresisting Kildare. They led him to another packing case and left him facing Gladden.

"Doc," I said, "a question: have you ever explained to your patient what would happen if his blood sugar got out of control?"

He looked at me and then at Gladden and back again. "Of course."

"I mean, specifically. In detail."

Doc's face, normally pallid, was now the color of putty. He drew breath to speak and then, reconsidering, lapsed into silence.

"It's a simple enough question," I said. "Have you ever spelled out to him what would happen if he was deprived of insulin? And how long it would be before he died?"

"No."

"Then tell him now."

Gladden broke in. "What the hell is this? More of your god-damn games?"

"Tell him."

Kildare's hands were in his lap. He was massaging them as though scrubbing up. The perpetual frown had drawn into a deep pucker. He looked up at me. "May I have a glass of water?" Kate went to a bucket, dipped a mason-jar and brought it. He drank thirstily.

I pressed. "Tell him."

He took another sip of the water, flashing a glance at Gladden. As he began, his voice was phlegmy and he had to clear his throat.

"Well." He shrugged. "Not much at first. It would depend, of course, but nothing right away." He turned to me, his arms wide, appealing. "He knows all about it. I've gone over it with him. He's read all the literature."

"Tell him," I said tonelessly.

There sat the two men, utterly antithetical. Doc, a skeletal figure, leaning on the packing case, his flamboyant clothes suddenly too big for him or he too small for them. Gladden, massive head up, jaw out-thrust, eyes smoldering. And beneath the handsome, imperious head, the grotesque body—flesh weighing on flesh, buttocks overflowing the tiny stool.

"Tell him."

Doc began again. "Thirst, of course, and the need to urinate. Headache. Some—let's call it raggedness of the nerves." He ventured a glance at Gladden from beneath his brows. "Nothing serious. Like the first stages of—"

"Shut up, Kildare," Gladden said.

Doc's eyes ranged furtively over the women, his gaze fixing on Kate. I didn't know what she'd said or done to him, if anything, but it was obvious that he feared her.

"Like the first stages of influenza," he added. "Some fatigue. Nausea, usually—it all depends. Later on, abdominal pain. Vomiting—" He broke off, his eyes darting about like a cornered ferret's.

Gladden was sitting with his elbows on his knees, his head resting on his fists, an aspect of enormous boredom to his face. Kildare brought the mason-jar to his lips. It was empty. He looked toward Kate. Her muscular arms were folded across her great bosom. She didn't move so much as an eyebrow.

Kildare placed the jar on the floor, continuing to look at it as though he needed to rest his gaze on something. "Some dimming of the vision—"

"Shut up, Kildare!"

"Tell him!"

Doc seemed to have concluded that he was for it, and now his voice returned to near-normalcy. "There would be the possibility of coronary infarction, of course." He looked at me, spreading his hands and shrugging, as though to signal his inability to add to what he'd said. I made no response. "The symptoms simply intensify until there is the onset of shock and the patient slips into a comatose state." His eyes, conciliatory, found mine. "What else can I say?"

"The coma . . . leading to death in how many hours?"

Again, the slight lift of the shoulders, the out-turned hands. "It's not something you can be specific about. There are so many variables. A few minutes. A few hours."

I wanted Gladden to have time to think it over. The women led him off to a shed used to store grain and padlocked him in it. He wouldn't be uncomfortable. We gave him blankets, and there were sacks of grain on which he could sit or on which he could manage a bed. He was left naked; I wanted him to feel vulnerable.

I had decided to return to the estate. I would, at the very least, have to make an attempt to help Gus Longo; I knew from Gladden's response that he was alive. I made a rough but detailed sketch of the house and grounds and with Joshua and Caleb planned a course of action. We went over the crucial areas a half dozen times: the location of the gate-house, the coach-house and barn, the kennels, the fences, the television cameras. I walked them through the house, describing the general layout and the specific rooms. It was decided that we would wait until Sunday. With Gladden away, Bartholemew would be off and the kitchen staff reduced to one. I would find some subterfuge to ensure that Jo was out of the house.

She hadn't been in her studio when I'd called that morning and I hadn't talked to her since telling her that her father had tried to kill me. I heard the echo of her words, "Run, Tony, run!" and wondered what her aunt had told her. I reached her now from the telephone booth beyond the stockade and asked her to meet me for breakfast on Sunday. "At L'Auberge. At nine-thirty. In the garden."

"Are you sure you're all right?" she asked, concern in her voice.

"I'm fine," I said. "There's nothing to worry about. Truly."

"Sunday would be perfect," she said. "Susie and I are going

into the city to a mass at St. Patrick's. I'll light a candle for a perfect day.''

"Light another for me.''

"For *us*," she whispered.


It *was* a perfect day. We each arrived exactly at nine-thirty, meeting at the door. I'd reserved the table at which we'd sat the first time we'd eaten together alone. The sun was oblique but warm and was shining on our end of the garden. Jo's hair was drawn back softly, with tiny tendrils left loose. They caught the light and formed a nimbus about her head. As I ordered and we talked, I avoided any reference to the phone call in which I had told her that her father's men were after me, and although each of us was acutely aware that it was in the air between us, it was as though we'd formed an unspoken pact to avoid it.

She reached across the table and put a hand on mine. "I'm so glad you thought of here. This is where we began and from where we'll go on forever."

I felt a moment's guilt. I'd invited her to breakfast not only because I wanted desperately to be with her but also to get her away from the house. Now I urged her to stay on in the city and to have a late dinner with me at the apartment.

"Perfect. Susie and I are going to do some of the galleries. I was dreading going home. Father's away, and the house is so big and empty." The mention of her father sobered her. She was silent, slowly turning her glass of orange juice. "I've been avoiding it," she said, her voice very small, "but we should talk about my conversation with Aunt Marg. And about Father."

"If you need to," I said. "I wonder, though, could we postpone until tonight? We'll have more time, and things will be clearer in my mind by then." But even then would I be able to tell her that, as we spoke, her father had been locked in a rude granary, deprived of his insulin, and that I was planning a raid on her home? I added, "As you said a minute ago, this is where we begin again, and I don't want to make any mistakes."

"Nor do I," she said. She raised her head to look into my eyes and managed a smile. Then, saying nothing, she raised her glass and touched the rim to mine. Neither of us spoke, but our eyes locked, my heart overflowed with love.

At eleven-thirty, when I opened the door to the shed in which Oscar Gladden had spent the night, he was seated cross-legged on a heap of grain sacks, one of the blankets we'd given him against the cold wrapped about his hulking body—like a swaddled Buddha, I thought. There were some dishes set to one side, cleaned of food except for a few crumbs and some peach pits. He squinted into the sunlight, scowling as he saw that it was I. There was a grizzle of dark beard on his jaw and his hair lay untended on his brow. The skin was gray beneath his eyes.

"I brought you a cigar from the city," I said.

"Keep your goddamn cigar," he said, but then reached for it. I passed him a match and he lit it, flipping the still lighted match toward my face. He drew deeply on the cigar, expelling the smoke through tightly pursed lips. When he spoke, he fixed his eyes on mine.

"I don't know what you think you're going to accomplish with all these juvenile heroics," he said, "but you had better realize now that you won't get away with it. They know where I was heading. They'll find me." His face hardened. "And when they do—don't doubt it for one minute, Carpenter—you and your goddamn Hollywood Indians will wish you'd never heard of Oscar Gladden."

"They won't be here today," I said cheerfully. "I had Doc call Knee-Hi and tell him you wouldn't be back until Monday."

He made no response, looking off, continuing to puff on the cigar. "How do you feel?" I asked.

"A hell of a lot better than you will."

"Doc tells me you last had your insulin yesterday morning. There'll be no more. You know he's going with me to the estate? We're taking both limousines. Doc will drive the lead car. Joshua and I will be with him to see that he does what he's told. Caleb will drive the ICU unit—"

"The Indian who runs this pest-hole?"

"Yes. Joshua's brother."

"He probably doesn't even know they've invented the wheel."

"While we're gone, the women will look after you. Any questions?"

He sat, hunched and silent on the sacks of grain, his face as stone. At the door I said, "While we're gone—and I have no idea when we'll be back—think about that body of yours. It's your enemy now. Doc tells me the headaches have already started. And the thirst. It's only the beginning."

The Indian women took Gladden from the granary to the longhouse. There they fed him and spread-eagled him on a sturdy communal table, naked, his wrists and ankles loosely bound. Ready to leave for Long Island, I stopped in to see him.

"Let me talk to Kildare," he said.

Doc, who had become almost embarrassingly servile, was brought to the longhouse. He stood by the table, anxious, his brow twisted in a worry-knot. He looks, I thought, like an aged fisherman contemplating a beached whale.

Gladden said, "Kildare, you will go with this prick and you will do whatever he tells you."

Doc bobbed his head.

I seized the moment. "Okay: let's begin now. Tell me where Gus Longo is."

Doc looked at Gladden. Gladden said, "Tell him."

"The storage room over the kitchen."

"Is he being guarded?"

"By Diego."

I said to Joshua, "Take him to the car. I'll be there in a minute." When we were alone, I stood where Gladden could see me. "Is there anything you want to say to me?"

"Yes. You should get cancer of the face."

I said, "When you're ready to talk, Kate will give you a pen and some paper."

He exploded in a snort of disbelief. "My god, the man is certifiable." He raised his massive head to where he could look at me. His body was awash with perspiration. The shape of it was outlined on the table where the sweat had dropped. He shook his head to fling aside the pools of moisture in his eye

369

sockets. "Now you listen to me, Carpenter. You don't have the guts to let me die. I know that. You know that. You're soft. You haven't got the stomach for it." He dropped his head and stared at the ceiling. "It's the flaw in you and in your ridiculous plan. Now get the hell out of here and leave me alone."

# THIRTY-THREE

As Doc Kildare turned the limousine into the driveway, Rocco spotted us and ran from the gate-house. The barrier rose. As we passed, Knee-Hi appeared in the doorway, exhibiting the seed-pearl grimace he wore as a smile, and saluted. I was grateful for the one-way window glass. They had seen nothing amiss.

We swept on to the house. Kildare activated the remote-control mechanism, and the door to the parking bay rose slowly. Inside, we turned off the engines and closed the door. Joshua, Caleb and I got out of the cars to stand motionless, listening.

Silence.

I led Joshua into the house, leaving Caleb to guard Kildare. In the trophy room, I flipped a number of switches and the television monitors flickered to life. There, on the second floor at the end of the hall, was Diego, in a chair tilted against the wall, reading a newspaper. I led Joshua to the kitchen. Cao Thieu, the Vietnamese chef, was preparing vegetables.

"Mist' Tony!"

It occurred to me that he might have learned of my flight from the barn and would wonder at my reappearance. "Cao," I said matter-of-factly, "there will be two of us for lunch." I held up two fingers, put my hand to my mouth and made chewing motions. "Okay?"

He nodded vigorously, holding up two fingers. "Two?"

I pointed to myself, to Joshua and then to the door of the dining room. "Lunch. Okay?"

He smiled broadly, the nodding almost a paroxysm. "Yes, yes. Two. No Mr. Gladd'?"

"No Mr. Gladd. Mr. Gladd away. Two."

He returned to his vegetables. I nodded to Joshua and led the way up the back stairs, a finger to my lips signaling caution. At the head of the stairs, I mimed the words, *one, two, three,* and on *three* threw open the door. Joshua's move through the doorframe had the swift efficiency of a predator's strike. Before Diego could rise from the chair he was on his face on the floor, an arm twisted up his back, a forearm-bar on his throat.

I took Diego's gun, gave it to Joshua—who jammed it against the guard's jaw — and went down the hall to the bathroom where I knew there was a roll of adhesive tape. With it, I sealed Diego's mouth and lashed his wrists and legs to the chair. I went through his clothes looking for the key to the room in which Gus was imprisoned, but found nothing. I asked him where it was but he shook his head sullenly. Joshua's look plainly asked, Do you want me to work him over? I shook my head.

Twice Joshua and I threw our combined weight against the door, but it remained secure. Joshua moved me to one side, stepped back, appraised the distance and drove a foot against the panel beside the handle. The frame splintered and the door swung inward, smashing into the wall and rebounding. Gus lay on a cot in a canvas straitjacket. He grinned when he saw us.

Now, back in the trophy room, Joshua stood watch at the narrow casement window while I scanned the monitors. Cao Thieu was no longer in the kitchen. He had undoubtedly fled to the gate-house. His message would be confused, but Knee-Hi would grasp that Mist' Tony was in the house and was not alone.

Joshua called me to the window. Rocco and a guard I recognized as Joey Podertz emerged from the gate-house and, guns in hand, went around to the back of the house. On a monitor I saw the door to the kitchen fling open and the two of them rush in. After a moment's consultation they went cautiously up the back stairs. Podertz released Diego while Rocco spoke urgently on a transceiver. After a moment, they went racing down the back stairs and out of the house.

"They're back at the gate-house," Joshua reported from his post at the window.

Five minutes passed. Knee-Hi and the other guards were

standing, talking, looking toward the house, occasionally pointing. There was the distant sound of dogs yelping with excitement.

"They're waiting for reinforcements," I said. "And they've loosed the dogs into the fenced area. There's no way out by the main gate."

Joshua grinned at me slyly. "As I keep telling Caleb, if it's the white man's world, take advantage of it." He picked up a telephone and held it out to me. "Call the cops."

I smiled with chagrin and put the receiver to my ear. It was dead. "Score one for them," I said and glanced at him archly. "You're delegated to send up smoke signals."

"What we *should* do is get in the cars and make a run for it," he said.

I shook my head. "Too many guns."

Gus broke in. "Maybe we should check on Caleb and Doc."

He and I went quickly through the entry hall to the parking bay. Doc Kildare was slumped in the front seat of the limousine, listening to the radio. Caleb was idling about on the loading dock. He started as I opened the door. I went to the car.

"Doc," I said, "Knee-Hi knows we're here. We may have to get out of here in a hell of a hurry. Are you with us?"

He shrugged. "I work for Mr. Gladden."

I turned to Caleb. "Keep the car running, ready to move out. And give me the remote-control for the garage door."

Gus and I scurried back to the trophy room. "Somebody else just arrived," Joshua reported. "A big black guy."

"Say."

"Say what?"

"Sacred Heart Saywell. That's his name."

He shook his head in mild bewilderment and turned back to the window. "Look out!" he whispered urgently. "Here they come."

And indeed they were coming. Saywell remained at the gate. The others broke into two groups and moved past on each side of the house. On the monitor, I saw three of them enter the kitchen, Knee-Hi in the lead, an excited Cao Thieu dancing about. The others joined them. On the second floor, guns at the ready, they separated and, working toward the front of the house, began to check each room.

"We've got to get out of here," I said. "We'll be trapped."

"That black guy's still at the gate-house," Joshua reminded me.

We went through the entrance hall to the front door. "Careful," I whispered and eased it open. There was a heavy planting of shrubbery to the right of the porch and, seizing the moment, we scuttled behind it.

In a few minutes the front door opened and Knee-Hi came onto the porch. He put two stubby fingers to his mouth and whistled. Saywell came running. "They're not inside," Knee-Hi told him. "We've been through every room. They've got to be on the grounds. Diego, Say, go get the dogs. We'll meet at the gate-house."

After they left, I whispered, "We're going back into the house."

"Jeezus, Tony! Are you nuts?"

"They've just searched it," I said. "They won't be back."

In the trophy room I studied the television panel, my excitement mounting. An idea had begun to gestate. I began experimenting with the controls. After a moment I shouted, "Got it!"

Gus and Joshua came to stand beside me, looking at the control panel as I flipped switches and set dials.

"Okay, men," I said. "Here's what I want you to do. You guys are going to run up the stairs and along the hall on the second floor. Duck into each room and out again. Make it look as though you're looking for a place to hide. Understand? When you're finished, come back here."

Joshua was frowning uncomprehendingly. "We make it look like we're looking for a place to hide but we don't hide?"

"Exactly. But for god's sake, make it look legit."

"This is one hell of a time to play games," he muttered, shaking his head dubiously. Gus tugged on an arm and off they went.

"And smile," I said grimly, mostly to myself. "You're on candid camera."

I pushed the record button on the control panel and switching from camera to camera followed their progress on the monitors. They dashed up the staircase and raced down the hall, opening closet doors, scurrying into rooms and out again. Soon they were back, panting and wet with perspiration.

"Academy Award stuff," I said. "Now we suck 'em in."

The dogs had arrived at the gate-house, lunging and barking at the ends of their leashes. We could see Knee-Hi giving instructions to the group, gesticulating with his stubby arms.

"Stand by," I said, and went through the hallway onto the porch, slamming the door behind me to get their attention. One of the dogs began to bark, straining toward me. Someone shouted, "There he is!" As they started toward me, I ran into the house, closing the door and locking it.

Back in the trophy room, I said, "Into the closet! Both of you! Leave the door open for me."

Through the window I could see the men and dogs mounting the porch. Rocco tried the door. "Break it down!" Knee-Hi shouted. There was a series of crashes, the door burst open and the men charged into the entry hall. I pushed the play button on the control panel, turned up the volume, and as the videotape began to roll, leaped to join the others in the closet. From behind the door we could hear the playback of Joshua's and Gus's amplified voices and the sound of their feet as they raced up the staircase and began to dash in and out of the rooms. Knee-Hi came to the trophy room. From behind the door we could hear him shouting, "The second floor! They're on the second floor, heading for the back stairs!"

There was a rush of feet on the staircase and an uproar from the dogs. It as quickly faded. I left the closet, went to the monitors and switched the controls so that I could follow the search. Damn! Knee-Hi had remained in the entry hall with one of the dogs. He was standing, gun in hand, at the foot of the staircase. As I watched, the dog pricked up its ears and turned to look toward our hiding place, its nose questing in the air.

"The dog knows we're here," I hissed. "We're trapped!"

"The window," Joshua whispered.

It was a casement-style window, barely wide enough to squeeze through. But once clear we would be able to leap to the porch.

The dog had begun to growl and was pulling on the leash in

our direction. Knee-Hi turned, his brow beetled. I opened one of the gun cases on the wall and removed a double-barreled shotgun. I checked to see that it was loaded and stepped to the door to the entry hall. Gus had been watching me, frowning. Now he put a hand on my arm.

"No, Tony. Don't!"

I shook him off. "On my signal, pull the door wide. Then be ready to slam it shut again."

"*Now!*"

Gus jerked the door open. One leap and I was in the hallway, feet planted, the gun to my shoulder. The dog lunged, breaking free. My fingers found the triggers. I fired both barrels at the aquarium and scrambled for the trophy room. There was a thump as the dog crashed into the door closing behind me.

On the monitor I watched the aquarium collapse with an unreal majesty, almost as though in slow-motion. First, there was a surging gout of water and a bulging outward of the entire glass wall. Then, suddenly, a tumbling, clanging maelstrom of crashing glass, frothing water and threshing fish. I heard a scream from Knee-Hi as the waters rose.

Gus and Joshua were already out the window. I scrambled after them. As we dashed across the driveway I reached for the remote-control unit in my pocket and depressed the button. The door to the parking bay rose like a theatrical curtain.

# THIRTY-FOUR

On the return trip to the settlement, Gus talked about the smuggling operation.

"It's foolproof. Tri-Nat trucks cross the border every week, year in, year out. The guys at customs know them. So whenever there's a shipment ready—"

"A shipment of what?"

"Gladden buys all kinds of stuff in Mexico. Health food, office furniture, body-building equipment. It's cheaper. Whenever a shipment's ready, one of us—Rocco, Joey or me—takes over from the driver on the Tri-Nat run from Los Angeles to Tijuana.

"I'm talking about the cash. The gold."

"No problem. The money's in one of the tires. We're light-loaded, so we can run with the lift-axle up. It's a regular run, remember, and we're haulin' goods waybilled to a legit destination. I make my delivery, lay up overnight and pick up the return shipment. Just before I leave Tijuana, along comes a tow truck carrying a spare wheel and makes the switch for one of the wheels on the lift-axle. If the police come by, no sweat. I'm havin' tire trouble."

"And at the border?"

"Like I said—no sweat. I show the waybills and off I go. Back in the USA, another tow truck makes the switch and takes away the tire with the gold in it."

"But how do you know there's gold in it?"

Gus grinned. "If you were driving a rig that was always

377

changing tires there was nothing wrong with, wouldn't you do a little investigating?'' He nodded. ''It's gold.''

We were approaching the turnoff to Caleb's village.

''Gus,'' I said, ''will you tell all this to the police?''

''Do I have a choice?''

''I'm sure we can make a deal, if you tell them everything you know.''

He was silent for a moment. ''Oscar Gladden's got a long arm.''

''Not any more,'' I said. ''Don't worry. I'll talk to some people I know at the FBI before either of us says anything.''

A sudden sense of relief almost overwhelmed me; we didn't need Oscar Gladden's confession. Gladden, spread-eagled on the table, had been at the back of my mind throughout the day. His words had echoed in my head again and again: ''You don't have the guts to let me die!'' I knew he was right, that however I might stiffen my resolution it would weaken if I saw him dying. And I knew too that, if I let him die, even accidentally, I would never be able to explain my actions to Jo, not even if she accepted the entire truth about him.

Kate met us as we got out of the limousines. ''Fat man chicken-shit,'' she said, handing some papers to Caleb.

He glanced at them and passed them to me. It was Oscar Gladden's handwriting, scrawled in an erratic hand.

''Doc,'' I said, ''go take care of your boss.'' I turned to Kate, ''What happened?''

Her mouth drew down in disdain. ''Nothin'. Then, maybe an hour, he say he got belly-ache. He gonna throw up. He groanin' an' cursin' an' sweatin'. A little while an' I tell him I get phone call and that all you been killed dead at this big house you bin talkin' 'bout.'' Her lips tightened in a smile. ''I know this kin' of man.''

''What did he do?''

''He say I gotta get him hospital right away. I tell him, 'All I been tol' is keep him at longhouse.' He scream an' yell, 'I gonna die! I gonna die! You gonna kill me!' I say, 'Not me, fat man. I don' kill you. I jus' gonna keep you here till I thing what I do.' He say, 'You can' do this.' I say, 'Oh yes I can,' and I go 'way.

But I watch. He lie on table shiverin' like he very col'. He shiverin'. Pretty soon he cryin'. Cry like baby.''

"So what did you do?''

"He say, 'Lemme go, I give you thousan' dollar.' I say, 'What I do with thousan' dollar, fat man?' He say, 'Ten thousan'.' I go 'way. But I watch. He throw up. Jus' once. Nothin'. Pretty soon he yell paper and pencil, paper and pencil. I tell him I don' know nothin' 'bout paper and pencil. He say, 'If I write ev'rythin' on paper, can I go hospital?' I say, 'I don' know nothin' 'bout no writin' an' no hospital,' but I give him paper and pencil and I go 'way. But I watch. He have trouble writin'. Droppin' pencil, shakin'. Like that. Women bring writin' to me." She laughed. "Fat man don' know I don' able read." She looked at me with brown, static eyes. "Fat man chicken-shit."

There had been an unbroken flow of activity at the village. Leaving the Gladden estate, I had stopped to call Mordecai Green at the FBI. He had dispatched a carload of agents and called in the state police. A half-dozen patrol cars arrived even as we did. For more than an hour, policemen in uniform and in plainclothes moved around, making notes, asking questions. Finally, a convoy of police cars was formed with the two Gladden limousines inserted in the middle. Oscar Gladden, Doc and the Spick were put in the ICU car, handcuffed to each other and to the dialysis machine. I caught a glimpse of Gladden as he was led to the car. When he saw me he jerked his hand upward in a vicious middle-finger salute that was undiluted malevolence.

After many delays and much consulting and waving of arms, the cavalcade moved off in a Fourth of July display of flashing lights and whooping sirens, sounding not unlike my painted Indians of the day before.

Had it been only yesterday?

I found a moment to telephone the apartment and beep my answering machine. There were calls from every branch of the news media, and other messages, including one from Dunc— "Hoorah for our side!" Finally, there was Jo's constrained voice asking me, please, to call her at her studio.

379

"I was in town with Susie," she said, her voice unsure. "I called home and that's when I got the news. I didn't know what to do, didn't know what to think. I tried to reach you, and finally I thought the best thing to do would be to come back here." It was a moment before she was able to continue. "The reporters! They kept shoving their cameras in my face, pushing, shouting. And the police! The house was swarming with them. They were in the library, in Father's office, going through his desk, his files, putting everything in cartons. They even searched my rooms." She was silent for a moment.

I wanted to say something but couldn't think of anything that wouldn't sound empty.

"Oh, Tony!" she said, and her voice was heavy with despair. "I don't know what to do. I don't know what to think." Her reserves gave way and there was a silence on the line.

I tried to comfort her, feeling impotent, knowing that much of what I was saying wasn't registering. I started to explain what had happened but gave up on it; it couldn't possibly be done on the telephone.

"I'm sorry, my darling," I said. "I can't tell you how sorry I am."

We arranged to meet as planned. "At your apartment," she said. "I couldn't bear it here."

After perhaps ten minutes, with an impatient line forming behind me, I hung up the receiver and, after a brief, solitary walk to compose myself, went in search of Joshua. As he walked with me toward the road, I saw Roger Zachs. He was at the center of a boisterous crowd of reporters. Even as we approached, two more cars and a van pulled up, and men carrying cameras and sound paraphernalia spilled out. A helicopter hovered overhead, scouting a place to land. The media firestorm had begun.

"We may not see each other again," Joshua said.

"I hope that's not true," I said.

"It will be. The one thing we had in common is gone."

"No, we'll see each other," I said and gave a short, arid laugh. "If nowhere else, in court. It'll be years before the dust settles. Do you have any plans?"

"I don't know. I'll have to think about it. A lot has happened.

There's a new office tower going up on Fifth Avenue. They'll be coming out of the hole in a couple of weeks.''

The reporters spied us and deserted Roger, breaking toward us in a scrambling run. As the first of them arrived — an old friend from my days on the *Register* — and was about to speak to me, he paused, looked at Joshua and frowned, puzzled.

"Hey, wait a minute," he said. "I know you. I've seen you somewhere. You're — you're. . .''

"Mr. Nobody," Joshua supplied with a grin.

"No," I said, "Mr. *Somebody*.''

The reporters had run their last quarry to ground. The chaos had eased. Cars, trucks and vans jostled impatiently at the gate as they funneled from the field. Suddenly, feeling utterly depleted, I turned my back on it all and, wanting nothing so much as to be alone, followed the river bank. Unexpectedly, I came upon the sweat-house and, on a sudden whim, shucked my clothes, pulled aside the deerhide covering the door and slipped into the dark, muggy interior.

There was a residue of hot coals in the pit and some water in the gourd. I splashed it on the fire. It hissed and spat and vaporized. Within a minute the air was thick in my nostrils and heavy in my lungs. I inhaled deeply, expelled the breath slowly and willed my body slack.

What now, Tony Carpenter?

Jo! . . . My poor, darling Jo. What she must be feeling! The house ransacked and overrun with strangers. Her father under arrest. His face on the front page of every newspaper, his image on every television screen: disheveled and in handcuffs.

She must be despairing — not only about her father but about her home. Undoubtedly, the estate would be secured by the IRS and barred to visitors. There would be no-trespass signs stapled to the doors and chains on the entrance gates. The manicured lawns would soon grow ragged with weeds, and the fallen leaves would drift into untidy windrows. Silence would tenant the rooms and shadows darken the halls. The ceiling of her studio would lose its luster to a film of dust.

Somehow I had to find the courage and the wisdom to help

her. But how could I justify to her what I had done? Where would I find the words to confess that, in my zeal, I'd had her father kidnapped, stripped naked and imprisoned? And that, to increase his sense of vulnerability, I had cut off his insulin. But there would be no option; I would have to tell her everything. Better that she hear it first from me; the full story would be in the newspapers within hours.

Beyond that, there was the matter of my own future.

I had no job. The Swiss bank account was a dream aborted. For a few weeks I would be a media celebrity—The Man Who Brought Down Oscar Gladden's Spiritual Empire—and then I would be yesterday's news. I might be able to get taken on by one of the papers, but even that would be difficult to arrange; much of my time for the next few months would be spent in talking to a grand jury or the Justice department or the IRS or whomever. And such monies as I had managed to put aside would probably go to the lawyers.

Pretty grim prospect, Tony Carpenter.

But hold on a moment: perhaps I could at least solve the money problem. I could write a book about Oscar Gladden. . . .

Yes.

I roused myself, left the hut, rubbed myself down with sand as I had seen Caleb and Joshua do, and plunged into the river. The waters were cold. As I came up from them I was shivering, but my mind was clear.